SEP   2002

The Second Coming of
LUCY HATCH

(a novel)

Marsha Moyer

wm

WILLIAM MORROW
An Imprint of HarperCollins*Publishers*

HarperCollins books may be purchased for educational, business, or sales promotional use. For information please write: Special Markets Department, HarperCollins Publishers Inc., 10 East 53rd Street, New York, NY 10022.

FIRST EDITION

Designed by Kris Tobiassen

Printed on acid-free paper

Library of Congress Cataloging-in-Publication Data
Moyer, Marsha.
    The second coming of Lucy Hatch : a novel / by Marsha Moyer.—1st ed.
        p. cm.
    ISBN 0-06-008165-1
    1. Widows—Fiction.   I. Title.
PS3613.O93 S43 2003
813'.6—dc21   2001054623

02 03 04 05 06 WBC/QW 10 9 8 7 6 5 4 3 2 1

For Randy Field
and
Michael B. Hejl,
who taught me how to recognize a cowboy man

(acknowledgments)

Thanks to:

My agent, Barbara Braun, and my editor, Carrie Feron, for their faith in and dedication to *Lucy Hatch*;

The many people, writers and "civilians," who looked at early portions of the manuscript or otherwise offered support: Mark Anthony, Brenda Blanchard, Lisa Brant, Larry Brill, Darrell Bryant, Janet Christian, Elaine Hrissikopoulos, Rob Lallier, Geoff Leavenworth, Barbara Burnett Smith, and Richard Willis;

The judges of the 2000 Austin Writers' League (now the Writers' League of Texas) manuscript competition for pushing me off the high board, and my many champions in the league, particularly the phenomenal Sally Baker;

Kathy Fitzgibbon, friend and teacher, in whose workshops the first pieces of this book saw the light;

Diana Gabaldon, for her uncommon generosity in sharing guidance with a new writer;

Michael Fracasso, songwriter extraordinaire, whose noble attempt to tutor me in his craft served to underscore my conviction that some jobs are better left to professionals;

My pals at the Cactus Café in Austin, Texas—for eight years my second home—including but not limited to Ginny, Bill, Susan, Griff, Derrall, Zane, Rafiq, George, and Spot; and especially my buds Chris Lueck (world's best bartender and honorary Cowboy Man) and Eric Spinks, who offered inspiration and input for "Jesus—The Missing Years";

Sylva Billue, Julia Lacey, Barbara Carroll, and the women of the late, great Syvenna Foundation, who provided early financial and moral support, as well as my introduction to northeast Texas, an experience that planted the seed for this book;

My oldest and best friends, Cynthia Burdick, Celia Kay Claybourn, and Mary Smith, for their unwavering encouragement and enthusiasm;

And to my family—my parents, Vance and Barbara, my brother, Tim, his wife, Yvette, and their son, Andrew Vance, and daughter, Gabriella Marie—for their love.

(*one*)

I was thirty-three years old when my husband walked out into the field one morning and never came back and I went in one quick leap from wife to widow. I wasn't the one who found him; that was Sam Gill, who'd come by to ask Mitchell to help him load a horse. He'd fallen off the tractor and under the blades of the mower—my husband, Mitchell, not the horse; I guess we'll never know how. Try as I might, and I have a thousand times on a thousand nights, I cannot imagine such a thing; my mind creeps up on it, then turns and bolts. I can't let myself think it, a man shredded like a handful of husks, bleeding dry in the sun. I've never much liked machines, never trusted them, but Mitchell could drive anything, repair it, make it run, and he was not a careless man. I didn't love Mitchell, which you'd think would help but it doesn't, really, not when you've been with someone fourteen years and worn their presence next to you so long it's like a favorite old shirt, come to take for granted its smell and its feel. I didn't love Mitchell, but he was mine and that was something.

I never expected to be a young woman alone. I'd left home for Texarkana to type for an import-export company the week I graduated from high school, and wouldn't you know I'd meet a farmer and wind up not six months later, back in the country. It seemed like all I ever wanted, getting up while the sky was still purple velvet with just a rim of pink in the east, Mitchell in his overalls already headed for the barn when I carried my coffee cup out onto the porch to watch the horizon as one by one the fields went a slow, shimmering gold. Even in the heart of the summer I liked the windows flung open, filling the house with the smell of hay and horses and the sweetbriar roses that bloomed wild along the porch rail. The nights were as black and bottomless as water in a quarry, and when the moon rose over the pines the countryside seemed cast in liquid silver.

Mitchell was twenty-seven to my nineteen when we married and I admit I was taken in by it all, by the pull of the land, by Mitchell's years, his size and sureness, by the silence I mistook for a mark of masculinity. Still waters run deep; I'd heard it all my life and so I believed it, went on believing it, and accepted it because I'd been raised to fear the Lord and stand by my man. That Mitchell never particularly drew me was so far down the list of qualities I, at nineteen, found important in a man, I'd have laughed if you'd even put it on the list. Mitchell was big, quiet, constant. As opposed to my daddy Raymond Hatch, who, legend had it, was quick and sleek and loved to laugh. Who left on a sales trip and never came back. So I married stability and virtue, and virtue, as we know, is its own reward. On the one hand, I can say in truth that in fourteen years Mitchell never raised hand nor voice to me; on the other, I have to admit that he never grabbed me up hard in passion, and rarely laughed. But like anything that's not too uncomfortable, you find you can live with it. I became, in time, without even noticing, someone whose life she's learned not to mind.

Still, I went a little crazy when he died. It was so swift and so awful—

one minute I was wiping my hands on a dish towel at the kitchen sink, looking out between the curtains with their neat little rows of yellow teacups at the pear tree just starting to bud out beside the barn and thinking nothing much past what I'd cook for supper and tapping my toe to the radio. The next thing I knew, Sam Gill was standing outside the screen door with his CAT cap in his hands, his face bleached white under the tan, and even before he got his mouth open I knew. I'd never seen death before, not up close and grinning, but when it walked in I recognized it right away, no one had to introduce me. I don't remember what Sam said to me that morning, the words, although I can see every petal of the painted roses on the china cup sitting on the drainboard, a ring of cold coffee in its saucer, and I can hear as clear as anything the voice of Ernest Tubb, 'round and 'round, walking the floor over you. One look at Sam's face and I went to ice all over, and when he finally spoke I heard myself let loose a wild bark of laughter, my shock was so deep and so unspeakable—as if Mitchell's silence was a crime deserving that hard a punishment.

I sat down at the kitchen table, still twisting the dish towel in my fists, while Sam lifted the telephone receiver off the wall. Pretty soon his wife, Mary, was there, and I started to laugh all over again when I saw the tears swimming in her round blue eyes. She went rummaging in the pantry until she found the bourbon and poured me a glassful, then pulled up a chair and circled me with her doughy arm; she smelled of yeast and cinnamon, like a fresh-baked sweet roll. The sheriff came, and then the long black car from the funeral home. I didn't stop laughing until Dr. Spikes arrived and gave me a pill, and made me wash it down with another gulp of bourbon. Mary Gill put me to bed, pulling the quilt up to my chin, and all the rest is as soft and blank and shapeless as I supposed death must be, a straight white tunnel into nothing.

When I woke it was dark out and my Aunt Dove was sitting in the corner in the rocking chair where Mitchell sat every morning to pull on his boots, every single morning since our wedding day. Not till I saw Aunt Dove's face did what had happened come up on me in all its fullness; my lungs were thick with it, my chest so tight I could barely breathe. "Oh, Lucy. Oh, honey," Dove said, and I flung back the quilt and stumbled past her, half on my knees, and threw up in the bathroom sink where Mitchell's safety razor still rested, his toothbrush in the holder alongside mine. Trapped in the teeth of the razor was one of his coarse dark hairs, every bit as alive at that moment as he. I didn't feel like laughing anymore, or for a long time after.

On a cool blue Saturday afternoon, when I might have been climbing into the pickup beside my husband to make our weekly trip to town for feed and groceries, instead we carried what was left of him down the aisle of the Calvary Baptist Church in a wooden box, and put it in the ground. Back at the house, while my sisters-in-law and neighbors laid out platters of ham and whole fried chickens and bowls of okra and sweet corn and salads made up of green Jell-O and pecans and Cool Whip, I took the last two inches of Mitchell's good bonded bourbon and carried it out onto the front porch. The moon was up, a fingernail silver of white over the trees, and I put my head back and opened my throat and let the whiskey burn straight down, all the way through fourteen years of history. At the bottom, finally, I met my complacency, the hard fact of how I'd settled for shelter in place of opportunity. I'd been a bright girl, I'd read books and run track and conjugated French verbs and played Emily in *Our Town*. My hair once fell to the seat of my jeans; I was a good dancer, a member of the pep squad, and a homecoming princess. How had I let go of possibility and run instead straight to Mitchell? What thing out there in the unexplored world had had me so fearful that I gave up without beginning? Mitchell was a steady, decent man; he'd have stood by me, in his wordless way, all our days. But he'd taken a wrong step, made some undoable mistake, and here I was, swaying on the porch in the moonlight, brought up hard against the rest of my life. Somewhere in the woods a dog howled, a long high-pitched sound that ran right through me the way the far-off sound of a midnight train can make you feel like the only beating heart on the planet. When my brother Bailey stepped out the front door and said my name, the sound of it spooked me so, I fell off the steps and snapped my wrist as quick and clean as the wishbone on a chicken.

Two days later my family packed me a suitcase and drove me the eighty miles back home to Mooney, Texas, back to my old bedroom full of ruffled yellow organdy and stuffed dogs and a mirror framed with photographs from long-forgotten dances and football games. The girl in those photographs did not much resemble the person whose face now floated in the mirror glass, looking for a sign of what to do next. I had a lot of time to think about it. No one talks about the fringe benefits of mourning, but one of those is that you are, at least for a while, absolved of responsibility. Laziness, indecision, even lunacy—all are forgiven, if not sidestepped completely, and people treat you gently and remind themselves not to expect anything.

It didn't suit me long, though; I hated the endless cups of soup and tea and the way everyone's eyes dropped when I came into the room, and Mama's constant hovering and mindless, humming activity set me on edge, made me want to burn all those yearbook pictures and rip the frilled curtains from the walls. Whatever life with Mitchell had made me, I was not that girl anymore. I didn't know what I wanted from the rest of my years, not by a long shot, but whatever it turned out to be, I was determined it would not be what someone else expected from me.

I t was my Aunt Dove who rescued me, the way she had when I was six years old and my daddy Raymond Hatch left us, leaving my mama flapping like a loose shutter in a breeze and my two brothers and me to fend for ourselves. Dove, Mama's elder sister by a dozen years, was the most truly solitary person I knew, fond of claiming she preferred her own company to that of anybody else—anybody else in Mooney, Texas, at least—she'd ever met.

But I wondered, sometimes, if such a state was her true inclination or the inevitable consequence of her early life. When she was fifteen, her brother, Garnett, two years older, was killed in a hunting accident. Other than Dove herself, there was no one aboveground anymore who knew the details, and she would never, ever, talk about it, although his picture—gangling, grinning, a shotgun cocked over his shoulder like some awful omen—sat on top of the TV in a gilt-edged frame, and she drove to the Mount Pilgrim cemetery faithfully twice a year with flowers for the grave. Her parents never got over it. Together, then separately, they let go the strands of their everyday lives; they stopped working, stopped speaking, stopped caring for themselves and then for each other, and the only time they left the house was for the hospital, Granddaddy six weeks behind Grandma, both dead not two years after their son.

So Dove, at the time in her life a girl is thinking of boys, and parties, maybe even college, had her broken parents to care for, and her baby sister, Patsy, my mama, to raise, and then, finally, two more stones to tend at Mount Pilgrim on Remembrance Day. She turned over her daddy's bookkeeping business to his young protégé, enrolled Patsy in the first grade a full year early, and, fresh out of high school herself, went to work in the administrative office of the Mooney public schools. Whether she had time for regret or grief at the way her life had turned, I don't know; she did all she knew to do, I think, which was to pay the bills, to fix Patsy's lunches and her homework, to hold her head up until no one in town could remember her any other way than remote and proud. She was middle-aged when Raymond Hatch finessed his way into Patsy's life; and by the time he slithered out ten years later, Dove had had plenty of practice at persevering in the face of misfortune. She had, time and again, functioned as the glue that held our wobbly little family together until Mama was finally able to pull her head up again and let Jesus take her by the hand and guide her back into the world; and I could only guess that, over the past twenty years, Dove had come to treasure her privacy as a reward for all she'd sacrificed, that, after a lifetime of mopping up behind the rest of us, her own company was a blessed relief.

It would not be true, exactly, to say that Aunt Dove had raised me, but it would likewise not be true to say that she hadn't been the sanest voice and the firmest hand through most of my girlhood. So, two weeks after Mitchell died, it was no real surprise to find her, with her froth of snow-white hair and a T-shirt that read, SPAMFEST '96, standing at the foot of my yellow canopy saying, "Get up off a there. We're goin' for a ride."

I'd barely been out of the house since I'd gotten there, and the sunlight fell into my eyes the way it must on a prisoner's face the first time he's turned out the front gate. It was the first week of March, and the dogwoods were blooming everywhere, showing through the pines like scraps of old lace as we rode out the highway north of town in Dove's Lincoln Town Car. Springtime in East Texas is a hard thing to resist, like an ache in my blood for something I wasn't even aware I'd been missing. Dove was silent behind the wheel, propped up on a couple of sofa cushions to see over the dash, her chin pointed forward and her teeth gritted in concentration, a sight so familiar to me that I felt a rush of relief and then pleasure; it was the first time since the accident that anything in my life was recognizable to me. Unlike my brothers and their wives, Dove didn't seem to mind the quiet, didn't seem to be gauging my state of mind by every word I did or didn't utter. There is something to be said for the balm of pavement moving under you, miles gliding by without destination beneath your wheels. Something lifts. It occurred to me that my life would go on, move forward, after all. That maybe I could learn to be glad about this.

We turned off the highway onto an unpaved county road. The big Town Car fell heavily into the red clay ruts, but Dove didn't slow down or otherwise coddle the car, and it jostled and balked as she worked the steering wheel like Richard Petty, like her eye was on the checkered flag. It wasn't until we reached the end of the road that I realized we'd had a destination, all along.

I knew without asking that the little house was empty; it had the feel of being uninhabited, though it was not an unfriendly feeling, but rather one of expectation. It seemed to droop a bit from neglect, but as we rolled to a stop in the yard I took one look at the hawks looping lazily through the tops of the pines against the blazing sky and the snowy petals of the dogwood beside the front door, and I knew this was at least the start of what I was looking for. I glanced over at Dove, who shrugged. "Shirley Tinsley at the real estate office told me about this," she said. "I thought it might be a good place to get used to the sound of your own voice. Lord knows it ain't gonna happen at your mama's house."

"I'm not sure I have a voice." I sat gazing at the sagging porch steps, the row of rosebushes, green but not yet budding, that lined the rail. Someone else might have been put off by the crack in the front windowpane, the missing shingles. But that dogwood beside the porch was like a beacon to me, those dormant rosebushes a sealed envelope containing a sweet invitation.

" 'Course you do," Dove said as I pushed open the car door and got out, inhaling the sharp green air. "You just ain't heard it in a while." Fourteen years is a very long time to keep quiet; there's an art to learning to hone that kind of silence, to camouflage it as contentment.

Dove followed me up the porch steps and through the unlocked front door. Inside, the four small, square rooms were bare and bright; dust danced in the bars of sunlight from the uncurtained windows. "Nothing a bottle of bleach and a dust mop won't cure," she observed as

I stood looking into the kitchen at the old porcelain stove, the enamel table with its peeling oilcloth patterned with ivy. A clock in the shape of a sunflower ticked steadfastly above the stove, keeping time for no one. Like it had only been waiting for me. There was a narrow iron bedstead in the back-corner bedroom, a ticked mattress just wide enough for one body.

We drove straight into town to Shirley Tinsley's office, and Dove wrote her out a check for five hundred dollars, for a deposit and the first month's rent. "You can pay me back when you get your money," she said, driving me back to Mama's house. My money was a big topic of conversation around the living room most nights among my family. I would be getting a settlement from the insurance policy Mitchell carried, and the farm was for sale. A couple of buyers had expressed interest; it was expected to fetch a decent price. I didn't care about any of that. No matter how I felt about Mitchell—and my feelings, just then, were all over the map—what I grieved for most, those first weeks, was not Mitchell's face across from mine at the breakfast table or his body giving off its sealed heat in bed at night, but that his death had cost me the home I'd loved.

That weekend, my brother Bailey's wife, Geneva, drove me out to my new house, with a box full of secondhand dishes and brand-new sheets, to help with the fixing up. My left wrist was in plaster, but we got straight to work, scouring floors and polishing windows with newspaper and ammonia and laying no-bug shelf paper in the kitchen cabinets. At night I dropped onto the mattress in my work clothes and plunged into dreamless sleep, not waking until the sun cracked the window sash and slid across my cheek and I got up to start it all again.

I'd known Geneva all my life, but until Mitchell died I never knew her well. She'd been in Bailey's class in high school, three years ahead of me, and had had a reputation for being big and wry, loud, and into everything, one of those girls whose multiple orbits spin and intersect to encircle almost everyone. She and Bailey must have known each other then—in a class of fewer than forty they'd have had to—but as far as I knew he'd never taken particular notice of her, little bubble-headed cheerleaders being more his style. He'd gone off to rodeo right out of high school, and by the time he got thrown and broke his hip and his collarbone and punctured a lung and retired from the circuit and came home, I was gone myself, married to Mitchell.

If anybody was more surprised than me to hear that Bailey had proposed to Geneva Clooney, I don't known who it could be, except maybe Geneva herself. I'd been at the wedding, naturally, had seen her standing up there in the gown she and her sisters had made, white taffeta with what must have been three thousand seed pearls on the skirt and bodice, every single one sewn on by hand, saw her gazing at Bailey with her wide, lively face for once gone slack and a little addled, and I knew she was wondering how she'd landed him, handsome and reckless as he was known to be, and how she would hold him. I approved of Geneva for Bailey, mightily so, but I admit that I drove back to the farm that night after the reception wondering, too.

It turned out to be one of those mysterious, inexplicably solid matches, so plainly wrong that it can only be right, and I never ceased giving my brother credit for sense I didn't know he had, for marrying her. Bailey hadn't changed all that much, really, in spite of the fact that his bronco-busting days were over; he was still inclined to be hot-headed, inclined to use his mouth and sometimes his fists before his brain had a chance to kick in, still liked to move through a room showing his fine teeth beneath his mustache, tipping his cap to the ladies and calling them "darlin'." He and our older brother, Kit, had their own contracting business, and Bailey never went near a horse anymore

other than to lead the town kids around in a ring on the back of a Shet-
land pony at the annual Jaycees Fourth of July fish fry; but then there
are things so entrenched in a man that he never sheds them, no matter
how domesticated it seems he's become. It was Geneva's saving grace
that she never tried, never cared to break Bailey but was wise enough to
stand back and give him his head, and he gave her hers in kind. They
were more alike than first appearances would suggest: stubborn, opin-
ionated, full of noise and mischief. It wasn't anything at all to see them
hollering at each other in public, in the Food King or the Texaco or
even, once, the All Faiths church supper, and it wasn't unusual either
to see them just as publicly making up, steaming up some dance floor or
the windows of their big dually pickup.

In the twelve years they'd been married Geneva had put on a little
weight, thickened some the way big girls tend to, and she was nearly as
tall as Bailey, so that they made an impressive, if unlikely, couple, the
kind who caused you to stop and look twice, and then smile. She had
the kind of laugh that carried across rooms, and the kind of glare that
could freeze you in your tracks. Her tongue could be a weapon, sharp
and acidic; but her patience was limitless, her generosity unbounded,
her heart as sweet and sticky as pinesap. She was wonderful with kids—
the herd of nieces and nephews she seemed always to be surrounded by,
offspring of her three sisters and of my brother Kit—though she and
Bailey had none of their own.

It was something I was curious about and didn't have the nerve to
ask; Mitchell and I had never succeeded in that department, and I
know I'd have been mortified if I'd been called upon to explain. At first
I supposed we were just unlucky; then I supposed (and Mitchell never
sought to correct me) that there was something lacking in me. Of
course we never talked about it—talked above and below and in sweeping circles around it, but never face-to-face, never spoke aloud the cold,
hard "Why?" Talk of sex made Mitchell redden and choke up like his

collar was binding him, even the harmless jokes the old retired farmers told around the domino table at the feed store; the thought of actually discussing our failure to procreate was something I never allowed to cross my mind. Our lovemaking even after all those years was hasty, furtive, two bodies colliding gracelessly in the dark and then rolling apart with a kind of desperate relief that seemed to stink of sin and shame. He was always gruff afterward, aloof, slightly irritable. But there was never anything that suggested that the arrangement didn't suit him; if Mitchell had desires beyond what I was able to satisfy, they never once broke the cool, placid surface. Whether or not it suited me was not an issue. The very thought that I—a woman, a wife—might have desires of my own would have been as foreign to him as the Chinese restaurant I dragged him to the night of our tenth anniversary, just that unfathomable, the outcome predictably disastrous.

But I knew, without being told, that it was not like that between Bailey and Geneva, understood—from their easy pleasure in each other's company, the way they looked at each other when the other wasn't looking—the depth and breadth of their connection. Even when they were furious at each other, fighting like cats and dogs, even when Bailey totaled the truck and Geneva didn't speak to him for nearly a week, there was no mistaking they were a duo, a unit, a team. "A match made in hell," Geneva would say, grinning at Bailey, who'd growl and nuzzle her and bite the tip of her nose. "Babe," they called each other, "sugar," "angel," "doll." The fact that he was my brother and she my sister-in-law didn't keep a pang from shooting through me at the sight of them, dancing slow with their beer bottles in the small of each other's backs, strolling arm in arm through the parking lot, climbing into the dually and heading home. Nobody had to spell out for me what happened when they got there.

But until Mitchell died and I moved back to Mooney, those images of Geneva and Bailey were fractured ones, scenes glimpsed and barely recalled; my memories of him were mostly from our shared childhood, and those involving Geneva tended to be concentrated around events and holidays: sharing the dishes with her after Christmas dinner, wrapping presents together for a baby shower for Kit's wife, Connie (who'd done her single-handed best to make up for her sisters-in-law, having borne her first two less than eighteen months apart, and twin girls twelve months later). So I greeted her wholeheartedly but not completely easily, those first mornings at the house in the woods; I wasn't yet sure of myself in the role of widow, was only just learning how to put on that face for the world. In the beginning she didn't seem to mind that I didn't feel much like talking. The old house had been vacant for more than a year, the prior tenant an elderly bachelor, so there was work enough around the place to keep the two of us busy for days ahead. If my reticence bothered Geneva or seemed odd to her, she never let on; and there is much to be said for getting to know someone through elbow grease and companionable silence.

It was not till the second day that she ventured a comment. She came into the kitchen, where I was scrubbing between the counter tiles with an old toothbrush and a bottle of Clorox; she'd been in the bathroom, going after the old tub with a tube of caulk. She stood looking out the window toward the lopsided, three-walled toolshed, wiping her forehead on her sleeve, and made the offhand observation that the pipe under the sink was badly rusted, would probably need replacing. I nodded agreement, and asked if she wanted something to drink. I was pouring tea over two tumblers full of ice when Geneva turned and said, "You're absolutely sure this is what you want? This place, I mean."

"I'm sure," I answered slowly, wondering to myself why she'd asked.

"Because—well, I know if I lost Bailey . . ." She hesitated, considering this for a moment, apparently found it too awful to contemplate for long, shook her head to dislodge the image. "It would just be too much for me, I think. Starting over like this. Out here. All alone."

"But Mitchell wasn't Bailey. It wasn't like that." I handed Geneva her tea and watched her reach across the table for the sugar bowl.

"Yeah," she said, tipping sugar straight from the bowl into the glass and stirring it with her forefinger. "I've been wondering about that."

"About what?"

"About why you don't seem more—I don't know. More heart-broken." She looked up at me, her gaze frank and uncritical. "You don't even seem all that sad," she went on. "If I had to put my finger on it, I guess I'd say you act more bewildered than anything else. But somehow you don't strike me as very, well, *bereaved*."

"What are you saying, Geneva?"

She sighed and set her tea on my clean countertop. "Now, don't get all bristly on me. All I want to know is if you're okay. I know the boys are looking after the estate and the farm and everything, and I know we've seen you every day, but I can't help wondering if it's enough."

I stared at Geneva, the general vicinity of her chin. I stared until my eyes blurred and, to the surprise of us both, I started to cry—soft at first, then hard and loud. I'd hardly cried at all since the funeral, not from sadness or shock, from exhaustion or my terrible confusion. It seemed I'd been saving my tears, storing them up for something, though this was not, I think, the moment either Geneva or I had expected.

"Lucy," she said, and stepped forward and took me in her arms. Her embrace was as sure as anything I'd ever known from a man; there was more in back of it than Mitchell in all of fourteen years had had to give me. How could I tell her that those tears were not from the grief they all expected and understood, not from loneliness, but from pure, rushing relief? How could I explain the way it felt to find myself, unexpectedly and perhaps undeservedly, turned loose from a life I hadn't even known had swallowed me whole? That in this little rundown house on the edge of nowhere I'd begun to wake in the mornings with a fluttering in my belly that I'd only just allowed myself to admit was exhilaration? With the loss of Mitchell's life I'd had mine handed back. How could I hope to convey my gratitude for this unmeant gift? All I knew was that it felt wonderful to cry, to lean into Geneva's bulk and soak the shoulder of her stained pink T-shirt, to have her pat my back and say out loud what I knew in my bones: that the years lay before me like fallow ground in all directions, rich with secrets underneath the soil; that everything would begin again.

(two)

W e've got to get you out of this house," Geneva said. She'd been pestering me about it for days, but lately she'd taken a more determined tone. The truth was, I didn't want to leave. I'd accompanied her a few times into town for groceries, and once as far as Wal-Mart on the bypass, but most days I felt as rootbound as an old swamp cypress; I thought if you tried to move me I might shrivel, turn to dust, disappear, doomed to roam the earth with the spirits of the Indians who'd once lived in these woods, looking for a place to call home.

I was, as she supposed, bewildered, puzzling out my way alone, interested, in a detached, clinical way, in this new woman in my skin, her thoughts and reactions. The isolation Geneva found so oppressive made me giddy. I had no television, no diversions but an old Delco radio and a box full of my high school lit books; the country itself was all I needed in the way of entertainment. The view from the front porch changed hourly. Spring was early that year, bursting, overbearing green against a sky so dense and blue it seemed bent on burning itself into my retinas. Every afternoon when I walked the half mile out to the main road for my mail—supermarket sale flyers, Dairy Queen coupon books, nothing more intimate than the electric bill—I saw things I hadn't noticed in my whole thirty-three years in East Texas: foliage I'd never taken the time to study, insects I couldn't name. Against the backdrop of my solitude, events were thrown into crisper focus, took on an urgency that had me flying to the window at every unfamiliar sound, standing in the middle of the road at midnight caught up in the pleasant futility of counting stars. That the days had no structure struck me as luxurious, even decadent; I could have ice cream for breakfast, cornflakes for supper, stay up half the night reading detective novels, sing at the top of my lungs in the tub.

Anyway, I was hardly alone. I had visitors daily: Bailey, Geneva, Dove. Even my mama came out once, with Dove, mincing around the place in her heels and clanking jewelry, patting at her hair like she was checking for cobwebs or bat droppings.

"Go ahead, Mama," I said finally, watching her try to make herself comfortable on one of the hardback chairs at my kitchen table as I poured tea, "you don't have to hold your tongue. I can tell it's killing you."

"I just want what's best for you, Lucy," she said. "I always have."

Dove and I exchanged a look. "This *is* best for me right now," I said. "Maybe you just need to adjust your expectations."

"As you have plainly done," she said. She picked up her teacup and sniffed it, like maybe I'd spooned in a little arsenic. I got up from the table and snatched the cup out from under her nose and tipped the tea down the sink.

Mama pushed back her chair and trained her hard blue gaze on me. "Have you asked Jesus for forgiveness?" she asked, her voice so fluttery and strange it made the hair on my neck start to prickle.

I opened my eyes wide. "What for?"

"For whatever it is you've done that made Him take your husband from you." And before I could get my mouth open, she marched out of the house and parked herself in the front seat of Dove's car.

"Don't listen to your mama, Lucy Bird," Dove said. "It ain't like she wrote the book on losin' a husband."

"How can she blame what happened on me?" I said. "Mitchell was killed! It was an accident!" I set the teacup shakily on the counter and let cold water stream over my wrists. "Mama wants me to live like I'm ashamed, Dove. She wants me to walk around like she has for the past thirty years, embarrassed by being left behind. I won't do it. Damn it, I won't."

In the doorway, Dove was grinning. "See there?" she said. "There's that voice I was telling you about."

I smiled back. "It's your fault," I said. "Everything I know, I learned from you." I pictured myself then proudly, fiercely solitary, cruising around the county in a big old car, tending my garden, bossing my nieces and nephews around. There were worse fates than growing old alone in Mooney, Texas. There might even be a kind of grace to it.

"That's my girl," she said, giving me a hug. And, to my relief, they drove away.

I was surprised, a few days later, to get a call from Bailey inviting me to supper at Mama's. "I get the feeling there's been some kind of falling out," he said.

I laughed. "She wants me to apologize for my heathen ways," I said. "Living out in the country, all alone, in a little falling-down house. I mean, it's bad enough if I'd been forced into it, but doing it of my own free will . . ."

"She thinks you're gonna turn out like Dove," he said.

"I should be so lucky," I answered. "Better than turning out like *her*.

Sitting around in pumps and pearls, waiting for Jesus to show up and ring the doorbell."

"Or our daddy Raymond Hatch." We both snickered. "Stand your ground, Lucy," Bailey said. "You're not the same person you used to be. Just remember, you're not the only one who needs a little time to get used to it."

As a peace offering, I decided to get some flowers to take along to Mama's supper. I drove into town in one of Bailey and Kit's old company trucks—I'd let Mitchell's two pickups go with the farm, to be auctioned with the rest of the place later that month—and parked at the curb in front of the redbrick shoebox that was Faye's Flowers, a block off the main square. The original proprietor, Faye Waters, had been dead twenty years, and her daughter, Peggy Thaney, had been running Faye's ever since. Peggy's display windows were a kind of legend in Mooney, geared as they were around local events: school dances and sports events, weddings and births. This week, I saw, was a tribute to the retirement of old Judge Markham from the bench; there was a full-size store mannequin dressed in robes and holding an open legal brief, and Peggy had fastened what must have been the hair and beard from a Santa Claus costume to the head, making the mannequin look less like the distinguished judge and more like a cross between Moses and Clarence Beadle, the Vietnam vet who'd lost his mind because of Agent Orange and lived in a hut in the woods outside town, coming in once every couple of months to pick up his mail and snarl at people like a rabid dog. THANKS, MARKY, FOR 40 GREAT YEARS! read a red-and-black tempera-paint banner that hung, slightly askew, over the mannequin's featureless head.

I pushed open the shop door, jangling a string of sleigh bells on a silver ribbon. An enormous person in a turquoise-flowered muumuu stood behind the counter, scribbling on a yellow pad. It wasn't until she looked up and met my eyes that I recognized Peggy Thaney. I hadn't seen Peggy in more than ten years, I guessed, and while she'd always been a big woman, she was now better than big—the word "giantess" came to mind. Her dress looked like it had been cut from a circus tent.

"Hi," I said. "You probably don't remember me." It was my standard greeting, what I said the first time I walked into the True Value or the Dairy Queen. It was surprising, though, what people did remember, stuff you might just as soon they'd forget. "I'm—"

"Lucy Hatch," Peggy said, laying her pen on the counter. "I'd have known you anywhere. You still look just like your senior picture."

"Oh, I hope not," I said with a laugh. It was funny, I thought, how the minute I landed in Mooney I was back to being known by my family name, like my marriage to Mitchell Breward had been nothing but a quick side trip. Funnier still the way "Hatch" seemed to fit my skin, the way "Breward" never had.

"They said you were back in town," she said. "You lost your husband, I heard."

I swallowed hard, took a second to let the whirling in my head die down. Every now and then the news seemed to sneak up on me and strike me fresh, like Sam Gill had just stepped onto my doorstep with his cap in his hands and I was hearing the words for the first time. "Yes, last month," I said. Sometimes it seemed like the oldest story in the world, and sometimes it seemed it had happened just minutes before. I came unmoored easily, drifted in time. Where was I, now, today? Faye's Flowers. My hometown. Mitchell was gone. Okay.

"How were the flowers?"

"Excuse me?"

"At the funeral. Were the flowers nice?"

"I honestly don't remember." Had there been flowers? Yes, I recalled plainly a wreath of something white at the altar, the bitter scent of chrysanthemums, before I had to pull back and retrieve my equilibrium.

"So, then," Peggy said, "what can I do for you today? Excuse the clutter. My helper quit last week, and I've gotten a little behind in keeping up the showroom."

She was right; the place was a mess, with dried and silk arrangements jammed onto shelves, lengths of ribbon cascading off their spools, and a cooler stuffed full of flowers in what could only be called haphazard fashion, roses and daisies and carnations all mixed together in tubs. Still, there was something cheerful about the place; I guessed it would be hard to be depressed surrounded all day by things that were fragrant and in bloom.

"I'd like to get something for my mama," I said. "I just moved into a little old place outside town, and she's kind of put out with me over it."

Peggy came out from behind the counter, her bulk swaying gently, gracefully, inside the muumuu, and walked over to the cooler. "What do you suppose your mama would care for?" she said. "Such an, um, *proper* lady. Roses are always nice, of course. What about lilies? Goodness, where are the lilies." She wandered into the back for a while, came back out carrying a huge armload of ivory lilies, graceful as swans' throats on their long green stems. "How about a few of these? They do kind of put me in mind of your mama. Refined, you know?"

The phone rang, and I waited while she went into the back to answer it. I stood at the door and watched the traffic on Front Street, what there was of it. It was hard for me to believe sometimes I'd ever lived anywhere else; all I could remember was the gentle, plodding pace of Mooney, where everyone knew everything within minutes of its happening, where football victories and new babies were honored with window displays, where a woman could walk into a store fifteen years after she graduated from high school and still be recognized from her yearbook photo.

Peggy came back into the shop looking flustered; her silver-blond curls had gone a little frizzy and were plastered to her forehead and her neck. "What's the matter?" I asked.

"I don't know what to do," she said. "I've got orders for three arrangements for Billie Clutter's birthday—Dr. Tolbert's nurse, over at the clinic—but I'm waiting on UPS to bring me a big delivery for a banquet tomorrow. Oh, I could just flog that little Raeanne for doing this to me."

"Raeanne was your helper?"

"If you could call her that. Spent most of her time on the phone in the back, filing her nails and gossiping with her sisters. She would drive the van for me, though. I sure miss that."

"Why'd she quit?"

"Got pregnant," Peggy said. "Some airman she met from the base in Bossier City. Decided to move over there and set up housekeeping. Can you imagine? No notice, none."

"I'll give you a hand." No one could have been more surprised than me to hear myself say it.

"You will?"

"Sure," I said. "I can drive the van. Or wait for the UPS guy, if that's what you want. Maybe help you straighten up the shop a little." Peggy was just staring at me, gap-mouthed, like I'd sprouted a second head. "Look, I could use a part-time job," I said. "I know you didn't offer, but I guess I'm asking you." I smiled. "I promise you I won't be getting pregnant."

"I can't pay but minimum wage," Peggy said. "No benefits." I nodded my head. "Nine to two, every weekday but Tuesdays," she said. "Every now and then I might need you on a Saturday for a couple hours." She sucked in a deep breath. "Lord, are you sure about this?" she said. "It seems awful sudden."

I wasn't about to tell her all I knew about sudden, how, if you even looked away for an instant, your whole life could turn. That finding myself behind the wheel of a delivery van for a flower shop didn't seem any more peculiar to me than waking alone in the middle of the night, swimming up through layers of consciousness wondering where I was and how I'd gotten there, the long, spun-out moment of panic as I struggled awake knowing something had happened, that something was not right. One instant I'd been someone's wife; the next I was not. It put a twist on "sudden," which told me that, from that point on, all bets were off.

"What about that?" Peggy asked then, nodding at my wrist, still in a cast.

"Oh, this comes off in about a week," I said. "The van's not a standard, is it?"

I waited while she put together the arrangements—two mixed spring bouquets, one bunch of roses and baby's breath—and together we carried them out to the van. Across the street, at the corner house I remembered as belonging to Mrs. Tanner, a couple of men, one white, one black, were cutting lumber on a sawhorse in the yard. I felt their eyes on me as I climbed up into the old Econoline and started the engine. Oh, well, I thought, better get used to it, as I felt the little seismic shift: Mooney, Texas, rearranging itself under my feet, making a place for me. A citizen, one foot back in the world.

Y ou're the one who said I needed to get out of the house," I said to my sister-in-law Geneva that night at Mama's house. She and I were setting the table in the dining room, laying out Mama's wedding china. Three lilies, in a Waterford vase, presided serenely over the table. My mama was an old pro at keeping up appearances. No one would ever have believed the chaos that had gone on beneath the surface here, the nights after my daddy Raymond Hatch left, when she wandered the house in a dirty satin peignoir drinking Four Roses out of a jelly glass and wailing like a banshee, the way the solar system had seemed to spin out of control around my two brothers and me. Oh, Mama had rallied, finally, to the extreme, thanks to Dove and Jesus. If you'd caught her in the last twenty years with a hair out of place, it would have made the local news, or at least Peggy Thaney's window.

Geneva smiled at me gently, shaking her head. "Your mama's gonna go ballistic," she said. "You know that, don't you?"

"Lord, Geneva, it's a flower shop, not a strip club. It's a perfectly respectable job."

"Driving a delivery van?"

I shrugged. "I don't know, I kind of like it. A way to get reacquainted with the community, you know?"

"Ballistic," she said again under her breath. Mama was in the kitchen fussing over the roast beef, and Bailey and Kit and Kit's family were in the living room, competing with the TV to see who could make the most noise. Dove wasn't coming, citing a "prior engagement," so Geneva and I looked up at one another curiously when the doorbell rang.

Mama came trotting out of the kitchen patting her hair. She wore a pale-blue suit with a heavy gold necklace and dark pumps, not a hem crooked nor a smudge to be seen. Her lipstick was Fire and Ice and her perfume was Youth Dew, as they'd been for as long as I could remember. Even when her breath had reeked of Four Roses, Mama's skin smelled like Estée Lauder. "That must be our guest," she said breathlessly, heading down the front hall.

"Who—?" I began, just as the door opened and Mama stepped aside to welcome the Baptist preacher, Reverend Honeywell. Geneva and I exchanged another look. "What's he doing here?" I whispered, but she just shook her head, and we finished sliding the linen napkins through the silver-plate napkin rings and laying them alongside each place setting. In the living room the TV went off, and in a couple of minutes Mama and Bailey and Kit and the preacher came into the dining room. Kit's wife, Connie, tagged along behind, herding their four kids, who scrambled and fought for the choicest seats at the table.

"Lucy," Mama said, touching the back of my arm, "you remember Reverend Honeywell."

"I do," I said, staring at the man's starched white collar, nervous about meeting his eyes. This had something to do with me, I knew it. Maybe driving a delivery van for a flower shop was the eleventh "thou shalt not."

Reverend Honeywell reached out and lay a pinkly groomed hand on the cast that held my broken wrist. "God hears you in your pain, Lucy."

"It doesn't hurt anymore, actually," I said. "It's pretty much healed."

He smiled at me like I was a terribly stupid child. "That is not the pain to which I was referring." I knew that, of course, but I thought he ought to have to work a little for his supper.

Mama seated me right next to the preacher. All through the meal I kept my head bowed over my plate, raising and lowering my fork, barely tasting my roast beef and potatoes and peas. Most of the talk consisted of the boys, my brothers, regaling us with business stories, and Reverend Honeywell told about a missionary family the church was sponsoring, but I could feel them all, my family and this near-stranger, this man of God, drawing the wagons close around me. At the first lull in the conversation I looked up and announced, "I got a job."

Everyone stared at me—all but Geneva, who kept her eyes on the gravy boat. "Yeah?" Bailey asked finally, lightly, tearing a dinner roll in two. "Where?"

"Faye's Flowers," I said. "Driving the delivery van."

"Oh, for goodness' sake," Mama said, laying her fork across her plate. "You're joking, I'm sure."

"No, I'm not. I went in this afternoon, and Peggy was in a bind. Her helper quit last week without any notice, and she's had her hands full ever since, trying to keep up the shop and get all the deliveries made. I offered to help her out, and she's going to pay me for twenty hours a week. I started this afternoon, actually, but I'm going in for real in the morning."

"How can you possibly deliver flowers?" Mama said. "You've only got one arm!"

"Only for a few more days," I said. "And I can drive just fine with one arm. Anyway, I like it. It makes me feel . . ." *Alive*, I wanted to say, except that it sounded so pitiful. It was true, though. The idea that people would be glad at the sight of me, that I might play a part in commemorating someone's affection or remorse or sorrow, appealed to me greatly.

"You're determined to do this to me, aren't you?" Mama asked, dabbing the corners of her mouth with her cloth napkin. I wished I knew how she always managed to eat a full meal and finish with her lipstick on. It seemed like a trade secret, one more thing she'd never taught me. My Aunt Dove had never worn anything in her life but Chap Stick, and was no help at all.

"Do what, Mama?" I said, my voice rising higher than I'd meant for it to, so that everyone, even the kids, stopped chewing and swung their faces my way.

"It's shameful behavior, Lucy, and you know it," Mama said. "It is not befitting your . . . your . . ."

"My what?" I said, the taste of anger as sharp and unexpected as a copper penny on my tongue. "My husband died! What do you expect me to do, wander around in my nightgown getting drunk and carrying on twenty-four hours a day? Or maybe you think I ought to dress up and sit around all day waiting for Jesus to save me!"

"Lucy," the Reverend Honeywell said, but I turned on him and the sight of his smug pink face made me want to hit something.

"Have you ever seen a man killed by a mower, Reverend Honeywell?" I asked. He cleared his throat, stared at the scarlet juice that remained of his roast beef, and admitted he hadn't. "Well, I haven't either. They wouldn't let me see him, there was nothing *to* see. One minute he was standing in the kitchen in his overalls drinking his coffee, heading out the back door, and the next thing I know somebody's telling me he's gone. Torn apart. Nothing but scraps and bone."

My two nephews, seven and six, sat staring at me across the table with their eyes bugged out. "Connie," Kit said, one low word, and she got up and started hustling the kids away from the table, protesting that they hadn't gotten dessert yet.

"The ways of God are not always ours to understand, Lucy," the Reverend said. "Sometimes all we can do is to have faith that there *is* a reason."

"Oh, and I suppose I'll find that out when? When I meet Mitchell again, over on the other side? Everybody keeps telling me he's gone to a better place, but you know what? I don't believe it. Mitchell had everything he wanted, in *this* life. A piece of ground, a house, a few cows. There *is* no better place for him than that one was. For me, either, but you know what? I'm not going to lie down and let the world run right over me because my husband's gone. If that's what Jesus wants me to do, well then, I guess He's no friend of mine."

"Lucy, you apologize to Reverend Honeywell right now," Mama said. It was interesting to see Mama get really mad, the way rage interfered with Christian tolerance and forgiveness. In Mama's worldview, there would be a separate room in heaven for people like herself, who'd been devout and God-fearing all their lives—even when she'd been sloshed, she was quoting the Gospels—and the born-agains would go to another, slightly shabbier room, so as not to taint God's right-hand servants with their cigarette smoke and their sordid stories, the drug busts and aborted babies and acts of adultery they'd committed before they finally saw the light. I could tell she wished I was eight and she could just smack my bottom and send me to my room.

I pushed back my chair and stood up. "I'm sorry," I said. "I'm sorry you're disappointed in me, and I'm sorry I've spoiled everyone's supper. But I hope to God Mitchell's not in your heaven, and I hope there's no place for me there, either." I actually laughed, a little. "I guess I don't have to worry about that, though, do I? Enjoy your pie," I said, and I marched out of the house and wrestled open the door of the borrowed pickup and drove myself, with my one good arm, home.

(three)

My first morning in the shop was a trial by fire. Peggy was doing the flowers for a Kiwanis banquet that night, and in the midst of preparing the arrangements and loading them into the Econoline, a call came that there'd been an accident at the Golden Years retirement home; the driver of the van that carried the wheelchair patients on their weekly round of errands had forgotten to set the parking brake and the van had rolled backward into a laundry truck, and four senior citizens were in the hospital, none seriously hurt, but jostled and bruised and understandably mad as hell. The administrator of Golden Years was pulling out all the stops, ordering armloads of extravagant bouquets for the injured folks, probably, Peggy said, in hopes no one would investigate the claim that the van driver—the administrator's nephew—was seventeen, unlicensed, and had a couple of convictions for possession of a controlled substance.

Till that day, I'd never done more than stick a bunch of cut flowers in a vase and pour in a little water, but I had no choice but to learn, fast. It wasn't so hard; you just had to stand back and let yourself see the whole arrangement in your mind, then start adding and subtracting until the thing achieved its natural balance. Or something like that, anyway; I had an affection for purple ranunculus with yellow statice that Peggy didn't especially share, but all she said was "We'll take that one to Lorna Shepherd, she can't see too good anyway," and left it at that. All in all, I was feeling pretty pleased with myself, carrying my work out to the van in preparation for the trip to the hospital. It seemed to me that if you didn't set your expectations too high, it might be possible to achieve a sort of karmic symmetry in Mooney, that maybe through a careful blend of work and home you might construct a net around yourself that would bear you up and keep you aloft. Not safe, exactly; I'd seen too much, the past few weeks, to believe anyone, anywhere, was ever truly safe. If death wanted you, it would reach down and snatch you up; there was nothing in the world you could do about it. In the meantime, I was learning to sleep alone, to cook for one, to smile at strangers, to arrange flowers. It was early March and still chilly at night, but I believed I could figure out a way to keep myself warm.

Peggy came out of the shop carrying two last sprays for the Kiwanis banquet, and handed them to me as she leaned into the van, arranging things this way and that. Across the street, at Mrs. Tanner's, one of the workers I'd seen on the lawn the afternoon before was climbing behind the wheel of a beat-up white Chevy pickup, backing down the drive. He swung out into the street and for a moment eased off the accelerator and sat idling the engine, looking right at me through the windshield, which had a crack in it like a spider's silver thread. Through the glass his eyes were so dark they looked black, and something in them seemed to kick me in the gut with a little boot of recognition, although I didn't think I'd ever seen him before, but then I was always having this kind of moment since I'd gotten back to town, people I thought I'd known in another life. I stood on the curb holding the van door open with my foot and a couple of bunches of gladiolas in my good arm while the old truck's engine chugged and sputtered and the driver just sat with his wrists draped loose over the wheel, watching me through the wind-shield, until a car drove up behind the pickup and tooted its horn, once, then again, and the driver, in slow motion, with all the time in the world, put the truck in gear and eased through the intersection and turned the corner onto Main Street, and I let go of the van door with my foot and decapitated a whole spray of gladiolas.

L uckily, things in Mooney moved at such a glacial pace that most of the landmarks were still as I remembered them, many from my grade school days. The county hospital had a new wing, and cardiac care and psychiatric units, but it still stood on the same plain-vanilla grounds west of town, rising from a flat brown field like spacemen had dropped it there and then abandoned it. I wondered, not for the first time, if the people who designed these buildings were sadists, intent on prolonging rather than relieving the suffering that went on inside. But then, a lot of Mooney looked like that. The coun-tryside was the most beautiful you'd ever hope to see, but the architec-ture was, for the most part, bland and unimaginative, seemingly created with the sole purpose not to offend.

On my way back through town, to the courthouse annex where the Kiwanis banquet would be held, I passed my brother Bailey in his big dually truck. He waved like mad, and I pulled over and so did he, and he hopped out and came running across the street, slicking his hair up under his ball cap. My brother was a sight for sore eyes no matter how you figured it; sometimes I just liked to gaze upon him and be reminded that maybe there was a God, after all, so long as there were men in the world who looked like this. He always, no matter what the climate or occasion, wore a button-down oxford-cloth shirt and starched jeans and polished Ropers, and most of the time a cap that said HATCH BROTHERS CONTRACTING. He never seemed to sweat. Our coloring was similar, except that our hair, which might best be described as auburn, came up with rust-colored highlights in Bailey, and though we both had brown eyes, Bailey's were gold around the irises, like a cat's. He was grinning at me with his long white teeth under his mustache as he came up and leaned his elbows in the window of the van.

"So, this wasn't just some story you concocted to piss off Mama and the preacher," he said. "You really are driving a delivery van."

"I'm surprised you stopped to talk to me," I said. "Seeing's how I'm going to the devil and all."

"Actually," he said, "I stopped to see if I could corrupt you a little bit more."

"Yeah?"

"You remember the Round-Up? Dub Crookshank's old place, where everybody used to go to dance when we were in school?"

"Sure I remember." The Round-Up had been the backbone of our social lives, both in high school and after, a real Texas honky-tonk with cold beer in long-neck bottles and a great jukebox filled with country standards, and sometimes live bands on the weekends. Even the kids who didn't drink went to the Round-Up, to flirt and fight and rub up against each other, test-driving our shiny new hormones on the big, dark dance floor while Dub smiled and looked the other way. Old people and little kids and everyone except the true hard-shell Baptists went to the Round-Up. I hadn't thought of the place in years, but the second Bailey mentioned it I could smell it, the spilled beer and sawdust, sweat and perfume. "My goodness, you all still go there?"

"Every Wednesday and Saturday," Bailey said. "Geneva's nuts about this singer . . . Oh, she'll tell you all about it. What do you say? You about ready for a night on the town?"

"Tonight?"

"We'll pick you up around seven, if you're game." He saw my hesitation, and smiled. "Come on, Lucy, you're already going to hell—what have you got to lose?"

Y ou've got guts, I'll grant you that," Geneva said, turning to look at me over the seat back as the big truck roared through the dusk. We weren't entirely finished with winter in East Texas, but you could feel the earth warming gradually underneath you, a little more every day, and it was possible to go out some evenings, like this one, in nothing but your shirtsleeves. "I mean, I can't abide that preacher of your mama's any more than you can, but I've always kept my mouth shut around him. But you, Lucy, practically came right out and told him to screw himself."

"I honestly didn't set out to be rude," I said. "But I just don't have any patience for that stuff anymore, you know? His or Mama's, either one. Why does everybody want me to go to pieces? I'm tired of faking what I don't feel."

What I felt, though, was pure, blade-sharp loneliness, walking behind Bailey and Geneva, their arms threaded lazily around each other's hips, through the familiar cedar-plank entrance of the Round-Up. I hung back a minute in the doorway and let the essence of the place wash over me, a hundred nights of illicit beer and dances with boys I knew were bad for me, boys I'd never speak to or even see outside these walls. Truth be told, the best sex I'd ever had was clothed and upright, sliding around this dance floor holding some sweet-smelling boy by the belt, the kind of sex that's all clutch and promise, with no possibility of conclusion, its inevitable disappointment. It had been a big shock, getting married and finding out that what husbands and wives did together had nothing at all to do with pushing slowly against each other in a beery haze while George Jones sang about a heartbreak any of us had yet to know.

And yet here I stood, one of a hundred females in jeans and boots, missing Mitchell. I dreaded the thought of smiling, socializing, strangers' hands on me. Maybe I was not ready to be part of the world, after all. Maybe I ought to wave the white flag, turn around and run back to Mama and Reverend Honeywell and their close personal friend Jesus. That sensation of coming dislodged in time washed over me again, with the accompanying wave of dizziness. Was I thirty-three, or seventeen? Had my husband just died, or was I here to meet Tommy Rupp, the mechanic at Orson's Texaco with the blue eyes and the black hair combed like Elvis's? How could everything be so familiar and at the same time feel like no place I'd ever seen? The worst part of waking up with that terror jammed up in the back of your throat is the realization that, when you turn on the light, the bad dream isn't going away. How many nights until I understood, in my darkest subconscious, that Mitchell was gone?

"Hey," Bailey said, his hand a welcome, steadying guide under my elbow, "how you doing?" He stood looking down into my face, his brow furrowed the way I'd seen it, too often, these last few weeks. Maybe the care of just one solitary person was enough to keep you afloat in the world. But I didn't think so.

"Oh, Bailey, I don't know . . ."

"Listen," he said, bending over to put his mouth against my ear, "I know this is tough, Lucy, but give it a chance, okay? One set, one hour. If you want to go at the break, we'll go. Fair?" Spots danced before my eyes. Merle Haggard was singing about swinging doors, a jukebox, and a barstool. "I'll keep an eye on you every minute, okay?" Bailey said. "Anyway, Gen wants you to see the man of her dreams. She'll be disappointed if you bail on her now." I managed to nod, and Bailey patted my arm. "I'm gonna get us some beers. That table there's our usual spot."

The room was exactly as I recalled it, untouched by age or progress. It was still dim and smoky and jam-packed, even on a weeknight, and the beer signs over the pool tables were the same ones I remembered, the Budweiser Clydesdales circling in an endless procession, the Falstaff waterfall still bubbling blue and eternal over that same old cliff.

I followed Geneva to one of the long wooden tables that lined the back of the hall, perpendicular to the stage and the dance floor, and slid onto the bench across from her, but she wasn't paying any attention to me; her eyes were aimed at the front of the hall, where the members of the band were stepping onto the platform, taking their places under the lights. At center stage a man shielded his eyes with his hand, squinting into the glare of the spot; someone let out a long, low whistle and he laughed, adjusting the strap on a shiny black guitar.

Geneva reached across the table and dug her nails into the back of my good wrist. "Check it out," she said, nodding toward the stage as the drummer kicked a rhythm with his foot pedal against the taut skin of the bass drum, making my bones rattle.

"What?" I shouted as the crowd noise rose, cresting like a wave, breaking across the hall.

"Don't tell me you don't remember him!"

"Who? Remember who?"

"Ash Farrell."

A flashbulb went off, illuminating the face onstage, igniting an image from some dim, long-buried corner of my memory. Ash Farrell. I remembered a skinny boy a few grades ahead of me in school, mute and remotely handsome behind a shank of dark hair. He rode a motorcycle—nothing big or showy, a trim black Kawasaki—and lugged a silver metal-flake helmet from class to class the way the rest of us did our algebra books. I never had a class with him, he was too far ahead of me for that, and so the picture I carried of him was of defiant silence, though I recalled that he had performed in the school variety show my freshman year, singing "Tequila Sunrise" in a trembling tenor, tossing his hair out of his eyes with a careless aplomb that made a handful of girls down front squeal, like they'd actually taken him for one of the Eagles. That spring there was some minor scandal about his graduation; he'd skipped the ceremony and was supposed to have taken a bottle of Old Crow and the Grace Bible Church preacher's daughter, Neely Craig, who was as wild as they come, and gone to Caddo Lake under the full moon. Neely was shipped off to private school in Fayetteville after that, so the rumor that he'd gotten her pregnant was never confirmed or denied but carved itself into tantalizing small-town legend, and as far as I knew, Ash Farrell had never come back across the county line. If I'd given it any thought at all, I'd have pictured him on his bike, flying down some wooded highway with his guitar strapped to his back, his hair whipping clean back from his face as the center stripe beneath him blurred to solid white, taking him away from the rest of us and our small, finite lives; I would not have thought East Texas could hold him.

I remembered Ash Farrell, all right, but the man up there grinning into the spotlight bore my memory so little justice I could hardly believe I'd heard Geneva right. Ash Farrell had been a slight, sullen kid, but this man, though lean, was muscled all over, with ropy cords of brown tendon below the rolled-up sleeves of a denim work shirt, his legs slender but sturdy in worn Levi's and cowboy boots. He had the look of someone who worked outdoors, with his hands; the skin at the corners of his eyes pleated like old leather when he smiled, flashing a mouthful of teeth. Had I ever, once, seen Ash Farrell smile? Maybe, for an instant, as the cheers and whistles rose into the rafters of the gymnasium on the dying chord of "Tequila Sunrise." Maybe so, or maybe it was just a mental embellishment, some trick to help bridge past to present. It wasn't until he tossed his head to shake the hair—falling thick over one eye, the brown now heavily marbled with silver—from his face that I felt the sudden shock of connection, the recognition of a thing once familiar. Or, in this case, twice familiar; Ash Farrell's was the face behind the wheel of the white Chevy pickup, the eyes through the windshield that had cost the lives of a spray of yellow gladiolas.

The band swung into Hank Williams's "Hey, Good Lookin'," and I knew right off that Ash Farrell had traveled a long way from "Tequila Sunrise" in the Mooney High gymnasium. I had no knowledge of music to speak of, an ear trained by nothing but the radio, but I recognized as soon as he opened his mouth that he had something special. It wasn't just his voice, although it was first and mostly that; it was richer than I remembered, seasoned, I guessed, by eighteen years of living, until it had achieved a depth, a layered and polished sheen, like a good piece of wood, well cared for. A remarkable, a distinctive voice, no matter how else you described it. But there was something else besides his singing; it was nothing more or less than the ease with which he owned his space, the luster that seemed to emanate from the circle of white light in which he stood, moving his feet in time to the music, smiling at the other players and at the occasional dancer who slid by under his gaze. He seemed self-possessed to a degree that was a little unnerving to someone like me, having to reinvent myself every single morning in the bathroom mirror. Till that night I'd have bet money that my brother Bailey was the best-looking man in Mooney, Texas, but I'd have been wrong.

The next tune was one I'd never heard before, something jaunty and upbeat, with a Bob Wills feel, and the two-steppers were out there with a vengeance now, scooting around the floor in well-oiled pairs. Geneva and Bailey were in their midst, twirling with the best of them; if I hadn't known better, I'd have sworn they were on their first date, they looked so fresh and happy. The words to the song were about an old couple learning to fall in love with each other just like the first time, and even though they had nothing to do with my situation, they gave me a pang just the same. One thing I'd learned about widowhood is that it tends to turn you into a revisionist; I spent a lot of time correcting feelings I thought were mine, when in reality they were just something I'd heard Reba McEntire singing about on the radio. Mitchell had never made my knees go weak, had never swept me off my feet, literally or otherwise. He was just there. And now he was not; and I was sitting in a dance hall, all alone. *Mitchell, if you can hear me*, I said in my head, *I hate your guts for this. I hope you're in the shabby room, the one with all the smokers.*

Geneva collapsed on the bench alongside me, perspiring and out of breath. She took a swig of her Miller Lite. "So, what do you think?" she hollered in my ear. "Pretty great, right?"

"He's good," I admitted.

"Too good for *this* dump," she said. "I keep telling him and telling him. He oughta be in Nashville." She had a point; from where I sat, Ash Farrell seemed to have the whole package: the looks, the talent. He seemed to shine too bright for the Round-Up, to make the room look a little dingy by comparison. "He *writes* these songs, some of 'em," Geneva said, with what sounded like pride by association. "Tell me why he isn't on CMT, right this minute."

"Maybe he likes it here."

"He likes it, all right," Bailey put in; I hadn't even realized he was listening. "Likes being a big shit in a little bitty field. Likes screwing secretaries and farm girls. Likes being a *handyman* for a living." He made it sound one step down from "gigolo," which, for all I knew, it was. Geneva smacked him lightly on the arm. She didn't really seem mad, though, which made me think that what Bailey had said must be, at least partly, true.

"Anyway, who would you ogle if Ash went to Nashville?" Bailey said. "You might even have to start paying attention to me, for a change." A ballad, a love song, started up, and she grinned and grabbed his hand, and they waded out into the pool of dancers and soon they were in a slow clinch, shuffling around the floor. I watched Ash Farrell for a while, his eyes closed in the spotlight, his guitar slung onto one hip, his voice digging down low and then arching up into the smoky rafters, and when I couldn't take the tale of loss and woe anymore I got up and went to the ladies' room and shut myself in a stall. I cried for two or three minutes, careful not to let myself get too red or puffy; then I blew my nose on some toilet paper and brushed my hair and repaired my lipstick. The rest of my life seemed to unfurl ahead of me like a roll of blank white paper, without a single feature or impression. Where were the colors? If Mitchell had been a color I supposed he'd have been one of the muted ones—gray, maybe, or denim blue. Still, color was color. Where was I supposed to find it now?

I thought the break would never come, and the second it did, I was on my feet. "Please," I said to Bailey, "I've got to get out of here." He gave me a long, appraising look. "You promised," I reminded him, and he nodded.

"Come on, Gen," he said as Randy Travis came roaring out of the jukebox. "We're gonna run Lucy home."

"Uh-uh," Geneva said, "no way. Come here, Lucy. You're gonna meet him."

"Who?" I said, before I realized she meant Ash Farrell. "Oh, Geneva, give me a break. I don't have anything to say to him! I just want to go home, okay? Come back afterward if you still need your fix."

"We'll just say, 'Hey,' " she said, taking me firmly by the elbow. "He usually comes to the bar for a drink about now. Come on."

"I feel like an idiot," I said as we parked ourselves along the bar, me facing the bartenders, Geneva turned toward the room, scanning it like a spy. "I feel like I'm seventeen and laying for Tommy Rupp." It didn't help that there were at least half a dozen other women lined up like a row of sideshow prizes along the bar, in bright blouses and too much makeup, their eyes trained on the backstage door. "Geneva, honestly," I whispered, nodding down the rank of glassy-eyed, candy-coated hopefuls. "This is pathetic. I mean, what does he do, just walk up and pick, like he's at Baskin-Robbins choosing a flavor? I don't want any part of this."

I needn't have worried about it, though; when Ash Farrell did finally show up, he was already accessorized. A bony blond in a white hip-hugging skirt and tank top was poured across his shoulders; if she could have found a way to have herself surgically attached, she'd have saved herself a lot of trouble. Her hair was piled on her head in an elaborate arrangement of loops and whorls, and a pair of silver disks the size of yo-yos hung from her earlobes. The fact that she'd gone to such effort made me look closer, and the second glance bore out what I'd suspected: that she wasn't any older, or not much, than I'd been when I'd come here to meet Tommy Rupp, and that Ash Farrell could probably get busted for statutory rape, if anyone cared.

Most of the bar groupies slunk into the shadows, leaving Geneva and me standing there like a pair of sore thumbs. Ash leaned his elbows on the bar and said something to Dub, who laughed and set a glass of amber-colored liquid in front of him. The girl was either whispering into or gnawing on his ear, her arm still looped across his shoulders, and with the look of a bull standing with perfect dignity in a field with a ridiculous-looking white egret perched on its back, he picked up the drink and downed it in one shot.

"Hey, Ash," Geneva said, and with careless diffidence he pivoted his face her way. He did smile to see her, though. He looked a lot happier than he did about what was going on at his other elbow, in fact. "There's somebody I want you to meet," she said, and stepped back and motioned with her chin to me. "My sister-in-law," she said. "Lucy Hatch."

For a second, it looked like he wasn't even going to bother to shift his gaze, that to move his eyes the fraction of an inch that was required to take me in was more than he could manage. They flicked over my face, preparing in one blink to dismiss me. Then, just as quickly, swung back.

"You," he said.

There it was again, the click of recognition I'd felt seeing him at the wheel of his truck, dialing into focus: something known.

"The flower girl," he added, and smiled, or was it a smirk? Hard to say in that light, with a teenager's tongue in his ear.

"You were holding up traffic."

"It was a worthy cause."

"Wait a minute," Geneva said. "Y'all know each other?"

"No," I said as Ash, at the same time, said, "Yes," and laughed. He turned his back on the girl and cocked his hip against the bar, signaling Dub with his eyes, I guessed, to hit him again, since that's what Dub did. "You live around here?" he asked me, picking up his whiskey, swirling it gently in the glass. "How in the world did I miss that?"

"I grew up here, if that's what you mean," I said. "I've only just been back a few weeks. I remember you, though, from school." His eyebrows shot toward his hairline; they were exceptional, as eyebrows went, heavy and black and ending abruptly before the outer corners of his eyes, like truncated parentheses. "The senior talent show?" I said. "You sang 'Tequila Sunrise.' All the girls screamed."

"Pretty good memory. It was 'Peaceful Easy Feeling,' though." He smiled into his drink. "And it wasn't *all* the girls."

"No, I'm sure it was 'Tequila Sunrise.' "

"I wouldn't have touched 'Tequila Sunrise' with a ten-foot pole."

I didn't know what the difference was, but I wasn't about to say so. "Were you this pretty in high school?" he asked, sending a flush into my face I couldn't arrest. "How come I don't remember you?"

"She was only a freshman when we were seniors," Geneva piped up. "You wouldn't have had any reason to know her."

"Or maybe you would have," I said, "if that's the sort of thing that stirs your, um, interest." I cut my eyes over his shoulder to the girl, who stood staring into her drink with what was quickly ramping up into full-blown pique. What in God's name was this stuff coming out of my mouth? Last night Mama's preacher, tonight a virtual stranger in a dance hall. The next thing you knew, I'd be one of those lunatics with my own late-night radio show, barking out profanities and bad advice in equal measure to people I'd never met.

Ash grinned. "Pretty *and* mean," he said. "Is that what happened to your hand? Aimed a left hook at your old man?"

The air seemed to leave in a rush from my lungs. I opened my mouth but nothing came out. I'd only had half a beer, but my head was whirling; the floor seemed to pitch under my feet. The girl had snaked her hands beneath Ash's armpits from behind and was headed for his big silver belt buckle, in this case surely the most redundant adornment ever modeled by man. "We have to go," I managed finally. "You were good, up there. I hope you get everything you want." This seemed to amuse him, or maybe he was just ticklish.

" 'Night, Ash," Geneva said, "see you Saturday," as I grabbed her elbow and steered her toward the door.

"Lucy Hatch."

I turned back around. He stood there like one of those multiarmed Indian gods, the blond's sharp little chin parked in the side of his neck. She hadn't unzipped him yet, but it seemed imminent. "What?" I said.

He took his time answering. "I just wanted to see what it felt like in my mouth."

"I wouldn't get too used to the taste, if I were you," I said, and jerked at Geneva's arm.

She glanced back toward the bar as we walked away. "Lucy!" she whispered. "He's looking at your *butt*!" She sounded genuinely thrilled by this.

"What a prick!" I said. "He's so full of himself, I'm surprised his head doesn't explode."

"He was coming on to you!"

I snorted. "He's a show-off, Geneva. An exhibitionist. All he's looking for is someplace to plant his flag. Did you see that belt buckle?"

"Maybe his girlfriend needs something to look into to touch up her lipstick afterward," Geneva said, and I shrieked and swatted her arm. When we met up with Bailey next to the door we were hanging all over each other, staggering with laughter. For that, at least, I could thank Ash Farrell. I hadn't laughed so hard as far back as I could remember.

That night I had a dream about Mitchell—a silly, unimaginative dream, transparent in its symbolism. In it I saw him walking out into the field as he had that last morning, his big head down, shoulders slightly stooped in his ragged overalls, scuffing his boots through the long grass. He just kept walking, moving steadily away, and though I had the distinct sensation that there was something important I should tell him, I couldn't get my mouth open; it was filled with something damp and gritty, wet ashes or sand. Mitchell just walked on until he disappeared into the yellow haze of the horizon, and I woke to find my pillow soaked, my throat swollen with tears.

I sat up in bed, disoriented, saying his name, hearing it ricochet around me in the dark. I said it again—a stranger's voice, loud and filled with terror as I realized he was not going to answer me. That there was no one to answer me.

I got up and switched on the bedside lamp and leaned over the bureau to look at myself in the mirror, running my fingers over the planes of my face until they began to take on their old familiar contours. After a few minutes I went into the kitchen and held the kettle

under the tap, then set it on the burner and lit the blue flame underneath. As I reached for the tea canister, I saw by the sunflower clock
that it was just past two. The silence of the house was huge, as black as
the night outside my window and as filled with things I couldn't place
or name; when the heat pump kicked on out back I gave a little cry,
scalding my wrist on the steam from the boiling kettle.

When my tea was good and strong I unlatched the screen door and
stepped out onto the porch, the boards beneath the soles of my bare feet
scarred and creaking, my good hand wrapped around the steaming cup.
A breeze blew wisps of scudding silver cloud across the moon, and in
the dark beating heart of the night I felt for the first time how it was to
be absolutely alone. Some beast could spring out of the trees and take
me in its jaws and no soul would hear. I could wander out to the highway and stick out my thumb and no one would miss me for hours,
maybe days. The only person of consequence in my life had left me, and
though the leaving was unintentional it all came out the same. If the
night wanted me it could have me—there was no one to dispute the
claim.

From the highway I heard the distant drone as a semi worked its way
up through the gears, caught a flash of headlights through the pines as it
whizzed by carrying its load of lumber or turkeys or propane, bound for
Texarkana, Shreveport, Little Rock, Memphis. The moon slid behind a
cloud and I found myself thinking, abrupt and unbidden, of Ash Farrell.
Ash Farrell was not alone, I knew, not that or any night; at two A.M. Ash
Farrell was just getting nicely tucked in by some long-legged, tempestuous girl half his age. I wondered then about the chances I'd missed,
whether by giving my hand so young to Mitchell I had closed forever
some untried door. What would it be like to offer yourself that freely,
with so little thought to design or consequence? To pick a companion
the way you picked a drink from a cooler, with no more expectation
than what would taste sweetest at that moment, never mind tomorrow

or a week from now? The only man I'd ever been with had been my husband, and fourteen years of marriage had only served, frankly, to make
me wonder what all the fuss was about.

Oh, there was something to it, I knew, from all the stories and the
songs. Just look at Bailey and Geneva. Look, for that matter, at Ash Farrell. I thought, as I had so many nights as Mitchell dozed beside me, that
I wasn't wired like other people, that I lacked some vital piece of cir-
cuitry. Now, for the first time, it occurred to me that I was not just a
widow, but a single woman. Would there be expectations, assumptions?
How long until I found myself one of that desperate crew lined up at
Dub's bar, makeup piled on and teeth bared, praying someone would
choose me? I decided, rinsing out my teacup and heading back to bed,
that tonight had been a warning, a lesson in disguise; and I made a
pledge to spend all my free time from here on out with my Aunt Dove:
watching, listening, learning what it took to live alone, without apology.

(four)

Peggy and I spent most of the next morning straightening the showroom, taking things off the shelves, dusting and Windexing, and placing the silk arrangements back in orderly rows, then set to work neatening the disarray in the cooler. Under the counter I found a stack of colored index cards, and made a series of hand-lettered signs that we fixed to the cooler's glass doors, naming the various flowers available and the cost per stem. Every now and then the sleigh bells on the front door chimed as a customer came in, or, more often, some acquaintance of Peggy's dropped by to drink a cup of coffee and gossip. In three hours in Peggy's shop, I learned more about the infrastructure of present-day Mooney than I would probably have learned in three months on my own: who was divorcing, expecting, building a house, declaring bankruptcy. I was aware that a lot of the folks who were showing up were there to check me out, to see how the new widow was bearing up, but I didn't mind; it seemed a fair exchange for being allowed to reenter the world, and their voices moved through me like familiar music as I worked, a cadence I'd known all my life, that I hadn't even known I'd been missing. Hardly anyone bought anything, but Peggy didn't seem to expect them to. "They'll be back," she said when I asked her if she didn't care. "When someone dies, or they have a fight with their sweetheart, they'll think of me."

I was just back from the day's only delivery—another round of bouquets for the victims of the retirement home accident—and was hanging up my sweater in back when I heard the front door jangle, and the murmur of voices. UPS had been there while I was out, and I was looking over the deliveries, which seemed unusually heavy on daffodils and irises, when Peggy called, "Lucy, that you? Get on out here a minute."

Her voice sounded peculiar, a little higher than usual, almost girlish. I poked my head around the door frame and there, with his elbows on the counter, was Ash Farrell.

"Afternoon," he said. I just nodded, pushing back my hair. I'd noticed his truck over in Mrs. Tanner's driveway when I'd gone out to the van, but I'd made sure I didn't look too hard. "I was hoping you might give me some advice," he added.

"I don't know how helpful I can be," I said. "I just started day before yesterday."

"Oh, I need a woman's point of view, not a florist's," he said. "Let's say you were a man, and you'd had a sort of misunderstanding with a young lady. What would you buy to try to make it up to her?" His face, in the light through the big plate-glass window, looked different than it had the night before in the Round-Up: less smug, more affable. His T-shirt was faded green and salt-stained, and there was sawdust on his forearms and in his hair. His eyes were not truly black, not quite, but the darkest brown I'd ever seen, like Cajun coffee.

"Maybe you don't need to buy her anything," I suggested. "Maybe you just ought to try cleaning up your act."

"Well, I plan on giving that a shot," he said. "But I thought the flowers might make a—you know. Statement."

I hated to tell him, but I didn't think there was a flower on the planet that would make an impression on the girl I'd seen draped across him last night like a sofa cover. A dozen French ticklers, maybe. A weekend at the Piney View Motor Court, in the waterbed room.

"So," he said, "what do you say?"

"Oh, I don't know . . ."

"What's your favorite flower?"

"Mine?" I thought for a few seconds. "Pink roses. But I'm not—"

"Great," he said, turning to Peggy. "I'll take a dozen."

The two of them made small talk—he and his partner were remodeling Mrs. Tanner's den, Ash said, installing floor-to-ceiling shelves to house her late husband's collection of stuffed wildlife—while Peggy took the flowers out of the cooler and arranged them with the usual greenery and spray of complimentary baby's breath in a sheet of cellophane. He wasn't paying any attention to me, and I was struck, as I'd been the night before, by the enviable ease with which he seemed to inhabit his skin. I wondered if it was something learned or if he'd been born with it, a mantle he'd inherited. Other than those scraps of memory from high school, I didn't know anything about him. He had to be thirty-six, thirty-seven years old; surely something, somewhere, had bounced him around a little, had knocked him back a time or two. How had he arrived at this place, then, cloaked in confidence, like there was nothing in the world he wanted that he couldn't reach out and lay his hand on? He dug into his hip pocket for his wallet and handed over two twenties, which Peggy passed to me to make change while she tied the base of the bouquet with a length of silver ribbon. She had, I saw, taken pains with the arrangement, and I wondered again if the girl it was destined for possessed the capacity to appreciate it.

"Now, Ash, this little plastic do-thingy will keep these fresh for a few hours, but you tell the, um, young lady to get them into water as soon as she can," Peggy said. As soon as she gets off her back and you come up for air, I added silently. It looked like a waste of $27.50 to me, but what did I know? Maybe she'd go for the thorns.

"Thanks a lot," he said, opening his palm as I counted out his change. His hands were brown and battered-looking, blisters across the base of his fingers, calluses on the pads. Everything worthwhile is worth doing with your hands, Mitchell always said. He'd lived that way, and he'd died that way, too, I guessed; I would never know. Ash pocketed his change and lifted the bunch of roses off the counter. "You've been a big help," he said, "Lucy Hatch." He didn't seem to be trying out the sound of it so much as rolling it around like a chocolate, letting its soft center melt on his tongue. He stood smiling at me until I looked away. Prick, I thought. Show-off. Flag planter.

"Good luck," I said. "I hope this accomplishes your goal, whatever it is."

He nodded. "I'll keep you posted," he said, and let himself back out the door into the March sunshine, the bells jangling behind him.

"So," Peggy wanted to know, her voice dropping half an octave, the second things were quiet again, "how do you know Ash?"

"I don't," I said. "Geneva introduced us last night at the Round-Up. I'm surprised to hear he's having female trouble. He had a whole row of them set out like windup dolls, including one who was already halfway to the motel room. She didn't strike me as the type for pink roses, to tell you the truth."

"Well, you never know," Peggy said. "Maybe Ash has finally decided to play by the rules. Straighten up and act like a gentleman." I didn't ask her what she meant by that.

We checked in the UPS order and restocked the cooler, and by that time my shift was up. As I walked around back to where my borrowed pickup was parked, I saw that the white Chevy truck was gone from

Mrs. Tanner's. Well, hell, why work when you could play? I remembered that sexy old James Taylor song: "Hey, baby, I'm your handyman."

I opened the door to climb into the pickup. On the driver's seat, in a cone of cellophane tied with silver ribbon, were a dozen pink roses.

I couldn't tell a soul. I thought immediately of calling Geneva, then realized just as immediately that I couldn't. She'd read all kind of things into it that weren't there, or worse, that were. She'd have me parked at the head of the bar at the Round-Up the very next night, in a fringed cowgirl vest and four shades of eye shadow, waiting to stake my claim. She'd needle and needle me, forcing me at Ash until I was as sad and frantic as that girl in the white outfit with her ribs sticking out, her need as oversized and gaudy as her jewelry. And for what? If it was a statement he was making, it might have done him some good to be a little clearer about it. I actually considered some gesture of refusal—leaving the flowers in the parking lot, or on Mrs. Tanner's front lawn—but decided that would give the act more weight than it warranted. Better just to appear nonchalant about the whole thing, like I was too busy, too imperious, to be affected by such folly. By the time I got home and stuck the roses into an old milk bottle in the middle of my kitchen table, I was more annoyed than anything else. I could almost hear my mama's voice, telling me how *shameful* it was. If he thought I was going to call him up, to hunt him down and thank him, he'd better think again. No matter what happened, I swore, I would not let myself be beholden.

Still, it was all I could do to keep the news to myself when Geneva and I met for lunch the next afternoon at the Mooney Café. We had just gotten our sandwich orders when Geneva started rummaging in her purse underneath the table.

"Our anniversary's next week," she announced, pushing a piece of paper across the Formica at me.

The magazine ad showed a long, underfed teenage girl in a black lace-up corset and net stockings, a riding crop poised on one hip. Her hair hung in lank strands, and her mascara was dark and gluey, like someone had socked her in the eye. "Well?" Geneva asked. "What do you think?"

"I don't know," I said. "Bailey doesn't really ride much anymore."

"Funny," she said, retrieving the ad to ponder it herself. "The *outfit*, girlfriend. Don't you think it'll knock Bailey's socks off?"

"That depends," I said slowly. "Who's going to wear it?" I didn't want to say so outright, but the girl in the photo was probably six inches taller than my sister-in-law and a good sixty pounds slimmer.

To tell the truth, I didn't especially want to be having this conversation—it was bad enough having to bear witness to the hands-on aspects of Bailey and Geneva's relationship in public, much less hear the private details—but I was relieved that the topic of the other night at the Round-Up hadn't come up. It was a mild, sunny Friday, the café was full of the lunch crowd, and I felt oddly content with my lot at that moment, given the circumstances that had planted me there: content with my little job, my little house, my grilled-cheese sandwich and greasy fries. It didn't seem possible that anything could ruffle it; and that thought had no sooner formed in my head than the café door opened and Ash Farrell walked in.

"Well, shit," I said. I was facing the door; Geneva had to swivel her head all the way around to see him. Her face went instantly electric, sparks of excitement shooting from her eyes. I didn't suppose he'd miss us, but just in case he did, she was half out of the booth already, waving like a maniac. He headed straight for us. I wondered how it was that in a day and a half Ash Farrell had managed to insinuate himself into so many aspects of my life, when we hadn't exchanged twenty sentences between us. It was the price you paid, I guessed, for living in a town of twelve hundred people.

"Hey," he said, sauntering up beside our booth, smiling down on us like some self-crowned prince. "Mrs. Hatch. Miss Hatch." His eye fell on the magazine ad in the middle of the table. He cocked one brow to give it his full concentration, then looked up, with newfound keenness, from me to Geneva and back again.

"Were you in English class the day they taught the word 'ubiquitous'?" I asked. I took a bite of my sandwich. It was useless, though. He just kept smiling.

"Sure," he said. "Means 'almighty,' doesn't it?"

I set down my sandwich and touched my napkin to my mouth. There was my lipstick, all right, every last bit of it. Ash just stood there, blocking the aisle, his hands in the pockets of his Levi's, watching us with a lack of self-consciousness that seemed entitled and complete. I took a sip of tea, cleared my throat.

"You're probably waiting for me to say thank you for the roses." I tried not to notice Geneva's jaw drop. She would crucify me for this, if not now, later. "I'm not sure I really understood the need, though. I mean—there *was* no need. You know that, don't you?"

Ash shrugged. "I got the notion you took me for a little bit of a drunken shitheel, the other night. I was just hoping to correct your first impression."

"Why should you care what I think? It didn't look like you were hurting too bad in the popularity department." The corner of his mouth twitched, not quite a smile. "Anyway, I'm the last person you owe an apology to," I said. "I don't even know you."

"Well, hell, Lucy. Did it ever occur to you that maybe I'm trying to change that?"

I couldn't look at Geneva, even though, under the table, she was digging the heel of her shoe into my instep.

"Look," I blurted. "I guess nobody told you this, but my husband just died."

"Actually, somebody did tell me," he said. "But not till yesterday, not till I asked around. I would never have made the crack I did at the bar, if I'd known." I gazed down at my plate, the half-chewed sandwich, a scattering of fries. "I don't usually drink when I play. It's just—well, there were some other things going on that night. Things that didn't have anything to do with y'all."

"Had to do with a white skirt and a tank top, I bet," Geneva murmured, but Ash didn't even acknowledge the remark. I could feel his eyes on me.

"I apologize for offending you," he said. "And I'm sorry about your husband. I don't even know what to say about something like that. It's the worst thing I've ever heard."

I stared at the tabletop until my eyes blurred, begging, silently, *Please, just don't say anything.* I had a feeling there were thirty or so folks within shouting distance of our table who would love for me to break down right there at lunchtime in the Mooney Café, in the grand family tradition.

"Maybe," Geneva said in a cautious tone, "that's enough about that subject for now."

"Sure," Ash said lightly. "I guess I'll pick up my lunch and get on out of here. So, I'll see you tomorrow night, huh, Gen?"

"It's Saturday, isn't it?"

"Lucy? How about you?"

"No," I said quickly. "I can't."

"That reminds me, though," Ash said, stepping over to the counter, where Carol, the waitress, had a couple of to-go bags ready for him. "I

was talking to Emmitt Fowler this morning, over at the co-op. He mentioned that that compost you ordered came in."

Geneva met my eyes across the table. "How did that particular subject happen to come up?" I asked, but Ash just took out his wallet and
handed some bills across the counter to Carol, who was following the
conversation with unusual interest. I guessed it, whatever "it" was,
would be all over town by suppertime.

"You planning on putting in a garden this spring?" he asked.

"Nothing fancy," I said. "Just some beans and tomatoes."

"I've got to run back out there tomorrow morning," Ash said, dump-
ing his change into the tip jar next to the register. "How about if I load
up that compost for you and bring it out to your place? It's more than
you're gonna be able to manage, with that wrist."

"I—" Geneva's heel again, grinding my toes under the table. "Well,
sure, I guess so. If it's not too much trouble."

"Nah, like I said, I'll be there anyway," he said. "And your place isn't
that far from mine."

He picked up his bags off the counter and stepped back over to our
table. I stared up at him, but his face never changed. Did anybody, ever,
tell Ash Farrell no? "How do you know where my place is?" I asked, but
he just smiled.

"I'll see you tomorrow," he said. "Ten o'clock okay?"

What if it wasn't? Would I have said so? Geneva and I watched as he
lifted a hand in farewell, then made his way leisurely toward the door,
stopping to exchange greetings with a couple of old farmers. We
watched through the window as he stood at the curb waiting for a car to
pass, then trotted across the street and climbed into his truck, which
was parked in front of the bank, and backed out, the tailpipe spewing a
cloud of exhaust.

Geneva leaned across the table until her forehead was nearly touching mine. "You *bitch*," she whispered gleefully. "You realize, I'm gonna have to kill you for this."

I shook my head vigorously, back and forth. "No, no, no, Geneva. This isn't what you think."

"I'm pretty sure it's not what *you* think, either," she said, picking up her yet-untouched turkey sandwich. "He gave you *roses*? When did that happen? And how could you not have told me?"

"Yesterday," I said. "He left them in the truck. And I didn't tell you because I knew you'd flip out. Just like you're doing now."

"I'm not flipping out," she said. "That comes later, after I've had some time to think about it." She bit into her sandwich and chewed for a while. "You know, maybe this is the perfect thing for you right now," she said. "A roll in the hay with Ash Farrell. Just to sort of, you know, get you back into the swing of things."

"I'm not rolling with Ash Farrell, Geneva!" I whispered. "Not in the hay or anywhere else! My God, Mitchell died—what, five weeks ago?"

"Yeah, but you told me yourself, Lucy, that things weren't like that, with Mitchell." I stirred my iced tea, dumped in more sugar, kept stirring. "So, maybe this *is*," she observed. "Like that." She drummed her fingers on the girl in the corset for emphasis.

"It isn't," I said. She cocked an eyebrow. "You think just because he bought me some flowers, that changes what happened the other night? You think I want to turn into one of those pitiful women hanging around the bar, hoping he might smile at me? Anyway, you saw what he goes for. What he takes home with him at the end of the night. What makes you think somebody like me would even show up on his radar?"

"I'm telling you," Geneva said, "I'd go home and shave my legs and put clean sheets on the bed. Just in case."

(five)

The next morning I got up late, rolling the stiffness out of my shoulders, and headed for the bathroom, where I stood under the shower, shampooing my hair as well as one hand would allow, then pulled on a clean T-shirt and jeans. I was nursing my coffee at the kitchen table, feet bare on the linoleum, my hair still damp down my back, when I heard the sound of a vehicle making its slow, determined way up the unpaved road, rattling its way toward the house. I looked at the sunflower clock over the stove: ten o'clock, straight up.

I went to the screen door and watched the white pickup rock to a halt, watched the door swing open and Ash jump down in a cloud of red dust, slapping his palms on his thighs. He stood for a few seconds surveying the landscape, laying back his head to take in the black jut of the pines against the sky, filling his lungs with the mild green air. He looked satisfied somehow—like he'd ordered the morning exactly to his specifications—and it irritated me so that I stepped out onto the porch and let the screen door bang behind me.

He wheeled at the sound. "Hey! Hi," he said as I pulled my cast across my chest and cupped the elbow in my good hand. "I brought you something. To see if I could get back in your good graces." He was leaning into the cab of the pickup, reaching across the seat.

"You were never in my good graces to begin with," I said as he lifted out a small, squirming puppy, round as a little pig, with swirls of black through its gray-blue coat. "Oh, no."

"I was loading up your compost," Ash said, setting the puppy on its stubby legs, "and some lady came by with a whole boxful of these guys. He's an Australian cattle dog," he said proudly. "His name's Steve Cropper." I must've looked blank. "You mean you never heard of the greatest southern guitar player of all time? The guy who played on all those great old Stax records in the sixties, with Booker T. and the MG's? 'Knock on Wood'? 'Green Onions'?"

"Sorry."

"Anyway, I happened to think of you, out here all alone, and I figured . . ." His voice trailed off. The puppy scrabbled around and over his work boots, nipping at the laces.

"You figured what?" I asked. "You figured I needed protecting? Me and my Australian cattle?"

Ash shook his head as the puppy abandoned his bootlace and began to sniff around the pickup. "We all need protecting, Lucy," he said. "You, me, everybody. Hey!" he exclaimed as the puppy turned and lifted its leg against the rear tire.

"I'll bet you taught him that, didn't you?" I said. "A little welcoming show, just for me. I don't guess you thought to bring him any food or anything like that."

"Twenty pounds of puppy chow, two bowls, a collar, and a couple of chew toys. He's had his shots, too, before you get all over me for that."

I set my shoulder against the porch post and held Ash's eye. "You do make it hard to say no, don't you?"

He smiled. "Well, I sure try."

I knelt on the step and the puppy bounded over and hurled himself against me, his tail lashing my calves, and pushed his nose hard into my crotch. "Lord," I said, blushing, scooping him up with my right arm, but not before Ash could say, "Yeah, I taught him that, too."

"I might've guessed," I said, standing red-faced to meet his grinning gaze. "Such charm and subtlety." The puppy began to lick my neck enthusiastically.

"So, what do you think?" Ash asked. "You want to give him a try?"

I looked into his dark eyes, wondering what in the world I was taking on as I felt myself fighting a smile. "Okay."

He gestured over his shoulder at the truck. "I've got your compost. Four hundred pounds, Emmitt said you ordered." It was a special blend from Austin that my Aunt Dove swore by. I set the puppy on its feet and went over to look into the pickup, where the forty-pound bags were stacked two deep along the length of the bed. "Where do you want it?" Ash asked, swinging the first sack onto his shoulder like it was five pounds of sugar.

"Around there." I pointed with my cast, and Ash set off around the house. I followed, picking my way carefully in my bare feet, the puppy leaping at my heels.

"Where?" Ash called as I caught up. "Here?" He motioned with his head to the plot Bailey had cleared for me with the push mower a few days before, maybe fifteen by thirty feet in diameter. He cocked an eyebrow at me. "Just exactly what are you planning to do with all this compost?"

"Well, I wasn't expecting it so soon," I said. "I haven't had a chance to break the ground yet. You can just stack it right there, for now."

"Someone going to till this for you?" he asked, dropping the heavy bag at one corner of the patch of ground.

"I can handle it."

Ash spun and looked at me. I sneaked a glance toward the house and his eyes followed mine, landing on the shiny new Craftsman hoe leaning beside the back door. "With *that?*" he said incredulously. "Are you crazy? You think you can work this ground with one arm in a cast and a goddamned *hoe?*"

He marched back around the house, hauled the puppy's food and supplies out of the truck bed and set them on the porch, then climbed into the cab and turned the key in the ignition.

"Where are you going with my compost?" I called as Ash pumped the gas pedal and the pickup sputtered and then roared to life.

"I'll be back in half an hour," he shouted. "Go on, feed your dog. And don't you touch that hoe." He jammed the truck into gear, executed a wide loop in my front yard, and headed off down the road, three hundred and sixty pounds of compost shifting and sliding behind.

It took me most of twenty minutes just to wrestle open the big bag of Purina and fill the stainless-steel bowls with kibble and water. I was sitting on the front step watching Steve Cropper finish his breakfast when the truck turned in off the highway and came bumping back up the road. Ash leaned out the window and called that he was going to drive on around back if it was okay with me, and I picked up the puppy and went after him.

"I really can't let you do this," I said as Ash hoisted a complicated-looking mechanical tiller out of the truck bed.

"Well, I'm not about to let you do it with a Sears hoe."

"I'll have to pay you, then," I said. He set down the tiller and looked at me. "Really. I insist." I could feel little beads of perspiration popping up along my hairline. "It's how you make your living, isn't it?"

"Right. Ash Farrell, hired hand." He bent and cranked the tiller hard; it started with a roar that made the puppy bolt from my grip and shoot straight under the house. I stood watching as Ash laid into the patch of hard ground like he was wrestling some wild beast into submission; the tendons in his forearms tensed and trembled, his jaw was set, and he didn't look at me. After a minute or two I went into the house and splashed my face with cold water until I felt my heartbeat go back to normal.

The telephone rang, and I stepped into the hallway and took the receiver off the hook. "Hey," Geneva said.

"It had to be you."

"I'm not interrupting anything, am I?" she asked, and I laughed. "So, did he show?"

"Oh, he showed." I dragged the phone the length of its cord down the hall and looked out the back door. Ash's T-shirt had already gone dark between the shoulder blades. "As a matter of fact, he's out back, tilling my garden."

"What?"

"When he found out I was planning to break the ground myself, he went home, or somewhere, I don't know exactly, and he brought back this machine, this tiller. He's out there right now, tearing up the dirt."

"Lucy!"

"I'm going to pay him," I added quickly. "At least I said I would. I think it made him mad."

"Oh, Lord."

"Well, what was I supposed to do?"

"Barter," Geneva said. "Offer to take it out in trade."

"He brought me a dog."

"This is a joke, right?"

"Some lady was giving them away at the co-op. He said he thinks I need protecting."

Geneva laughed. "So, train it to bite him on the ass. Listen, I called to see if you wanted to strip the paper off those bathroom walls this morning, but maybe I'd better stay clear. I wouldn't want you to miss a golden opportunity."

"Geneva, you're crazy. It's not—I mean, I'm not . . . I mean, come on out if you want to. He's just doing a job."

"He's doing a job, all right," Geneva said. "And you don't even know it." She hung up.

I stayed inside, busying myself with small, mindless chores until the tiller fell silent. I looked out the back door and saw Ash draw a forearm across his brow, his shirt soaked through.

"I've got lemonade, if you want it," I called through the screen. He turned at the sound of my voice.

"Thanks," he said, and I poured him a big glass over ice and carried it down the back steps. I watched him tilt the glass, his Adam's apple bobbing rhythmically in his throat, one deep swallow after another, until he'd drained it dry. "You've got beer, I hope," he said, handing the empty glass to me, "for later."

"I think there might be a Bud or two," I said. They were Bailey's, actually, but this didn't seem like a time to split hairs.

"Well, write my name on them." Ash looked out across the garden, half of it newly turned, and said, "I can't believe it's not even the middle of March and already this damn hot."

"Shouldn't I be doing something?" I offered. "It doesn't feel right, standing by while you take care of all this."

"You can keep the beer cold," he said. "Look, I'll be done in an hour. Anyway, you hired me, remember?" He bent and lifted the tiller and gave it another hard crank. I figured it might be weeks before we'd see poor Steve Cropper again.

Geneva didn't come, and so I wandered the house, looking for some undone task. Finally I took a quart bag of Aunt Dove's peaches out of the freezer and started to roll out, with a Coke bottle and a good bit of difficulty, a pie crust on the kitchen table. I managed to fumble it into a glass plate, and turned on the oven. Before long the kitchen was like a furnace and smelled of heaven, of rich, sticky summer sweetness.

As I was peeking through the oven door to check for brownness, the tiller stopped, and Ash came up the back steps and rapped at the screen.

"Smells good in there."

I went to the door, mopping my forehead with the back of my arm. "I don't know what I was thinking," I said. "It's too warm for this."

"Want to come take a look?" He pointed with his chin over his shoulder.

"Sure." I wrapped a dish towel around my fist and slid the pie out of the oven and set it on one of the burners to cool, then stepped out the door and followed Ash across the yard.

He stood looking with satisfaction over the rectangle of fresh-plowed ground. "What do you think?"

"It's a whole bunch of dirt, isn't it?" I said. He glanced at me, and I shrugged. "Well, it's the truth—what am I supposed to say?"

"You know, this soil isn't great for tomatoes," he said. "You need to make sure you've got enough phosphate, a little bit of nitrogen and potash, before you plant." He pushed a hank of silver hair out of his eyes. "You probably know all this, right? I mean, you must have learned one or two things from your Aunt Dove."

It wasn't surprising that he would know this; Dove had what was widely regarded as the best garden in the county, in her front yard. Not only did she grow most every type of vegetable and annual known to man, but the plot was a sort of charmed space, dotted with fat little stone Buddhas and other emblems of Eastern religions, and instead of scarecrows or rubber snakes to scare off pests, she'd hung the borders with rows of Tibetan prayer flags. No one in Mooney knew what to make of this, and Dove wasn't telling, but you couldn't dispute that, whatever it was, it brought her magic. When I was a little girl, I'd thought the spot was as enchanted as any fairy tale. My mama wouldn't set foot in the place; she was terrified Jesus might happen to glance down and take her for a pagan.

"Not as much as I should, probably," I admitted. "How do *you* know this stuff?"

"My stepmom was a big-time gardener," he said, squinting off toward the row of pines at the back of the property. "The lady I called my stepmom. The lady who raised me." I shook my head; I hadn't heard this story. "Did you know the Kellers, when you were growing up? Bob and Christa, lived on a big spread out east of town? Their kids were Tessa and Bob Junior. Come to think of it, they were older than you. Well, the Kellers were the people who took me in. After my dad took off and my mama—"

His voice stopped unexpectedly, like someone had lifted a needle off a record in the middle of a song. His eyes were narrowed, glittering, still aimed at those trees like he could see right through them and beyond. "On second thought, maybe that's a story for some other time," he said, turning his chin back toward me, his gaze coming slowly into focus. "Meanwhile, I'll take my pay."

"I . . ." How in the world did you negotiate something like this? "My checkbook's in the house."

"I was talking about the beer."

"Oh. Well, come on inside, then."

"You go on and crack one for me, okay?" he said. "I'll be in in a minute."

I took one of Bailey's Budweiser longnecks out of the icebox and carried it to the back door. Through the screen I watched as Ash walked over and turned on the hose that was hooked up to the faucet at the outside corner of the house. I held the beer bottle in the crook between my rib cage and my cast, and in the time it took me, with my good hand, to get the cap twisted free, Ash had stripped off his T-shirt and bent himself under the hose, aiming the stream along his bare torso, the back of his neck. The water sluiced over the graceful wings of his shoulder blades, and he shook his head under the cool spray, sending rainbows in all directions. His skin was the color of a butter rum Life Saver, a shade darker below the biceps, and the hair on his chest was dark and downy, powdered with gray. In spite of the heat a shiver ran through me at the pure foreignness of it, another reminder of all that my marriage, and now my widowhood, served to shelter me from.

Ash turned off the hose and patted himself dry with his shirt, then walked back over to the truck and reached into the cab and pulled out a fresh T-shirt and slipped it over his head, stuffing the tail into the waistband of his Levi's. He worked a hand through his wet hair as he came up the back steps, stomping the dirt off his boots on the mat.

I opened the door and put the beer in his hand, and he hoisted the bottle and drank. "Ah," he said, wiping his mouth with the back of his hand as he followed me into the kitchen, "born again." I watched his eyes tour the room, the ancient gas stove, the ivy-patterned oilcloth on the table, the battered linoleum under his feet. I felt no obligation to apologize for the shabbiness, and Ash's manner didn't invite it. "I remember when this was old Lowell Ellson's place," was all he said. "Man, it's a sight cleaner now than it was in those days."

"I hope so," I said. "Geneva and I used up two whole bottles of Clorox on this room alone."

"You planning on staying here awhile?" he asked, taking another sip of beer. "Or is this just temporary? Until you get your feet back under you?"

The shape of the room seemed to shift, the scope of my gaze to elongate so that things, for a second or two, went wildly out of perspective; the stove seemed too tall and narrow, the table to vanish altogether. *What?* I thought, reaching for the back of a chair. *What is he talking about? What happened?* "Lucy?" Ash said, and I blinked my eyes, and gradually things slid back into their expected places. My kitchen. My rent house. My husband was dead. Still. Forever.

"That depends," I answered finally. "We had a farm, down toward Morseville. Four hundred acres, a house, a couple of barns. Cattle.

Machinery." I drew a breath; I had never stopped to think, not once, about what had happened to the mower. "It's all getting auctioned off at the end of the month. I guess a lot of what happens next depends on how that goes." Bailey had warned me, already, that the debt we'd carried on the place might well balance out any profit from the sale. There was a life-insurance policy that I knew would pay out, but I didn't expect to be able to live on any of it forever.

"Well, I admire you," Ash said. "It can't be easy, doing what you've done."

"What else could I do?" I said. "What were my choices?"

"Fold up," he suggested. "Cave in. Spend all day in bed with the covers over your head. Lots of people do."

"Nope," I said, shaking my head. "Never. Not an option."

"Glad to hear it," he said, draining his beer, setting the bottle on the countertop. "Otherwise, I'd never have met you. Could I trouble you for that other Bud?"

"These belong to my brother Bailey," I said, reaching into the icebox for the remaining beer and passing it to Ash. "If he finds out I let you have them, there'll be hell to pay."

"I imagine there might be that anyway," Ash said, "if he finds out I've been here. While we're at it, how about a piece of that pie?"

I cut us each a slice—the filling was still bubbling as the knife pierced the crust—and we carried our plates out onto the front porch, where a couple of webbed lawn chairs stood folded against the house. Ash set them up and we sat. The breeze off the pines across the road was sweet-scented and inviting.

Ash forked up a bite of pie, against my warning, and promptly burned his tongue. "Good," he insisted thickly, chasing it with a swallow of beer, and I laughed and set my piece on the porch rail to cool for a minute.

"Can I ask you a question?" I said. He smiled at me curiously. "Did

you really get Neely Craig in trouble? Everybody said that was the real
reason her daddy sent her to Fayetteville."

Ash laughed. "Neely Craig probably got sent to Fayetteville to keep
her out of the Texas Department of Corrections," he said. "Jesus, that
girl was wild. A lot worse than me. I was a little bit scared of Neely, to
tell you the truth. She could drink half a bottle of bourbon like it was
Kool-Aid and never miss a beat." He propped one boot on the porch
rail and balanced his pie plate on his knee. "I'll tell you something I've
never told anybody before," he said. "I never even did it with Neely
Craig. And the only girl I ever got in trouble, I married."

"You were married?" I was surprised that Geneva hadn't mentioned this.

He nodded. "For a couple of years, when I was barely twenty-one. I
was living in Dallas then." He sipped his beer, held up the bottle to the
light. "My daughter still lives there, with her mama," he said. "She's
fourteen now."

"Do you see her?"

Ash stared straight ahead at the trees across the road. "No, I don't,"
he said. "Not for seven and a half years." He glanced over at me. "I
know. I'm an evil, stinking bastard."

"I didn't say anything."

"You know, I wish people would just . . . " he began, then stopped. "I
did try to see her, for the longest time," he continued. "Let's just say her
mother made it difficult. Marlene was the most beautiful thing I'd ever
laid eyes on, but crazy as a bedbug from the day we met. And man, did
she ever end up wrecking me."

"Not permanently, though," I said, which made the corners of his
mouth turn partway up. "Why'd you marry her," I said, "if you knew she
was crazy?"

"Who knows?" he said. "Maybe it's in my blood." I just stared at him;
I didn't know what he was talking about. "Marlene got pregnant," he

went on. "I was twenty-one and Catholic. Forces conspired, I guess you could say." He drank his beer. There didn't seem to be anything more to say about it.

"So, how'd you end up back in Mooney?" I asked after a minute. "No offense, but it looks to me like maybe you'd burn a little too hot for this place. Your music and all," I added when he swung his eyes toward me.

"My stepmom died," he said. "Marlene and I had separated, the baby wasn't quite two. Bob—Christa's husband—tracked me down in the apartment where I was staying in Dallas, trying to get my shit together, figure out what to do next. Christa had breast cancer." I watched the shape of his mouth while he talked, the lower lip square and full, a scar in the form of a checkmark, pale and slightly raised, in the hollow just beneath. "Bob sounded like he'd lost his mind. You'd have to have known Bob to know how scary that was; I mean, the man was a rancher, a deacon in the church, president of the Toastmasters, one of the most stable, together guys you'd ever hope to meet, and he was completely unglued.

"Well, I didn't even think twice, I just loaded up my truck and came back. When I got to town, I went straight to the hospital. They'd taken off both of Christa's breasts that morning." His voice trembled. "The most stupid fucking pointless surgery in the history of Western medicine," he said. "The cancer was everywhere—her liver, her spine. Christa had always been this big, sassy, proud lady . . ." Ash looked over at me. "And now they'd carved her up for the sole fucking point, I guess, of saying they'd done all they could do. I tell you what, if I ever hear some doctor telling me I've got a terminal disease, I'm going right out and lie down in front of the first train I see. No knives and tubes and chemical cocktails for me.

"Anyway," he said, sucking in a breath, "I stayed there with her, in the hospital, for most of the next three weeks. Her own kids didn't even come; Tessa was in the middle of final exams or some bullshit like that, and Bob Junior was off on a Greenpeace boat somewhere, saving the whales, and didn't even return his father's phone calls. I mean, I grew up with these kids, you know? And they'd always seemed okay to me— never exactly treated me like a brother, but we'd gotten along all right, all those years—but now they were nowhere to be found.

"And Bob Senior was completely useless. He'd show up at the hospital in his bathrobe, with shaving cream all over his face, or one time carrying this beautiful sexy lace nightgown in a fancy bag. When Christa saw that nightgown, I thought she was gonna give up and die on the spot. You know what she did, though?" I shook my head. "She laughed. She knew she was dying, that her breasts were gone and her husband was cracking up and her kids were AWOL, but she laughed about the whole thing. Not like a crazy person, either, and not from the morphine. The doctors didn't have any idea what to make of it. They said she was delirious, from pain and the drugs, but they didn't know Christa. She wasn't delirious. She just thought it was all funny. Some weird, wonderful joke."

Ash tipped back his head and drained his beer and set the bottle on the porch rail. "She left me ten thousand dollars," he said. "I hadn't even stopped to think about what I'd do after she died, but as soon as they read the will, I knew I was gonna stay. Get myself a little piece of land with some trees, build me a house, and find some kind of work I could do with my hands. Write the best music I could and play it as often as I could." He looked over at me. "Those aren't very grand ambitions, I guess. It's suited me pretty well the past twelve, thirteen years, though. I don't guess there's too much I want that I don't have."

"I've decided there's an art to it," I offered after a minute, "living like you do. My Aunt Dove is another one. The point seems to be to let yourself be content with what's under your nose."

Ash smiled. "You sound like you've got it all figured out."

"Well, I don't," I said. "It's different for you. You have your music.

Not to mention the, um, fringe benefits." He laughed. "I don't even know what I want. I never expected this—to have to come up with my own interests." I picked up my pie and dug my fork into it. "That sounds terrible, doesn't it?" I said. "Being thirty-three years old and not even knowing what you like?"

Ash shook his head. "I think it's a lot more common than you might expect. Especially around here," he added, and we both smiled. "Anyway, at least your mind is open. You're looking. That's a start."

"I'll tell you something I haven't told anybody, either," I said. He was lifting a forkful of pie to his mouth but stopped halfway, his mouth open. "I like living by myself. I really, really like it."

"You mind if I ask you something personal?" he said. "Since we're in true-confession mode."

"Okay."

"Were you in love with your husband?"

"Well, he never really made me go all tingly inside, nothing like that. That's not really what being in love is about, though, is it? Being tingly all over?"

Ash balanced a scrap of crust on the tines of his fork. "Well, if it isn't, I don't know what is."

"It'd be hard to sustain that, though, wouldn't it, for fourteen years?"

"Shit." He laughed. "It's hard to sustain for fourteen *days*."

"I guess I thought he was my shot, you know?"

He lowered his foot from the porch rail to the floor. "What are you talking about?"

"Everybody gets a shot, right? So, Mitchell was mine." I looked off across the road, but I was aware of Ash watching me.

"Is that what you believe?"

"Oh, I'm not talking about that business you do," I said. "The king bee, buzzing up and down, pollinating all the flowers on the vine."

"You know," Ash said, "I don't recall ever once discussing the details of my love life with you. I wish I knew where you're getting this stuff."

"I was at the Round-Up Wednesday night," I said. "I have two eyes. The word 'smorgasbord' comes to mind." He was looking right at me now. "Does that girl know you have a daughter almost her age?"

"For your information, Misty is twenty years old."

"Good Lord, her name is *Misty?*"

He had to smile. "It suits her, don't you think? And for your further information," he added, "I'm not seeing her. Anymore," he added quickly, when I looked doubtful.

"Really? Since when?"

"Since I decided to clean up my act." He polished off the last bite of his pie and set the fork in the middle of his plate. "Meanwhile, you might want to think about listening to your own advice."

"What's that?"

"Maybe what you're looking for is right under your nose."

I propped open the screen door for him, then followed him through it and into the kitchen. He ran the water from the tap over the plates and then stacked them in the sink.

"You know," he said, turning to look around him, taking in again the room in its proud dilapidation, "there are a few things I could do around here for you, Lucy. To make this place a little more . . ." He scouted around for the right word. "Habitable?"

"I appreciate that," I said, aware of my face burning hot under his gaze. "But I'm not sure it's a good idea."

"Why not?"

"Well, for starters, this is a rent house. I'd have to clear any improvements with the real estate company."

"Yeah? And?"

I focused my gaze on the window. "I don't know how else to say it but right out. I honestly can't afford it. Until Mitchell's estate is settled, I'm living off savings. Peggy's only paying me a hundred dollars a week; I'll be lucky to make my rent." I shook my head. "I wish I could do it, but I don't see how it's possible."

Ash was smiling. "Oh, I imagine we could be creative. Work something out."

I looked him straight in the eye. "Something like what?" Geneva's words—*Take it out in trade*—echoed in my eardrums like a mockery. Suppose he expected something in addition to money in exchange for tilling my garden? What if he wouldn't take a check?

"I don't know," he said. "There must be something you're good at. Something you could do for me. Cook me dinner sometime, maybe?"

"I'm not much of a cook."

"You make a damn fine peach pie."

"Let me get this straight," I said. "You would work on my house in exchange for a pie?" Ash shrugged. "Anyway, what makes you think I want my house improved?" I said. "What makes you think I can't take care of things perfectly well on my own?"

"Because, let's face it, Lucy," he said, "I've got skills you don't have, I've got tools you don't own, and most of all, I've got two arms when you've got only one. You can be proud and foolish if you want, or you can be sensible and let me help you."

"My cast comes off on Tuesday," I said, "thank you just the same."

"Suit yourself," he said then, lightly, and stepped over to the back door. "I've gotta run," he said. "My band practices Saturday afternoons. Anyway, I wouldn't want to wear out my welcome, and I can feel it getting real, real thin." He opened the screen door and started down the steps.

"Wait a minute," I said, following him into the yard as he picked up the heavy tiller and heaved it into the bed of his truck. "What about the work you did today? I said I'd pay you."

"You can give me some of those tomatoes when they come up, how's that sound?" Ash hoisted himself into the driver's seat and reached for the key in the ignition, but he didn't turn it.

I stepped up next to the window. "Actually," I said, "there is something else you might be able to help me with. You wouldn't happen to know where I can get a cheap old car, would you?"

"Sure," he said. "How old? How cheap?"

"I need something that will carry me back and forth to work every day," I said. "Otherwise, I'm not particular."

"Five hundred dollars? Two hundred? A thousand?"

"What kind of car can you get for two hundred dollars?" I wondered. "Is that even possible?"

"Well, it might be lacking a few of the basic automotive amenities," Ash said. "A roof. Tires. A steering wheel."

"Closer to five hundred, I guess. I'm going to have to borrow the money."

"My buddy Isaac King has a brother who buys old junk cars and rebuilds them. For sale, sometimes, but mostly just because he likes to. I usually see J. D. on Sundays. You want me to find out what he's got for you?"

"If it's not too much trouble."

Ash cranked the key, and the engine coughed a couple of times and then caught and bellowed; exhaust poured out of the tailpipe. "J. D. got me my truck, as a matter a fact," he said, grinning over the engine's roar. "I don't know what finer recommendation you could want."

I pushed my hair out of my face. I felt, in spite of my admonition to myself, beholden. "I appreciate all your help," I said.

"Sure you won't reconsider and come to the Round-Up tonight? I'm telling you, I'm a changed man."

"I bet," I said, laughing.

"Gotta see it to believe it."

"Trust me. Thirty seconds at the bar, you'll forget you ever met me."

For a couple of seconds, Ash's eyes held mine. He opened his mouth like he meant to say something, then thought better of it and shook his head. He wrapped his hand around the gearshift and slipped the transmission into reverse.

"I'll let you know about that car," he said, and with a flick of his wrist on the steering wheel, he was gone.

I sat down on the back steps and listened until I couldn't hear his engine anymore. The stillness seemed to hang over the house like an apparition. The puppy crept out from under the steps, wagging its tail uncertainly.

"Come on out from there," I said. "There's nothing to be afraid of." He didn't quite trust me yet, though, and I couldn't say that I blamed him. You never knew what people's real motives were. What looked like kindness might be something else, in disguise.

(six)

I'd been feeling guilty about my behavior at Mama's earlier in the week, so Sunday morning I got up and put on what she called a decent dress—navy blue, long-sleeved, without a pleat or a flourish from my neck to my knees—and went with her to church. She didn't have much to say to me on the short drive from her house to First Baptist—she drove with a deliberation other people reserve for things like brain surgery—but she did offer some semblance of a smile as I slid into the pew next to her and picked up the hymn book. Every Sunday for the past thirty years Mama had been sitting in the middle of the third row, right under the preacher's consecrated gaze, and today was no different. Except that, today, all through the service, I felt Reverend Honeywell's eyes focused especially on me. You can't tell me it was a coincidence that the first hymn, not listed in the program, was "What a Friend We Have in Jesus." The theme of the sermon was redemption. It seemed to me that, for a so-called holy person, Reverend Honeywell enjoyed a little too much seeing people squirm.

I turned down Mama's offer of tuna salad for lunch, and hot-footed it over to Dove's instead. Bailey and Geneva were already there, in the kitchen, everybody up to their elbows in pork ribs. "Nice to see you, Lucy Bird," Dove said as I sat down and helped myself to a plateful. "Maybe you can clear up a coupla things for us."

"About what?" The ribs were heaven, dripping with spicy sauce, the meat falling off the bone. I knew for a fact that they'd come from Willie B.'s stand up near Marietta. Dove drove out there almost every Sunday morning, and I'd go with her sometimes when I was a kid; you could smell the wood smoke and the pig flesh for five miles in any direction, and my mouth would be watering before we even parked the car. Willie B. used to lift me up to watch the meat spitting and crackling in the big black pits. "See there?" he'd say. "That there used to be a little girl just like you." And I'd scream, like someone had run an ice cube down my spine, and then Willie and I would laugh and laugh together.

There was silence for a minute as everyone chewed and swallowed. Nobody spoke; they all seemed to be waiting for somebody else to go first. "About what?" I said again, irritably.

Dove wiped her hands on a square of paper towel. "Your brother seems to think you got somebody sparkin' you."

"What?" I glanced at Bailey, who stared at his plate. "What are you talking about?"

"Give me a break, Lucy," he said. "He was hanging around our table last night like a stalker. Lucy this, Lucy that." Bailey looked up at me, hard, and I felt myself flush. "Geneva said he was at your house all day yesterday."

"He wasn't there two hours," I said. "Three, tops. He was working, Bailey. He tilled my garden."

"Did you pay him?" It was my turn to avert my eyes. "Well, did you?"

"Not exactly." I could see they were expecting some further explanation, Geneva in particular. "I gave him some pie and a couple of beers," I said. "He wouldn't take any money."

"My beers, I bet!" Bailey exclaimed. "You gave him my fucking Buds, didn't you?" He threw a rib bone onto his plate in disgust.

"Bailey Hatch," Dove said. "I'll not have language like that around this table, on a Sunday or any other day."

"Geneva said he gave you roses." Like it was a social disease.

I looked at Geneva, but her eyes were fixed on the far wall; she seemed to be in some sort of ruminative state. "It was a misunderstanding," I said. "Bailey, honestly, what's this all about?"

"I'll tell you what it's about," Geneva said in a dreamy voice. "Bailey figures there's only one woman in this town that Ash Farrell doesn't have wrapped around his little finger—two, I guess, counting you, Dove—and he's afraid he's watching her get lassoed right before his eyes."

"Are you talking about me," I said, "or you?"

"Oh, I'm already a goner, sweetie," she said.

"This isn't a joke, Gen," Bailey said. "Lucy's husband just died. She's living way out in the country, all by herself, and now Ash is out there, sniffing around like a tomcat . . ."

"Don't you think I know how to run off a tomcat?" I set down a rib bone and licked my fingers; it was common knowledge that Willie B.'s sauce was too good to waste. "You throw water on him." As I said it I pictured Ash peeling off his sticky T-shirt, turning the hose over his head.

"Well, you sure as hell don't invite him in for pie," Bailey said. "You don't give him beer upon beer, ones that aren't yours to give."

"He did some work for me, and I was repaying him. We sat on the porch for a while and talked. He knows about Mitchell, for goodness sake. It was all completely respectable."

"He's laying for you," Bailey said darkly. "Hide and watch."

"Well, you know what?" Geneva said, sitting back in her chair. "What if he is? I mean, exactly what would your objection to that be, Bailey?" To my surprise, he turned pink, beginning with his ears and spreading into his collar. "Yeah, that's what I thought," she said. "Takes one to know one, isn't that what they say?"

"I don't know what you're talking about," Bailey said, shoveling another rib onto his plate. "I'm a happily married man."

"Well, you weren't always," she reminded him. "You used to be a rodeo cowboy. Remember, hon?" Bailey ripped into the meat with his teeth, and Geneva sat back with a big, slow smile on her face.

"Look," I said, "this whole conversation is ridiculous. I don't care if Ash Farrell is a wolf or as pure as the driven snow. Don't you get it? It doesn't make any difference to me. Nothing's happened. Nothing's *going* to happen."

"Are you honestly telling me," Geneva said, "that you haven't even thought about it?" She held my gaze just an instant longer than necessary, and in it I swore she saw, as plain as I did in my mind's eye, the pads of muscle in Ash's stomach contracting as he leaned over to turn off the faucet, the brief flash as the metal button at the waist of his Levi's caught the sunlight.

"I'm sorry to disappoint you," I said, "but no, I haven't."

"You know something?" she said, getting up to pour more tea. "You Hatches are lousy liars. Every last one of you."

"Do you have any books on growing vegetables?" I said to Dove. "I'm going home."

"Law, honey, what do you need a book for? I'll tell you what you need to know."

"Ash says I need something for my tomatoes," I said. "Nitrogen, I think? Phosphate?"

"Sure, that's easy. I'll give you some a my special mix. Come by next week and I'll have a batch made up for you. You want me to set aside some seedlings for you, while I'm at it? I got Better Boys this year, Sunmasters, some a those Yella Pears."

"I was hoping you would."

We walked together to the front door. "How you gettin' along out there, in your little house?" she said to me on the step. "It seems to suit you, I'll say that. Put a bloom in your cheeks."

"Dove, do you remember Ash Farrell's mama?"

She considered me for a second, her mouth turned up. "A minute ago I thought you said Ash Farrell could go spit."

"He can. That doesn't mean I can't be nosy, does it?"

"I reckon not." She stepped down into the garden and bent to examine a row of cabbages, the heads swollen and purple, ready to bolt; it had been such a warm winter that everything was out of whack, blooming weeks ahead of schedule. " 'Course I remember her. She and his daddy were quite the couple when they moved to Mooney. Just married, I recall, and Frank had a job with the Missouri Pacific. Such nicelookin' people, kinda glamorous—like movie stars, almost. Seemed wild as all get out about each other, there at the start. Ash come along a year or so later, and you never saw a prouder mama. You know what that boy's full given name is, on his birth certificate?" I shook my head. "Ashton LeGrande Farrell. Don't that beat all? Can you imagine, hanging that kind of name on a tiny little baby?"

"Ash the Grand," I said, laughing. "No wonder he's got such a swelled head."

"I don't rightly know what happened to Lynette. Could just have been bad luck, the way it is for some women. Oh, I know it has some fancy doctor name, but we used to call it the baby blues."

"Postpartum depression," I said.

"Yup, that's the thing. Anyhow, I don't know if it was that or if she really was nuts, all along. Them two—Lynette and Frank—started to fight. Not just in their own house, behind closed doors, mind you, but right out in the middle of things: Frank's office, the café. One time they got into it at Orson's Texaco, and he gave her a shove and knocked her into the gas pump. Had to have six stitches in the back of her head. It was a damned ugly thing, especially the way it was all out there for the whole town to see.

" 'Fore too long, Frank left. Just up one morning and packed a suitcase and took off. Left Lynette with the baby and a houseful of furniture and not much else. Well, she wouldn't come outta the house, not for the longest time. I mean, days went by and nobody saw her. Finally the neighbors had Lester Pinnell—you prob'ly don't recall, he was sheriff before Bill Dudley—come out and take the door off the hinges. There was Lynette, just settin' in a chair, starin' out the window. The place was kind of a mess, dirty dishes and such, but the baby seemed okay, and even though Lynette wouldn't say much, Lester couldn't charge her with anything, so he left. No crime against havin' a broken heart, I guess, or else the whole town would be in jail."

"All but you," I said, and Dove smiled.

"Things went along okay for a while," she said. "Lynette got a job at the feed mill, and Ash seemed like a happy little boy. My goodness, he was a sight, even as a tiny child, had a smile that would bowl you right over, like you'd been grinned at by Clark Gable. As far as anybody knew, they never heard word one from Frank. But they seemed to be gettin' along.

"And then, when Ash was about four, I guess, it all fell apart for real. Later on people would say Lynette had been gettin' quieter and quieter, for a long time, and the things she did say didn't make sense. Then she didn't show up for work one day, and the next. None of the neighbors had seen her, neither, so Lester had to come out again and take off the door. This time it weren't so pretty. There was all kinds of different stories people told—that Lynette was in the chair, in the bed, on the couch, on the floor. That she was in a nightgown, an evening gown, buck naked. You know how folks talk. Bottom line was, the door wasn't the only thing that was off its hinges. They found Ash in a closet, settin' there proper as you please, eating dog biscuits out of a box. They took Lynette to the hospital, and from there they took her to Rusk. And Ash got turned over to the county.

"He was blessed, really. The Kellers heard the story and rushed right over. You never saw a soul as tender as Christa Kellers', and their two kids was about Ash's age. They just took him into the fold. Them stories your brothers used to tell, in school, about Ash runnin' around hellbound? I never believed the half of it. Oh, I reckon he'd get a beer in him and drive too fast or chase after some girl, but you always knew that Christa's hand would be right there on his shoulder when he needed steadyin'. I believe in a way she cared for him more than she did her own kids. You know, Ash was the only one who sat with her the last few weeks before she died? Them two of hers never even showed their faces. Christa showed them, though, I reckon. Left everything in her will to Ash. It weren't much, I don't think, but she give him all she had."

"What happened to Lynette?" I asked. "Is she still down at Rusk?" The big state hospital was there, just a couple of hundred miles to the south, and had been for as long as I could remember. When I was growing up, one of the worst threats you could make to someone was to "send them down to Rusk."

Dove looked at me in surprise. "Why, no, honey. She got out just a coupla years later, and came back to town. Ash wouldn't have a thing to do with her, though. Far as I know, he still don't. She lives over on a big old tumbledown place out near Daingerfield, used to belong to her people. You see her now and again, drivin' around in her old Chrysler, dressed to the nines, like she's still the glamour puss. Last time I run into her in the bank, I said, 'Why, hello, Lynette, how you gettin' on?'

and she hollered that I was tryin' to grab her purse and that she'd have me arrested."

I don't know what was in my face, but Dove reached out and patted my arm. "You see, Lucy Bird, maybe you and the boys didn't have it so bad, after all. At least you didn't lose your daddy and your mama both." A hot bolt of shame sliced through me for all the times we kids had joked, thoughtlessly, as kids will, about how our mama *should* have been sent to Rusk, the way she acted when our daddy Raymond Hatch left. It was because of Dove, I knew, that none of us had wound up in a closet eating dog biscuits out of a box.

"He told me he thought maybe he married his wife because she was crazy and it was in his blood," I said. "I didn't know what he was talking about."

"Nah," Dove said. "I reckon Ash married his wife because she turned his head. Same as you." I blushed and opened my mouth to say something, but Dove waved her hand in the air to cut me off. "Don't you say one word about it," she said. "I expect what Bailey says is true, more or less. It don't make you obliged to nothin' you don't welcome. If I was you, I believe I might just set back and enjoy the view."

"You sound like Geneva." I ran a finger over the belly of one of the little Buddhas. "Anyway, I like being on my own. It's restful." Dove nodded sympathetically. "I decided I'm through with that other foolishness."

Dove laughed. "The question ain't whether or not you're through with it," she said. "The question is, is it through with you?"

Т he phone was ringing as I let myself in the front door of my house. I kicked off my high-heeled church shoes and ran for it, sliding up the hallway, fumbling the receiver to my ear.

"Lucy? You sound like somebody's after you."

You ought to know, I almost said, but didn't. He didn't even bother to identify himself.

"I heard the phone from outside," I said, leaning against the wall to catch my breath. "I just got home from church."

"You wouldn't have struck me right off as the church type."

"I had some, um, unpleasantness last week with Mama and her preacher," I said. "I thought I'd better go with her and see if I could atone for my sins."

"Did you?"

"No," I said. "I went to my Aunt Dove's and ate pork ribs instead. It was a lot more religious than anything the Baptists have dreamed up."

Ash laughed. "Willie B.'s pork ribs, I bet."

"Those would be the ones."

"You want to take a look at a car?"

I was balancing the phone between my ear and my shoulder, trying to wrestle one-handed out of my panty hose. "My, you work fast."

"So I've been told." I imagined, on the other end, the skin crimping at the corners of his eyes. "Seriously," he went on, "J. D. has this particular car. Been working on it for two months, almost. Says he's been saving it for something special. I think I managed to convince him you just might qualify in that category." I didn't know what to say to that. "Isaac and I usually drive over to his folks' place in Louisiana for Sunday dinner," Ash said. "We could stop by on the way and let you see the car. It's not ten minutes out of our way."

"Okay," I said, "sure."

"You gonna be around awhile?" he asked. "It might take us an hour or so to get out the door and on the road. Stick the keys in my hand and I'm good to go. Isaac's got a wife and five kids, though. It takes him a little longer to disentangle himself."

I changed out of my dress into jeans and a white shirt. In front of the bureau mirror I stood for a few minutes and studied the angles and hollows of my face. I tried to be objective, but I couldn't; I knew it all too well, the sweep of the cheekbones, the way my nose looked straight ahead and in profile, the dusting of freckles, the frank brown eyes. I was reminded of the spiral-bound notebook we'd passed around in junior high school in which we'd graded each other's body parts, the idea being, I guess, to compose, out of our flawed masses, one perfect, composite human being. I'd been chosen "Best Nose"—an honor I'd probably been a little too pleased about, though not as pleased as if I'd gotten "Best Breasts," which went to Karleen Taylor.

I thought of Ash standing at the bar of the Round-Up wondering if I'd been this pretty in high school, and it made me mad: at him, first, then at myself. I was thirty-three years old, a widow. I didn't want to have to care what anybody thought, of my nose or anything else. My mama used to catch me staring into the mirror when I was a teenager and tell me that Jesus would rebuke me for my vanity. I'd thought that was pretty funny, coming from a woman who permed her hair within an inch of its life and never even went to the mailbox without a coat of Fire and Ice. Well, none of it mattered now. I was through with that foolishness. I left on the mascara and blush and lipstick I'd worn to church, though. Let Ash, let anybody, think what they would.

It was a cool, sunny afternoon, and I sat on the steps and threw the chew toy for Steve Cropper and let him lick my toes. He was a sweet dog but, in spite of the breed's reputation, not very smart; I figured the purity of the lineage must have gotten watered down somewhere on its way from Australia to East Texas. In fact, living with Steve Cropper reminded me a lot of living with Mitchell. All he required from me was a meal now and then and a dry place to sleep.

I heard them coming well before I saw them; it was a contest as to which of the motors was louder, and both chassis clattered and complained on their way up my unpaved half-mile road. I sat and waited for them to come into view, an ancient olive-drab Buick followed by a rickety orange-and-white GMC pickup. The Buick pulled ahead into the yard, and the old truck quivered to a stop behind it. Ash was at the wheel of the Buick.

"Oh, my Lord," I said. "You can't be serious."

"You said it had to get you to town and back," he said through the open window. "You said you weren't particular about the rest. That's a direct quote."

I stood up and walked over to the car. It was as big as a bass boat, with fins in back like angels' wings. A fine layer of red dust had settled over it from the trip, but that didn't do much to disguise the original paint job, which looked like something the army might use to camouflage tanks in the field. A glance inside revealed cracked vinyl upholstery, and a backseat the size of a motel bed. "You could put six people back there," I said wonderingly, to which Ash grinned and replied, "Or at least two. Real comfortably."

"This," I said, "is a five-hundred-dollar car?"

"Seven, actually," Ash said. "J. D.'s willing to cut you some slack, though, seeing's you're a poor widder woman and all."

"I'm not asking for slack," I said. "I'm asking what, exactly, makes this car worth seven hundred dollars? Or five, for that matter?"

"Isaac?" Ash called, his head out the window. "Get over here and help me defend my integrity."

The door of the two-tone truck swung open, and the man I'd seen working alongside Ash in Mrs. Tanner's front yard all week stepped down. He was shorter and stockier than Ash, his shoulders stretching the neck of the muscle shirt he wore, his biceps like cannonballs beneath the short sleeves. He smiled a broad, gap-toothed smile at me as he came over with his hand out.

"Afternoon," he said. "Isaac King. Pleased to know you."

"Likewise," I said, shaking his hand. "I'm Lucy Hatch."

"Law, I guess I know," Isaac said. "Fact like that be hard to miss."

"Oh, how's that?" I said, but Ash cut me off.

"Tell Miss Lucy here, Isaac," he said, opening the Buick's door, "why your brother believes this car is worth seven hundred dollars." He unwound his legs and got out. There was a can of Miller High Life in his hand.

"Shoot!" Isaac exclaimed. "Worth more than that, prob'ly. This car is a classic, can't you see that?"

"For your information," Ash said, "there's four hundred and twenty-five horses under here." He patted the hood with the flat of his hand. "You push the pedal down on this baby and she *goes*."

"That doesn't really answer my question."

Ash telegraphed Isaac a look, some sequence of masculine code I couldn't have cracked with a crowbar. "I'll be honest with you, Miss Lucy," Isaac said then. "The car ain't much to look at, it's true. But my brother, J. D., he spent two months rebuilding this engine. I ain't gonna tell you the transmission don't slip a little, or that the shocks is the smoothest in the world. But it'll get you there, safe and of a piece."

"Yeah? For how long?"

He shrugged. "Few years, you keep the radiator full and the oil clean."

"Seven hundred? Really?" It seemed like highway robbery. At the same time, I had to admit, there was something enticing about the car. My mama would faint at the sight of it, this was probably 90 percent of its appeal.

"Five-fifty," Ash corrected, "for you. Listen, J. D. doesn't expect his money today. He said keep the car for a few days, drive it, see how it treats you. You decide you like it, you pay him, if not, he takes it back, no questions asked. Sound fair?"

"All right." I bent and looked through the driver's-side window. "I don't guess it has an air conditioner."

The men burst out laughing. "Sure it does!" Ash said. "Right there, next to the CD player and the security system. Jesus Christ, Lucy. See this?" He grabbed the window handle and cranked the window partway up, then down again. "There's your air conditioner."

"Okay, okay," I said, red-faced, over their laughter. "I'll drive it for a couple of days. Let you know what I decide. It'll take me that long to come up with the money anyhow."

"No rush," Isaac said kindly. "Take your time. Anyway, I expect Ash will know where to find you. He seems to have a talent that way."

Ash pulled the key out of the ignition and handed it to me. "We're riding over to Rodessa for dinner," he said. "You want to come along? Ladies always welcome."

"That's your motto, isn't it?"

"Isaac's mama and sisters are the best cooks you'd ever hope to meet," Ash said. "After dinner we all sit out in the yard and drink a little beer and pass the guitar around."

"You all aren't drinking and driving, are you?" I said, nodding at the can in Ash's hand. "Rodessa's forty or fifty miles."

"Isaac's the designated driver," Ash said. "Anyway, we have too much fun, we just spend the night on the living room floor. Won't be the first time. Sure you won't come along? I guarantee you a fine old time."

"No, I'm . . ." *Not ready*, I almost said, but stopped myself in time. "Not ready" would imply that at some point I *would* be ready, and I couldn't say that, not with any certainty. Dove was right about one thing, though; the view from where I stood was very, very fine. "You all go on," I said instead. "You wouldn't want to miss anything. I think I'll go for a drive."

A fter they left I climbed into the front seat of the Buick and sat behind the wheel for a while, soaking in the car's ambience, such as it was. For all its age and disintegration, it was at least tidy; it reminded me of my house, in that respect. Maybe this was what widowhood was all about, a sort of descent into glorified decay. If there was, in fact, a grace in accepting this, then I supposed I'd better get on with it.

I rolled all the windows down and put Steve Cropper in the front seat, where he ran back and forth, barking excitedly; it seemed to remind him of something, a past life, I guessed, since it didn't have anything to do with Australian cattle. I stuck the key in the ignition and turned it, and the big V-8 fired right up and then sat there, rumbling contentedly. Steve Cropper had his feet on the passenger-side door handle, his head already in the breeze. "You ready?" I asked. "Here we go."

I had trouble, at first, locating forward gear—the letters on the column didn't seem to have any connection to the transmission, at least none the car understood—but I found it at last, and we executed a neat, if wide, circle in the front yard and headed out the road toward the highway. The car rocked and jostled on what must have been the loosest suspension ever, but once we hit the paved road and turned toward town, the engine grabbed and the ride was as I'd always imagined ice skating would be, like gliding effortlessly across a flawless surface, propelled by some unseen hand. Steve Cropper was hardly big enough to see out the window, but his ears stood straight up, his teeth bared in ecstasy. On a whim, I reached down and twisted the knob on the dashboard radio, and Carla Thomas's voice jumped out, life-size, from the speaker: "B-A-B-Y, baby, you look so good to me, baby."

"What do you think?" I yelled over the wind through the open windows as we pulled in at Orson's Texaco and turned around. "You think it's a keeper?" I steered back out onto the highway and eased the pedal down. The road opened up underneath us, thrumming with possibility, and we roared into the blue.

I t was warm enough now that I'd taken to sleeping with the bedroom window cracked, and I was drifting that night, halfway between wakefulness and sleep, when I heard the sound of tires on the unpaved road, crunching over the occasional stone or branch, approaching the house.

I sat up in bed but didn't turn on the lamp. My heart was racheting; I knew, in the space of ten seconds, what it meant to have your life pass before your eyes. Every word of doom and warning from my mama's and my brothers' lips ran through my mind: disgrace, danger, a woman alone. I didn't own a gun, or anything more lethal than a steak knife and a pair of nail scissors. I wondered, stealing out of bed in the dark and down the hall, if my mama would grieve for me, or if she would stand over my headstone with her hands on her hips and complain that she'd told me so.

Whoever it was kept coming. I checked that the front door was locked, then sneaked into the kitchen and over to the window. It was a little before midnight, pitch dark out, overcast. If the truck hadn't been white, I don't know if I'd have been able to identify it so easily.

The thought crossed my mind, as he pulled in beside the Buick and cut the engine, that maybe there was a side to Ash Farrell no one in Mooney knew. Maybe, all these years, behind the well-lubricated facade, he really was a lady-killer, in the literal sense. Who knew what happened to all those women he met, week after week, at the Round-Up; there was such a surplus, surely one could disappear every now and then without being missed. I crept over to the drawer beside the sink and groped around until my fist closed on the steak knife's handle, then carried it to the window. It, too, was open a crack, and slowly, silently, I knelt beneath the sash and waited for something to happen.

Nothing did, for the longest time. Finally, the driver's-side door opened. Ash's shirt was light-colored, which didn't seem too smart for sneaking around trying to murder people, but it did make it possible for me to see him. He lifted something out of the cab of the truck, then went around and let down the tailgate, which screeched a little on worn hinges. He seemed to be talking to someone, though I couldn't make out what he was saying, until I saw him crouch in the dirt and realized he was petting Steve Cropper. So much for protection, I thought; the puppy was leaping on his hind legs, slathering Ash with kisses, and hadn't barked one time.

Ash sat down on the tailgate, his shirt a pale swatch against a black satin drape. It was quiet for a while, just the wind in the pines and the hoot of some far-off bird. Then I heard the strum of a couple of guitar chords, and finally his voice, like a lick of flame against the backdrop of the night.

> *Along the Red River where the sweet waters flow*
> *Where the stars they burn bright and the soft wind does blow*
> *There lives a fair maiden, the one I adore*
> *And I'll court my dear maiden on the Red River shore.*

And without warning I was eight years old, lying in the warm dark with a starched sheet pulled up tight to my chin, the box fan in the window ticking time behind a woman's voice soft as a brushstroke:

> *I asked her so kindly, "Will you marry me?*
> *I haven't a fortune." "No matter," said she.*
> *"Your love it is true and your heart it is sure*
> *And I'll marry you, dear, on the Red River shore."*

The palm that lay upon my forehead was dry and rough with work and scented with the cherry-almond Jergens lotion Dove rubbed into her knuckles every night after the supper dishes. My hair pricked up on the back of my neck, listening to Ash's voice carry the song through the night and lay it at my feet, like a gift I hadn't known I wanted. I sat at the window with my fist stuffed into my mouth, not knowing whether to laugh or cry as the verses spun themselves out, trying to make sense of the sad, dark beauty I was hearing. In the tune Aunt Dove had sung to me, the cowboy murdered his bride's father and they'd lived in misery ever after, but in Ash's version the couple seemed to settle instead into peaceful domesticity:

Now that I've won her, I'll wander no more
And live with my love on the Red River shore.

It was nothing but a simple folk song, an ordinary lullaby. Why did it seem to reach down into me and tear me open from toes to throat? How had Ash known? Was it coincidence, or something else?

He sang a few more tunes, nothing I recognized: one about a Civil War soldier, one about a man watching over a sleeping child. At some point I set the knife on the floor and sat back against the wall under the open window. I closed my eyes and it was just possible, with the drift of the night wind and Ash's voice through the window, to believe there was some kind of force at work here, a kind of impetus that kept us all moving forward, even though it seemed at times that the whole point of living was to wish for things we couldn't reach, to long for some state of completion we'd never know, or only in glimpses, a spark here and there. I'd had it once, I thought; and behind my eyes I saw, as plain as if I'd traveled there, the bedroom I'd shared all those years with Mitchell, dark and silent, dusty now with disuse. The rocking chair in the corner, the maple-framed mirror, the blue quilt on the bed that had belonged to one of Mitchell's forebears. It was still there, untouched, little more than an hour's drive away, but even though, in legal terms, I owned it—

for another couple of weeks, at least—it didn't belong to me anymore. It seemed Ash's music had loosed something in me, reminding me of the link that was mine to hold in the world's long chain of loss and sorrow, and I lay my head in the lap of my nightgown and let the tears come. When I sat up again, the pickup was making its usual start-up racket, enough to wake the dead, and by the time I could get to my feet and put my face against the window, Ash was gone.

(*seven*)

Peggy had warned me, when I started the job, that Monday was typically her busiest day. "I've been studying on it for twenty years, and I haven't figured it out yet," she said, "but everything happens on the weekend. People fall off ladders, wreck their cars, get drunk and argue with their girlfriends. Then, come Monday, they're all either in the hospital or the doghouse, or both. All I know is, everybody wakes up Monday morning thinking they've got to have flowers."

My first Monday in the shop, her prophecy appeared true. Before noon, I delivered arrangements to three people who'd been sent to County General over the weekend—a broken hip, an automotive mishap, an angina attack—and two to women who, if you could judge from their reactions when I walked in carrying their bouquets, had been wronged in some onerous way or another by men. "That son of a bitch," one of them actually said as I set the fifty-dollar vase of Traviata roses on the corner of her desk. "If he thinks this makes up for Saturday night, he's got another think coming." I said what I always said—

"Have a nice day"—and walked out to the van puzzling over the games people played. I was a little worried, frankly, that my job would make me cynical, watching people behave badly and then trying to gloss it over with offerings of sweet-smelling beauty. I resolved to keep my head above the fray.

Ash's truck hadn't been at Mrs. Tanner's when I left on my early rounds, but it was there when I got back. I glanced at her house as I climbed out of the van—just the slightest flick of my eyes, nothing anybody could prove in court—and saw him crouched over a stack of lumber on the driveway, sizing up something with a tape measure. I thought I might make a dash for the back door of the shop, but he'd seen the van.

"Lucy!" he called. He was less than fifty yards away; I couldn't very well pretend not to hear him. I turned, and he made a sweeping circle with his arm, motioning me over.

He came down the driveway partway to meet me. He wore a tool belt low around his hips like an outlaw might wear a holster, and walked with a languid confidence, almost a swagger, that made something sour rise at the back of my throat.

"Hi," he said. "How's the car?"

"Fine."

He seemed surprised. "You like it?"

"So far."

He looked a little harder into my face. "You okay? You seem a little out of sorts."

"I didn't sleep that well."

"No?"

"There was some kind of racket in my driveway, sometime around midnight."

"Racket."

"Then, when it finally stopped and I went back to bed, I kept having this dream. Water, and more water . . .

"A wet dream." He smiled.

"Very wet," I said. " 'Along the Red River where the sweet waters flow.' "

"Jesus," he said. "You know that song?"

"I . . . Yes." I looked out across Mrs. Tanner's lawn, to the tulip tree next to the front door that was already dropping its blooms. "My aunt used to sing it to me at bedtime, when I was little. I hadn't thought of it in years. It seems to me the story was a lot less cheery, though, the way she told it."

"Oh, I always try to tack on a happy ending when I can."

"What in the world put you in mind of that particular song?" I asked, and felt my face flush at what seemed like the audacity of the remark; neither one of us had officially acknowledged that what had happened last night, had happened.

Ash scuffed his toe along an oil stain on the driveway. "I have no idea," he said. "I've always loved those old songs, from the first time I picked up a guitar. I guess I like to think that cowboy might've been me, a hundred years ago. Sometimes I get the notion in my head and can't shake it loose. And sometimes I just fall in love with how things sound."

"Yes. I know." I tore my eyes off the tulip tree and looked at him. The sky over our heads was as blue and unblemished as the day God made it. Something passed between Ash and me, invisible, unnameable, but as real as if he'd placed an object in my hand, something hard and glistening, beguiling but built to last.

No, I thought.

I don't want it.

Take it back.

Mrs. Tanner's front door opened, and Isaac stuck his head out. "Hey, Ash!" he hollered, then saw me and raised a hand in greeting. "Oh, hey there, Miss Lucy! How's the car?" I gave him the thumbs-up. "Lunch," he said to Ash, and Ash waved.

"I have to go," I said. I'd never had a full-blown panic attack before, but this must be how they began: pounding heart, shallow breathing, sweaty palms, feeling of certain doom.

"Come on in and eat with us," Ash said, all offhand charm again. "Isaac's wife sent him to work this morning with half a brisket. It's not quite Willie B.'s caliber, but damn near."

"I can't. Peggy's expecting me back." I was already backing away, off the curb, into the street. I actually thought it would help to run away, that's how stupid I was. "Monday's our busiest day."

Ash nodded; whether or not he believed me, he'd decided to let it go. "See you, then," he said, unhitching the tool belt and dropping it into the bed of the truck, "sooner or later."

I turned and fled.

I t hadn't happened, of course. It was a delusion, a trick of the light. As the afternoon passed, I managed to convince myself of that with some certainty. I drove home at the end of my shift and spent the afternoon with a book in my lap but staring into space, thinking nothing. At six I tore open a Budget Gourmet and put it in the oven, but I couldn't eat. I went to bed at eight o'clock, and slept, and dreamed of blankness and blue, and by Tuesday morning everything had righted itself again.

Early that afternoon I drove into town to the Mooney Clinic and let the nurse of the town G.P. cut the plaster off my wrist. Dr. Platt came in for sixty seconds, examined the mend, pronounced it healed, and sent me off with a Xeroxed sheet of strengthening exercises. "That's it?" I said. The doctor shrugged. "Use your head," he said. "I wouldn't go right out and bench-press three times my weight, and you want to watch any vigorous movement, especially the twisting kind, for a while. Otherwise, have a blast."

I stepped out into the hall and ran into Geneva, who worked for the local ob/gyn. She had a pack of Marlboro Lights in her hand and a scowl on her face. "Look!" I said, waving my left wrist in the air. "Free at last, free at last, thank God almighty . . ."

"Come on outside with me," she said. "I need a smoke."

I sat down beside her on a concrete bench in the sunshine and watched her light up. Her nurse's scrubs were printed with teddy bears, whose cheerful faces were a marked contrast to Geneva's. She pulled the first hit of smoke into her lungs like it was life support.

"What's the matter with you?" I said. I held my wrist aloft and turned it this way and that in the daylight; it seemed astonishingly smooth and pale, like an anatomy-book drawing of a wrist.

"Never get married again, Lucy," Geneva said darkly, puffing on her cigarette. "You've gotta promise me that."

"What did he do now?"

"He . . . Oh, shit."

"Something serious?" I felt a small sinking in my belly; I hoped this wouldn't kill my opportunity to hit Bailey up for the money for my car.

She inhaled furiously, tracing her cigarette through the air like a kid with a sparkler on the Fourth of July. "Our anniversary's coming up, right?" I nodded encouragingly. "Well, there are these earrings—big old dangly diamonds, a couple of carats apiece. I saw them last time we were in Marshall, at Zale's.

"So, I ask the clerk for a little brochure—several copies of the brochure, in fact—and I circle the earrings with a big red marker and then I leave them lying around the house—next to the toaster, taped to the bathroom mirror . . ."

I laughed, and she glared and me and pulled hard on her cigarette.

"Anyway, I go to the bank this morning to cash a check, but when the teller gives me my balance, something doesn't look right. There's a great big chunk of money missing out of our checking account.

"My first thought is, my earrings! I was so excited I just about peed. And then all of a sudden here comes that fat old loan officer Morris Kirk, running out of his office in those striped suspenders he wears, telling me how excited Bailey is about his new John Deere.

" 'Excuse me'?" I say, like I didn't hear him right. " 'Why, Bailey was just in here this morning, talking about the new lawn tractor he ordered from Emmitt Fowler,' Morris says, just as jolly as can be. 'Showed me a brochure and everything!' And Lucy, damned if I didn't call up Emmitt Fowler at the co-op, and it's true! He said Bailey went in and paid cash for it this morning. It's on order from goddamned Kansas or something." Geneva stood up and ground her cigarette to ash under one heel. "Twelve whole years we've been married, and Bailey's idea of celebrating is a goddamned lawn tractor!"

"Gee," I said, biting my lip to keep my smile in check, "I guess there goes the black corset and the horsewhip."

"Ha! He'll be lucky to get a piece in the *next* twelve years. Aren't you working today?"

"Tuesday's my day off."

"Come on, I'll walk you to the parking lot. I need the air." It was a well-espoused theory of Geneva's that if you spent five minutes outside in the fresh air for every cigarette you smoked, the oxygen would somehow cancel out the coat of tar you'd just laid over your lungs. She claimed to have learned this in nursing school.

She did a double take when she saw the Buick. I grinned, dangling the keys.

"What do you think?" I said. "Kind of fits my new image, don't you think?"

"Would that image be white trash?" she asked. "Where did it come from? And don't tell me the assembly line in Detroit. It looks like maybe Dr. Frankenstein dreamed it up."

"Or General Patton," I said, a little proudly. "Isaac King's brother rebuilt it." She hesitated a beat too long, and I jerked my chin around and looked at her. "Ash procured it for me," I said. "Don't you say another word."

Her face relaxed into a smile. "How *is* Ash?" she said, letting his name unfurl like a pair of silk drawers.

"How should I know?" I said peevishly. "You think I keep tabs on him twenty-four hours a day?"

"He's right across the street at Mrs. Tanner's, isn't he?" she said. "Anyway, it's pretty much the impression of the whole town that he's keeping tabs on *you*."

I stared at her. "Excuse me?"

"They've got a pool going, Lucy, over at the café."

"What kind of pool?"

"You know—how long before . . ."

"Before what?" I felt the heat rising in my face. I knew "before what," I just wanted to make her say it.

"Before he plants his flag."

I opened the car door and got in, jamming the key into the ignition. Whatever made me think I wanted to move back to Mooney, made me feel it would open its arms and give me shelter? My whole life since Mitchell died suddenly seemed like a crazy quilt of desperate missteps, everything done either incidentally or on a whim. I'd known I couldn't stay on alone on the farm, but what on earth had led me to believe that anyplace else would ever feel like home?

Geneva leaned over and looked in the window. "Your brother's a madman," she said. "He marched over there straight off and threatened to sue Burton for defamation of character. Yours, of course."

"Let me guess," I said. "Burton told him it's a free country." Burton had owned the café for forty years, and "It's a free country" was his response to just about any kind of discord.

"All I know," she said over the grumble of the Buick's engine, "is that if I had somebody like Ash Farrell coming up that hard behind me, I think maybe I'd slow up a minute and let him tag me."

"You go after him, then," I said, revving the engine a couple of times, not because it needed it but because it made me feel good. "You and Bailey are having a snit, maybe what you need is a little diversion. I'm sure Ash would be happy to accommodate you."

"Don't think I'm not thinking about it. Meantime, Lucy, I hope you've got some good running shoes."

I smiled at a sudden memory. "I remember when I ran the two hundred meters at the state relays, my sophomore year," I said. "I almost won."

" 'Almost,' " Geneva said contemplatively. "Doesn't that mean somebody caught you?"

All I wanted was to go home and recover my equilibrium, maybe drag the hoe around the garden a little bit, or sit with a pad and a pencil and map out where the tomato cages and bean poles would go. I thought if I could just get through the rest of the day without seeing Ash or hearing any further mention of his name, I might be able to retrieve some of that feeling I'd had in the first few days in my little house, as if my life was something that could be ordered like a ledger, that it was mine to command.

At the mailbox I slowed the Buick and removed the handful of envelopes and flyers and laid them on the seat beside me. Steve Cropper came wiggling out from under the steps when he heard the car. "The man of my dreams," I said, picking him up and kissing him on his little snout. Ever since Sunday afternoon, he associated the sound of the car with the notion of going for a ride. "Maybe later," I told him, setting him down and reaching into the front seat for the mail.

I stood on the porch and shuffled through the stack, sorting with a glance the junk from the bills. I almost missed the envelope from Farmer's Beneficial Insurance. I stared at the return address for a moment, then slit the envelope with my thumb. "Dear Mrs. Breward," the letter began, and for a second I couldn't remember who that was.

The check was for thirty thousand dollars.

It felt like God had stuck his hand in my chest and was squeezing my heart, squeezing and squeezing until surely there was nothing left for it but to burst. Thirty thousand dollars. It was more money than I'd ever had at one time, more than Mitchell had ever earned in a year. And it was not enough to carry me more than a couple of years, even with a job. In a matter of months, then, I would be like Clarence Beadle, living in a hut, ranting in the post office; or like the woman we called the Rag Lady when I was in grade school, who wandered around downtown clad in a fantastic assortment of tatters and remnants, strung together God knows how but giving, somehow, the blended effect of refinement and poverty. Nobody knew who the Rag Lady was, but there were rumors she was an artist, and had been the wife of a wealthy man till she lost her mind, and had finally drunk herself to death under a railroad bridge. Why, I wondered, was there so much madness in this town? It was rampant in the streets; I was surprised 20/20 hadn't shown up to do an exposé. I would be part of a grand tradition, then: one of the demented souls of Mooney, Texas, pushing my belongings in a shopping cart, sleeping under the MoPac trestle, buried, unknown and unmarked, in the county graveyard. What bureaucrat in a suit down in Austin had decided that a man's life was worth a measly thirty thousand dollars?

I unlocked the front door and pushed it open, and water poured out.

"Shit!" I dropped the mail, then snatched it up again, making sure the envelope from Farmer's Beneficial was dry, and set it on the windowsill. The water was a couple of inches deep, and running toward the front door from the kitchen. I waded in, across the flooded linoleum, and opened the cabinet under the sink. The pipe, what was left of it, looked like antique lace, except that instead of cotton threads, it was woven of rusted metal. The water gushed, endlessly, almost defiantly, from the corroded pipe. There was no cutoff, at least that I could see.

A despair came over me then that was deeper than anything I'd felt since Mitchell died, a sense of powers conspiring against me. I thought of the lumbering old car, the house falling to pieces around me, the check that wouldn't begin to fix things. What kind of life was this? Wasn't there some Indian sect that, when the men died, just put the wives up on the pyre and let them burn alongside their husbands? Maybe this was why: not because life might not be worth living, but that sheer survival was too exhausting to contemplate. I might have put my head in the oven if I could have swum over there. I was too depressed to cry.

Think, think.

My mind latched onto a spontaneous image: The week before, a man from the water company had come out and shown me how to read the meter. I sloshed back out of the house and around the corner and there, as I'd remembered, was the black box in the ground. Thank goodness I had two hands now, even if one wasn't much help; I was able to pry the metal lid off the box and, sure enough, inside was a round handle, just like the kind for turning on and off the hose. I cranked the handle, which was stiff from disuse. Avoid vigorous twisting motions, the doctor had said. I twisted, vigorously. My wrist complained. Slowly, the handle turned.

What if it wasn't the right handle?

I dashed back around the house and up the steps, Steve Cropper dancing at my heels like this was some kind of frolic. The water still oozed over the door frame and dripped onto the porch, but the flow beneath the sink had stopped.

I took off my soaked sneakers and inched to the telephone and dialed Shirley Tinsley at the real estate office.

"I'm sorry," the receptionist, Tancy Burkhalter, said brightly, "Shirley's out with a client."

"I have two inches of water in my house," I said. "Tell me what to do."

I heard Tancy humming under her breath, what sounded like the *William Tell* Overture, though it had to be my imagination. "Okay, I'm calling Pep Walter," she said. "That's who Shirley uses on plumbing jobs. You sit by the phone and wait, and he'll call you back, all right?"

"Two inches of water," I said, and hung up.

A minute later the phone rang. I snatched it up and yelled hello.

"Lucy?" It was Ash.

"Oh, God. Not now," I said. "You're supposed to be Pep Walter."

"Why would I be Pep Walter?"

"Because I have two goddamned inches of water in my house, and a pipe that looks like somebody poured acid through it, and everything is a big goddamned mess and Pep Walter is supposed to come out here and fix it!"

"Pep Walter couldn't tell a drainpipe from a corncob pipe," Ash said. "Pep Walter is probably over at Lake O' The Pines with his pole in the water and his pager turned off. What in the hell would you want with Pep Walter?"

"I have to get off the line," I said. I didn't acknowledge that what Ash had said was probably true; I was sure Pep was trying to call me that very second.

"Tell me what the problem is," Ash said. He sounded like he was lying on a beach somewhere, woozy from the sun, having oil rubbed into his shoulders by a nymph in a bikini, which made my voice that much more frenzied by comparison.

"I just told you what the problem is! There's two inches of water in my house! I have to—"

"Is there a cutoff?"

"Not in the house, not that I could find. I turned it off outside, at the meter."

"The water is off?"

"Yes, it's off! Do you think I'm completely incompetent?"

A pause, one tick too long. "What's the pipe look like?"

"How should I know? It looks like a busted pipe! Look, I—"

"Is it metal or PVC?"

"Metal, I think. PVC doesn't rot, does it?"

"I don't guess you could wade over there and measure it for me."

"For you? What for? Pep Walter is coming out to fix it."

"Pep Walter has got a nice fat catfish tugging at his line," Ash said. "You won't be hearing from him till, oh, I'd say November. I'll be there in half an hour."

"What do you want me to do?"

"I believe I'd get out the mop." He hung up.

Hey, you got your cast off," Ash said. "Congratulations. Wow." He stood with his hands on his hips, surveying the flooded kitchen. "If you wanted me to come out here and sing to you, Lucy, you could have just asked."

"I've never known you to require an invitation," I answered. I was in a black mood. I'd rolled up my jeans and pulled my hair into a loose knot at the back of my neck, and everything, everything was wet. I'd wrung out the mop so many times I'd lost count, but there's only so much an eight-inch sponge can do.

"You need a string mop," Ash observed mildly. "The old-fashioned kind. Better yet, you need a Shop-Vac."

"Don't you dare tell me what I need," I said. "I'm already about to hurt something."

He reached out onto the porch and lifted a metal toolbox through the front door. "So, has Pep called yet?" I aimed the end of the mop handle at him, and he laughed and slogged into the kitchen. "This floor is ruined," he said, "I can tell you that right now. If there's plywood under the linoleum, it won't last six months before it rots right out from under you." I ignored him. Six months from then, I expected to be living under a bridge, and this floor would be somebody else's problem. "Jesus Christ," Ash said, his head inside the sink cabinet. "This pipe must be seventy years old. Didn't you check this stuff before you signed the lease?"

"Stop haranguing me," I said. "If you can fix it, fix it. If you can't, then go away and I'll get Pep Walter."

He straightened and looked at me, a moment longer than I'd have liked. "Something troubling you, Lucy?" he said. "Something besides a busted pipe?"

I took the mop out front and wrung it over the edge of the porch.

He spent the next hour under the sink, his Levi's sopping from the knees down, removing what remained of the old pipe and fitting on a new one, while I mopped and wrung, mopped and wrung. After a while, though, it started to feel like we were competing for air, like there wasn't enough in the room to go around, and so I went outside and sat on the front steps. The mop wasn't doing much good anyway. I wished I smoked; it seemed like exactly the right situation for a cigarette. I supposed I could take it up, since no one was likely to care if a poor homeless woman got lung cancer. Of course, in a year or two, how would I afford cigarettes?

Ash came to the screen. "I'll be finished up in here before long," he said. "What's for supper?"

"In case you haven't noticed, the kitchen's out of service."

"So?" he said. "Your car works, doesn't it? How about a pizza, or a couple of hamburgers? Jeez, Lucy, I give up an afternoon of paid work to come out here, bust my hump to get your plumbing fixed—"

"Nobody asked you to!" I cried, scrambling to my feet and facing him through the screen. "Who asked you to bust your hump, Ash Farrell? No one! You just called up and you . . . and you . . ."

"And I fixed it." He said this calmly, without anger. "I got it done."

"Pep Walter would have got it done."

"Pep Walter has been abducted by aliens," Ash said, and I started to laugh, and so did he. He was a mess—soaked jeans and work boots, rust on his T-shirt, his hair plastered back—none of which did much to dull the shimmer.

"Regular crust, or double-stuffed?"

I was still in my rolled-up jeans and untucked shirt and tumble-down hair and foul mood, so it was lucky I didn't see anyone I knew, not at Pizza Hut or at Wal-Mart, where I stopped to buy a string mop, or at County Line Liquor, where I picked up a six-pack of Bud and, on impulse, a pint of Jim Beam. I hadn't had a drink, a real one, since the night of Mitchell's funeral, when I'd fallen off the porch. It was a cliché, I knew, but I didn't feel like that person anymore. Not that I wasn't just as capable of falling. It was that I didn't care so much, anymore, where I happened to land.

When I drove up, Ash was sitting on the step with Steve Cropper between his bare feet. The plumbing must have been back in service, because he'd cleaned up; his shirt was fresh, and his hair was damp and combed back.

I opened the car door and tossed him the mop, which he leaned against the porch post. "I hope they got this right," I said, passing him the pizza box. "They were having a little trouble with the concept of 'half pepperoni.' "

"At this point I think I could eat the box."

"Here," I said, pulling the six-pack out of the brown paper bag and handing it to him. "Unless you'd rather have some of what I'm having."

I sat down beside him on the step and took out the whiskey, twisting off the cap. I wadded the bag into a ball and tossed it into the yard for the puppy, but he was more interested in the pizza. Ash stared at me as I lifted the pint bottle and drank.

"Were you drinking that in the car?" he said.

"Only one shot. What's it to you?" I offered him the bottle, but he shook his head and took the cap off a Bud. "Didn't you ever have one of those days when you just don't give a shit?"

Ash was quiet awhile, drinking his beer. "You know, Lucy," he said, "this may be none of my business, but I'd really like to know what's going on."

"Why?" I said. "So you can fix it?" He didn't say anything. "That's what you do, isn't it? Fix things?"

"Well, I wish I knew why you make me feel like apologizing for it. Give me that," he said, neatly intercepting the bottle as it was on its way to my mouth for another round. "Here, eat something," he said. "If you're gonna be puke drunk, it's a lot better to have something in your stomach first."

"The voice of experience," I said. He just smiled and handed me a slice of pizza, the crust thick and oily, dense with cheese and sauce. I hadn't thought I was hungry, but I was. I was starved. I ate one piece, then another, then I licked the sauce off my fingers. I got up and went inside for a Coke. Patches of the linoleum had started to separate from the plywood beneath, but I didn't care so much about the whiskey anymore. I was starting to feel better: not happier, exactly, but less like there were snakes crawling around under my skin.

"Pep called," Ash volunteered, opening his second beer. I looked at him in surprise, and he smiled.

"You're kidding. While I was gone?" He nodded. "What did he say?"

"He wanted to invite you over for a big old fish fry."

I punched Ash lightly on the forearm. "Seriously. What did you tell him?"

"That I had the situation well in hand."

"I'm not sure the real estate company will reimburse you for what you did," I said slowly.

"Thirty-four fifty for parts. It's not likely to break me, one way or the other."

"What about the labor, though?" I said. "You said yourself, you lost an afternoon of work . . ."

"Hey, don't sweat it," he said. "It all works out in the end, doesn't it?"

"How?" I said, looking at him over my Coke. "How does it work out in the end? Ash, we can't . . . I can't . . ." I shook my head at the futility of ever getting the words I wanted, when my head seemed full of ones I couldn't say. "The whole town is talking," I said finally, and was glad it was getting dark so he wouldn't see me blush. "They think something's going on, and . . ."

Ash looked up. "And what?"

"And nothing is."

He sat looking at his beer bottle for a while. At his side Steve Cropper gnawed happily on a pizza crust.

"I guess if that hurts you, then I'm sorry," Ash said. "I never thought about it that way. The whole town's been talking about me since I was three years old. I don't guess there's too much left anybody could say that wouldn't bounce off by now." He smiled down the neck of his beer, but there was no pleasure in it. "I expect I've heard every crack about Milk-Bones there is to think up."

"Can I ask you something?"

"Is it about dog biscuits?"

"Indirectly, I guess."

"Go ahead."

"Why don't you see your mama?"

"My mama gave me up." He took a swallow of beer.

"No, she didn't," I said. Ash looked at me sharply. "They took her to Rusk."

"Nobody took her," he said. "She committed herself. Before she did, she signed a piece of paper. Made me a ward of the county. Relinquished all rights and responsibilities."

"No."

"Yes."

"But . . . If she really was—you know. Crazy. Overwhelmed. Depressed. Whatever it was. Maybe she didn't know what she was doing! Maybe someone coerced her, maybe she—"

"She signed the paper, Lucy! She let me go, so I let her go." I listened to him draw a breath and hold it. "Anyway, I got lucky, if you think about it. My stepmom really loved me." He put his head back and stared up at the sky, where the first faint stars were beginning to show themselves against the deepening blue. "You want to hear something funny? When I get lonesome—really lonesome, not just wanting somebody to rub up against—it's Christa I think about. I think if I could find somebody who cared for me like she did, and then add the sex part without messing it all up, I'd have everything I need."

"How many times have you been in love?" I asked.

"Define 'love.' "

"Oh, not the rubbing-up-against-somebody part," I said. "My Lord, I doubt you can even count that high. I mean—I don't know. I guess it's where you don't mind staying over for breakfast the next morning."

"Three," he said. "Maybe four. There was this one girl who kept burning the toast." I laughed. "Is that more than you would have expected," he said, "or less?"

"More," I said. He looked surprised. "I expected you might just say your wife."

"Nah," he said, polishing off his beer. "My wife, I'd have to say, was number two. She wasn't even the love of my life."

"Who was?"

"Well, I'll make a deal with you," he said. "You'll have to come back to the Round-Up sometime, and I'll play you a song about her. Listen," he said, as far off, through the woods, the six-thirty freight hit its whistle as it cut across the crossroads at the place we called The Corners. "If that isn't the bluest sound on the planet, I don't know what is."

"You think so? I like it," I said. "It makes me feel like, if things ever got too bad, I could just—go." I was aware, in the gathering dark, of him looking at me. "I got a check in the mail today," I said. "For thirty thousand dollars."

Ash whistled through his teeth. "I like to think I'd be a damn sight more cheerful than you if thirty thousand dollars turned up in my mailbox."

"From the insurance company," I said. "Compensation for Mitchell's death." I took the pins out of my hair and shook it loose. "You know, I thought I'd been handling all this pretty well. It wasn't till I saw that check that I started to get scared. Thirty thousand dollars sounds like a lot of money, but it isn't, really. Not when you think that it's . . ." I couldn't say it: *all I'll ever have.* "Oh, it makes me so mad! At first I was mad at the insurance company—I mean, who decides these things, that the value of someone's life is thirty thousand dollars? Then I got to thinking about it, one of the million times I was wringing out the mop this afternoon, and I realized, *Mitchell* was the one who decided. He's the one who took out the policy."

"Nobody ever expects to need it."

"But why be half-assed about it? You know what the difference in the premiums on a thirty-thousand-dollar policy and a three-hundred-thousand-dollar one is? It's just a few dollars a month! I don't know if he was stupid, or thoughtless, or if he just plain thought he was never going to die. Or maybe this is just his way of getting even with me."

"What for?"

"For everything I didn't feel."

"You think he knew?"

"I didn't make him feel any more tingly than he did me," I said. "I guess we were a good match, that way." I looked at Ash. "This is Reverend Honeywell's fault," I said. "I think he put the gris-gris on me in church on Sunday. I saw him doing it."

Ash started to laugh. "I'm pretty sure Baptists don't practice voodoo, Lucy. Anyway, you know what I would say about your gris-gris?" he said. "*C'est la vie.*"

"Easy for you to say. You have skills, a trade. You won't wind up on the streets like the Rag Lady, freezing to death drunk under the bridge."

"Well, now, I might," he said thoughtfully, like it was an option he was mulling over. "But I don't imagine I will. You know why? Because someone would look out for me. And someone would do the same for you."

Steve Cropper was chewing the corner of the pizza box, and Ash tucked the lid shut and set the box on the porch rail. "There's a lot of hazards built into living in a town of twelve hundred people," he said, "but one thing you'll always know is that you have a place here. My mama gave me up, but the Kellerses took me in. Didn't your aunt practically raise you, when your daddy left?" I nodded. "People do have tiny little minds sometimes, and great big mouths. But there's something else to most of these folks. Under all the meddling and the gossip, they really will do their best for you. Sometimes it may be something trifling, like fixing a busted pipe. And sometimes it's something bigger."

"Nobody looked out for the Rag Lady," I pointed out.

"That's because the Rag Lady didn't belong to anybody," Ash said. "And you do."

He stood up and shook the kinks out of his legs. "To tell you the truth, I expect that having my name and yours paired up over at the café is bound to help more than hurt my reputation. I can't say it makes me entirely unhappy. Still," he said, "maybe I ought to be getting on home. Somebody comes along and sees us sitting here like this, no telling what kind of bets will be flying in the morning."

"I'm pretty sure my reputation is shot to hell anyway," I said. "I haven't done anything right since I got here. Who knows, maybe getting linked up with you will elevate me a little." Ash was still standing there, looking down at me. "That's okay," I said. "Go on home, if you want to."

"I don't want to, particularly," he said. "I was just saying maybe I should."

I gazed at his bare feet on the porch step, like a couple of silvery fish in the dusky light. The word "no" was so near the tip of my tongue that I knew the devil had put it there, and so I bit down hard on it until I tasted blood, until the commotion in my head died away and clarity prevailed. It seemed to me that Ash had done nothing but heap my arms full of beneficence since I'd met him, that I would never get out from under the obligation.

"Maybe you should," I said, standing to meet his eyes, wondering if he could see, in the shine of those first scant stars, that I hadn't yet found the courage of my convictions. But I was looking. It was a start.

(*eight*)

The next day, on my lunch hour, I went to the bank and deposited the insurance check, taking out seven hundred dollars in cash. Then I drove over to the real estate office and walked in and laid the plastic True Value hardware bag containing the remains of my kitchen's original plumbing on Shirley Tinsley's desk.

"Here's the receipt for the replacement," I said. "Thirty-four fifty, plus tax. And I want a hundred dollars for his time."

"Whose time?"

"Ash Farrell's."

Shirley sat back in her capacious executive-style chair and studied me. She was a big black-haired woman given to two-piece knit pants outfits decorated in fancy rickrack and sequins; today's ensemble depicted a casino theme, glittery dice and playing cards with beaded hearts and spades. "Tancy was supposed to call Pep Walter," Shirley said. "Pep's who we use on these jobs."

"Pep didn't call back," I said, then, with a stab of conscience, "not for several hours. It was an emergency, Shirley. If you don't believe me, go out to the house and take a look. The kitchen floor is ruined. I was lucky, Ash was . . ."

"Ash was what?"

"Handy." Why *had* Ash called, in the first place? Till that moment, I'd never thought to wonder.

"Oh, yes," Shirley said slyly, "Ash is *handy*." Something kicked like a mallet against a tom-tom in my gut as she reached into her desk drawer and brought out a heavy leather-bound account book. "I want you to understand, Lucy," she said, "that I'll go along with this, this time, since, as you say, Pep was unavailable, and Ash was, um, handy. But in the future, I'll have to ask you to clear these things with me ahead of time. I mean, I don't think it's fair, do you, to expect me to subsidize your little . . ."

"My little what?" I stared right at her, but she didn't even blink.

"Honey, I wouldn't begin to know what to call it," she said, and I stood there with the blood roaring in my ears, clenching my fists at my sides, while Shirley wrote out a check to Ash for a hundred thirty-six dollars and sixty-six cents.

"The kitchen floor's going to have to be replaced," I said. "The plywood's rotting under the linoleum."

"I guess Ash told you that, too."

"I don't think it's debatable, Shirley," I said. "Send Pep Walter to check it out if you don't believe me."

"I'll just do that," she said, checking the calendar on her desk blotter. "How about tomorrow at four o'clock?"

"Fine," I said, and snatched the check out from under her pen before the ink was dry. I left the chunk of rotten pipe on her desk like a gratuity.

Ash and Isaac were eating sandwiches on the tailgate of Isaac's truck in Mrs. Tanner's driveway when I got back to the flower shop. I parked the Buick next to the delivery van and walked across the street, both of them silent, chewing, watching me come.

I handed Isaac the envelope with the seven hundred dollars. "Here's the money for the car," I said. "Can you get it to J. D. for me?"

"There's seven hundred dollars here," Isaac said, peering into the envelope.

"You said it was a seven-hundred-dollar car."

"Seems like it was s'posed to be five-fifty," Isaac said, glancing at Ash, "for you."

"I don't even know J. D.," I said. "He surely doesn't owe me any favors."

"The favor was to me, Lucy," Ash said; he wiped his mouth on a handful of paper napkins. "A friend for a friend."

"Well, you've done me enough favors in the past few days to last a year or so, already. This is for you," I said, and handed him the check from Fairview Realty. He seemed to be puzzling over the numbers like they made no sense to him. "I didn't know how much to charge for your time," I said, "so I said a hundred dollars." Ash didn't say anything or even raise his head. "I hope that was enough."

He looked up, and his eyes seemed to slice right into me, a stealth attack, quick and deadly. "It's enough," he said, the pitch of his voice causing Isaac to look over at him sidelong.

"I've got to get back," I said. "Enjoy your lunch." And I started out of there as fast as my legs would carry me.

"Lucy."

His hand was on my arm before I knew it, and I pulled loose and cried, "Don't!" making him draw up short in surprise. "What is it with you? Why can't you just let things be?"

He frowned at me, pushing his hair off his forehead. "Hang on a minute," he said. "Did I miss something here?"

I looked at the tulip tree in exasperation. I realized that, in my mind,

I'd been arguing with Ash all night, that I held him responsible for my lying sleepless till three in the morning, laying out in a string that seemed to stretch to the horizon all the reasons he needed to slide back out of my life and let me alone. My taking it out on him in person the next day seemed like a perfectly logical extension of this; I had to force myself to recall that the arguments had been hypothetical, one-sided. "I got you your money," I said. "Can't you just say thank you and forget about it?"

I watched my words settle over his face. It was funny, in a way; I guess he'd been refused so seldom in his life that his features didn't quite know how to assemble it.

He studied me hard for a few seconds, then nodded, once, and held up the check as if to say, "Thanks and forget about it." Then he walked right past Isaac and the truck and into Mrs. Tanner's house, and closed the front door behind him.

Well, I thought. That's that.

My life seemed to compress again, to shrink itself into the trim silhouette I'd begun winnowing out so carefully before the week just past. Aunt Dove drove out with a load of her special fertilizer and a couple of flats of tomato plants. Shirley and Pep Walter—who had a bumper sticker on his truck that said, EAT, SLEEP, FISH—came and bickered over my kitchen floor. Bailey called to go over a few points about the auction of the farm, which was coming up in less than two weeks, and to discuss investing my insurance money. Geneva dropped by the shop Thursday at lunchtime, just to chat. Ash's name never came up. His truck was in Mrs. Tanner's driveway, off and on, but it was remarkable how, in a matter of minutes, I'd managed to excise him from my life, the way you might a prickly thorn. Like with a thorn, though, there's a hole afterward, and it stings, even if I would never have admitted it, not even to my own face in the mirror.

Friday morning, I was heading out of the parking lot with a delivery just as Ash came around the corner in his truck. I let off the accelerator and he slowed as he approached me, rolling down his window. We sat that way in the street for a while, eyeing each other behind the wheel.

"How you doing?" he asked after a second.

"Good. You?"

"All right." He turned his gaze to the windshield and squinted through it. "Can I say something? Without you going and getting yourself all in a swivet?"

"I don't know," I said, "probably not," but when he looked at me I smiled to show him I'd been joking.

"I thought you and I were getting to be friends," Ash said. "And I guess something happened to mess that up." I just looked at him. "Well, I miss it," he said.

"Me, too."

"Yeah?" I nodded. "Then maybe we could take a step back. Try again."

"What did you have in mind?"

"I've been thinking of driving up to Willie B.'s at noontime and sitting under those big pine trees and eating some ribs," Ash said. "That idea hold any appeal for you?"

I don't know why you took the trouble to build yourself a house," I said, climbing into the passenger seat of Ash's truck. He had to sweep an armload of junk onto the floor in order to clear enough space for me to sit.

"What are you talking about?"

"Seems like you could make things simple by just sleeping in the truck. Everything you own must already be here." The space behind the seats was crammed with papers and clothes and fishing gear, and the floorboards were littered with tapes and empty soda bottles.

"Well, I've thought of that," Ash said, sliding in behind the wheel. "Not much leg room, though, and there's no place to plug in the microwave."

We rode out 1399 north, toward Marietta. It was a cool morning, overcast, but the green of spring lay like a plump quilt over everything. We slowed as we passed the house on the hill of the Grace Bible Church preacher, Reverend Craig, father of the notorious Neely; it was famous for the cross erected in the yard, thirty feet tall and painted white. "He's got a couple of spotlights trained on it at night now," Ash said. "In case, I guess, Jesus decides to come back at two in the morning and can't see to land."

"I think Jesus already came back," I said, staring at the cross in the rearview mirror.

"Yeah?"

I nodded. "He works at the Qwik Mart. He's married to a beautician with varicose veins."

"Named Vonda," Ash said.

"They have two kids, Crystal and J. J. . . ."

"Jesus Junior . . ."

"And he has a gambling problem. And a sister who's addicted to crack cocaine . . ."

"Who's a table dancer at the Bon Ton Room . . ."

"And everybody says their mama's crazy 'cause she sits outside the courthouse telling how she got knocked up by God."

Ash laughed out loud. "*Jesus—The Missing Years.*" He glanced over at me. "I hope this isn't the conversation that got you in trouble with Reverend Honeywell."

"No, but I just might bring it up next Sunday. Ah!—smell that?" I turned my face to the open window. "Dead pig."

It was a quarter past noon when we pulled off the highway into the dirt patch in front of Willie B.'s stand, and every single one of the picnic tables in the clearing under the trees was filled. Willie's son Lam was inside the shed, handing out the plates of ribs and chicken, his big old laugh carrying over everything.

I left Ash to stand in line at the window while I went around back where the pits were. Willie B. and his pit man, Marcus Strum, were doing what they usually were, poking at things inside the metal cookers. Marcus nodded when I came around the corner, and Willie turned around and saw me. He looked baffled for a second or two, then his face split like a dark nut, his teeth as square and white as Chiclets in his pink gums.

"Lord above," he said, "an angel rode down from heaven and landed right beside the highway at Willie B.'s." He hugged me so hard all my bones cracked.

"I wasn't sure you'd remember me." I felt, inexplicably, like crying. Since Mitchell died I was unusually responsive to small acts of charity.

"I always recollect the comely ones," he said. "You been gone awhile, seems like. You back, or just visitin'?"

"No, I'm—my husband passed away." I looked at the ground. "I guess I'm back to stay."

"Well, I'm surely sorry for the circumstances, but glad for the result," Willie said. "Maybe we'll start seein' you out here Sunday mornin's again, with your Aunt Dove."

"Maybe you will." Ash appeared at the corner of the shed, a Styrofoam plate in each hand, which he raised aloft. "There's my lunch," I said. "Come out and sit with us if you get a minute. That is, if we can find a place to sit."

"You just leave that to Willie," he said, and I trailed him around the stand to the cluster of picnic tables under the trees, motioning with my head for Ash to follow. "You there!" Willie barked at a couple of guys in shirts indicating they worked for the cable company in Atlanta. "What y'all doin' dawdlin' around, takin' up my table space when there's people about to pass out from hunger here?" He smacked one of the two on the butt, in a friendly way, with the back of his hand. "Get on up offa there and get back to work. Gotta be somebody someplace settin' around just waitin' on you to show up so they can have an excuse to set on the couch the rest of their life, fryin' their brain like an egg."

"It's Friday, Willie," the guy who'd gotten smacked said. "We just wanna sit awhile and drink some beer." Willie B.'s was BYOB, and they had four left of a six-pack in a cooler.

"And there's any number of fine establishments up and down this highway where you can do it," Willie said. "This here's the VIP table and these here is VIPs. Now move your asses somewheres else." The cable workers picked up their cooler and got off the benches, grumbling as they made their way toward their trucks. "Here we go," Willie said cheerfully, taking the plates from Ash and setting one on either side of the table. "You all need tea or somethin'?"

"Please," Ash said, and Willie stepped over to the shed and came back with two tall paper cups of sweet tea over ice. "All set?" he asked. "I got to get back to my pits."

I nodded. "It's so good to see you, Willie."

"My, how the little girls grow up." He looked at Ash. "You ever want any lessons on how to make this one squeal, I'd be glad to give you a coupla pointers." He turned and walked off around the stand, chortling under his breath.

"Seems like that would take the fun out of finding out for myself," Ash said, sliding onto the bench across from mine. When I looked up he was sipping his tea, watching me over the rim of the cup.

"I hope you don't think I'm about to get all undone over a plate of pork ribs," I said, tearing open the little packet of plastic utensils. "I wouldn't want you to have spent four ninety-nine for nothing."

"I doubt that's possible," he said, and bit cheerfully into a rib.

The joke, though, was on me. I did come undone: over a plate of pork ribs and potato salad, under a stand of pines off the Marietta highway, listening to Ash relate some ridiculous childhood story about stalking a chicken with a rubber machete, telling him the tale of Pep Walter and Shirley Tinsley standing around my poor blighted kitchen arguing about how replacing my floor was going to keep him inside for a week just when the bass were biting up at Wright Patman Lake. Something that had been wound up tight started unraveling at the middle of me. I wasn't even aware of how much I'd eaten or how hard I'd laughed until Ash had to get up and go to the window for more paper napkins for me to wipe my eyes.

"My goodness, Lucy Hatch," he said, pressing the napkins into my hand as he slipped back onto the opposite bench. "If you could see yourself."

"I bet I'm a fright," I said, dabbing at my eyes.

Ash shook his head. "You look—well, like you're having a good time."

"I am," I said, and then was immediately stricken by the sound of my own voice. My husband had died just six weeks earlier. I was on a direct track to the homeless shelter, and from there to the street. What was the matter with me? What did I have to laugh about?

"Uh-oh," Ash said. "There it went. Poof, up in smoke."

"I feel guilty," I said, and then looked into my tea to avoid his eyes across the table.

"Why?" He had this way of disarming you, of leading you off the garden path while something in his voice promised you'd be all right.

"I'm not supposed to be here." I wasn't sure if I meant it literally or figuratively, or both, and Ash didn't ask.

It had started to drizzle, and people were finishing their lunches, tossing their plates and cups into the big galvanized barrels next to the shed and getting into their vehicles and driving away. Before long, we were the only ones left, and Lam pulled the metal shade down over the window to indicate the stand was closed.

"Can I ask you something?" I said to Ash. "It's just—oh, never mind. It's crazy."

"Ask me."

I sat for a moment and studied the way the moisture pooled on the surface of the table, but I finally couldn't think of any way to say it but straight out. "When you first met me," I said, "did you have this sort of, oh, feeling, like we already knew each other? Like maybe we'd met somewhere before?"

Ash didn't answer me directly, although his lips parted, like he meant to. He sat watching me across the picnic table, a way he had sometimes of looking into my face like he was hunting for something, like he'd set it down and then forgotten where he'd put it and there might be something in my eyes that would help him remember. I felt the heat rush to my face, even in the misting rain, and looked away.

"Never mind," I said. "I told you it was crazy. Maybe it's just some past-life thing. Like maybe we were Egyptian slaves together, or Chinese peasants. Or maybe we're supposed to meet up in some *future* life. Maybe it's a premonition."

A smile played across Ash's lips, so faint that if you blinked, you'd miss it. "Damn," he said. "Remind me to ask Willie what he puts in his sauce."

"I said, never mind." I stood up and gathered up the remains of our lunch and put them into one of the cans, then went over and got in the truck. Half a minute later, Ash climbed into the driver's seat. The windows were open but the air in the cab seemed charged, that you'd only have to twitch for everything to detonate. It was a long way down from the spot where I teetered, and I knew, though I didn't know anything else, that the fall would be both swift and hard.

"Did you ever sleep with Shirley Tinsley?" I asked. The rain made patterns like netting around the crack in the windshield. It seemed like it might be a relief to finally hit bottom.

"Jesus Christ, no. What made you think that?"

"She more or less accused me of letting my house get flooded as an excuse to lure you over for some sort of dalliance," I said. "I thought there might be a story there."

"Not in any lifetime I remember," Ash said, smiling, which made me turn my face back to the window. "Wait a sec," he said. "Here, look at me." I cut my eyes sideways. "*Look* at me," he said, and got my chin between his thumb and forefinger and tilted my face toward him. He held my chin in one hand, then wet the thumb of the other with his tongue and ran it slowly over my mouth. "Sauce," he said, and put the pad of his thumb into his mouth and sucked it clean.

"That," he said, turning me loose, "was worth the price of lunch, all by itself."

"Why are you doing this?" I blurted, seemingly from somewhere outside my body. "Why don't you just go find Bambi, or Mitzi, or whatever her name is? Somebody . . ."

"Somebody what?"

"More—unencumbered. Without so much baggage."

"I like baggage," Ash said. "Baggage is how you carry the good stuff." I looked at him doubtfully. "If you're trying to scare me," he said, "it isn't working. Back to your question," he said, and at first I couldn't remember what question he meant. "I did feel like I knew you, the first time I saw you. It was like I recognized you, somehow. A countryman. Isn't that what you mean?" I nodded yes. "But I'll tell you something else," he said. "I want to know you in *this* lifetime, Lucy. I'm not willing to chance that we might not come around again. What if one of us goes one way and one of goes the other and we never get another try?"

"You mean, I could come back as a Chinese peasant and you could come back as . . . as . . . ."

"As a rat in the gutter. Yep. Meanwhile, here we are. Right now." He was quiet a minute. "Do you understand what I'm talking about?"

"If you're trying to scare me," I said, "it's working real well."

"Look, I . . ." He placed his hands on the steering wheel. "I know what people say about me, and I won't try to deny there's some truth in those stories. I might even admit I've done a thing or two to invite them. But . . ."

"What?"

"I don't know how to say it without scaring you more." He looked over at me. "This isn't just about wanting somebody to rub up against," he said. "This is something else."

I lay my head back against the headrest and closed my eyes. It was just possible, if I held my breath and kept very still, to feel the planet turning. There was so much natural momentum in the universe, so many things that just kept moving, whether you encouraged them or not.

"I need to get you back to work, I guess," Ash said finally. "Peggy's probably having a fit." I nodded without opening my eyes or lifting my head, and listened to him put the key in the ignition and turn it. The engine fired.

I t was raining hard by the time we got back to town, and Ash rode me right up to the front door of the shop. We hadn't talked on the trip back, and as he sat now behind the wheel, his foot jittering on the pedal to keep the motor idling, I looked over at him and didn't know where to start. If I'd had more experience with men, if my husband had been more demonstrative or loquacious, would I have been able to rattle off something light and fluffy, or was this, by anyone's terms, too big for that, too weighty? I had no standard to measure it by except my own long, empty past. All I knew was that something burned in me that hadn't before, like a tiny white star behind my breastbone.

"Aren't you ever coming back to the Round-Up?" Ash asked at last. "I've been working on something I want you to hear."

"As a matter of fact, I'll be there tomorrow night."

"You will?"

"Uh-huh. I have a date."

Ash watched me for a while while I studied the front of the shop. This week's theme was the upcoming entry of the Mooney Wildcats into the district basketball playoffs. "Go Cats!!!" read a banner in purple and gold, the school colors, and Peggy had managed to acquire from the collection of Mrs. Tanner's late husband across the street an actual stuffed wildcat, which bared its teeth at us, glassy-eyed, through the window.

"Stop looking at me like that," I said finally. "My brother arranged it. It's a double date with him and Geneva. Some young guy who just started a couple of weeks ago with the company. He mentioned he'd like to go dancing, and Bailey set it up."

"I bet he did," Ash said, making eye contact with the wildcat like they were adversaries in crime. "Your brother's been ready to spit in my eye since the minute you showed up in town. How young?"

"Excuse me?"

"You said 'some young guy.' How young is 'young'?"

"I don't know, it's just something Bailey said. I assume he's old enough to drink." I smiled at Ash, who didn't smile back. "Look, you've been bugging me for a week about going back out there to hear you sing, and now I'm doing it. How was I supposed to know there were strings attached?"

He gunned the engine. "I hate to seem rude," he said, "but I have to run. I need to see if Misty's got any plans for tomorrow night."

"I'm sure Misty would be ready in a heartbeat for anything you'd care to name." I opened the door and dropped out lightly onto the curb. "Thanks for lunch," I said through the open window. "I hope you got your money's worth." He cut his eyes at me with what looked like vexation. "So, I'll see you tomorrow night, then. This song you mentioned," I added. "How will I know it?"

"You'll know it." Ash smiled grimly and eased away from the curb. I noticed he turned right, toward Main Street, instead of toward Mrs. Tanner's.

The shop was empty except for Peggy, who was sitting at the counter eating Nutter Butters out of a bag and reading a paperback romance novel, something with a muscle-bound, half-clad jungle warrior on the cover. "Goodness," I said, admiring the hero's flowing locks, "I'd like to know his hairdresser."

She set down the book and looked at me avidly. "How was lunch?"

"It was Willie B.'s," I reminded her. "Best pork ribs in East Texas, if not the world."

"You know I'm not talking about the ribs."

"It was fine," I said, opening the cooler to fuss with a tub of anemones that were leaning sideways into the snapdragons. "Fun. Ash is . . ." I glanced over at Peggy, whose face brightened expectantly. "Ash is good company."

"Ho ho." She broke a cookie in half and scraped off the filling with her teeth. "Is that what you're calling it?"

"Good Lord," I said, slamming the cooler door. "You're a widow, Peggy. When you lost Duane, did you run right out and start fooling around with the next man you met?"

"Noooo," Peggy said, chewing thoughtfully. "But the next man I met wasn't Ash Farrell." I rolled my eyes. I was getting a little sick of this, to tell the truth—like sex was something you did with your retinas.

"Mitchell's been dead six weeks." I said this with a kind of amazement; it seemed like that life had belonged to someone else, something I might have seen on TV or in a tabloid newspaper. Somewhere, I knew, Jesus must be laying for me, waiting for me to trip up; He and my mama and Reverend Honeywell were coming after me together, crawling on their bellies like snakes through the grass.

"Makes no difference," Peggy said. "Your number gets called, that's it."

"What number?" I asked, reaching for a cookie. "Nobody's calling any number."

Peggy grinned. "Funny, isn't it?" she said. "Seems like everybody can hear it but you."

(nine)

I'm not sure this is a good idea," I said to Geneva, studying myself in the bureau mirror. I'd changed my clothes three times, from a scoop-necked pink dress and high-heeled sandals to starched Wranglers and a pearl-snap shirt, to well-worn Levi's and a plain white T-shirt and boots. It was a look that fairly promised to disappear on a crowded dance floor, which is what I'd finally decided I was after.

"Relax, would you?" Geneva said. "I told you, Lucy, I've met the guy. He's nice, a gentleman. Nothing to be afraid of. Cute," she added.

"How cute?" I fooled with my hair in the mirror. It was still raining out, and the humidity made it more unruly than ever.

"On a scale of, say, one to Ash Farrell?" she said, grinning at my reflection over my shoulder. "He's a seven."

"Ash being what?" I said, and then blushed when she laughed.

"Ash being the real reason you're in a tizzy about tonight." I plucked and plucked at my hair, to no avail. "One of Bailey's crews was eating lunch up at Willie B.'s yesterday noon," she said, sitting down on the bed to study her manicure.

"Shit," I said. "You know, maybe I should just strap a video camera to my head. It would save everybody a lot of trouble."

"Now, that's some footage I'd like to see." She started to peel the polish off her thumbnail. "Except, if everything's like you say it is, all there'd be to look at is Ash chewing on an old pork bone. Am I right?" In the amount of time it took me to blink my eyes I saw Ash's thumb drawn across my mouth; it didn't seem possible it had happened the way I remembered, that I'd come away from it with an actual memory of the taste of his skin.

Out in the yard, Bailey tapped the horn. One of the conditions of the evening, on my part, had been that they'd pick me up; I wasn't about to get into a car with an absolute stranger, no matter what his credentials or where he fell on the one-to-Ash-Farrell scale.

Geneva stood up. "Stop futzing with that hair," she said. "He's gonna think he's died and gone to heaven when he sees you, in any case."

I picked up my purse and turned off the bedroom light. I didn't ask Geneva who, specifically, she meant by "he."

We were early, and so my date—Ron, his name was—wasn't there yet. Geneva and I claimed their regular table while Bailey went to the bar for a pitcher of beer. The room was, as always, smoky and crowded, the voices of the patrons rising to compete with the din of the jukebox. I closed my eyes and listened to the crack of someone's pool cue against a rack of balls, a couple of guys arguing about the Houston Rockets' chances for the playoffs, the jostling of the preshow jam-up at the bar, Marty Stuart singing, "This one's gonna hurt you for a long, long time."

Geneva nudged me in the ribs, and I opened my eyes and there was

Ash, over on the other side of the room, talking to some fellow under a Jax beer sign. I sucked in my breath and held it. He was wearing a black turtleneck with the sleeves pushed up above his elbows, tucked into black Levi's, and a pair of shiny pointy-toed black boots. Could that possibly be the same belt buckle I'd poked fun at not ten days earlier? It was big, all right, and silver, but against all that black it looked like a jewel on velvet in a shopwindow, exactly right. The streaks of silver in his hair and the belt buckle caught the light and threw it back like one of those mirrored disco balls. "Goodness," I said, which was all I could manage.

"I'll say," Geneva replied.

"He looks like Johnny Cash."

"If Johnny Cash could knock your eyeballs out." In my peripheral vision I saw her glance over at me. "Did he know you'd be here tonight?"

I nodded. "I told him Bailey fixed me up."

"He was real glad to get that news, I bet."

"He's supposedly got a date with that Misty girl. I guess the gun-slinger look is for her."

"I wouldn't count on it." Ash shook hands with the man he'd been talking to and came toward the bar.

"Is it my imagination, Gen, or is there something about his hips?" He hadn't spotted us; I was free to stare all I wanted, and this dusky stranger seemed to have no connection to the Ash I knew.

She let out a whoop of laughter. "Something like what?"

"I'm not sure, exactly. See how he keeps them tucked, when he walks? Like a dancer, almost." She didn't say anything, and I looked over at her and almost fell into her open mouth.

"Lucy!" she gasped. "I believe you're infatuated!"

"Half the room is infatuated. Take a look at that." I nodded in the direction of the bar, where already the female faction was jockeying up in their fringe and tassels and war paint, laying their traps.

The discussion was cut short when Bailey walked over, a pitcher of beer in one hand and a fair-haired young man in a button-down shirt and Wranglers at his side. I shot Geneva a look, but the young man already had his hand out. "Hi, you must be Lucy. I'm Ron." I nodded hello. He *was* cute, I guessed, in a country-club way, like he belonged at the helm of a speedboat or a golf cart. He looked like he was about twenty-two. He sure didn't look like a gunslinger, but then nobody had promised me a gunslinger, had they? I hadn't even known, till about two minutes before, that I'd wanted one.

Ron slid onto the bench next to me, and Geneva switched sides to share a bench with Bailey. "Your brother tells me you lost your husband," Ron said, lifting the pitcher to pour us plastic cups of beer. His hands were clean, steady. "I'm sure sorry to hear that."

"Thank you." *Goddamn you, Mitchell, this is all your fault. If you hadn't died, no one would be fixing me up with twenty-two-year-olds. If you'd loved me when you were alive, I'd be grieving now, missing you, instead of seeing outlaw hips every time I close my eyes.*

"So, Mooney's your hometown?" Ron handed me a cup of beer. "I've only been here a few weeks, myself. Seems like a nice place. Quiet."

"Quiet?" This was uproarious to me. The town buzzed in the background of my life all the time, a constant drone, like a swarm of bees down inside a tree you always know is there, even when it can't be seen. "Depends on your definition, I guess."

"Bailey says you like to dance."

"I used to," I said. "I haven't had much practice lately."

Ron picked up his beer and smiled at me. I was being too hard on him. He was polite, gallant. He was doing Bailey a favor. I glanced across the table and saw my brother watching me with a sort of smug approval, and I realized with a start that Bailey had orchestrated this whole thing as a ploy to turn my head away from Ash, to do it right under Ash's nose.

"Well, we'll have to work on that tonight, won't we?" Ron said, and we looked toward the stage as the band took their places under the spotlights, Ash smiling at the rush of welcome from the crowd, strapping on his black guitar. "One. Two. One, two, three, four," he counted into the mike, and the band sparked right up, a quick, jazzy fiddle working nimble-footed in and out and around the rest of the music as the crowd jostled and surged as one body onto the dance floor and then paired off into individual grooves.

Ron and I followed Geneva and Bailey onto the floor, and the minute Ron swung me into position I could see that Bailey was getting whatever it was he'd paid for. The boy could dance, not in the flashy way some of the men had, the ones who moved their feet like little Swiss clock parts, who you could tell thought everybody was watching their every twist and turn, but in a way that knocked you out with how subtle it was. It was like he had me on a lead, and he spun out that lead a little bit at a time, the way you do when you're first letting a dog have its head, when you want to see if it knows the code.

I was rusty at first, and so Ron kept the lead, not tight, exactly, just firm, a guiding, not a controlling, force. Then, as my confidence returned, he started playing it out until it was at its full length and we were equals, or almost. I would never have his innate grace, his body's second sense for movement, but we were a good match, physically; he wasn't too tall or long-legged, and his stride matched mine so that, just by association, he made me look good. I forgot a little bit about Ash, to tell you the truth, even though we were circling right under his gaze as he sang a song about Cinderella and the cowboy man. There was a cluster of girls in little spring skirts gathered in front of the stage, swinging their hips to the music, their earrings flashing like strobes, but if Ash was aware of them, or me, or anyone, he never gave a sign. He smiled and tapped his toe under the lights. He seemed to have shed his old persona and slipped into this new, dark and gleaming one: Cowboy Man.

We danced three or four fast songs in a row, and were headed back to the table for a breather when I heard Ash say into the microphone, "Okay, folks, we're gonna do a little survey. How many people in this room right now were at Mooney High School eighteen years ago?"

There was a chorus of hoots and catcalls from the crowd as I slid onto the bench and Geneva pushed a beer at me. "And how many of y'all remember the senior talent show?" More crowd noise: a few groans, but mostly shouts and whistles of approval.

Ash continued. "Well, at least one of you does, I know for a fact. Except that her version of events is a little—how should I put it?—contorted."

Geneva leveled her eyes at me across the table. "I didn't know the young lady in question at the time," Ash went on, "but it seems like maybe the song's a little bit more relevant now than it was eighteen years ago."

He nodded to the guitar player, who started the familiar twanging intro to "Peaceful Easy Feeling," and I started to laugh, ignoring Geneva kicking me under the table with the spiky toe of her Nocona boot. The dancers rushed onto the floor as Ash grinned and leaned toward the mike. I couldn't take my eyes off him, the way he tossed his hair off his forehead, just as I remembered from high school, the way he handled that black guitar like it was a prized thing, a conspirator in this overture that was at once personal and utterly public. It seemed to me that all my life I had sold myself short, that the part of myself I thought had begun and ended with Mitchell was cupped now in Ash's palm, unfolding in layers, each more ornate and extravagant than the next, like the panels in a Japanese fan.

Maybe all I had to do was put out my hand.

 beehive blond was washing up at the sink as Geneva and I pushed through the heavy wooden door of the ladies' room, but otherwise the place was empty.

Geneva leaned against one of the sinks and shook a Marlboro Light out of its pack. She lit it and took a puff, and I plucked it from her lips and put it between mine and took a deep drag. I didn't quite choke to death, but almost. Geneva leaned over, exasperated, and snatched the cigarette back.

"He's crazy," I said, coughing and fanning my face. "The song was 'Tequila Sunrise.' Old age has addled his brain."

"Well, *something's* addled him, that's for sure." She crossed one ankle over the other and drew contentedly on her Marlboro. "What difference does it make what the song was? Lord, Lucy, he's done everything but tattoo your name on his forehead!"

I leaned over and peered at myself in one of the flaking old mirrors. I looked feverish, my eyes glittering, wild. My hair was all over the place. Geneva sighed theatrically, like I was a trial to her mortal soul. "What am I supposed to do?" I whispered, even though the blond had departed and there was no one but my sister-in-law to hear. Through the crack in the door I could hear Ash singing an old Marty Robbins song about being in love with a Mexican girl.

"That depends," she said. "What do you want to do?"

"Nothing!" I exclaimed, then watched my cheeks go rosy in the mirror. "Oh, God, that's a lie." I pushed my hair off my face with both hands. "I can't tell you," I said. "I don't even think there are words in the dictionary."

"Oooh," Geneva said, "now we're getting somewhere." She tapped her cigarette against the rim of the sink.

The door opened, letting in a wedge of neon and music, and two plump ladies in jeans and vests fashioned after Indian blankets edged past us and into a couple of stalls.

"I'm scared, Gen," I said, meeting her eyes in the mirror just as she opened her mouth. "Please don't say something smart. I've never been in love in my life, unless it was with Tommy Rupp when I was seventeen, and we never did anything but feel each other up a little. Mitchell didn't . . . It wasn't . . . I mean," I mumbled, "what if something's the matter with me?"

"Do you honestly mean to tell me," Geneva said, "that you think it's possible you could lie down with Ash Farrell and nothing would happen?" I shushed her, motioning toward the stalls, but when she laughed, I let her. "Trust me, sweetie, anything you don't know, you'll figure out. I'm betting Ash has tricks you've never even *thought* about."

"But that's exactly what I—"

The door opened again and two girls came in, hip to hip. I didn't recognize Ash's date until her eyes were level with mine in the mirror.

I stood up straight, and so did she, and for half a second her face fell apart. She composed herself faster than anyone I'd ever seen, though, like an awning dropped over her heavy-lidded yellow-green eyes, keeping anyone from seeing inside. She stepped up to the far end of the row of sinks and held out her hand to her friend, and the friend passed her a cigarette. I glanced at Geneva, who smiled faintly and stubbed out her Marlboro in the sink.

"You're probably feeling like pretty hot shit right about now, huh?" the girl said, striking a match.

I took my eyes off the mirror and looked directly at her. "Excuse me?" Her features under all that paint were shockingly young, and beneath the hair and the jewelry and the short, tight skirt she looked whittled to the bone. Had Ash done that, or was it her natural state?

"Lucy, right?" She lit her cigarette and drew in a rattling chest full of smoke. "Everybody knows he was playing that song for you. He *wants* everybody to know. That's what he does."

"Could you excuse us, please?" Geneva said. "We need to get back to our dates." She put her arm around my shoulders, but I seemed to be in some sort of thrall to Misty, could not get myself out of that weird chartreuse gaze. I'd never seen eyes that color on anything, human or other-wise, in my life.

"Let me save you a little wear and tear, okay?" she said. "This is Ash: He'll say whatever he thinks you want to hear. It's like this gift he has, you know?—finding the soft spot. Then, as soon as he's got you roped up good, he'll cut you loose. And the next thing you know he's up there under the spotlight singing about somebody else."

"Come on, Lucy," Geneva said, tugging at my arm.

"If you really knew what was good for you, you'd walk out there right now and tell him to kiss your ass," Misty said with a joyless little smile. "You're not gonna do it, though, are you? Nobody ever does. Oh, well, maybe you'll have a little fun. One thing I will say, it's a hell of a ride."

The first set had ended, and I let Geneva steer me back toward our table, against the surge of the crowd in the direction of the rest rooms and the pool tables and the bar.

"Stop," I said to Geneva, just short of the table, "wait." She pulled up alongside me and looked into my face. "I feel like I might throw up."

"You weren't actually listening to that little tramp, were you?" Geneva said.

"I don't know," I said slowly. "What she said makes sense, doesn't it, if you think about it?"

"Sweetie, don't you think she'd say just about anything if she thought there was half a chance you might tell Ash to take a hike?"

I shook my head. "This is what I was talking about, Gen," I said. "I don't know how to play this game. Nobody ever told me the rules."

The stage was empty now, the instruments sitting in their stands under the spotlights, awaiting the second set. All around me couples laughed, leaned together, stood with their hands in each other's hip pockets, danced to the jukebox. There was a whole language here I'd been part of once, but I'd lost it with Mitchell, and I didn't believe I could claim it back. It was like I recognized the sounds but couldn't pull them together into anything I understood, couldn't form the words with my mouth. When I was seventeen, this room had seemed to encompass all the world I'd ever wanted, every possibility, but all I felt now was shut out, a stranger in my own territory.

Bailey and Ron had stood up beside the table and were motioning us over. "We were starting to think maybe you'd gotten lost," Ron said, and I smiled apologetically at him. Ash was in the room; I could feel him coming, like a change in the weather. "You want to step over to the bar with me," Ron said, "help me carry the beer?" I wanted to go home and crawl under the mattress and stay there for a week until it all blew over, but I said okay.

Ron ordered two pitchers of Miller and laid a twenty out on the bar, then stood with his foot on the rail, surveying the room. His expression was calm, detached; he was a blank to me, like if I took my eyes away for a second I'd forget completely the assemblage of his features. It occurred to me that it would serve Bailey and Ash and everybody right if I grabbed this boy by the hand, right this minute, and took him home and tied him to the bedposts. If no one would tell me the rules, I would just have to invent my own.

Dub slid a shot glass full of whiskey across the bar, and the black sleeve that reached for it didn't even try not to graze mine. He'd squeezed in behind me, and when I turned around we were hip to hip, my chin level with his chest. I couldn't quite bring myself to lift my eyes. I could smell him, his soap, shaving cream, something else I recognized but couldn't name. He swallowed his whiskey, and I could smell that, too. "Please help me, I'm falling," Hank Locklin was singing on the jukebox, which might have been funny if I'd felt anything like laughing.

"I had a chat with your date in the ladies' room," I said.

"What date?" Ash put back his head and let the rest of the whiskey go down.

"Misty. Isn't that her name?"

"I don't have a date with Misty."

"You don't?" He shook his head and set his empty glass on the bar. "But when you dropped me off yesterday after lunch, you said—"

"Aw, hell, Lucy. You blind-sided me, telling me you were coming here tonight with a date. I had to say something to even it up." He signaled Dub for another drink.

"What's she doing here, then?"

He shrugged. "It's a public place. Anybody gets in who's got two bucks for the cover charge. I didn't invite her, though. I thought I told you, I cleaned up my act."

"You told me a lot of things." I watched him pick up the fresh glass and take a sip. "That you don't drink when you're playing, for one thing."

"Only when I'm trying to work up my nerve," he said as, on the other side of me, a voice said, "Lucy?" It was Ron. Our beer was ready.

"You want to go on and take one pitcher?" he said. "I'll get the change and some cups and bring the other one." He looked over my shoulder to Ash. "Hi," he said, offering his hand. "I'm Ron."

Ash flicked his eyes at me, then Ron, then back to me again. Ignoring Ron's outstretched hand, he reached past me for a pitcher of beer. "Here," he said. "Let me give you a hand."

"Ash, no," I said, but he was already headed to our table. Ron picked up the second pitcher and the cups, and there was nothing for me to do but follow them.

"Hey," Geneva said, leaning across the table as Ash set down the beer so that he could kiss her cheek. "Loved the old Eagles song, Ash. We were all just sitting here trying to guess who the young lady was who made you think of it." Bailey, the boy who'd won more deportment awards than anyone in the history of the Mooney public schools, stayed on the bench with his hands out of sight, like maybe there was a gun in his lap.

"You all having a good time?" Ash asked. "Looks like Lucy and her date have been trying to win the dance contest."

"She claimed she was out of practice," Ron said, pouring beer, "but I think she was just holding out on me."

Ash smiled at me slowly. "You wouldn't do that, would you, Lucy?" he said. "Hold out on a man?" Bailey started to his feet, but Geneva laid a hand on his arm and he sat down again. "Well, now that you're nice and primed, how about giving me a turn?" Ash said, and before I had a chance to respond his hand was in the small of my back. *It's like this gift he has—finding the soft spot.* He looked at Ron. "You don't mind, do you, if I dance with your date? I'll have her back before you know it." And before Ron could open his mouth, Ash was steering me, like some child's remote-control toy, onto the dance floor.

He led me thick into the crowd, until we were well away from the group at the table, and pulled me around in front of him. I might have hoped for something with a tempo, something that would keep us moving briskly around the floor, but an old Clint Black song was playing, one with a slow, sad fiddle. As teenagers we'd called these grope songs; technically it was considered dancing, since your feet were moving, but it would get you kicked out of most of the school dances I remembered. I raised my face close to Ash's throat and I thought the scent of him would bring me to my knees; I *knew* this, oh God, how did I know it? His fingers spread low in the curve of my back and he worked his other hand into my hair, not gently, but hard, up against the scalp.

I did what I'd done with Tommy Rupp: I grabbed Ash's belt with both hands, and his knee slipped between mine and he took a step and

I followed, him guiding me with only the careful, insistent pressure of his thighs. His shirt was damp, and against the sweet darkness of his throat I opened my mouth, remembering the taste of his thumb between my teeth; in my head it was all mixed up with Willie B.'s sauce, the idea that I would never get enough of it, and I felt more than heard the sharp intake of Ash's breath as he raised his head and looked at me. Before that moment, there was a chance, I guess, that he doubted me, but there couldn't be, after that. It was like he opened his eyes and watched me step across the line. My husband hadn't wanted me, and had died. What did I care anymore, what things cost? Ash leaned his chin against my forehead, and my hand found his belt buckle and rested there, and for a single beat his feet stopped moving, and then began again.

"Lucy?" His breath was warm and smelled of whiskey.

"What?"

"Are you drunk?"

"Not a bit. Are you?"

"Oh, no, ma'am."

"Your date says you have a gift for finding the soft spot."

"What the hell would she know about it? She doesn't have a soft spot, inside or out." He shifted his chin an inch, and his lips grazed my hair. "Anyway, she's not my date."

"Does she know that?"

"Probably by now."

"She said you'd tell me anything I want to hear."

"What do you want to hear?"

"The song was 'Tequila Sunrise,' " I murmured, fitting my chin into the hollow of his collarbone. "I don't know why you won't admit it."

We were quiet then; the last verse was winding down. The odds of my having Ash Farrell by the belt or anything else in another thirty seconds were slim to none. I pressed my face against his throat for a moment, drawing in one last hungry breath of him, and Ash turned his mouth against my ear.

"If I were to stop by later, do you think the front door might be open?"

I didn't answer right away, and he lifted his head and looked at me. "I'm not sure I have your nerve," I said, which made him smile.

"Don't worry." His thumb found the tender place at the base of my skull, under my hair, his hand on my spine pinning my hips to his without a quarter inch to breathe. "I've got plenty for both of us."

I turned down Bailey and Geneva's invitation to join them, along with Ron, for their usual post–Round-Up pancake breakfast at IHOP. "I have a headache," I said, looking Bailey right in the eye. I heard the two of them arguing beside the truck as I came across the parking lot after saying good night, forever, to Ron. "He didn't even pay her way in tonight," Geneva was saying. "She doesn't owe him a god-damned thing."

"That's not what I'm talking about, and you know it."

"Listen here, Bailey Hatch," she said. "If you think you can stop a train by lying down in front of it, go ahead. The train's already rolling, though. You'd save everybody a lot of mess by just getting out of the way."

The rain had stopped and a slice of white moon hung over the pines as they dropped me at my door. "Lucy," Bailey said over the rumble of the dually's diesel engine as I stood on the step hunting in my purse for my keys, but when I looked back at him over my shoulder he just shook his head and turned his face away.

"What are you going to do, Bailey, post a guard on my front porch? You can't keep the world out, no matter how hard you try."

"You don't know Ash Farrell," Bailey said. "You haven't watched him work. He'll . . ."

"He'll what?"

"He'll take what he wants, for as long as he wants it. And then he'll leave."

Like every man I've ever know but you, Bailey, I thought. *My husband; Ash's daddy; our daddy Raymond Hatch.* One thing about all that leaving is that it makes you real clear about the here and now.

"I just want you to be safe, is all," he said.

"My husband got chewed up by a farm machine," I said. " 'Safe' is a word that's gone straight out of my vocabulary."

"Leave her alone, Bailey," Geneva said from the passenger seat. "She's got a headache." She giggled, and Bailey threw the truck into reverse, and they drove off. I stood for a while on the porch, listening to their engine fade and Steve Cropper thumping his tail under the steps. There was a stillness in me I wouldn't have expected, one that comes, I suppose, from knowing that you've chosen your path, that the destination, if not quite in sight, is at least in mind. I pushed open the door and went inside, leaving it unlocked behind me.

(ten)

I don't recall at what point that night I started wondering what had become of Ash. I had no idea how long he might have to stay at the Round-Up, whether he'd wait to collect his pay or talk to the band or load up his guitar. I was looking for him by one-thirty, and by two I'd begun to think I'd misread his cues, that maybe an open front door was not the invitation I'd believed. At two forty-five I stripped off my blouse and jeans and my one set of matching underwear and put on an ugly old granny nightgown and lay down on the bed and said every curse word I knew out loud to the ceiling, in case Jesus was listening, just so He wouldn't think He'd pulled one over on me, and at two forty-eight, the phone rang.

I almost didn't answer it. I had to, though; no one in my family has ever been able to ignore a ringing phone, even though the chances of it being any kind of good news on the other end of the line at two forty-eight in the morning are next to none.

"Lucy?" As usual, he didn't identify himself. I sat and listened for a second to the din in the background: men's upraised voices, Eddy Arnold singing "You Don't Know Me."

"Go to hell, Ash Farrell," I said. "Go screw yourself."

"Wait a second—don't hang up!" I didn't, more out of morbid curiosity than anything else. "Lucy, I'm in jail."

I started to laugh. Not because the idea of Ash in jail was so funny, but that he actually thought I'd fall for such a ruse. The open front door had been his idea; if he had to make up such a feeble excuse in order to get out of it, why had he bothered suggesting it in the first place?

"Come on, Lucy, you're my one phone call. You've gotta help me."

"Oh, Ash, honestly. If you want to hang out and drink with your buddies and have sex with twenty-year-olds, why didn't you just say so? Look, I appreciate your calling. For future reference, my front door is locked. Have a nice night, all right?" I hung up.

The house was so quiet it seemed I could still hear the hum of the telephone wire. Or maybe it was Jesus, chuckling out there in the dark. A pain began in my sternum like someone had inserted a blade and was twisting it, slowly, sideways, and I gasped and clutched my chest. *Woman spurned, has heart attack and dies.* Had Mitchell been just an unlucky draw, or something I'd deserved, that I'd lured to me like some rightful punishment? Why was the game so easy for everybody but me? Tears sprang to my eyes, and I willed them back, swearing under my breath that no man, Ash Farrell or any other, was going to make me cry. My brother Bailey would be so happy, even if he had been wrong on one point. Ash didn't always take what he wanted and then leave; sometimes he left without taking a thing.

Something I learned that night about anger is that it oftentimes functions to blunt the spikes of our other emotions, to take the edge off hurt or humiliation. I was so mad that I never made it to the pain and shame of the thing, but lay all night, alert and rigid, my fury stirring in my brain like a righteous stew. I tossed and twisted between the soft, soap-scented sheets, and when the sun slipped over the windowsill I got out of bed and made a pot of strong French Market coffee and drank most of it standing up at the kitchen counter. Then, when I was good and caffeinated, I put on cutoffs and an old torn T-shirt and threaded my ponytail through a Hatch Brothers Contracting cap and went out onto the front porch. The day had dawned clear and brisk, with a few wisps of fog close to the ground due to the previous days' rains, and I knelt on the steps and laced on my old track shoes. I whistled for Steve Cropper, and we set off up the road at a trot.

I was in no kind of shape, couldn't even pretend to be, and a sleepless night and a whole pot of coffee didn't do much to improve my wind, but it was wonderful just to feel the blood pumping in my veins, to feel my lungs expand and my heart open up all its throttles. I made it the half mile to the main road without having to break stride, tagged the mailbox, and turned back. I was halfway to the house when I heard a car coming up the road behind me. It was Aunt Dove, I knew without looking. One thing about living in the country, it hones your eardrums in a way you don't require in town; I believed I could recognize every single one of my acquaintances from a quarter mile off, just by the sounds of their engines.

Sure enough, here she came, zooming over the bumps and ruts in the clay road like Evil Knevil. I was huffing now, but I kept moving as she nosed up alongside me in the big Lincoln and the power windows went whirring down.

"Something the matter there, Lucy Bird?" she called. "What you runnin' from?"

"It's jogging, Dove," I said. "Didn't you ever hear of keeping in shape?"

"Must be nice," she said, "gallivantin' up and down the roadside, free as a bird, while your friend set up on the top floor of the courthouse, waitin' to make bail." I pulled up and looked at her. MUDBUGS HOCKEY, her T-shirt said. "I just came from the café," she said. "Everybody's talkin' about it."

"About what?"

"How you left Ash Farrell in the jail all night, high and dry."

"Good Lord," I said, jogging in place, trying to keep my heart rate up. "He's telling that cockamamie story all over town?"

"It ain't no story, honey," she said. "Ash got arrested last night, right when the Round-Up was closin'. I seen him myself when they let him out this mornin'. He come right on over to the café. Had a hole in his face like a woodpecker drilled him. Tellin' everbody how he give you a call at three in the mornin' and you hung up on him, left him there to rot."

"Got arrested, why?" I narrowed my eyes at her, like Ash had sent her to perpetuate this fable.

"Well, now, that depends who you b'lieve. Accordin' to Ash, he was assaulted. Accordin' to the girl, he came after her."

"What girl?" I said, bracing myself for the answer I already knew.

"I don't recollect the name," Dove said, pondering a minute, "although it seems to me it was some outdoorsy-soundin' thing. Windy, rainy . . ."

"Ash *assaulted* her?"

"Well, now, in his version, *she* came at *him*. In the parking lot, right after Dub turned off the sign. Smacked him in the face with a high-heeled shoe; damn near put his eye out. Then, he claims, she started screaming bloody murder, about how he'd been layin' for her. Didn't have a mark on her, or a single witness, but that dumb ole deputy, Dewey Wentzel, come out to write it up and wound up draggin' Ash up to the jail, all the same. Bill Dudley's on vacation, you know, gone to Orlando with the grandkids. Dewey don't know what the hell to do without Bill holdin' his hand, I'm surprised he managed to get Ash locked up. Ash said he called you but you slammed down the phone in his ear. That part sounded a little peculiar to me, I have to say. I mean, why, at three o'clock in the mornin', would Ash Farrell be expectin' you to make his bail?"

I stared over the roof of the car, chewing my lip. The coffee coursed through my veins like rocket fuel. In some alternate universe, some beautiful past life, Ash and I were best friends, soul mates, kin. In this one, it was clear, we would never get it right.

"Lucy?"

"What?"

"You done heard a word I've said?" I shook my head. "You wanna jog up to Willie B.'s with me, pick up some lunch?"

"No, thanks," I said. "I'm a new woman. No meat, no booze, no cigarettes. No men," I added. "Today's the first day of the rest of my life."

Dove pulled the car forward into my yard and swung it around. "Weather turnin' this evening," she said on her way out. "Big storm pushin' down outta Oklahoma."

I put back my head and stared up into the china-blue sky. "I don't believe that for a minute," I said.

"You listen to me," Dove said. "Tuck up your skirts. Somethin's comin'." She put a hand out the window and waved, and drove away.

I went inside and drank a quart of water, then made myself an egg-white omelet. It tasted like cardboard, but I congratulated myself on my new healthy habits. The phone rang seven or eight times, then stopped. I told myself I was made of sterner stuff than this, and switched my track shoes for old sneakers and went out into the garden.

The ground was too wet to be worked, but I worked it anyway, chopping big, hard clods of mud with the side of the hoe, pretending with every single chop that Ash Farrell's neck was on the block, that I was watching his head cleave neatly from his shoulders and roll. There was something deeply satisfying in flinging around all that dirt, and I looked again at the dazzling sky and then hauled out of the shed the flats of tomato plants Dove had brought earlier that week. I pulled out an old pitchfork and worked in the special fertilizer she'd given me, then got down on my knees and started laying the plants in the ground, and that's when I heard Ash coming. I wasn't surprised; the phone had been ringing all morning, and you'd expect, wouldn't you, that he'd have to have the last word?

I listened to the truck pull in and chug to a halt in the yard. I could hear his boots on the porch and his knuckles rap against the screen door; both front and back doors were open, so his voice carried through the little house, calling my name, but I kept on with my work, and sure enough, in thirty seconds here he came, straight through the house, in the front door and out the back.

He didn't look, at first glance, like someone who had spent the night in jail. He walked with as much purpose as I'd ever seen, all coiled energy, like a cat on the prowl, taking the steps two at a time down into the yard.

I sat back on my heels in the dirt. "I'm not believing this," I said. "You just let yourself into my house."

"It was wide open."

I stood up, dragging a hand across my face, feeling the trail of mud I was painting across my forehead. "What are you doing here, Ash? I told you—"

"You told me the front door would be locked."

"It was a metaphor." The gouge in his face would be hard to miss; a hairsbreadth from the socket of his left eye, it was bruised more than bloody, though the skin was swollen and purple clear back to the temple. "What happened to your face?"

"Don't tell me you haven't heard!"

"I just want to see if you stick by your story."

"Misty Potter whacked me with her goddamned shoe and then managed to get me arrested! What story do you think I could come up with that could top that?"

"Why would she do a thing like that? It doesn't make any sense."

"Because she's a goddamned maniac? How the hell should I know? It makes as much sense as you leaving me to sit up all night in a jail cell, listening to Dewey Wentzel crack his gum and work the crossword puzzle out loud." Ash crossed his arms over his chest. "What's a five-letter word for 'heartless woman'?"

"Does it begin with *b*?" I stood up and brushed off the front of my shorts, although everything from the hips down was pretty well caked in mud.

"Jeez, Lucy. My bail was only a hundred bucks."

"So that's what a night with you goes for, does it? A hundred bucks?"

He dragged the toe of one boot in the dirt. "If you're interested," he said, "five hundred is your going rate."

"For what?"

"That's what I offered Dewey Wentzel to spring me last night," Ash said. "Five hundred dollars."

"You're joking, right?"

"I would've said more, but I just spent two-fifty on the transmission on the truck."

"You bribed an officer of the law while you were already under arrest for another crime?"

Ash shrugged. "You'd already hung up on me. I didn't see how it could get any worse, sitting up on the top floor of the courthouse and thinking about you out here with your door unlocked. Metaphorically or otherwise."

I pulled the tines of the pitchfork out of the dirt and pointed them at him. "Go away," I said. "I don't even think you're telling the truth. I heard voices, when you called. I heard Eddy Arnold."

"You heard the Shannon brothers hollering in the drunk tank. As for Eddy Arnold, that was Dewey's old transistor radio, sitting right up next to the phone." He tipped back his chin and closed his eyes: " 'You give your hand to me and then you say hello—' "

"Stop!" I cried, brandishing the pitchfork, and Ash lowered his head and looked at me like I'd broken his reverie. "You act like everything is some, some stupid nineteen-forties musical, that all you have to do to patch things over is burst into glorious song!" He knew I'd nailed him; he didn't have a retort for that. "So, you told everybody in the café that you called me to bail you out of jail at three in the morning," I said. "What's more, you bribed Dewey Wentzel to let you go. In other words, the whole town knows that you intended to spend the night with me." Ash smiled, and I said, "What?"

"Old Claude Pope sure was mad at Dewey. If he'd sprung me at three A.M., Claude would've won the pool."

I stared at him. "This is all a big brag to you, isn't it? Just one more notch in your gun."

He shifted from one foot to the other, his eyes tracking off across the garden, toward the woods. "I thought . . ."

"You thought what?"

"I thought we understood each other."

"I did, too," I said. "I guess both of us were wrong."

"So you're saying I missed my window of opportunity."

"The window's closed, Ash. The windows, the doors, all of it." He took a step toward me, but I waved the pitchfork at him. "You better watch out, one pissed-off woman already put a hole in you."

"I'm leaving," Ash said.

"Good."

"Town."

"What?"

"I'm going to Austin," he said. "Not that you'd give a damn."

I stuck the pitchfork in the mud. "All on account of me locking my doors?"

"It's nothing permanent. Just for a couple of days."

"Let me guess," I said. "You're tangled up with the law."

"No, I'm tangled up with too many foul-tempered females," he said. "I know for a fact the girls down in Austin are friendlier than here. A *lot* friendlier."

"I'm sure they're unlocking their front doors as we speak." I knelt and began packing dirt around a tomato plant.

"You don't want to put those tomatoes out," he said. "It's gonna storm tonight."

"Bullshit. There's not a cloud in the sky." There was, though, one little pinkish-looking one off in the distance, over Tiny Marlow's barn.

"Mark my words. Those plants are gonna wash away."

"Gloom and doom. Hadn't you better be getting on the road?"

"Yes, I better had." He studied his feet awhile. "Somehow I don't feel this conversation has ended up where I meant it to."

"Well, look on the bright side," I said. "Maybe you'll write a song about it."

I lifted a seedling out of its paper cup and loosened the root ball with my fingers, then laid it in the trench, tapping the dirt back in with a trowel to fill it. Ash stood and watched me repeat this act three times before I got aggravated and turned and looked up at him. "What?" The sun was behind him, and even though I put up a hand to shade my eyes, I couldn't see his face.

"Come, go with me," he said. I laughed out loud, like he'd suggested we jump off the roof and fly like Superman. "When was the last time you did anything wild and impetuous, just for the hell of it?"

"Last night," I said. "It didn't exactly make a believer out of me."

"Aw, come on, Luce. Go hose yourself off and grab your toothbrush. We'll paint the town red."

I stood up slowly, letting his features come back into focus. "No, thanks," I said. "I guess I'll just stay here and try to rebuild the shambles of my good name." The funny thing was, I could picture it. Or rather, I could picture two people who looked like us, strolling around Sixth

Street in Austin, sitting by the river, eating Mexican food in a place with mariachi music, lying down together in a motel bed. It seemed that at that very moment it was all happening somewhere, a parallel universe where there was one common language and doors were always open and no one, ever, cared more about her good name than she did about learning to fly like Superman.

"I'll call you when I get there," Ash said, turning to go.

"I'm sure you'll be much too busy for that," I said. "Buddying up to the natives. Painting the town."

"I'll call you," he said, and walked off around the house, this time, instead of through it, and drove away.

I'd just brought out the last flat of tomatoes when I heard Bailey's truck coming up the road. "Back here!" I called when he cut the engine, and presently he came around the side of the house, looking like he always did, neat and upright and respectable, too handsome for anybody's good, my sweet brother who loved me. Short of my mama or Reverend Honeywell, there was no one I wanted less to see.

He gazed at me for several seconds, at the churned-up plot and my muddy clothes. I figured the state of my garden and of my person were a pretty handy allegory for my life in general, that morning.

"What, you don't answer your phone?" he said.

"I can't think who might be calling today that I might possibly want to talk to." I took off my cap and shook my hair out of its ponytail. "I hope you didn't come out here to gloat," I said. "I've got this pitchfork handy."

"I wash my hands of it," Bailey said, displaying his two palms. "He's been here already this morning, hasn't he? I see his goddamned footprints in the yard."

"Well, you know Ash. He couldn't sit still till his side of the story was told."

"What *was* his side?" Bailey asked. "If you'll pardon my wondering."

I looked for a few moments at the cloud over Tiny Marlow's barn, the way the top had started to billow like a lady's bouffant hairdo. "Now that you mention it," I said, "he never exactly said."

"I ran into Saul Toomey at the Texaco this morning," Bailey said. "Saul said that Claude Pope said that Dewey Wentzel said that Ash offered him five thousand dollars to let him out of jail last night."

I let out a shriek of laughter. "Five thousand dollars!" I leaned on the pitchfork, which threatened to topple me headlong into the mud. "I don't think Ash has that kind of money, not for me or for anyone. It was five hundred," I said. "Five hundred dollars."

"Good God, Lucy, listen to you!" Bailey exclaimed. "Five hundred, five thousand, what difference does it make? He put a *price* on you! Doesn't that make you feel just a little bit . . ."

"A little bit what?" I asked, drawing myself upright. "Let me tell you something, Bailey. I lived for fourteen years with a man who didn't think our whole life together was worth more than thirty thousand dollars. Not even the price of a truck like yours, or a down payment on a decent house. By Mitchell's standards, two months with me wasn't worth what Ash would have laid down for one night. If you think what Ash did should make me feel like a whore, then go ahead and think it. You don't have any idea how I feel."

"Well, I'm beginning to," Bailey said. "That's what worries me."

"Why?"

"Because I think you think you're in love."

"I think no such thing!"

"You haven't admitted it yet, maybe. But you think it. My Lord, the man starts wooing you like some gooney teenager, buying flowers, singing songs, then he goes and gets into a fight with a girlfriend, knocks her around a little and gets a black eye for it—"

"He didn't touch her!"

"How do you know?"

"She clobbered him and then started screaming! It was a setup, pure and simple. If you knew this girl . . . Oh, it doesn't even matter now," I said, sweeping my hair back into the cap. "Ash is gone."

"Gone, where?"

"Austin. Don't look so hopeful. It's just for a day or two," I said. "Unless maybe he makes up his mind he likes it down there and decides to stay. He's already decided the women here are too uppity for him."

"Well, I can't say I don't agree with him there," Bailey said, and smiled at me for the first time since he'd been here. "You know, the weather's supposed to turn ugly this evening."

"I've lived in East Texas my whole life. You think I don't know how to ride out a little thunderstorm?"

"This might be a bad one. There's been tornadoes already, up in Oklahoma. Two people killed, golf-ball-size hail, eight inches of rain."

"Oklahoma's a long way off."

"Not that long. And you know these spring storms, Lucy, they're just like a runaway train, gathering steam." Like another train I could mention, but didn't. That other train was rolling to a stop now anyway, maybe even jumped the track for good. I felt weary all of sudden, like my bones ached, the way I'd felt right after Mitchell died and I walked around the house sometimes yearning for something I couldn't put my finger on, that didn't seem to have a shape or a name.

"What are you telling me? Get to higher ground?"

"I would, but I know you won't do it, will you?" My brother smiled as I shook my head. "Geneva and I plan to stop by Wal-Mart after church, stock up on a few things. Is there anything you need? Candles, batteries? Have you got plenty to eat? What about bottled water? You don't even have a TV!"

"What, so I can watch all those pretty color radar pictures showing me how I'm about to die? I've got a radio, Bailey. I'll be fine."

"You put that puppy on the porch, it starts to storm," Bailey said, nodding to where Steve Cropper lay in a patch of sun next to the steps, chewing on a paper cup. "And for goodness sake, Lucy, pay attention. Keep the radio on. Don't you stay in this house if it gets to blowing. Remember what they taught us in school?"

" 'Get in the ditch,' " we said in unison. "Look," I told him, "I managed to stave off a charge from Ash Farrell, I guess I can handle some thunder and lightning."

"I wish you'd change your mind. Come into town with Gen and me."

"I can't," I said. "It's such a gorgeous day. I have to get these tomatoes in the ground."

I sat down on the back steps after Bailey left and watched the top on the cloud over Tiny Marlow's barn; it rose taller and taller and looked lit from within, like the clouds in all those Renaissance paintings we'd studied in school, bands of angels descending with wings unfurled. I would probably look back on this one day and laugh, but right now it felt like there was a bullet hole in my soul. I wanted Ash. I wanted him. I wanted everything I knew would happen between us in the dark, what should have happened last night but that Misty Potter and Dewey Wentzel and Jesus and I myself had foiled. I closed my eyes and let it wash over me like a black wave, drawing me down, until my lungs filled up and my brain went blessedly blank.

The phone rang. Probably Mama, calling to tell me to build an ark.

"Do you miss me yet?"

I almost couldn't find my voice. "You haven't been gone thirty minutes." There were highway sounds in the background.

"I stopped in Jefferson to fill up the truck. Listen, I forgot to give you my pager number."

"Why in the world would I need your pager number?"

"Why, for all your home repair and building needs?" Ash said. "I don't know, Lucy. Maybe you'll decide you want to unlock that door after all."

"You never did say why you're going to Austin."

"Didn't I?"

"Just tell me if it's business or pleasure."

"Well, now, you're presuming those two things are mutually exclusive."

"Somehow I doubt even you would drive three hundred miles just to get laid." He laughed at that. "Anyway, why leave town when there's such a pool of willing talent right in your own backyard?"

"Don't start with me," he said. "I spent the night in a jail cell, instead of with the woman I love. You don't know how little it would take to set me off."

"The woman who what?"

"I have to go. I want to beat the rain. I'll tell you all about it when I get back—Wednesday afternoon, evening at the latest. Got a pen?"

I went into the bedroom and sat down on the bed. I was getting garden dirt all over the quilt, but I didn't care. Maybe sometimes what you're looking for is right under your nose, and maybe sometimes you let it get into a pickup truck and drive away. My eyes burned; it felt like years since I'd slept.

I stood up again and stripped off my muddy clothes and let them fall in a heap on the floor. In the bureau mirror I faced my reflection like it was reckoning day. No one, not even my husband, had ever seen me this way, bare naked in the hard light. I had nothing to compare myself to; on the one hand were the women of Mooney, most of whom tended to plump up and spread at an early age, and on the other were the women I saw in movies and in magazines, so spare and fleshless they seemed bred on another planet. What if what was here was less than Ash expected, not what he craved? Suppose there was some enigmatic combination of girth and cup size and skin tone that kept him, like that

king bee, hopping from one vine to the next in search of, always searching for, that next, perfect flower? What if, as I'd always suspected, there
was some essential lack in me, some missing flash or spangle?

I stood under the shower and scalded myself clean, then put on a
fresh nightgown, even though it was barely afternoon, and crawled
between the sheets. There was so much I didn't know, steps it seemed
must be necessary before you could call it love. Or maybe it was as simple as unlocking your door. I closed my eyes, turning the word "love"
over and over in my mind like some magic stone, like if I only rubbed it
long enough and hard enough I would break the whole mysterious
code, and the next thing I knew it was six hours later, and the wind had
changed.

(eleven)

I stepped out onto the back steps in time to see the empty plastic tomato flats go sailing across the yard, toward the woods. The pink cloud over Tiny Marlow's barn was long gone, replaced by a sky full of skittering dark-blue thunderheads. I pulled on a pair of old rubber Wellingtons and walked around the house calling and calling Steve Cropper, but even though I could hear him whimpering under the porch he wouldn't come out. In the kitchen I turned on the radio. Eddy Arnold was singing "You Don't Know Me." I thought to change the station, but I was sure that, no matter where I set the dial, the same song would be playing, like on some old episode of *The Twilight Zone*. Lightning flickered in the distance, echoing as a report of static across the airwaves, followed by a far-off rumble of thunder. Raindrops began to spatter against the metal porch roof.

I liked weather, always had. In grade school, whenever there was a tornado warning and we kids were supposed to huddle under our desks, the teachers had to pry me away from the window instead, scanning the skies for funnels. I was the star pupil, year after year, during Severe Weather Awareness Week; it took a lot to spook me. I turned on all the lights in the kitchen and made myself a cup of tea, but even though it had begun to rain steadily, the radio announced no watches or warnings. The windows were open, and the rain mixed up with the clay and the pines smelled like something primitive and necessary, the way I'd felt with my face up in Ash's throat.

I wondered idly if Ash was in Austin yet, going about his furtive business. The long afternoon nap had calmed me, restored my perspective. He was a cad, pure and simple. How else could you explain him boasting that he'd offered five hundred dollars for a night with me? What kind of man would've gotten into such a scene with a girlfriend in the first place, and with such a girl? What kind of man rattles off the word "love" as casually as a phone number, without a thought to how hard it might land?

Sitting at my kitchen table listening to the thunder grumbling and the rain pinging on the roof, all the watches and warnings I'd heard about Ash in the past ten days seemed to rise to the fore, letting me take them out and hold them up to the light. Maybe last night, instead of a reproof, had been the step back I needed, away from the lure of his voice, the dark scent of his skin. You didn't get the kind of reputation Ash had, I knew, without at least some of the framework being true. Maybe he really would find some friendly girl in Austin, and my nights would be quiet again. I got up and went to the screen door and watched the rain lash the tops of the trees across the road, and that's when the phone rang. I never even thought about not answering it.

"Don't you know you're not supposed to talk on the phone during a thunderstorm? You could bust your eardrum."

"How do you know it's storming here?" *Because*, he'd say. *Because I turned around and came back. Because I'm right down the road, just a few miles away. I'll be there in a couple of minutes.*

"I'm watching you on the TV," he said. "The whole northeast corner of the state is lit up like a bad acid trip, yellow and orange and red . . ."

"You drove all the way to Austin just to watch the Weather Channel?"

"Well, it's either this or the dirty movies on the pay-per-view."

"Sounds like a high-class place you're staying."

"Huh. Tell that to the drag queens out front on the sidewalk."

I pulled the phone cord into the kitchen and sat down at the table. "Seems like you might've used a little of the five hundred dollars you saved last night to get yourself a decent room."

"Oh, this one's decent enough," Ash said. "Anyway, I don't know that I might not need that money somewhere else."

"Like when you need to bribe your way out of jail later tonight, after you meet some girl you can't live without."

"I only ever met one girl like that in my life," Ash said. "Wait, make that two. The first one divorced me. And the other one was pretty put out the last time I saw her." I was quiet a minute, listening to the rain on the roof. "Anyhow, it's nice here," he said. "Sun going down over the river. You should be here."

"Why should I?"

He laughed. "Well, jeez, Lucy. Because it's Austin. Because we could be listening to music somewhere, eating supper under the stars. Because this motel has a hot tub and Magic Fingers."

"And dirty movies."

"I don't expect we'd need the dirty movies, if you were here."

"My brother came by this afternoon, just after you left."

"Ah, shit. I'm not gonna like this, whatever it is."

"He said that Saul Toomey said that Claude Pope said that Dewey Wentzel said that you offered him five thousand dollars to let you go last night." I listened to the yelp of laughter that burst from Ash's lips. "That's what I told him. That you didn't have that kind of money."

"If I had, Dewey'd have turned me loose, wouldn't he?" Ash said. "I doubt even such an upright defender of the law could have resisted that kind of bait."

"You'd have paid Dewey five thousand dollars?"

"After the way you grabbed hold of my belt on the dance floor? Five hundred, five thousand—how do you put a price on something like that?"

I got up and stood at the window, watching the rain come off the roof. My throat felt so tight I wasn't sure the words I wanted could squeeze through. "Ash, I . . ."

"What?"

"Would it surprise you if I told you I've never been in love? Not once in my whole life?"

"Well, yeah, it would. Surprise me. I mean, I guess I know about your husband, but what about before that? Not even some smooth-talking guy in a letter jacket in high school?"

"Oh, I never could stand that type. I was always interested in the ones I wasn't supposed to be, the older guys who pumped gas and built drywall, who had a little dirt under their fingernails."

"Damn," Ash said. "I left for Dallas too soon. Seems to me you and I might should've run into each other seventeen, eighteen years ago."

"You would never have looked at me eighteen years ago," I said. "You were too busy being led around by the short hairs by Neely Craig."

"I would have looked at you anytime, anywhere," Ash said. "In any life, for that matter. And don't be so quick to blast Neely. You and Neely are a lot alike."

"You said she was wild! You said she was so wild you were scared of her!"

"Well, now, there's wild and there's wild. I didn't say you should get sent off to Fayetteville. Neely went about it different from you, is all. If I had to put a name on it, I guess I'd say it's that you both have something in you just aching to bust out."

"Is that what scared you?"

"Well, Neely was a little psychotic about it. In your case, though, I aim to be right there in the front row when it happens. I wouldn't want to miss a thing."

Lightning flashed somewhere nearby, crackling in the phone line, and the thunder followed close on its heels; the heart of the storm was getting closer.

"You must be getting ready for a big night out," I said. "All those girls with their doors unlocked, waiting on you to paint the town."

"Nobody's waiting on me."

"Yes," I said softly, "somebody is." He didn't say anything. "Ash?"

"Hang on a minute," he said. "I'm digesting what you just said."

"If I could undo last night, I would. Whatever it cost."

"You should have come with me. You should be here. Right here."

"I'd undo that, too."

"It's the Lone Star Motel, on South Congress," Ash said, "if you feel like putting your money where your mouth is. So to speak."

"I'd need water wings to get there."

"Yeah, it's supposed to be raining here by morning."

"Why can't you tell me why you had to go there?" He didn't answer me. "It has to do with music, doesn't it?"

"It's just a superstition of mine, is all," he said. "I don't want to jinx it."

"Can I wish you luck?"

"Yes, you can," he said. "Meantime, I plan to roll right over here and go to sleep. Just as soon as I figure out how to turn off the dirty movie."

"I thought you were watching the Weather Channel!"

"I am," Ash said. "This movie's the one in my head."

I t stormed all night. Steve Cropper, with more sense than I thought he had, came up on the porch around midnight and huddled against the screen door, looking at me with reproach, like the rain was something I'd arranged purely for his inconvenience.

I didn't even bother to go to bed; I knew I wouldn't sleep. At four in the morning I was still sitting at the kitchen table, listening to the gutters empty into the yard, watching, in the porch light, the rain sluice in silver sheets off the roof. The radio played dark tangled Louisiana swamp music, gravel-voiced black men long dead who'd sold their souls to the devil. In thirty-three years I had never known what it felt like to make that kind of deal, but I thought I knew now. Who would have guessed that, after all those fallow years, Lucy Hatch was a creature of the flesh after all? The answer, of course, was sleeping under the roof of the Lone Star Motel, three hundred miles away. I closed my eyes and imagined I was a bug on the ceiling, an angel on his shoulder, watching Ash sleep. I believed I could see the flicker of his eyelids, the pulse beating in his temple, his skin the color of buttered toast under the thin sheet. His heart, fearless enough for both of us.

At seven-thirty the phone rang. It was Peggy, calling to tell me that the Little Sandy bridge was out. "It's senseless for you to drive all the way around to The Corners just to get to town today," she said. "Nothing will be open anyway, except maybe the courthouse and the café. I'm not even sure UPS can get here. Everything's floating away."

I went and looked out the back door at my garden, where the long trenches I'd dug the day before for my tomatoes held nothing but rainwater; not even a leaf or a root ball remained. I swiveled the radio dial until I found a voice reading off a list of business and road closures in a hundred-mile radius. The Sabine was out of its banks and over the highway above Carthage; no school in Marshall, Longview, Jefferson, Atlanta. Bailey called to say that Geneva was going to work, but he and Kit had cut their crews loose until the rain let up, whenever that might be. There seemed no end in sight. He wanted to drive out in the dually and fetch me. "Were you planning on swimming across the Little Sandy?" I asked. "The bridge out west over Flat Creek is open," Bailey said. "I'll go around." "You'll do no such thing," I replied. "My house is four feet off the ground, Bailey. If the water gets in here, we'll all be in a lot more trouble than we can run from."

I stayed in my nightgown all day, wandering from window to window in my bare feet, eating ice cream out of the carton, watching the yard fill up. Every now and then the rain would ease and a patch of pale sky would appear, then a low growl of thunder would start up in the distance and the sky would blacken again and the rain commence. Steve Cropper whined and twitched on the porch, and wouldn't touch his supper. I had a book open in front of me on the kitchen table, but the words just danced on the page. I put the radio back on the bayou station, where they didn't bother with such foolishness as weather reports. Yes, by Jesus, it was raining and we'd probably all wash away; what else was there to say about it? The devil was bound to get you, some old way.

It was nighttime again when Ash called, more than twenty-four hours after the storm began. He sounded tired, played out. "I don't know if I have the stuff for this," he said when I asked him how his day had been. "I don't know if I'm cut out to jump through hoops."

"I guess it comes down to how bad you want it."

"You remember that day I came over and tilled your garden? That song and dance I gave you about being content with what's under your nose?" I said I did. "Well, that wasn't exactly the whole truth and nothing but the truth, as far as I was concerned."

"I know that."

"You do?"

"Sure. I knew it the first time I heard you sing."

"The thing is, I know I'm good enough. I *know* it. The question is, can I stoop down low enough to kiss enough ass to get where I want to go?"

"Where *do* you want to go?" I asked, but he didn't answer me right off. "Ash?"

"Right now?" he said. "Home."

"Come on, then."

"I can't. I have to meet a fellow Wednesday morning."

"Just as well, probably. Everything's underwater."

"Yeah, I saw helicopter pictures on the TV. The Trinity's three miles out of its banks, they said. It's been raining here since daybreak. Maybe the whole state is just gonna break loose and sail away." I listened to him breathe into the phone. "Lucy?"

"What?"

"If you've never been in love, are you sure you'd recognize it if you saw it?"

"I'm not sure. That's why I'm saving your seat. Front row, isn't that what you said?"

A long silence spun out; the line crackled, whether with lightning or something else I didn't know. "That does it," Ash said. "I'm heading back tomorrow."

"You just said you had to stay till Wednesday!"

"I'll move my meeting up to tomorrow morning. I can be on the road by noon."

"Ash, no. The bridges are washed out. You won't even be able to get through!"

"I'll get through."

"I don't think it's safe," I said, which made him laugh.

"Shit, it's not safe for me to stay here. I'm feeling real twitchy."

"You said yourself, the Trinity's over the road! And it's still raining."

"I don't want to hear one more word about the weather," Ash said. "Do you want me, or not?"

The words seemed to drop through me like a sinker on a line, landing with a *thunk* at the bottom. "I . . ."

"Answer the question, Lucy."

"Yes." It didn't sound the way I meant it to, but waffly, conditional. I tried again. "Yes."

"It's settled, then. I'll call you when I leave."

I might have slept an hour, maybe two. I went to bed, I know that, and watched the water track like tears down the window glass. Eventually the sky paled, and I got up and took a bath and made a pot of coffee. All I could see from any window in the house were mud and trees and angry sky.

It was my day off, but I called Peggy at noon just to see if the shop was open. "Well, I'm here," she said, "but nobody else is. This place looks like a ghost town. Practically no way in or out except the west route. Not even FedEx is running. I can promise you, nobody's buying flowers." I hung up, and not long after the phone rang.

"I'm on my way," Ash said. "I just have to fill up the truck."

"I don't think you should come. It's still pouring."

"The Weather Channel shows it ending in the morning."

"Wait till morning, then."

"Listen, I've been driving in every kind of weather since I was twelve years old. I drove across Dallas in the middle of a tornado, practically, to get to the hospital when my daughter was born. If that storm didn't carry me off, I don't guess this one will."

"But half the roads between there and here are flooded! How will you get here?"

"Why, I'll go around."

"Around where? Louisiana?"

"If I have to."

Silence. "Ash, I'm scared."

"I'm scared, too. Scared you're gonna bust out and I won't be there to see it. Scared you'll sell my seat to somebody else. Anyway, nothing can happen to me."

"Oh, God, take it back. Cross yourself, or something. Don't you know it's a curse to say that?"

"I'm only gonna ask this one more time, Lucy. Rain, snow, sleet or hail—do you want me, or not?"

"Yes." In any weather, any time of night or day, yes. "But please, please be careful." It sounded ridiculous, like something you'd tell a kamikaze pilot strapping himself into the cockpit.

"You just leave the light on for me." He hung up.

S till the rain came. Afternoon dragged into evening, evening straggled into night, and along about ten o'clock the wind picked up again and the lightning flashed and the thunder rolled, and finally, after a noble two-day stand, the electricity went out. My little Delco transistor continued to sputter in the dark, Blind Lemon Jefferson shouting his Texas blues as I walked around the house lighting every candle I could find. Under no circumstances should it take ten hours to drive the three hundred miles from Austin to Mooney. Something terrible had happened. Had to happen. Ash, swept off the road in the dark, his face against the windshield as the cab filled up with water and the river carried him away. Suppose that, just by knowing me, he'd become, like Mitchell, a marked man? Suppose death was something I drew to me the way sugar draws flies, a sweet, sticky trap that would trail me the rest of my days? Suppose he was driving around out there, looking for my light and not finding even a flicker? I had two boxes of red and green votives, after-Christmas markdowns Dove had picked out of the remainders bin at Wal-Mart, and I sat at the kitchen table and made little boats out of aluminum foil and lined them up in the front windows. Four dozen candles is a lot of fire. Maybe the house would burn down and he'd see the blaze.

At midnight I started making deals with God. I bargained for Ash's safety with everything I had: my happiness, my own selfish desire. *Send him home and I'll do whatever You want. Keep him unharmed, and I promise not to touch him.* Don't you think God knows when He's being hood-winked? Don't you imagine He's pretty much heard it all? God knew there wasn't a chance I meant to keep my hands off Ash Farrell. *All right, then, send me to hell if You want to, but let me have this first. Just one time.*

I could barely make out the sound of the engine over the rain still hammering the metal roof. I ran onto the porch in my nightgown and listened as hard as I could, but before I could trust my ears I saw the twin pinpricks of headlights, making their slow, irregular way up the road. It's the Red Cross, I thought; they're here to evacuate me. It's the high-way patrol, coming to tell me they've found the body.

It was Ash's old white truck, though, splattering mud up to the wheel wells, the water leaping up in silver arcs in his headlights. I stepped into my rubber boots and flew down the steps, into the yard. In the thirty seconds it took him to cut the engine and open the door, I was soaked to the skin, my hair plastered to me.

He slid down from the driver's seat and almost collapsed in the mud; his legs folded under him, and he grabbed the door handle and managed to brace himself against the side of the truck. His face in the backwash from the headlights looked a hundred years old, peppered with a day's stubble, his eyes a glazed, lustrous black. He didn't seem entirely sure where he was. I took a step toward him, and he scraped his wet hair off his face and smiled, as it were, to see me.

"I couldn't find your light," he said.

"The power's out. Don't you see the candles? I lit every one I had." His head bobbed, maybe yes, maybe no. "Have you been on the road, all this time?"

"The Little Sandy's over the road," he said. "I had to go around."

"Up to Flat Creek?"

"Over to Waco," he said. I didn't think he was kidding.

"Why didn't you pull over? Why didn't you wait till morning?"

He shook his head slowly. It seemed to be taking everything he had just to keep himself upright. I stepped close to him and held out my hand, and he took it and wrapped it in both of his and brought it up against the front of his shirt. His heart tripped like a jackhammer beneath the wet fabric, his lungs rose and fell, and he pulled me closer and then put his arms around me and I fell like a refugee into the circle of his heat.

His hands touched me like they'd been plotting every move, my hip curving exactly the way he'd planned it under his fingers, my breast fitting into his palm just as expected, and I tipped back my face to the rain and let Ash's mouth trace my earlobe, my jaw, the line of my throat where my blood pulsed with the same red rhythm as my heart. I raised my head and his mouth caught mine, and I came up on my toes in the tall rubber boots and then half out of them as Ash drew me against him, his tongue parting my lips, sliding deep and absolute into the corners of my mouth. Our teeth collided and I tasted blood inside my lips as all my weight rocked against him, just enough to offset his balance, and without warning he let me go and staggered back hard against the truck and slumped south, until he was half seated on the running board.

"Ash, my Lord—you can barely stand up!"

He tried to smile. "Well, get me off my feet, then."

I led him onto the porch and stepped out of my Wellingtons, watching as he propped himself against the door frame to tug off one muddy boot, then the other. He followed me through the screen door, and paused to thread the hook through the latch. In the narrow hallway we seemed to be all heat and breath; the wet magnified the sharp, explicit smell of him, and I let it impel me to him, lifting my face to his in the dark, hunting and then finding his mouth with mine as we surged together, our hands all over, wild and blind.

We knocked into the wall, revolved, knocked into the opposite one, making our way back the hallway like a couple of waltzing drunks, stumbling finally through the bedroom door, and Ash turned me loose long enough to tear the tail of his T-shirt from his jeans and yank it over his head, then reached for me again and half walked, half carried me backward the four steps to the bed. We fell in a skein of limbs, getting each other by handfuls of hair and fabric and skin, touching and kissing whatever we found, hungry and indiscriminate. I could feel the shape of him inside his jeans, the single-minded way he strained against me, and as the racket of our breathing threatened to drown out the rain pounding on the roof, I wrestled away from him and peeled off my wet gown and lay back in my panties, damp and shivering, across the bed.

A nearby strike of lightning lit the room like a flurry of flashbulbs, spangling my skin with a hundred jagged streaks of silver and white and gold, and for a beat or two Ash drew back and looked at me as he came to grips with whatever it was he was coming to grips with, a kind of bedazzlement that seemed to have pinned him there in the strobing light. I hoisted my hips an inch to slip out of my panties, but, "Stop right there," he said, and dropped into a crouch at my feet. They were everyday panties, white cotton with an unassuming little bow front and center, and Ash bent his head and planted one soft, reverent kiss there and then, breathing deep, hooked his thumbs inside the elastic and rolled them down.

"A real redhead," he mumbled, and I laughed and sat up, getting his face between my hands.

"Is that all you drove twelve hours for, to find that out?"

"No," he said, nuzzling the inside of my knee, "not all by a long shot." His voice was blurred with fatigue or something else, and I curled my fingers around his wrists and pulled him to his feet.

"Then get back up here, while you still can."

So he undid the buttons of his Levi's and left them where they fell, stretching himself out alongside me. It occurred to me that maybe all men were this beautiful in their pelts, that it had only been Mitchell's reticence that kept me from knowing. This was the one who was here, now, willing and warm under the palms of my hands.

"Jesus, Lucy." A ribbon of lightning split the bed as I slid underneath him. "Do you have any idea—"

"Hush," I said. "Yes."

"All the ways I thought about it, I never pictured it happening like this."

"This is exactly the way it's supposed to happen," I said, and took him in my hand and brought him into me. I couldn't remember the last time with Mitchell, didn't remember how long it had been, and I was tight but so wet that what I'd thought might hurt, didn't, though the immediate, profound chord of pleasure I felt made me gasp, not at its foreignness but its familiarity: *I know this.*

Ash raised his chin and looked at me. "Okay?"

"Okay." In fact I was far, far beyond okay, looking down on it from a great height. I recalled telling Geneva: *I don't think there are words in the dictionary.* No wonder what people always said was, just, "Oh, God."

He cupped my bottom in one hand and drew me tight against him, planting himself deeper inside me; I heard myself moan, and Ash kissed my forehead and asked, "Good?"

There was a dry click in my throat as I swallowed. "Oh, God."

For a second Ash lay motionless over me; and then a single faint sound—"Ahhhh"—broke loose from the back of his throat, and he started to move, gently, then not gently, and I moved with him, rocking him, matching his rhythm, my hips cradling his. It felt like all our life-times—past, future, the here and now—were trying to converge, to work their way to this, one perfect moment of symmetry. We rolled, shifting positions, once, then again, and I gave a little cry as he slipped out of me and then, just as suddenly, came inside again, on top of me, driving my knees up and back. His breath was ragged, his head thrown back and a vein jumping blue and alive in his throat, and I knew he was close, and I let my legs fall open as far as they would go and arched myself like a bent bow against him, and Ash bucked, then shouted like he'd been pierced, and fell down over me. The only way I'd known Mitchell was finished was by the tiny, muffled noise he'd made in his chest, the way you might suppress a coughing fit or some other impolite sound, and that yell of Ash's almost rent my heart. I thought if I had a recording of it I'd play it to myself every single morning to remind myself how, at least once in my life, I'd given rapture to another human being.

He turned onto his side and pulled me with him, our legs still twined; his lips roamed lightly across my face, in my hair, and I lay my head against his chest and listened to the chambers of his heart empty and fill. I thought of him like a child's paper boat in a rain-swelled gutter, borne across hundreds of miles of water to land here: safe, at home. What was it Ash had told me that day on the porch, about the reasons he'd married his wife? *Forces conspired.*

"So, is this real," he murmured, "or just another one of my road hallucinations?"

I lifted my head to look at him. "That didn't feel real to you?"

"The line's real fuzzy where I'm at right now."

"You need to sleep."

"I think I will, a little." He stroked my face with his palm, and I turned my mouth toward it and kissed the base of his thumb. He smiled. "You all right?"

"Never better."

"Stay with me?" Already he was wrapping me in a cocoon of limbs, enveloping me in a nest of such exotic temptation I could hardly breathe. "Ash, wait," I whispered against the warmth of his neck, but he only sighed against my shoulder and fell, straight as a stone through water, into sleep.

He slept like a dead man, never stirring, although he did smile, once or twice, as my hands skimmed his tawny skin, taking advantage of the glorious contraband that had washed up in my bed. Mitchell would no more have slept without his drawers than he'd have slept past six A.M., and having a naked man at my disposal, even an unconscious one, made me giddy. With the tips of my fingers I traced the incline from Ash's shoulder to his waist, walked them across the plate of his stomach, stroked the smooth scythe of his hip. He was as neatly arranged as an alley cat, everything designed for utility, without an errant line or an ounce of flesh to spare. I worked my face into his armpit and drank in his luxuriant, dark smell, the smell that made drums beat somewhere down in my marrow. I wondered if I would ever get used to this, if his body would ever become predictable to me, or if there would always be this note of fascination, of something familiar but illicit. I wondered if he'd be around long enough to find out.

Ash's lids trembled, and he opened his eyes. "Lucy Hatch," he said drowsily. "I must be dreaming."

"No," I whispered, and kissed his shoulder.

"Was that you with your little butterfly fingers all over me?"

"Go back to sleep," I said. "I'm just playing."

"Without me? No fair," he said, and rolled on top of me.

As the sky grew light outside the window I saw that the rain had let up, and I unwound myself from Ash's humid tangle and carried a candle into the bathroom and splashed cold water on my face and brushed my teeth and worked a brush slowly through my hair. In the golden wash of the candle's flame I looked hard at my eyes in the medicine-chest mirror and waited for the voices—Mama's, Bailey's, Reverend Honeywell's—that promised I would get what was coming to me, but nothing happened. There was, in fact, a nearly perfect quiet at the center of me. I felt like I had a clear glass bubble balanced inside my chest, that I had to do whatever it took to keep it steady. I didn't know what was inside the bubble, if it was happiness or hysteria. I didn't know how I felt.

It was still overcast out, and the room was just beginning to glow at the corners with the first trace of day. I sat down on the edge of the mattress and waited for my eyes to adjust, for Ash's form to emerge out of the gloom.

"Lucy?" He lay his hand on my hip, and I jumped.

"What?"

"I woke up and you were gone. I thought maybe you took off on me."

"Don't be silly, it's my house."

He worked his legs out from under the quilt. "I need to go out to the truck, get my kit. Clean myself up a little."

"There's no hot water. The lights are still off."

"I don't guess a little cold water will hurt me." He sat up and swung his legs over the side of the bed, resting his hand for a second on the back of my neck, under my hair. "Everything all right? You think you can live without me ten minutes?" That scent again, laying a path straight from his marrow to mine.

"You've got five."

He stepped into his Levi's and padded down the hall, then let himself out the front door. I heard him talking to the puppy on the porch, and in a minute he was back, shutting the bathroom door behind him. The bedroom window was open an inch, and I lay down and pulled the quilt over me, but I couldn't stop shaking. The room did its slow dissolve from charcoal to steel, and Ash came back and left his jeans on the floor and crawled up under the quilt and burrowed against me. His core temperature seemed to be three or four degrees higher than mine, and I felt myself open to his heat the way you'd spread yourself before a fire, obliged and welcoming. He tasted like peppermint.

"This bed," Ash muttered against my mouth.

"What about it?"

"Is too damn small."

"One of us has to get on top, is all."

He laughed, throwing back the quilt, and pulled me down over him. "You first. I want to see what I almost died for last night."

In the half-light I could feel my cheeks burn, but I sat up proud as Ash slid his hands over my rib cage to cup my breasts, my nipples jutting under his thumbs.

"Well, I hope it was worth it." I barely recognized my own body this way, poised above his and every inch the opposite: round where he was planed, white where he was brown, smooth where he was furred.

"Words can't begin," he answered, lifting his mouth to circle one nipple, then the other, with his tongue, and I made a little sound low in my throat and jerked away from the hot blue flare of sensation, but Ash held me fast. In the tiny room my breathing rasped like he had me at gunpoint, and by the pearly light I watched the whole length of my body quake as Ash drew me to him, running his callused palms down my rib cage, over my hipbones, up the insides of my thighs, his fingers finding the swollen, slippery place between.

In one deft move he flipped me onto my back, kneeling on all fours over me. I felt seared by the look in his eyes. We were close to something, some line was about to be crossed, and though it scared me through and through, I did not look away. Instead, in the clean-washed light of morning, I ran my gaze over him, his man's body, honed by work and time, and what had often, in another lifetime, seemed clumsy or farcical suddenly presented itself as a marvel of biological engineering. *Oh!* I said with fresh, unfettered understanding as Ash scooped my hips into the bowl of his two hands and I lifted myself to him and took him inside, grip against thrust and some channel slowly cracking open in me from head to toe as we moved together, fingertips touching every place we joined, our eyes blasted wide; a channel opened, and in the brave new daylight world, my afterlife rushed in.

(twelve)

Ash slept, again. This was wondrous to me, like sleeping through a house fire or an air raid. How did he do it? Where did he go? I felt bound to the earth in a way that I understood demanded diligence, my constant, watchful attention. To sleep was to let the devil in, although it was possible, I was starting to realize, that the devil was already here, one arm flung over his head, his legs bound up in my great-grandma's Star of Bethlehem quilt. Sleeping, like everything was regular, like the world was the same place it had been yesterday, and the day before.

The phone rang, and though Ash never even twitched, I slid away from him and dashed into the hallway and snatched up the receiver. One of my psychic family, probably, their radios tuned to the sound of sin. It was Peggy, though, calling to tell me that the power was out at the shop as well as most of the rest of town, and not to bother even trying to come in until tomorrow. It was past eight A.M. and it had never

occurred to me that this was, or should have been, a workday. I hung up
and stood in the bedroom doorway and stared at Ash for a while, boring
my gaze into his blameless face, but he wasn't feeling particularly psychic either, apparently, and went on dreaming.

I pulled a nightgown over my head and went into the kitchen and
opened the refrigerator, which was dark inside, still cool but not cold. I
took out a carton of eggs and cracked a half dozen into a skillet and put
it over the flame of the gas stove and scrambled them up, and when I
turned to pull a platter out of the cabinet, there was Ash, lounging
against the doorjamb like a gangster in his Levi's and unbuttoned shirt,
his arms folded over his chest.

I scraped half the eggs onto a dinner plate and slapped it down on
the table. "Here," I said. "You must be starving to death."

He watched me a moment before coming into the kitchen and sitting down at the table. "Good morning to you, too, merry sunshine,"
he said.

"Go ahead. Eat."

"A fork would be handy." I passed him one, and he took two or three
slow bites, chewing thoughtfully, his eyes on me like he was waiting for
me to pull a dagger out of my skirts and cut him from ear to ear. "Aren't
you eating?" he asked. Female spiders have it right, I decided, the ones
who kill the males after they mate, probably so they don't have to make
small talk over breakfast.

"I'm not hungry." I set the skillet, still half filled with eggs, in the
sink. Ash laid his fork across his plate. "The rain's stopped," I said,
going to the window. "I guess you won't be stuck here after all."

"Nobody's stuck anywhere," he said. "Don't you know what I went
through last night to get here?"

I closed my eyes and saw his grizzled face in the truck's headlights,
the way his legs would hardly carry him. "I guess I was wrong, the other

day," I said. "When I said I doubted you'd drive three hundred miles just to get laid."

"Jesus Christ, Lucy!" He pushed back his plate. "Who do you think I am?"

"I don't know!" I cried. "I don't *know* who you are, I haven't even known you two *weeks*, and here you are, in your, your bare feet in the middle of my kitchen eating my eggs and acting like you own the place, just because we . . . we . . ."

"Come over here," Ash said, pulling out the chair next to his. "Sit down." I did, and covered my face with my hands. "Breathe," he said. "Not like that, like something's nipping at your heels. Slow, and steady." I did, and after a minute my head stopped spinning. I looked up. "Okay?" he said.

"There's something wrong with me," I blurted, and then stared at my hands in my lap.

"Wrong with you, how?"

"I don't know," I said. "I just think you must be used to different."

"All the girls in my experience have been pretty much plumbed the same."

"I don't mean that," I said. "I just mean more—I don't know. Razzle-dazzle."

"You mean, like sequins?" he said with a quirk at the corner of his mouth. "That would itch, wouldn't it?"

"You're making fun of me."

"Listen to me," Ash said, picking up my hand and weaving my fingers through his, and the sight of our two hands laced together on the table-top pulled the breath straight out of me. "You were right there with me this morning, every second, all the way," he said. "What more in the way of fireworks do you think I want?" I gazed at the ivy on the oilcloth until it swam. "Look, I know it's not right to speak ill of the dead, but your husband was a fool, Lucy, not to treat you like you deserved. But that's not my way. I mean to give you all you're worth, all you can take, so you might just as well get used to it."

"I don't know what you mean," I murmured, like an idiot, like I didn't recognize that he was laying a carpet of emeralds and rubies at my feet. Like I didn't know razzle-dazzle when I saw it.

"You know damn well what I mean," Ash said. His thumb stroked the back of my hand. If this wasn't the devil's deal, then I guess I'd never heard one.

He stood up from the table and opened the cabinet and took down another plate, then transferred the rest of the scrambled eggs from the skillet and set the plate in front of me, and got me a fork. He sat down again and picked up his own fork. For a second or two it was almost funny, the scene was so homey, so mundane. That bubble still rested, though, pulsing and fragile, beneath my breastbone. His dark scent was still on my skin; his promise sat on the table like a shimmering prize. *All you can take.* How could I think of laughing?

We finished our eggs, and I got up to stack the plates in the sink. "There's one more thing we might ought to talk about," Ash said, "here in the daylight, with both feet on the floor." I looked over my shoulder at him. "It's not like me to be so irresponsible. What I mean is, I do carry, um, protection with me. I'm not usually so out of my head that I don't think of it till a whole night's gone by and I've already missed two opportunities for using it."

"Three," I said, and went back to scraping the plates.

"What?"

"It was three opportunities, not two. Not that anybody's keeping score." I was, though. In one night with Ash I'd had more sex than in any single month of my marriage.

"Well, damn," Ash said wonderingly. "You mean I lost one completely?"

"Seems so." I rinsed the dregs of our breakfast down the garbage disposal and hit the switch on the wall before I remembered the power was out. "Anyway, I can't get pregnant, if that's what you're worried about."

"You can't?"

I shook my head. "I'm . . ." Was there a word for it, I wondered, that didn't make it sound like a defect, a shortcoming? If there was, I'd never found it.

"Infertile?" he offered, and I nodded. Not a pretty word, but efficient. He seemed to ponder this for a second or two. "Well, all right," he said, and I guessed that was that; it never seemed likely to me that Ash was looking for a house full of heirs. "But there are other reasons for protection, Lucy. Diseases, for one."

"You think I have a disease?" And I'd thought "infertile" had an ugly ring.

I watched him tamp down a smile. "No, I think that's pretty unlikely," he said, "under the circumstances. I was thinking you might be worried about me."

"*You* have a disease?" My throat constricted. Is this the way it was done, a mild-mannered announcement, hours after it was too late to do anything?

"Well, no, I don't. That's what I'm trying to tell you. I went and had a test." I suppose I looked flabbergasted. "I'll show you the paper, if you want. I just wanted it out in the open, is all. So that you wouldn't think I was being—I don't know, heedless."

I had to bite my lip not to laugh. I could hardly imagine anything more heedless than the past two weeks had been; it seemed to me that my life since the moment I'd met Ash had been one long skid on icy pavement. What was this concept of "safe sex," anyway? Full body armor couldn't have protected me from him, from the look in his eyes as he came into me. *All you're worth*, he'd said. *All you can take*. I closed my eyes and shuddered, and he stood up and came over to the sink and put his arms around me with an ease that almost made me weep.

"When was the last time you slept?" I shook my head; I couldn't remember. "Come on in here a minute," he said, leading me into the hall and toward the bedroom.

"Sit down," he said, and patted the edge of the mattress. I sat, and he climbed up behind me and grabbed me by the shoulders so hard I yelled. "That's what I thought," he muttered, digging his thumbs into my trapezius. "You're as tight as a tick. Be still, Lucy. Let your neck go." I did, letting my head roll forward, his thumbs kneading deep into the muscle. "Does that hurt?"

"Yes."

"Well, good. Sometimes a little pain is a necessary thing."

"The master has spoken," I said, giggling, then, "Ow!" I cried as he drilled the balls of his thumbs into the base of my neck.

"You let me know," he said, his mouth near my ear, "if you want me to stop."

"No," I murmured. "No, I don't want you to stop." The funny thing was, I really was getting sleepy. At the same time, I felt roused, in a floaty kind of way, like his hands were hypnotizing me, turning me into some kind of rubber love doll. I didn't know quite what to make of the two contrasting sensations, so that when Ash whispered, "Lie down," I did what he said without thinking.

He rolled me onto my side and fitted himself into the narrow space between me and the wall. "Lucy?"

"Hmm?" He was pulling the quilt over us, tucking his knees into the backs of mine.

"This bed is ridiculous. Tonight, we're going to my house." He worked an arm around me and drew me back against his chest, his chin on top of my head. I could feel his heart beat against my shoulder blades. "Hey, aren't you supposed to be working today?"

"The shop's closed. No electricity," I mumbled. "What about you?"

"I'm in Austin," he said, "remember?"

"Oh, yeah." I smiled. *Forces conspired.*

"Go to sleep."

"I can't."

"Why not?"

"You're too . . ." *Close,* I wanted to say. *Present.* "All those arms and legs and things around me," I said. "It's too distracting."

His breath ruffled my hair. "I'll tell you what I told you at the breakfast table," he said. "This is it. Get used to it."

I came out of a dream of fire, my limbs heavy as stone, pinned, immobile, while flames licked the sky around me. The barn was on fire. I had to tell Mitchell, I knew, and yet there was a languor in my veins, a sense that it was out of my control, not my responsibility. The barn was on fire, and if Mitchell didn't take care of it, well, then he was a fool.

I turned toward the heat with a kind of subconscious recognition, lifting my face to its source. "Sssh," Ash whispered, pushing my hair to one side and kissing the side of my neck, "you're dreaming."

So I let myself slide under again, my mind floating somewhere between dark and light, aware of nothing but my skin under his thickened fingertips, the silken grit of his unshaved chin as it grazed behind my ears, the curve of my throat, the hollow of my collarbone. The quilt had fallen to the floor, and my nightgown worked itself into a tangle at my hips as I felt him move down over me, kissing and kissing, creating a smooth, undulating purl of response from my head to my toes; I felt boneless, helpless, as he knelt between my legs, everything caught up in that bright, burning core.

His breath was hot and his jaw rasped against my skin as his thumbs made a frame for his mouth, and I whimpered and then cried out at the first stroke of his tongue, feeling a balloon of panic rise up in me, but Ash held on, his hands a vise on my thighs, as panic dissolved into a towering white spume of sensation and my hips began of their own accord to follow the cadence of his sweet, determined mouth. This, surely, was some trap dreamed up by the devil; this, surely, would cost you heaven. But something inside me clicked and hummed, and the hum got louder and louder until it roared red between my ears, as Ash slid off the bed onto his knees and dragged me to the edge of the mattress, his shoulders wedging my thighs wide and his fingers moving inside me with the rhythm of his tongue; for a single beat my breath stopped, and then inside me the bubble burst, razzle-dazzle such as I'd never dreamed was in this world, and my whole body arced wildly, convulsively, and I let out a howl and fell straight off the bed onto the floor.

I opened my eyes to find Ash propped on one elbow over me, grinning and rubbing his jaw with his hand. Somewhere deep inside me a pulse throbbed like a memory, faint but persistent, and I reached for him and pulled him down alongside me, fumbling with the buttons of his jeans.

"Slow down, Lucy, you're gonna hurt somebody."

"Ash, please. Hurry."

"You don't want to rest a minute? Catch your breath?"

"I can breathe just fine. Oh, hurry."

He leaned over to kiss me, and I tasted myself on his face, and he brought his fingers to my mouth so I could taste myself there, too. I sat up and tugged my gown over my head and sent it sailing, and lay back with my knees bent and open as Ash, stone sober now, freed the last of

his buttons and got his Levi's to half-mast and, without further preamble, lowered himself and entered me; and with his first thrust, at the
first, delicious shock of penetration, a rush of contractions cascaded
through me, wave following wave, my body vaulted and shuddering
against him, all my senses fused and everything lost in the single, radiant point of contact.

Ash lifted his head and looked at me, and the word "lover" slid
across and into my vocabulary like a peg in a groove, like some expression in another language I'd heard all my life but had never grasped the
meaning of until now. *My lover.*

"Merciful God," Ash said as slowly, together, we began to move, and
that was the last thing in any language either of us said for a while.

I never had a honeymoon. Mitchell had owned the farm less than a
year when we married, and it was planting season; there wasn't
the time or money to travel, and so I spent every night from my
wedding night forward in the same bed in the same room, full of
Mitchell's family's heavy old maple furniture, the same faded ocher-
colored roses marching in rows up the wallpaper as I drifted off to sleep
looking at my husband's back, listening to his breathing.

I wonder now what my life with Mitchell might have been like if
we'd had a time like Ash and I did at the start, just to loll around, to
talk under the covers, to eat Cheerios out of the box, to discover the
feel and fit of each other's body. Would Mitchell have wanted me more
if we'd had the chance to get to know one another that way, if he hadn't
been rushing out the door every morning at six o'clock or falling into
bed dead to the world at nine-thirty every night, if his every waking
thought hadn't been directed, by necessity, at the seasons and the
weather and the land? By the time I got used to the idea of being married, I'd already put my appetites, unformed as they were, in a box and

stuck it off somewhere on a shelf. What a surprise it was, after fourteen years, to find that box and crack it open, to learn that what was inside had not shriveled and dried up after all but was instead nested, gathering strength, growing strong and green and ripe, just waiting for somebody to rip off the lid.

That first day with Ash, then, was the honeymoon I'd never had, and I felt blessed that I had the presence of mind to recognize it for what it was, and to prize it. Ash went out to the truck and brought in his guitar, and sat up in the bed in his Levi's and sang to me: "Now that I've won her I'll wander no more, and live with my love on the Red River shore." He spread out the map on the kitchen table and traced with a finger the route he'd driven the night before, four hundred and sixty miles, a meandering twelve-hour course through Central Texas looking for any bridge that wasn't washed out, grappling his way north and east, a county at a time.

We put on our boots and slogged out to the main road, exclaiming over the water everywhere, the mud so thick it looked like something alive, primordial. Ash had a big laugh over my garden, my vanished tomatoes. The Buick was stuck in the front yard, halfway up to its hubcaps; I guessed I'd have to call Bailey eventually, with his big truck and his winch and chain. Not today, though. Ash and I sat on the steps in the pale sunshine and split a warm beer and then went inside and went back to bed, even though it was the middle of the afternoon. Everything felt glazed and slightly surreal to me; I thought if I blinked it would all dissolve into the horizon, like an oasis that isn't really there. *Is this what I'm worth?* I kept wanting to ask him. Were we there yet? Would he let me know when I'd reached the limit?

Around four o'clock the phone rang; we were both half drowsing, but Ash threw back the quilt and I crawled over him and went into the hall to answer it.

"Hey," Geneva said. "I just thought I'd call and see if you floated off."

"Not yet."

"Do you have lights there? Ours just came back."

"No lights." I stepped into the kitchen and looked at my naked body in the rectangle of daylight from the window. I gasped, covering the phone with my hand. My thighs and rear were tattooed with imprints of fingers and teeth, and little red blood vessels bloomed like stars around my nipples.

"So, what've you been up to out there for two whole days?" Geneva said, and then immediately launched into a story about the power going off at the clinic and all the calamities that had ensued. I leaned against the door frame and let her ramble, and in a minute or so Ash came into the hall, pantomiming "Who is it?" with his hands, rolling his eyes when I mouthed my sister-in-law's name over the receiver.

I motioned him forward into the kitchen and gestured at my battered body in the light. I pointed at him, indicating, "You did this," but he didn't look even slightly repentant as he came at me in his taut cat's skin and dropped at my feet and kissed the inside of my knee.

"So," Geneva said finally, conspiratorially, "have you heard from Ash?"

"Huh," I said, and stumbled back and caught myself against the side of the table.

"Ash," Geneva repeated. "He went to Austin, right?"

"Uh-huh."

"So, I was wondering if he'd called. Seems to me things were a little testy between y'all when he left."

"Ah."

"He did call? Or he didn't?"

"Uh-huh. Did."

"And he said what?" I kept my hand over the mouthpiece, and after a moment she sighed and said, "All right, be that way. See if I ever tell you any of my secrets, ever again. Just answer me this. Did he happen to say when he's coming back? Because, you know this is Round-Up night, and Bailey and I . . . Lucy?"

"Uh."

"When is Ash coming back? Do you know something about this, or don't you?" There was a moment's silence, and then an ear-piercing screech that nearly made me drop the phone. "Oh, my God!" she cried. "He's there, isn't he? He's there, and you're doing it!"

"Well, not at this exact moment."

"Oh, my God! Well, I . . . How did he *get* there?"

"He drove. Four hundred and sixty miles, in the pouring rain. He was practically catatonic when he showed up." Ash made a face at me and stood up. "He revived just fine, though."

"Bailey will die," Geneva said with what sounded like relish.

"No!" I exclaimed. "You can't tell him."

She started to laugh. "You don't think he's gonna find out eventually?"

"I just—I think Ash deserves a head start, is all."

"Well, tell him to start running. Anyway, the whole town will know by this time tomorrow, whether you like it or not. Ask him if his band is playing tonight or if he's too busy being your sex slave."

I posed the question to Ash, who laughed and took the phone from me and stuck it between his chin and his shoulder. "Sex slave, definitely," he said into the mouthpiece. "What kind of a choice is that? No, listen, I talked to Dub a couple of hours ago. No show tonight. He doesn't have any juice." At first I thought Ash meant no liquor, then I realized he meant no electricity. "Yeah, it's rough, I admit. Lucy and I are gonna have to come up with something to do in the dark."

He was quiet a second, listening. "What are you talking about? You think I don't know how to treat her?" He met my eyes over the receiver.

"You tell your husband," Ash said, "that he can yell and cuss all he wants, he can come out here with a shotgun, even, but I'm not budging. In fact, you can tell him he'd save himself a lot of grief if he'd start realizing we're on the same side. All I want is what he wants. Lucy, happy." They talked a minute or two longer, then he handed the phone back to me, brushing his lips across my forehead, and walked out of the room. I stared after him like he was something I'd conjured, like he'd left a trail of gold bullion in his wake.

"*Are* you happy, sweetie?" Geneva's voice was uncommonly tender.

"I don't know," I said. "I think so." Happiness was Easter baskets and birthday cakes and bottle rockets on the Fourth of July. Happiness was Willie B.'s ribs. How could I put what I felt in the same category, like it had a size and a shape, a beginning and an end, a taste you could sink your teeth into? Every time I got into bed with Ash felt like an amusement-park ride: delicious, fluttering fear during the slow upward climb, followed by a shrieking, heart-stopping seven-story drop straight down into bliss. I felt exhausted, exhilarated, even, but happy?

I hung up the phone and went into the bedroom, where Ash was setting his guitar in its case. His duffel bag was open on the bed. "You talked to Dub?" I said, and he nodded, latching the lid on the case. "When was that? Where was I?"

"You were in an altered state of consciousness," Ash said, and smiled. "Come on, Lucy, let's get dressed. At the risk of ruining my reputation as the world's greatest lover, if I have to spend another night in this bed of yours I'm gonna throw my back out so bad I won't be able to work for a month. To say nothing of, well, extracurricular activities.

"Think of it as a sleep-over, if you want to." He turned to face me. "Grab whatever you need for tonight and in the morning, for work. You can ride into town with me, and tomorrow afternoon we'll find somebody to pull your car out of the mud. The guy J. D. works for has a wrecker, I think."

"But I don't even know where you live!"

"You think I'm a troll who sleeps under a bridge? I have a plain old ordinary house, with a normal, human-being-size bed. It isn't three miles from here. You can run away on foot, back to your own place, if things get too scary. Which I promise you, they won't.

"Now, go get your clothes on. I'm taking you home."

(thirteen)

ost of the rural roads in Cade County were numbered, but
we nearly always called them by some defining landmark
instead—Price Farm Road, say, or Turkey Creek. More
often than not, a road might be christened after one of the tiny clap-
board churches that sat back in the pines with venerable names like
New Prospect or Arcadia or Zion Hill, even if some of those churches
hadn't seen a worshiper in thirty years.

So it happened that Ash lived at the end of what was known as Little Hope Road, although Little Hope Chapel itself had burned to the
ground in the 1950s and nothing remained but a concrete slab and an
ancient, unkempt cemetery. The road itself was unpaved and rutted,
the clay churned into red, roiling mud. It was that hour before afternoon gives itself over to evening, and Ash's house emerged low and
sturdy against the woods darkening behind it. An orange bulb glowed
next to the front door.

"Your porch light is on," I said.

"I always leave it on when I'm gone," Ash said, steering into the yard and shutting off the engine. "Makes me feel like somebody's waiting up, even if nobody is."

"You have electricity, I mean."

"Huh—so I do."

We got down from the truck and a rangy black dog came running around the side of the house and hurled itself at Ash, lashing his hands and arms with its tongue. "Hey, buddy, you didn't swim off on me," Ash said, stroking the dog's head. "Lucy, this is Booker. Booker T., meet Miss Lucy Hatch."

"Your dog's name is Booker T.?" I scratched the dog under his chin, and he rolled his eyes adoringly. "And you named my dog Steve Cropper? Isn't that a little—"

"Serendipitous?" Ash suggested with a sly smile as he pulled my bag out of the truck and handed it to me.

"That's not the word that leaps to mind," I said, following Ash onto the porch as he unlocked the front door.

"I'm not sure if I mentioned it," he said, reaching inside to switch on the hall light, "but my house isn't quite—well, *complete*."

We stood on the threshold of a good-size living room, modestly furnished: plaid couch, beat-up recliner, coffee table, and one whole wall devoted to a stereo with a pair of big speakers and more CDs than I'd ever seen in my life outside a record store. The walls were fashioned of weathered old planks, shades of red and brown and gray, that Ash would tell me later had come off the sides of an abandoned horse barn. "What do you mean, not complete?" I asked. For a bachelor's place it seemed remarkably tidy, even snug; it had the stamp of handmade, of someone who knew and loved wood.

"I told you Christa left me a little money," Ash said, propping his guitar case in the corner. "Well, it was enough to get me started, to buy the land and lay the foundation, but not much more. I had some savings and I poured that into it and got myself four functional rooms. The rest of it, though, is a work in progress. You'll see what I mean." I don't know what was in my face, but it made Ash laugh. "Don't worry, I have indoor plumbing. I have electricity, as you can see. I have everything you need."

"What I need is a hot shower."

"You read my mind," Ash said, and picked up my bag and motioned for me to follow him.

The bedroom had the same plank walls as the living room; the bed was made of cedar logs and covered with an old wool patchwork blanket, and over the headboard was a small octagonal window with a Celtic cross etched into the glass. There were a heavy bureau and a night table with a small reading lamp, on which sat a well-thumbed Bible, open to Paul's letter to the Ephesians: "Awake, O sleeper, and arise from the dead, and Christ shall give you light."

Ash stepped through an adjoining door and flipped a switch. "You can come in, it's safe," his voice said from around the corner, and I dug my few toilet articles out of my bag and tiptoed into the room behind him.

It would be hard to say that I had any preconceived notions left about Ash by that point, but I admit that something fundamental in my understanding of him changed the first time I saw his bathroom. I can't say, exactly, what I was expecting, only that it would not have surprised me to find a Hollywood tub, marble sinks, ten-dollar soap in a hand-carved dish. The utilitarian aspect of the real thing was a bit of a shock. There was barely room for one person to maneuver, much less two, and the fixtures were almost austere: a plain fiberglass tub stall, toilet, single free-standing sink, standard-issue medicine cabinet mirror above the sink, a wall-mounted cupboard for towels. Ash had unpacked his travel kit; and his comb, his toothbrush, and a lowly disposable razor sat on the edge of the sink; a bar of Ivory rested in a plastic dish. I realized that, more than a shrine to Ash's repute as a host, I'd expected a monument to his vanity, but there was none. It didn't appear that he spent a second longer in front of that mirror than a monk.

He pulled back the plastic shower curtain and turned on both taps full tilt, then reached past me and took an armload of towels out of the cupboard. "What is it you do at a sleep-over, anyway?" he asked. "That's a girls' thing, isn't it? I mean, guys don't have a name for it. When we do it, it usually just means you drank too much and passed out on your buddy's couch."

"Oh, it isn't usually very interesting," I said. "Most of the time you just try on eye shadow and eat potato chips and stay up all night and talk about who you think you'll marry."

"Well, I don't know about the eye shadow," Ash said, "but I think there's a bag of Doritos lying around here somewhere."

"I guess we can skip the marriage talk," I said. "Seeing's how both of us already did our time."

"Hey, I liked being married," he said mildly. "It suited me."

"You told me your wife was crazy and wrecked your life!"

"I said I liked being married," Ash said. "I didn't say I necessarily liked who I was married *to*." He tweaked the taps one last time and then straightened and without a note of warning pulled his T-shirt over his head.

"I . . . Are you going first?"

"No, we're going together. Come on, before the hot water runs out."

We never did this at any sleep-over I've ever been to before," I said, once the basics—shampooing, soaping, rinsing—were out of the way and we'd moved on to other, nonhygienic items of business.

"No, it seems like you'd have mentioned it," Ash said, "right up there with the eye shadow and the potato chips."

"Sasha Davidson did steal her daddy's car once," I said. "We made it all the way out to Wright Patman Lake before she got panicky and ran us into the bar ditch. We'd have gotten away with it, otherwise."

"How old were y'all?"

"Twelve. Maybe thirteen."

"Ah," Ash said, "girls after my own heart." His hands, roaming, paused. "Can I just say something I've been thinking since the first night I met you? Lord, you have a delectable little ass. It makes me want to turn you over and get my teeth in the back of your neck and just . . ."

"Og," I said, someplace deep in my throat, and my knees gave a little and Ash had to catch me and manage to keep us both upright in our slippery, steamy skin. It occurred to me that this was the second time since he'd arrived in the rain the previous night that I'd almost knocked him over, and that once I actually had, even though he was already on the floor at the time.

"Bailey and Geneva were having sex in the shower on their honeymoon, and the tub mat slipped," I said, laughing as Ash winced. "It's funny now, but it was kind of awful when it happened. Bailey had to have twelve stitches in his forehead. To this day, my mama thinks he hurt himself parasailing."

"He's lucky it was his forehead." Ash turned off the shower and reached for a towel. "Okay, let's not let family history repeat itself. Dry yourself off and we'll see if we can't find something less hazardous to cook up."

It was nearly dark out now; a swath of pink-tinged sunset came through the little window over the bed and replicated the pattern of the cross on the middle of the blanket.

"I guess I'm not much of a sleep-over guest," I said, watching Ash turn down the blanket. "I forgot to bring anything to wear to bed."

"We'll just have to make do. Are you cold?"

"Not particularly, why?"

He grinned at me. "You're all puckered up." He covered my breasts with his hands, and I moved into his arms, offering my open mouth, offering it all.

"I haven't felt like this since I was about sixteen," he said into my neck.

"Like what?"

"Like I can't hold back," he said. "Like I'm about half a beat away from completely losing control."

"Then don't," I said. "Don't hold back."

He cupped my bottom, and I turned around and pressed myself against him and he groaned and tipped me forward on my knees onto the edge of the mattress and raised my hips with his hands. The first shot was blind and off the mark but the second slid into me to the root, making us both gasp, and on the eighth or tenth stroke I felt myself start to moan and then to spasm, and a half dozen or so deep thrusts later Ash sank his teeth into my shoulder around a muffled cry, spilling himself in great, spurting arcs inside my thighs, against my belly.

I let myself down onto the sheets, my heart galloping, my breath tearing from my throat. Ash had promised me, before we'd left my house, that nothing scary would happen, but he'd lied. Was this, then, the source of that affiliation I'd felt the first time I'd met his eyes through the windshield, the past lives, the secret pact? When I'd admitted to myself that I wanted what would happen in the dark between us, had I been imagining some sweet schoolgirl notion of sex or this, the roller-coaster drop into oblivion, the free fall with no net? Who had I really been dealing with last night, sitting in the candlelight with swamp music running in my veins, contracting for Ash's safe return; and at what point would they come calling, wanting to collect their share of the bargain? Ash snaked his arm around me and nestled against my back, pulling me into the heated snare of his embrace. Mitchell had always wanted to distance himself from me as quickly as possible afterward, to start that solo journey back to himself. But Ash seemed to want to loiter in the mingled zone, like there was comfort there. It took a long time for me to stop trembling, but Ash held on.

I rolled over to find him buttoning his jeans, handing me one of his old snap-front denim work shirts to wear. "Get up," he said. "I brought you a present from Austin."

He upended a shopping bag on the living room rug and about twenty CDs slid out, still in the shrink-wrap. He dug through the pile until he singled one out, peeled off the wrapper, then knelt and loaded it into the changer—it was one of those that held six at a time—and cued it up.

"Along the Red River where the sweet waters flow . . ." I heard as Ash held out his arms and I went into them, and we swayed together in the receiver's ghostly glow. The recording sounded ancient, the singer's voice unfamiliar, and I wanted to ask where he'd located it but couldn't find my own voice. "I'll live with my love on the Red River shore." Somehow, inexplicably, Ash and I were connected through this plain old cowboy's song, and though I wasn't sure I'd ever know why, I thought I understood the lesson: that you take your poetry where you find it; you learn to dance to what's playing.

The song ended and another CD shuffled into the slot, and Ash and I stretched out side by side on the rug as the furnace kicked on and the last bands of rose and apricot lit the walls through the west-facing window. There was no song, no artist, I recognized in the mix that followed, though I liked most of what I heard, and Ash didn't speak, except once, when he said, "I thought of you the first time I heard this," as the singer sang about being wrapped around your pretty little finger again. It was the first time since he'd shown up the night before that sex didn't seem to loom, infusing the air with its sweaty, tangled insistence. It was there but aloof, a honeyed possibility, a melodious suggestion.

I turned onto my side and looked at Ash's profile in the glow of the stereo receiver, and tried not to but could not help imagining Misty Potter curled against him on this same rug, his fingers wound idly in her pale hair; I saw her on her knees on his mattress, her back arched, and Ash . . . No. But something cold had pooled behind my breastbone and I couldn't shake it. I sat up, and Ash stirred and propped himself on one elbow.

"Something to drink," I murmured, "coffee or tea," but when Ash started to sit up I held my hand against his shoulder and told him I'd do it, that I was sure I could find what I needed.

His kitchen was almost as much a surprise as the bathroom; it was large and airy, with white-painted cabinets and a big rough-hewn blond table and gleaming appliances, including a refrigerator that looked like you could park a Volkswagen inside, with double doors and a built-in ice dispenser. An antique pie safe sat along one wall, and the window above the sink held an aloe plant in a terra-cotta pot. No teakettle was in evidence, but there was a saucepan in the dish drainer that I rinsed and filled at the tap, and I rummaged in the pantry until I found a half-empty box of Constant Comment, then took two blue-striped mugs down from the cupboard and set them on the table. A plastic flap hung over a space in the rear wall—evidence, I guessed, of what he'd meant when he said the house was incomplete—and I was dying, all of sudden, to lift it, to start opening drawers and cabinets, to see what sort of things he kept, but I fought the urge, and by the time the water started to boil and I lifted it off the flame, Ash was in the doorway.

"Find everything okay?"

I nodded and dropped a tea bag into each cup and filled them from the saucepan. "This is nice," I said. "Your kitchen."

"I like you in it," he said. "My kitchen."

"I made you a cup," I said, and he nodded thanks. "You want to take it in the other room?" I could still hear the stereo, somebody's disconsolate voice sliding around on top of a silvery steel guitar.

"Nah, let's pull up right here," Ash said, taking out a chair from the table for me, then another for himself. "I wouldn't want you to forget how to recognize me with the lights on."

I sat, arranging the tails of his borrowed shirt around my knees, and stirred my tea. Ash took a plastic honey bear down from the pantry and put it in the middle of the table, then sat down beside me.

"How do you like my table?" he asked, running his hand over the wood's pale surface.

It seemed like a curious question, so I answered noncommittally: "It's nice."

"I just finished it last week. It turned out better than I expected."

"You made this table?"

"With these two hands." He spread them wide on the tabletop, flexed his wrists.

"I guess I just never thought about it," I said. "About furniture having—you know—origins."

"Most people don't, I guess. It's been a preoccupation of mine since I was a kid," Ash said. "Something just makes me look at a piece of wood and picture what's in it, waiting to come out. Now then," he said, sitting back and picking up his tea, "maybe you want to tell me what's on your mind."

"I don't know what you mean."

He smiled into his cup. "You know, I try to avoid making too many generalizations about women," he said, "it only gets me in trouble. But one thing I *have* noticed is, the minute they get worked up about something, they start banging around in the kitchen." I opened my mouth to protest, but Ash held up his hand. "Don't you say a word," he said. "This morning you just about brained me with a skillet."

"I guess you'd know all about it," I said. "Lots of opportunities, I mean. To have women banging around in your kitchen."

"Well, now," Ash said slowly, removing the tea bag from his cup and stirring in a spoonful of honey, "that could mean one of two things. You're either assuming I've had a lot of women here, or that the ones I've had have all been mad at me."

"I'm sorry," I said. "I can't seem to shake the vision of Misty Potter."

"Misty Potter never set foot in this kitchen," Ash said.

"It isn't really the kitchen I was thinking about."

"Misty Potter never set foot within a two-mile radius of this house. Unless she's out there in the dark right now with binoculars and a deer rifle, which I wouldn't put past her." He picked up his cup and drank, watching me over the rim. "Jesus, Lucy, did you get the idea that Misty and I were—I don't know, having a thing?"

"Weren't you? My Lord, Ash, the night I met you, she was all over you like paint on a barn! Do you know what she said to me about you, last Saturday in the ladies' room? 'It's a hell of a ride.' " He had the good grace to drop his gaze. "That same night she almost put your eye out with her shoe, and then had you arrested! Doesn't that sound like some type of *thing* to you?"

"Yeah, the pathological, delusional kind."

"You're telling me you had no sort of sexual interaction whatsoever with Misty Potter."

"Well, I didn't say that." I stared at him, and he sighed and set down his cup. "Look, there are women you bring home and women you don't. Women you drink tea with in the kitchen, and women . . ." He thought for a moment, then decided that that avenue of narration was best left untraveled. "I look at it this way," he said. "Misty Potter was a, a sort of anthropology experiment."

"Oh, I see," I said. "Like mating with a Samoan, just to see what it's like."

"Exactly!"

"I feel sick," I said and got up from the table, but there was nowhere to go. Before I knew what had happened Ash had scrambled to his feet and I found myself trapped between the counter and his hipbones. He caught the back of my skull in his hand.

"Listen to me," he said. "What makes you think you and Misty Potter have one single thing in common?"

"Gosh, maybe because two weeks ago you were having sex with her, and now you're having sex with me?"

"I drove four hundred and sixty miles in the pouring rain for you!" Ash exclaimed. "I just about washed off the face of the fucking earth, twenty or thirty times! Does that sound like someone who was just looking for a hand job in the parking lot to you?"

"Oh, shit," I said, covering my face with my hands.

"Goddamn, Lucy, it was a—a figure of speech."

"This is a terrible mistake," I said. "You don't need me. You need a Samoan."

Ash smiled. "I've been to Samoa," he said. "I didn't much care for it. The natives have terrible tempers." I tried to twist my head out of his grip but he held tight. "Can I just say one more thing? Something else you'd probably just as soon not hear?"

"Can I stop you?"

"There haven't been that many women in my house," Ash said, "and fewer still drinking tea in my kitchen." He loosened his grip on my skull and wove one hand loosely into my hair, and I leaned forward and lay my face against his throat, the source of that enigmatic, urgent scent. "And only one I would ever have driven twelve hours across the state for in a twenty-year flood, whether she was waiting to take me into her bed or not."

I lifted my face and let him kiss my eyelids, my hair, finally my mouth. There was a kind of purity to it, an innocence of spirit that seemed untainted by the risk of anything more heated. A front had been breached, though; there was no real hope of going back, only these little way stations, temporary interludes where we could pause and get our bearings.

"Ash?" I lifted the tail of his T-shirt and walked my fingers through the dark hair that led like a trail of sweet bait into the button fly of his jeans. "I don't mean to talk this to death, truly. But there's so much I don't . . ."

I stammered silent, and it crossed my mind that there was more than a little irony in the ease with which I'd lain down with Ash compared to the difficulty I had expressing myself vertically. "What I'm trying to say is, will you teach me what I need to know? How to touch you, how to . . . All the rest?" I saw the gleam of his teeth, and I jerked my face from between his hands and ducked it against his shirtfront. "Don't tease me!"

"Why in the world do you think I'm teasing you?" He cupped my cheek in his palm and tilted my chin to his.

"Because! Because you're *smiling*!"

"I'm smiling because I believe that's the most intoxicating invitation I've ever had in my life."

"I doubt that seriously," I said crossly. "All those anthropology experiments. Trips to Samoa and such."

"You don't need lessons, Lucy," he said. "Just practice. You're what I'd call a natural." He ran his thumb over my mouth and I turned my head slightly to capture it between my lips, my back under the loose-fitting shirt molding itself to the hard curve of his hand. "See?"

"I think I just needed to find a countryman."

I watched the remark tell on Ash. For all that we'd passed through in the last few days, a disparity hung between us, the gravity of what he'd offered tipping the balance on one side, while the other—my end—still dangled weightless, unreciprocated, in the air.

"Well, you did," Ash said, holding me easily his arms. "You found him." "Him," I couldn't help but notice he said, like there was only one.

I ran my fingertips up his forearm, over the dark-gold curve of his biceps. In little more than twenty-four hours I'd gained a knowledge of male anatomy fourteen years of marriage had barely alluded to. Who'd have guessed there were so many ways to make a man quiver, to bring him to his knees?

"Tell me the truth," I said. "Is there anything you've never done?"

Ash smiled, his fingers playing over the snaps on the front of my shirt. "There must be *something*."

"Name one."

Circling my waist with his hands, he hoisted me onto the new blond table.

(fourteen)

We were quiet driving into town the next morning, taking in the countryside and the effects of all that rain. Overnight, wildflowers bloomed in plush carpets along the roadsides. A crew was working on the power lines outside Orson's Texaco. There was a sinkhole the size of a caboose in the middle of State Street, with barricades and flashing orange lights. Ash shot a glance at me as we passed the café. "Reckon we ought to stop in, make sure some joker gets his prize money?" I slapped his arm and he smiled sunnily and tooted the horn as we rode by, causing Saul Toomey and Jed Gilbert on the sidewalk to turn and look, and then look again.

"There we go," Ash said. "Might as well start the tongues to wagging."

I could hear Peggy humming in the cooler when I let myself in the back door of the shop. I hesitated, then propped open the cooler door. She had a doughnut in one hand and a bunch of wilted carnations in the other, and she looked completely astonished to see me.

"I wasn't hardly expecting you this morning."

"You weren't?" I glanced around at the tubs and bins of faded flowers, expired after two days with no light or refrigeration. "I thought we'd be busy."

She snapped one of the least-bedraggled blooms from its stem and twirled it in her hand. "I guess I thought you might be callin' in."

"Calling in?" I repeated. "You mean, sick?"

Peggy smiled. "Lovesick, maybe."

She stepped lightly forward and tucked the white carnation into my hair, and I felt the grin start behind my eyes and knew I couldn't hold it, felt it stretch my cheeks and ring in my ears.

"You want to tell me your version," Peggy said, "or do I have to make do with what everybody's saying over at the café?"

"Which is what?" I asked. Peggy cocked her head and considered me for a moment. "Well, honestly, Peggy, you don't expect me to walk over there and hear it for myself, do you?"

"I expect there's a few folks over there would appreciate it if you *did* walk over, so's they could find out when, precisely, it was that Ash got—you know. Back. To town." She cleared her throat. "There's about seventy-five dollars riding on it, in fact."

"He got back," I said, "sometime around the middle of Tuesday night. That's as precise as I care to be. No matter what's riding on it."

"So he was at your place till suppertime yesterday? Then y'all packed up and stayed the night at his house, and he rode you in to work this morning."

"How . . . ?" I began, then shook my head and shut my mouth. One thing I'd learned in the weeks I'd been back in Mooney, it didn't do to question how the local grapevine operated, only to rest assured that its roots were deeper and more entwined than any single person could hope to thwart.

"Never mind," Peggy said. "I expect you and Ash deserve a little goodness that's yours alone, 'cause the whole town will own a piece of it before long.

"Now will you look at this mess?" She gestured around her. "Only the second time in the history of Faye's Flowers that we have to throw everything out and start from scratch. Go on, get yourself a doughnut and get in here and help me. UPS will be here at ten with a whole truckload, so we've got an hour to get the dead stuff out of here."

We had only one delivery all day long, to Arlene Womack, who was in County General having her gallbladder removed, and so I was able to keep a blessedly low profile, although I did have to endure a couple of long looks from Ira Deacon and his stock boy behind the counter when I stopped to fill up the van at the Texaco. Peggy and I took advantage of the opportunity to get the cooler cleaned and swept out, and spent the rest of the day restocking the merchandise. Ash and I had planned to have lunch together, but he had to run to Marshall to the hardware store, which was bigger and more progressive than our dusty little True Value, and so I had to settle for thirty seconds of him through the window of the pickup, handing me half a Subway ham-and-Swiss sandwich and telling me that we were scheduled to meet J. D. and his tow truck at my house at four. My shift was over at two, and we arranged for him to pick me up at three-thirty at Aunt Dove's house. I had studiously, and successfully, managed to avoid every single member of my family, but I knew I couldn't do it indefinitely; I figured Dove was the least likely to either beg for salacious details or hold me on a stake over a roaring pit.

I walked the six blocks to her house after work and found her in her garden, fretting over the rain damage. For all her fuss, it wasn't much; she had an elaborate and ingenious drainage system in place, and it looked to me like all she'd suffered were a few yellow leaves from too much water, though she claimed the cucumbers would languish, a few weeks down the road. She led me into the kitchen and drew us each a glass of water from the tap, her customary offering of hospitality.

"Well, now, I'm glad you finally turned up," she said, pulling out a chair at the table. "The folks from the *National Enquirer* is bound to be here any second."

I watched her a minute before sitting down beside her, but her expression was circumspect. "So, who've you been talking to?" I took a drink of water.

"Law, honey, who *haven't* I been talkin' to? My phone like to ring off the wall the past twenty-four hours. I don't recall it was this bad even when your daddy Raymond Hatch run off and your mama took to the streets in her nightgown." She tilted her water glass to the light and examined it thoughtfully. "I just keep sayin' the same thing I kept sayin' then. 'No comment.'" Her eyes shone. It was plain she was enjoying this.

"Does Mama know?" It was the one thing that had been on my mind above any other, although I had to admit that the idea of facing down Bailey loomed large in its own right.

"Did Jesus rise from the dead?"

We were quiet awhile, though not uneasily so; we sipped our luke-warm tap water.

"I wonder what you must think of me," I said finally, and Dove looked up at me with surprise.

"You've always been my hero," I went on, "the person I've admired more than anyone else in the world. When Mitchell died I thought it was my chance to use everything I learned from you. How to be proud and self-sufficient. How to live as I pleased without a damn for what anybody thinks. And now . . . Well, you must think I've no spine at all."

Dove got up and refilled our two glasses, then sat down again. "I'll tell you, Lucy, what I think," she said. "I think you was married for a long time to somebody who never once saw you for *you*." It was my turn to look surprised. "I'll say this now, though I would never have said it then, you was so bound and determined to marry Mitchell Breward. But I knew the first time I met him that he would put out your light. It almost broke my heart, seein' you go off with him, knowin' you the way I do that you would honor your vow to him no matter what, whatever it cost you. It was so hard to see you, all those years; it was like you was always trying to put the brightest face on it, but I could just see you fadin', right before our eyes."

A knot had formed unexpectedly in my throat, and when I swallowed to dislodge it, my eyes filled with tears. "I'd never go so far as to say it's a blessing that Mitchell was killed," Dove said, "I don't believe the Lord works that way. But I can't help but think, when he did pass, that you got set down in front of Ash Farrell for a reason. Oh, I know what folks around here say about Ash, been sayin' it as long as he's been old enough to shave, almost, but I'll tell you this, I remember that young man who set by Christa Keller the days and nights before she died, and there's a glory shinin' at the middle of his soul; I've always felt that. The first time I set up here at this table and listened to Bailey and you arguin' about whether or not Ash was sparkin' you, I told myself what I hoped was true: that Ash saw that ol' shine down inside you, just like his, lookin' for a way up into the light."

I wiped my eyes. "You don't think I'm a slut?"

Dove gave a shout of a laugh. "I think you're human, Lucy Bird, as human as the next person, if not more so. As for wantin' to live as you please without a damn for what anybody thinks, I reckon you've already gotten your start. There's ways that livin' with Ash is gonna take a lot more grit than livin' alone ever would, mark my words."

"Nobody said anything about living with anybody," I said. She looked at me sidelong. "It's only been two nights."

"You mean to tell me you think that's it—the end of it?" she asked. I shook my head, smiling like a fool. "When's the next time you're s'posed to see him?"

"Three-thirty," I said. "He's picking me up here."

"Uh-huh," she said with a grin. "Anyway, knowin' what Ash did to get home the other night, it don't seem likely to me he'd be ready to cut you loose after two measly nights."

"I guess not."

"You want just one teeny piece of advice," Dove said, "from an old maid who don't give a damn what anybody thinks?"

"You know I do."

"Your mama, Lord bless her, made her whole life an altar to a man who left her. When Mitchell died, it about tore me up to think of the same thing happenin' to you. Now that I see it ain't, you got to promise me one other thing. You just take care not to make too much of an altar to a man who's still breathin', and you'll be okay." I nodded, still blinking back tears, and Dove patted my hand. "Now come on in the livin' room with me and watch *Montel*. I tell you, it'll give you a whole new perspective on your own little troubles."

It did, if only to bolster my determination never to take my little troubles in front of a camera crew and a studio audience. Half an hour later I heard Ash's truck pull up at the curb, and I jumped up and met him at the front door. "Dove would have greeted you herself," I said, admitting him to the living room, "but she's got to find out which one of the paraplegic twins is really a cross-dressing cabaret performer in his secret life."

"Hush," Dove said, her eyes glued to the screen; she flapped her hand at me. "It's the one in the blue, you hide and watch."

"Hi," I mouthed at Ash, and, "Hi," he mouthed back, and took advantage of Dove's attention being elsewhere to give me a whole-hearted, lingering kiss. "I see y'all back there, don't think I don't," Dove said without turning her head, as the blue twin emerged from the wings in a fetching chiffon garment and a dynel fall and began to sing the theme song from *Evita* from his wheelchair.

"I don't know which is worse," Dove said, "that he cain't carry a tune or he don't make a better-lookin' woman." She aimed the remote at the TV and punched the Off button. "Well, there, Ash Farrell," she said, getting purposefully to her feet. "What do you have to say for yourself?"

My Aunt Dove had been the attendance secretary for the Mooney public schools for forty-three years, and had a way, even ten years after retirement, of putting the fear in you with the most neutral phrase, just by the spin she put on it, the precise arch of an eyebrow. Ash had just driven twelve hours through a twenty-year flood, though; there didn't seem much left that could faze him.

"Not much, Miss Dove," he said easily. "How've you been?"

"Tryin' not to wash away," she said, "like everbody else. You run into a bit of weather, I heard."

"A bit. Nothing worth mentioning."

"I s'pose not. Considering what was waitin' for you on the other end." They both looked at me. I opened my mouth, then shut it again. "I guess I don't have to tell you," she said, leveling her eyes at him, "that you are the luckiest son of a gun in Mooney, Texas, if not the world."

"No, ma'am," Ash said, unsmiling. "You don't have to tell me."

Dove came forward and lay her hand on Ash's arm and steered him toward the door. "Step out here with me a second," she said, and I followed them into the garden, wondering what she was up to.

"I knew Christa Keller real good," Dove said as Ash looked up from fingering one of the little stone Buddhas. "We was president and president-elect of the garden club one time, when you kids was young. You prob'ly don't recall." He shook his head.

"She was quite the gardener. Had more nerve than I did, that's for sure. Not as much know-how, necessarily, but more nerve. She'd try anything—white pumpkins, purple asparagus. She had some a them sweet onions from Texas A&M before anybody else ever heard of such a thing, an' some a them mild jalapeño peppers, too, though what good a jalapeño with no bite ever was to anybody is somethin' I wonder to this day." Ash smiled. "You liked pole beans, I recollect," Dove said, "ain't that right? Kentucky Wonders."

"Yes, ma'am." He set the little Buddha back on its pedestal. "How did you know that?"

"Aw, we used to go in together and order seeds from the catalogs, save money on shipping. Ever single year Christa ordered pound upon pound of Kentucky Wonder seeds. She said no matter how many she planted, you couldn't get enough of them."

"I don't guess I've had them in fifteen years," Ash mused, fixing his eyes on the horizon.

"Well, you're in luck," Dove said. "I'm planning on puttin' some in the ground next week, just as soon as things dry out a bit. You behave yourself, treat our Lucy right, maybe you'll be around to reap the rewards, a coupla months from now."

T hat's the most pathetic bribe I've ever heard in my life," I said to Ash, once we'd said good-bye to Dove and were in the truck on our way to my place. "You mean now I have to wonder if you're seeing me because you want to be or just because of a couple of pounds of pole beans?"

"Well, it's better than thinking I'm in it for the cash or the real estate, isn't it?"

"Just wait," I said darkly. "Wait until Bailey starts making you offers to let me be. You haven't begun to *imagine* cash or real estate."

"Really?" Ash asked with interest, and I pinched his forearm and he laughed and turned on the radio. "Don't worry," he said. "I'll tell your brother you're the hottest piece of ass to come down the pike in twenty years, and unless he can compensate me for *that*, I'm not interested in his shoddy deals."

The tow truck was already in my yard when we arrived—EXTREME AUTO WHOLESALE, it said on the door—and the Buick had been pried loose and hauled twenty or so feet to a reasonably dry spot, and two men in coveralls were sitting on the hood of the wrecker drinking cans of Miller Lite and having what seemed to be a fine old time. I went into the house for my checkbook, and when I came out Ash was up there, too, cracking a can. I had never known a human being with such an ability to assimilate himself anywhere, with anyone; there seemed not to exist a social situation or gathering that found him at a loss, out of his element.

I wrote out the check and handed it over to the man Ash introduced me to as J. D., but they were deep in some shared recollection, har-harring away and tossing back the brew, and after a minute or so the testosterone got too thick for me and I went back into the house. The electricity was on, and I went around straightening things, making the bed, putting the candles away for the next twenty-year flood. Most of the items in the refrigerator were okay, though the milk was right on the cusp, and I poured it down the drain. I had no idea what was supposed to happen next. One advantage, I suppose, in having sex with people you're married to is that you don't have to wonder where you're going to spend the night.

After a while I heard the wrecker's big engine start up, and as it receded into the distance Ash came whistling up the steps and in the front door. I couldn't say, exactly, why that annoyed me, but it did. I pulled a handful of wilted salad greens out of the crisper and stuffed them in the garbage disposal and disintegrated them, but it didn't make me feel any better.

"You know, don't you, that I'm just gonna follow you straight in here and ask you what's wrong," Ash said behind me. "The minute you step into the kitchen—*any* kitchen—I'm gonna be right on your heels. No point trying to dodge it."

He crushed the empty beer can in his hand, his expression placid. "You got your wheels back," he offered as, I guessed, a jumping-off point.

"Okay," I said, leaning back against the sink to watch him. "Now what?"

"Meaning what? The next fifteen minutes? The next twenty years?"

"I mean, give me a blueprint here, Ash. Are we dating, going steady, what? Do we take turns shuttling back and forth between houses, or do you go home and I wait for you to call me? Do you work me into your harem? Do I have to stand in line at the bar? How does this work?"

"What are you talking about?" he said slowly. "We're . . ."

"We're what?"

He stared at the crushed can in his hand. "Well, jeez, Lucy. Do you want me to ask you to move in with me after two days?"

"Don't be ridiculous."

"Because I would, but I think you'd freak out completely."

"You're right, I would."

"See?"

"To say nothing of my family completely disowning me."

He held up his hands. "There you go."

I glanced around me, at the late-afternoon sun filtering through the pines, painting its dappled light on the oilcloth. "You hate my house," I said petulantly.

"I don't hate your house," Ash said. "I hate certain things *about* your house. Your skinny, lumpy little bed, to be specific."

"How can you hate my bed?" I said. "I took you straight out of four hundred sixty miles in the rain and into that bed!"

"So, we'll put up a plaque. Maybe get it listed on the register of historic places. Just don't ask me to sleep in it again."

"This is the first place that's ever been mine, alone," I said. "I can't give it up. I can't even think of it."

"I'm not asking you to," he said. "You need this place, Lucy. For reasons that make sense now and reasons you don't even know about yet."

"Then how . . ."

"Easy. You pack up a few things and bring them over to my house, and we just keep thinking of it as a sleep-over. One night at a time. Any time you need some space to yourself, I start working your nerves, you come back here."

"What about you? What if I start working *your* nerves?"

"Well, my tolerance is higher than yours, I think," he said, and laughed when a look of indignation crossed my face. "But if I do need a night off, I'll say so, okay? Same as you. Now get your stuff. I'm getting this overpowering urge to hear you squeal."

Out on the porch Steve Cropper pushed his nose against the screen.

"What about my dog?" I asked. "It isn't right, just leaving him here alone."

Ash stepped out the door and scooped the puppy up in one hand. "Hey, little guy," he said. "You all set to make musical history?"

We left the two dogs sniffing and circling in Ash's yard, and Ash unloaded a case of tools and carried it around back while I went into the house. He found me standing in front of the open refrigerator. "One thing might save you a lot of grief down the road," I said as he stood eyeing me from the doorway. "Sometimes when I'm banging around in the kitchen, it just means I'm hungry."

He came into the room and reached past me to shut the Fridgidaire's big double doors, then backed me up against one and pressed his hands flat against my hipbones. "Hungry? You mean, like, for food?"

"I was," I confessed. I wrangled his shirttail out of his jeans and walked my fingers across his middle. "It seems to be fading."

"Let me get a shower, Lucy," he said. "I'm all over sweat and dust."

"What's wrong with sweat and dust? They ought to find a way to put it in a bottle. I guarantee you women would go for it more than all that sweet, spicy stuff they make to cover it up."

It was my turn to back him up, out the doorway and down the hall. I pushed him onto the bed and worked his shirt up around his ribs. He just watched me, his eyes steady, his mouth curved a little, as I kicked off my shoes and crawled up over him. I leaned forward and kissed him once, lightly, on the mouth and he groaned and arced under me.

"Okay," I whispered. "How do you want it?"

He sucked in his breath. "Say again?"

"You heard me."

"Um, what are my choices?"

"Hard and fast," I murmured, "or sweet and slow."

Ash's eyes closed; his head fell back against the mattress. I watched his Adam's apple roll.

"How about both?"

I drove my own car into town the next morning, and had just pulled into the shop's parking lot when my brother Bailey turned the corner and eased his big truck, engine muttering, up to the curb. I didn't think he'd try anything in broad daylight, but I approached with caution just the same.

He didn't look at me, but across the street, where Ash and Isaac were unloading something from the bed of Isaac's truck. "Sorry to drop by unannounced this way," he said. "I've been trying to call, but I never get an answer."

"I haven't been home much."

"You staying at his place?" He jerked his head in Ash's general direction, as if I wouldn't know which "he" he meant, as if there was a whole plethora from which to choose.

"Uh-huh."

"He hasn't tried to marry you for your money yet, has he?"

"Not in so many words." I smiled as Bailey's face registered real surprise. "No, right now we're calling them sleep-overs. One day—well, night—at a time."

"Is that right." Bailey turned his head slowly and studied me. "Well," he said grudgingly after a second, "you look all right. In fact, you look good."

"Thanks."

"Mama's fit to be tied, Lucy. She had her Bible group over yesterday to pray for your soul."

I held my breath for a moment, hoping to still the buzz I felt building between my ears. "You tell Mama . . ."

"What?"

"You tell Mama, Ash found a glory in me. Tell her he's bringing it up to the light."

"Jesus," Bailey said. "Did he tell you that?"

"No, as a matter of fact, Dove did."

Bailey gave a long sigh, and looked at the backs of his hands on the steering wheel. "Truth be told, I'm here on an item of business."

"What would that be?"

"You know the auction's a week from today." I'd forgotten, but I nodded, like it was fresh on my mind. "Far be it from me to tell you how to live your life, Lucy, or to presume to know whether or not you owe Mitchell Breward, or his memory, a damn thing. But there are things in that house that have been in our family for three generations. I know you were too wrought up when Mitchell died to deal with it then, but I and Geneva and Mama and Kit cannot stand by and watch those things carried off by strangers."

"What are you saying?"

"I'm saying you have to pick a day, early next week, for us to drive down there and go through the house. To collect the family heirlooms, anything else you might want to keep."

I closed my eyes, and behind them swirled the image of Mitchell's and my bedroom, dust motes floating in the bars of sun through the curtains, the chenille bedspread and the old blue quilt tucked tight, everything orderly and undisturbed, as if any moment Mitchell would just walk in, tip his change into the Mason jar on the bureau, sink into the old rocker to pull off his boots. There weren't words to describe the dread I felt at the thought of going back, the certainty that something that had been waiting there in that room for me would wrap its runners around me and pull me, finally, into its dark heart, where I belonged.

"You know," Bailey said, "Mama will eventually come to terms with this thing." He nodded in Ash's direction, like it pained him to spell out the particulars. "Especially if it holds, which I'm telling you right now I wouldn't lay money on. But her grandma's Spode china is in that house, Lucy. Her own mama's Bible, from when she joined the church. Photographs that can't be replaced. If you don't do this . . ."

I clamped my hands over my ears. "All right. Tuesday," I said. "My day off is Tuesday."

"Can you be ready to go by seven?" I said I could. "Where should I pick you up?"

"Ash's, I guess. Assuming it lasts that long."

The wisecrack sailed straight over Bailey's head. "I expect you must be pretty excited about tomorrow," he said.

"Why, what's tomorrow?"

"Why, it's your big debut at the Round-Up, ain't it? Ash Farrell's new squeeze?" Bailey laughed at the look on my face and shifted the truck into gear. "We'll see you there, okay? Front and center." He made a point of turning around in Mrs. Tanner's driveway. I wasn't surprised when Ash raised a hand in greeting, but I was when Bailey returned the gesture. Especially since neither of them had a middle finger extended.

Y ou're awful quiet."
We lay under the patchwork blanket, Ash's chest against my back, his leg thrown across mine like I might be getting ready to blow away.

"Well, let's be realistic—I can't squeal *every* time."

"That's not what I meant, and you know it."

I rolled over and looked at him in the lamplight. My heart still lurched a little every time I saw his face at this range, and I ran my fingers along the plane of his cheekbone, into the salt and pepper of his hair.

"This wouldn't have anything to do with your brother stopping by this morning, would it?" Ash asked.

"Wow, pretty soon I won't have to talk at all; you can just read my mind."

"Now, that sounds like a dangerous concept."

I was quiet a minute, choosing my words. "I have to go down to the farm next week," I said. "Go through the house. Gather up the things that belong to my family, anything with any . . . sentimental value, I guess you'd call it."

"It's nothing to be ashamed of, Lucy. You were married for fourteen years. If you didn't want at least some memento of that, I might wonder if something was wrong with you."

"But that's just it," I said. "Something *is* wrong. I'm afraid, Ash," I said, and looked into his eyes. "I'm afraid to go back. Something will happen."

"Something like what?"

"I don't know. I feel it, though, like it's there, laying for me."

"Is Bailey going with you?" I nodded yes. "Well, you know he's not gonna let anything happen to you."

"I guess not."

"There's no place for me there—you know that, don't you?"

"I know." I lay my cheek against his throat. "Anyway, I'd rather just think of you, here. Like this."

"It's only for the day," Ash said, "right?"

"Right."

And then it will be over, I thought; and there would be nothing for me but this: the warm, solid length of Ash's body, his cryptic scent, scrolling out ahead of me, as far as I let myself see.

(fifteen)

We stayed in bed past noon Saturday, making love, drowsing, hour after hour. My nerves seemed parked just beneath the surface of my skin, in a constant state of alert. I was sure I'd lost five pounds since Wednesday; hunger, the prandial kind, seemed far down the list, like some household chore or civic duty. Things felt glorious and crazed and completely transient. I never took Ash into my arms one time without telling myself it might be the last, without believing I heard the devil on my shoulder, snickering in my ear, getting ready to call me out.

Ash had band practice at two, as he did every Saturday. I lay between the sheets and watched him emerge from the shower, dripping on the rug, and go into the closet and come out buttoning his Levi's.

"I thought I'd swing back by this evening and fetch you around seven," he said, sitting down on the edge of the mattress to pull on his boots. I didn't say anything, and he looked up. "What?"

"Do you realize we've never even had a date?"

"How about that time I took you to Willie B.'s for ribs? That time you were licking my fingers in the truck?"

"You stuck your thumb in my mouth!" I sat up, and the sheet fell to my waist, and I snatched it up and pulled it to my chin, which made Ash smile. "I was not the instigator," I said resentfully. "I was never the instigator."

"Huh," he said. "Who grabbed whose belt, the very next night, right out on the dance floor?"

"Who put whose hand on whose ass, on that same dance floor?"

"My hand was not on your ass! There were two men there, at least, who'd have ripped my arms off if I'd touched your ass."

"You propositioned me!"

"You accepted!"

"Not technically," I said. "I never actually said yes."

"Lucy," Ash said patiently, "everything about you said yes. Whether your mouth said it or not."

"So you think I'm easy. Is that what you're saying?"

"No, I think you were ready." He stood up and shook his jeans over the tops of his boots. "I think you recognized a countryman. You want a date?" he said. "Fine. I'm taking you to the Round-Up tonight. I'll pick you up at seven."

"Bailey made a joke yesterday," I said. "About this being our debut."

"You watch. Two thirds of the county will be there," Ash said. "I bet we even get a few nosy hard-shell Baptists."

"So, this has happened a lot of times?" I said. "You seem to know just what to expect."

"This has happened exactly never," Ash said, "which is why I think we'll draw a crowd."

"You never took a girl to the Round-Up before?"

"Not one like you." He smiled, letting me wonder, I guess, exactly what that meant.

"You don't think they'll stone me or anything, do you?"

"Nah," he said. "Probably just some rotten fruit and vegetables." He laughed at my expression. "Can I just pass on one thing I've learned in thirty or so years of being the butt of everybody's gossip? Hold your head up. Act like you made the rules. Trust me, Lucy, there's not a person on this planet, and surely not in this town, who thinks they're invincible. Just look 'em in the eye and smile. After a while, it gets to be second nature."

He bent over to kiss me, and I realized that Ash had just unlatched some door, that he'd given me a peek behind a front of his I'd marveled at since the first time I'd watched him in the Round-Up's lights.

"So, you're saying it's all an act."

"Not after a while," he said. "But that's how you start."

Geneva called around six. I'd been changing my clothes for half an hour, although most of my things were still at the rent house and so I was restricted to the ten or twelve pieces I had on hand, in their various combinations: skirts, tops, dresses, jeans. I couldn't stop thinking of that scene in *Gone With the Wind* where Rhett sends Scarlett into Melanie's party in the bodice-busting red dress after she's been caught kissing Ashley, advertising to the world that she's a tart. So, was it better to confess it and act proud, or to take the low road and make people wonder? Maybe, like Scarlett, I'd be rescued by my sister-in-law.

"Flaunt it," Geneva advised. "Sweetie, there won't be a woman there who wouldn't hop in a heartbeat into your shoes. I say, rub their noses in it."

"It doesn't feel right," I said uneasily. "It's not like I'm going there to gloat."

"Why not? God, I remember my first date with Bailey; it was at the

Round-Up, matter of fact. I spent two hours getting ready, not counting the trip to the beauty shop that afternoon to get my hair done. I wore the tightest jeans I had, and a push-up bra. Three-inch heels."

"No blouse?"

"The bra was *under* the blouse," she said, "jeez, get serious. Anyway, I was making a point, you see? I wanted everybody to know what Bailey was getting so they wouldn't get any ideas. I wanted it real clear he wouldn't be having any reason to look elsewhere. Not that night, or any other."

"You slept with Bailey on y'all's first date?"

"Well, we'd known each other twenty years, practically. Anyway, who are you to talk?" she said. "You've been sleeping with Ash for, what, four, five days now, and y'all haven't even *had* a date."

"Yes, we did," I said. "One."

"When?" Her voice was ripe with skepticism.

"That day we had lunch up at Willie B.'s."

"Yeah, so. What, exactly, made it a date?"

"Well, he paid."

"Okay, so he bought you lunch."

"And afterward, he licked his thumb and put it in my mouth." Geneva was uncharacteristically speechless. "He said I had sauce on my mouth, but—"

"Shut up," she said. "I'm about to hyperventilate."

"I'm scared," I confessed. "Suppose Mama sics her Bible group on me. Suppose somebody calls me a whore. Suppose Misty Potter wants to fight me in the parking lot."

"Let me just ask you one thing," Geneva said. "Are you ashamed of yourself, Lucy? Do you *feel* like a whore?"

"No, I don't." What I felt, in fact, was bulletproof.

"Go, then," she said, "and wear whatever you please. When you get down to it, this is between you and Ash, isn't it? Not a bunch of small-town biddies with flapping tongues. Anyway," she added, "once they get a look at me, nobody's gonna be paying any attention to you." There was a short, cryptic silence; then she added teasingly, "Our anniversary's tomorrow."

"Gosh, Gen, I forgot." I studied on this for a minute. "This isn't about that black corset, is it?"

"Oh, sure, you'd like me to wear *that* to the Round-Up." She laughed. "Take a little of the heat off you."

"I can take the heat," I said.

"Can you? Let's do it, then," Geneva said. "We are Hatch women, and here we come!"

The parking lot was filled to overflowing; we had to leave the truck in the vacant field across the road. Ash reached behind the seat and pulled out his guitar, and I felt the rush I always felt on the threshold of the Round-Up, of possibility, things to come. What could have been more fitting, really, than the second coming of Lucy Hatch being staged here, where the first part had begun, so auspiciously but to so little effect, half a lifetime ago? I wondered, not for the first time, what might have happened if I'd succumbed to Tommy Rupp when I was seventeen, what direction my life might have taken. Tommy had moved to Quitman, I recalled, and opened his own garage. Married, twice; I couldn't remember if the second one took. It was all foolish speculation, anyhow. Ash transferred the guitar case to his left hand. "Remember, now, what I told you?" I lifted my chin high, and he smiled. "Just like that," he affirmed, and reached for my hand with his free one.

Ash nodded to a knot of people outside the door, who parted for us like the Red Sea but didn't say a word, and dropped my hand briefly to shake hands with the doorman, Arless Cooper, who was eighty-five if he was a day but had been with Dub so long no one had the heart to dethrone him. It was common knowledge, even when I was in high school, that Arless was so blind kids could, and sometimes did, hand him Monopoly money for the cover charge. Fortunately, a fairly stringent honor system was in place and Dub took in only a few fake bills a night, which he patiently sorted from the real cash and threw out with the empty beer bottles, and as best I could tell, Arless never knew the half of it. Beyond the front door the hall beckoned, with its haze of smoke and neon, Hank Snow on the jukebox, the perfume of all those bodies drinking and dancing and fighting and flirting. I looked up at Ash, and he smiled, and his fingers squeezed mine. *Act like you make the rules; that's how you start.*

We made it unaccosted to Bailey and Geneva's table, where I was surprised to see not just my brother Kit and his wife, Connie, who went out about one Saturday night per year, but Aunt Dove, grinning and tapping her toe, a bottle of Lone Star in front of her.

"Wow," Ash said into my ear, "looks like you called for backup."

I didn't have a chance to tell him I hadn't; he went around the table shaking hands, squeezing Dove's arm and kissing Geneva on the cheek. She was all dolled up, two buttons on her blouse undone to display the bounty of her Wonderbra.

"Is this for me?" I heard Ash say, and watched as she leaned back to give him a long look from under her mascaraed lashes.

"You son of a bitch," she said. "I thought we had a deal, and here you are, messing with my sister-in-law, right under my nose."

"You introduced me to your sister-in-law," he reminded her. "Anyway, you know I love you, but not enough to die for you." He nodded at Bailey, who nodded back, his eyelids at half-mast, as if to say, *Damn straight.*

"Actually," she said, "it's our anniversary. Twelve years, tomorrow."

"Is that right? I'll have to see what sweet old song I can pull out of the hat for y'all later on."

"That'd be nice, Ash." She sat down and nuzzled Bailey, who smiled like a man resigned agreeably, if a bit drunkenly, to his fate.

"Now, if it's not too much of an imposition," Ash said, his hand on the back of my neck, "I'll turn Lucy over to you all for a bit."

Bailey cleared his throat. "I think you got that backward, pal."

Ash gave a faint smile. "I'm returning her to the fold, then. I want her back at the end of the night, though."

"I doubt you'll get much of a fight there," Geneva said wryly, and Ash leaned forward and kissed me with light, dry lips in front of half our hometown, then swung his guitar case from his left hand to his right and made his way across the room, toward the stage.

Geneva grabbed my arm and pulled me down on the bench next to her, beaming like a bride. "Aren't you gonna ask me about my new John Deere?" she asked, and flipped her hair off her face.

I gasped as the bar light spun prisms through the chunks of ice glittering from her earlobes.

"Does Liz Taylor know these are missing?" I leaned close to admire the stones, at the same time catching Bailey's eye. He gave me a conspiratorial wink. My brother was a lot of things, but stupid wasn't one of them.

"Turn around," Geneva said suddenly. "Let me see your face."

"What? Why?"

"I told Bailey on the way over here tonight," she said, "that I'd be able to tell by looking at you if you were—let's see, how do I put this? *Fulfilled.*"

"Lord, Geneva." I blushed, although it was too dark for her to see, and reached past her for a cup of beer.

"You want to hear what I think?"

"Do I have a choice?"

"I think you finally found out why God gave men tongues." I made a strangling sound, then slapped a hand over my mouth, but not before everyone at the table had looked at me. Geneva was rocking, laughing, on the bench. "Well, you didn't think it was for conversation, did you?"

"For your information, Ash does conversation just fine."

"So, you're saying he's multilingual." She was cracking herself up; it was a good thing the band was starting and no one could hear her but me.

Geneva and Bailey got up and slid onto the dance floor, followed by Kit and Connie. Dove sat beaming at me across the table, and ten seconds later some white-haired cowboy in a checkered shirt and a beat-up Resistol came over and offered her his hand and she, too, was up and gone, leaving me alone, gazing into my beer.

Nobody asked me to dance. Not once, the entire evening. It was like Ash had put his brand on me. Or maybe I really was too disreputable to be associated with, even in such a cursory way. All I know is that plenty of people slunk by the table, smirking and cutting their eyes away, and not a single one of them stopped or spoke a word. My brothers felt so sorry for me that they took turns with me on the dance floor, but I knew they were doing me a favor. I tried to probe Kit for his reaction—never an easy feat under the best of circumstances—but all he'd say was, "It's your life, Lucy," as Bailey, mercifully, cut in and spun me away in an easy two-step.

I smiled up at him as we moved across the floor. "You never ordered any lawn tractor, did you?"

"If I had, I'd be down at the morgue right now with a tag on my toe." My brother grinned. "Nah, but it sure was fun making her think I had. You should've seen her face when I drove her out to the co-op this morning. I parked at the loading dock, and we went inside, and I told Emmitt I was there for my new John Deere. He reached under the counter and handed Gen this little green toy tractor with her earrings wired to the driver's seat. I'm surprised you didn't hear her holler clear across town."

Bailey's eyes narrowed slyly. "On second thought, you were probably making so much racket on your own, I doubt you'd've heard her." I swatted his shirtfront, and he laughed. "You do look happy, I'll say that. He treating you okay?"

"Of course." I flushed at the implication.

"Oh, I didn't mean that," Bailey said, "that's Geneva's department. What I mean is—"

"I know what you mean, Bailey." How to tell my own brother what a mystery and a blessing it was to lie in Ash's arms and have him talk to me, consider what I had to say, hold me against his beating heart as he slept? Ash's very repose in his own skin seemed as much a gift as the way he offered it: with the basic tenet that we were modeled not just for function, but for joy.

"You promise you'd let us know," Bailey said, "if everything wasn't fine? I can't help but . . ."

"What?"

"It hurts me, that we all just sat by and watched you, well, *languish* all those years with Mitchell. Like there's something we should have done." We were both quiet awhile, considering this. "It also makes me—I don't know, leery, a little, of this thing with you and Ash. Like maybe you were so hungry for someone to notice you that you sailed right into the first port you saw."

"Or maybe I just found a port I liked the look of." I smiled as Bailey shook his head. "I'm not saying I have the answers, either. I don't know what it is, any better than you. But I do know I wouldn't want to miss it, however it comes out."

He looked at me soberly. "I'll say this—Ash seems different, somehow."

"Different, how?"

"Aw, I guess I been watching him flirt and fool around for twenty

years, before he started singing here, even, and he always treated it
kinda offhand—a lark, I guess you'd say. In fact, in all that time, I don't
think I ever saw Ash go after a girl; it's always been the other way
around, and that seemed to suit him fine, Lord knows I never saw him
suffer a shortfall. That's why I sat up and took notice when I saw him
pulling up so hard behind you—because I realized I'd never seen it
before. He always used to just act like, you know, the girls came with
the territory, like it was part of his job not to resist. I never saw him line
up somebody in his sights before, the way he did you." This was so startling I couldn't think how to answer. "You recall what you told me Dove
said, about Ash seeing something in you and bringing it into the light?"
I nodded. "I can't believe I'm hearing myself say this, but I think I know
what she means."

"So, you don't think he's in this just to get laid." Bailey scowled at
me, and I laughed. "Before you worry so much about Ash's motives, Bailey, maybe it'd be a good idea if you took a look at mine."

"Do me a favor, would you?" Bailey said into my ear as the song
ended and Ash announced a break. "You're my baby sister, okay? You
just keep those particular motives to yourself."

We sat down at the table and Bailey passed a fresh round of beers.
"You'll never believe who I saw at the bar," Geneva leaned over the
table and said to me. "Misty fucking Potter."

"Seriously?" I looked around but couldn't pick her out of the throng,
the shiny young things in their brief skirts and their undeterred hope,
all the folks lined up for alcohol. "Let's hope Dub did a weapons check
at the door."

But if Misty had laid a trap for Ash, he wasn't making himself an easy
mark. Instead of his usual stop by the bar, he made a beeline straight for
our table, and pulled me up by the hand. "They're playing our song," he
said, and sure enough it was the same Clint Black tune from the Satur-

day before, the one I'd thought was going to change my life. Well, it had, ultimately; it had just ended up taking a few days longer than I'd expected. I hung on to his belt like my life depended on it, like he was pulling me into port. Ash lay one hand decisively on the curve of my rump; I raised my head and he smiled down at me like a cat with a canary wriggling in its jaws.

"Geneva saw Misty," I said. "Over by the bar."

"Like I told you, Lucy—it's a public place."

"She had you arrested!"

"She dropped the charges."

I studied him for a few seconds. "Are you sure there's not more to this story than you're telling me?"

He smiled off over my head. "There's a lot more I'm not telling you," he said. "Trust me, it isn't something you want to hear."

"I mean, maybe you've got this secret life or something. Like you're seeing Misty Potter on the side."

Ash tipped back his chin and laughed. "*What* side?" he wanted to know, drawing my face into his neck. "Lord, Lucy, where do you think I'd get the stamina for somebody else? I can barely keep up with you as it is."

"You keep up with me just fine," I murmured.

"Well, you haven't killed me yet."

The second set went much the same as the first, with me sitting in exile while the rest of my family lived it up on the dance floor. Near the end of the night, Ash mentioned Geneva and Bailey's anniversary and then dedicated a song to "everybody in the room by the name of Hatch." I sat on the bench watching my brother and sister-in-law circle the floor in the tightest of clutches and let Ash's voice work its way down through me, woven through with sweet tendrils of guitar: "Lovers like you and me will never say die."

I stood next to the table after the lights came up and watched Dove go off with Kit and Connie, already fretting about overtime for the baby-sitter, and Geneva and Bailey stroll out with their arms around each other's waists, him tickling her upper lip with his mustache; they'd decided to forgo their weekly trip to IHOP, other things presumably having taken precedence over pancakes. A handful of diehard females clustered at the bar until the last possible moment—Misty wasn't one of them—until finally Ash emerged, and stopped to exchange a few words with them before turning and giving Dub a look so pointed I could see the sharp tip from where I stood, and Dub leaned across the bar and said something and the girls let their eyes linger for a second on Ash's back and then sagged their shoulders and gathered their purses and skulked toward the door.

Ash came toward me with a shot glass of whiskey in each hand. Onstage the band members were loading up their equipment, but otherwise, except for Dub and his barbacks and cleanup crew, the room was empty. The jukebox played "Tennessee Stud."

Ash smiled and handed me a glass and bent to give me a kiss, abbreviated but full of promise. He clinked his glass to mine and drank.

"Do you have to stay long?" I asked.

"You tired?"

"No. Why?"

"This is our date, remember? I'm surprised you're so anxious for it to end."

Ash's lead guitar player, Derrall, came out and got a beer and sat down with us and talked awhile, while the team of college kids Dub employed scraped bottles into plastic garbage pails and wiped down the long tables and swabbed the floor. I took a sip of my drink and felt it scorch my throat and land in the pit of my belly like a small blue flame.

Before long the band had packed up and left, and Derrall stood and said good night, and then it was just Ash and me alone at one of the long tables, Charley Pride on the jukebox, the last of the cleanup crew, Dub behind the bar.

Ash's glass was empty, and he got up and crossed back to the bar. "How's your drink?" he called, and I held it up to show him I still had most of it as Dub set out another glass and filled it from a bottle. I watched Ash come toward me, sipping his drink, those hips like the deadliest weapon I'd ever seen.

"Where'd you learn to walk like that?" I said as he pulled me to my feet.

"Like what?" He drew my bottom lip between his teeth and I forgot the question, forgot everything but the way the tip of his tongue parted my lips and then withdrew, like a taunt. He finished off his whiskey in one shot and set the glass on the table. "Come on out here, Lucy," he said. "Dance with me."

I leaned against the Wurlitzer's lighted glass with Ash's hand on my hip and scanned the titles hungrily. I loved this music, all of it; it was such a part of my history, the sound track to my very first notions, however provincial, about love. No wonder our expectations were so vaulted, our assumptions out there somewhere over the moon. "He Stopped Loving Her Today," "I'll Share My World with You," "Walkin' after Midnight," "Behind Closed Doors." The selection was canted heavily to the side of heartbreak. I pointed this out, and Ash said, "Yeah, you know, the trouble with Haggard and Jones and those fellows is that they'll do just grand when you're coming off a love affair, but they ain't much help when you're going in the other direction."

"That's all right," I said. "I know which direction we're going. Don't you?"

"Man, I sure hope so."

And so, as teenagers stacked empty pitchers and collected trash around us and Dub counted receipts behind the bar, Ash and I hung on to each other and slid our feet to all those sad, silky voices. It was hard to remember that life was as cruel as the music wanted us to believe, that somewhere on the other side of the world right now it was dark and cold. It seemed, just then, that the nights all those years before when I'd had Tommy Rupp by the belt were just a premonition, a practice run. It was possible to believe that the span between then and now, fourteen years with Mitchell, had been nothing but a short, mournful song.

"Two Dollars in the Jukebox" cued up, and Ash groaned as I attempted to guide him in a gentle jitterbug; he knew the steps, but he wouldn't take his eyes off his feet, and after half a dozen bars he pleaded defeat and eased me back into his arms.

"You know, maybe you should've stuck with that Ron guy," he said. "That is, if it's a jitterbugging fool you're wanting."

"No, thanks," I said, inhaling the aroma of his throat. "I've got the fool I want. At least at this moment."

"Let's see," Ash said. "Either you mean I'm a fool at this moment, or you want me at this moment."

"Or both." I ran my thumbs over his forearms, down his damp back, through the loops of his belt. Behind the bar Dub hit a switch and the house lights dimmed until the brightest spot in the room was the old Wurlitzer.

"Okay, you all," he called, "this here's a family place. You want to keep headin' the direction you're headin', you better take it to the house."

"Mm," Ash murmured, slow and whiskey-voiced. "What a good idea."

The moon was a hairsbreadth from full, and rode fat and white over our heads as we walked hand in hand across the highway to the empty field where Ash's pickup sat. My heart felt as overfed as that spring moon, a single beat from brimming over and spilling its contents out over the landscape, drowning us in a torrent of light. I didn't know how to keep what I felt to myself, and at the same time I didn't have the words to offer it up. I'd never been in love, and was surprised by how much it felt like pure, rushing terror.

Ash reached past me to unlock the truck's passenger door, then eased his guitar case in behind the seat. I turned to face him, and he stepped forward and slid his arms around me like our skins were magnetized.

The liquor buzzed, unfamiliar, in my head and made me loose-limbed and bold. I pulled Ash to me and his mouth grabbed mine, forcing my chin back, his hands at my waist lifting me onto the seat. I circled his hips with my legs, working my boot heels into the backs of his knees, feeling the length of him from thigh to belly as he pressed his weight against me.

"There's an old army blanket in the back, I think," he said. "You want to go down to the creek?"

"What creek?"

"There's a branch of Flat Creek runs right across the bottom of this field." I pulled my face up and looked at him, and he smiled, not quite sheepishly. "At least that's what I've heard."

I put my hand in his and followed him down through the short grass, in the moonlight. Before long the grass petered out and we came out onto a stone ridge beneath which the creek tumbled and coursed, brimming almost to its banks after the heavy rain.

"Wow," Ash said, shaking out the blanket and spreading it on the wide, flat rock. "I've never seen it this full before. Most of the time it's not much more than a trickle." He glanced down, read my expression, and grinned. "Or that's how I imagine it, anyhow."

We lay side by side on our backs on the old green blanket. The coolness of the rock seeped through the scratchy wool and into my shoulders and the backs of my thighs. Frogs sang like a crazy choir, and the moon hung so near it seemed that with a single step we could scale its craggy face.

We were quiet a long time, nothing touching but the backs of our hands. The sounds and scents of the final days of March surrounded us: the heavy, moist air, sap in the trees, the steady hum of insects; Ash's blood running in his veins, his heart pumping strong, encased like a gem in his chest but belonging to me. I don't know how I knew that, but I did. It didn't matter, finally, whether or not we said the words, tonight or any other; it felt like he'd spent the past two weeks carving them into my flesh and bone.

He turned over and looked down at me, his eyes in the moonlight two dark pools in a starch-white face. "Lucy Hatch," he said.

"What?"

"Nothing." He smiled. "I just wanted to see what it felt like in my mouth."

"So, what's the verdict? Now that you've had some time to get used to it."

"Sweet," he said, tipping my face to his with one hand. "The sweetest thing I ever tasted." His mouth was tinged with bourbon and every lie he'd ever told.

I sat up and knelt to face him on the blanket and, holding his eyes with mine, undid the buttons on my shirt, bottom to top. I shrugged free of it and let it fall, then reached behind me and unhooked my bra. I would never know, God willing, the full range of ammunition Misty Potter carried in her arsenal, but I'd seen with my own two eyes that her chest was as flat as Kansas.

The moon was so bright it bleached the color out of everything, casting it in the metallic hues of an old negative as I tucked my hair behind my ears and threw my shoulders back, my body arching pale and cool as ivory in the silvered light.

"My Aunt Dove says you have a glory shining in you," I said. "She says you saw the same thing in me." Maybe my heart wasn't on my sleeve, but I had no doubt it was visible, that Ash could read the message plain as day in every liquid beat. I'd told my brother I didn't have the answers, but it wasn't true. I had one, the only one that mattered.

"Come and shine on me, Lucy," Ash said, drawing me down with his warm, sure hands. "Things have been dark for so long."

(sixteen)

I'd seen that darkness in Ash. Every now and then a door would close, a shutter would slam shut, as if caught by an unexpected gale. It never lasted long—sometimes it moved across his features like a shadow, and was gone—but when it did, it was formidable and I learned to let it pass, to stand clear until the light shone again. Ash liked to claim he was a simple man, but the truth was that he was too gifted to be simple. That darkness was the place the music lived in him, and I believe that in fact he would not have had it any other way, that he had made, at some point, his own devil's deal.

We hid out like desperadoes all day Sunday, with the screen door latched and the phone off the hook. I cooked pancakes, and Ash practiced the guitar. We walked the dogs. We drank beer in the porch swing. Sex ran like a secret spring underneath it all, one you dipped your cup into whenever you wanted a taste; it didn't necessarily lead to fruition, every time, but it was constant. When I thought about the two weeks between the night I met Ash and the night I first slept with him, what I remembered was primarily resistance—a sense of forestalling the inevitable, like trying to repel a force field. This was the other side of resistance, then, the eternally unfolding exhilaration of surrender. Sex was a spring, and my cup, as they say, runneth over.

As we were getting into bed that night I leaned over and picked up the Bible on Ash's night table. It looked like the standard child's catechism edition—pebbled-black cover, color illustrations of the Holy Land—but when I flipped to the flyleaf I saw it was inscribed to Francis Eugene Farrell upon his confirmation, nearly forty-five years before.

"This was your father's!" I exclaimed, then felt guilty, like I'd been caught going through a private stash, when Ash rolled over and looked at me.

"It's the only thing I have of his," he said. "I don't even know how I happened to come by it, just that somehow it was with my things when Christa and Bob took me. Divine intervention, I always thought."

"Did you ever know your father?"

"I never did. I was three when he took off, and I can't remember anything."

"You never saw him later? When you were older?" Ash shook his head. "Do you know where he is now?"

"Yeah, I do." He reached across me and touched a fingertip to the cover of the old Bible. "He's in Hilliard Memorial Park, in Dallas. Has been since 1980. I did see the stone one time." He was quiet a minute. "I expected some big reckoning, but it turned out not to be much of a moment."

"How did you manage to find him?"

"Oh, I checked around a little. You'd be surprised how easily most people turn up. I didn't know he'd died, though, when I set out looking."

"You were hoping to meet him, then."

"I was hoping to have a chance to look him in the eye. See what a man looks like who would walk out on a woman and a baby." Ash's voice had dropped until it was barely audible. "Now all I have to do is look in the mirror." Neither of us said anything for a while.

"I thought you told me your wife left you," I said at last.

"My wife divorced me. It wouldn't be fair to say that she was the one who did the leaving."

"Do you miss your girl?"

"Sure. I miss the *idea* of her, you know? Sometimes I try to think what she must be like, and I get to missing all the ways she might have turned out that I'm not there to see."

"Well, it's not too late."

"Trust me. It's too late."

"But it isn't! You could—"

He caught me by the wrist so hard that my fingers lost their hold on the Bible and it landed, splayed open, on the patchwork blanket.

"Stop it, Lucy. It's not open to discussion, all right?" My eyes filled, which I told myself was from his grip on my wrist. He must have thought the same thing, because he let it loose. "I just—I can't talk about this." He turned onto his side, away from me.

I moved up behind him, but there was no reaction, just the rise and fall of his breathing. "Can you at least tell me her name?" I said. "I won't ask you anything else."

He didn't answer me for so long that I was sure he meant not to, and finally I turned in the other direction and yanked the blanket up to my chin and we lay that way for a while, silent but vigilant, the two-inch space between our spines charged with friction. I'd spent most of four-teen years with a man's shoulders squared off at me from the other side of the mattress, though; if Ash thought he could chastise me through silence he had more to learn about me than he'd gambled on.

Finally he sat up and swung his legs over the side of the bed. I heard him open the bureau, and in a minute he came around the bed and sat down on the mattress beside me. There was a small plastic frame in his hand, which he passed to me.

The photo had been taken informally, in an outdoor setting; there were leafy green trees in the background, the roof of some sort of pavilion. It must have been a windy day, and Marlene held her long black hair off her face with one hand, laughing, while her other arm cradled the baby. Fifteen months old or so, I guessed, an ordinary small girl, moon-faced and startled-looking, with tangled brown hair and a mouth stained dark by juice or maybe a Popsicle.

It wasn't hard to see that the picture wasn't really about the child but the mother, her complete, jaw-dropping beauty. The baby seemed incidental, a last-minute prop, like an umbrella or a bouquet of flowers. Still, something in me went out to the girl, in a way that felt more comradely than maternal. Ash said she was fourteen now; maybe she had come to terms with being the plain daughter of two good-looking people, maybe she was clever and quick and had learned to compensate in other ways. Or maybe not. I knew, too well, what it felt like to lie in bed at night scanning the airwaves for some sign, any sign, of an errant father, the thought that if you just turned the dial one more time you might stumble upon his signal, the frequency meant just for you.

"Denise," Ash said. "Her name is Denise." He removed the frame from my hand and set it in the drawer, and climbed back under the covers. He lay on his back for a minute, then rolled over, away from me. Something needed to be said, but I didn't know what it was. I felt haunted by Marlene, even with what I knew had happened later, that she was crazy, impossible to live with, that she wasn't even the love of his life. I felt cowed by her and her untouchable beauty, perfectly preserved and eternal, tucked inside a drawer in a cheap plastic frame, like a sort of secret shrine. But the moment passed, and when I turned to

Ash and said his name he was asleep, or pretending to be, and I understood that that drawer, briefly opened, now was closed, that we weren't
to speak of it again.

W hen my shift at the shop ended on Monday, I walked
across the street to Mrs. Tanner's. Ash and Isaac were
working inside, but the front door was open. I stepped up
and tapped my knuckles against the door frame, and Isaac glanced up
from the shelf they were installing in the living room and said, "Hey,"
and Ash looked over his shoulder and smiled to see me. Something
exceptional must have been in my face, because he pushed his hair off
his forehead and said quickly, "What's up?"

"Sorry to interrupt. Have you got a second?"

He picked up a tall chrome thermos and we went out into the yard.
Under the tulip tree he twisted open the thermos and poured a cup of
water and gulped it, then another. It was a hot day, in the nineties. He
watched me over the rim of the cup. "Say something, Lucy, you're scaring me."

"I was just thinking it might be a good idea if I took the night off
tonight. Slept at my own place."

"Any special reason?" He stared into the empty thermos cup, his
voice measured, careful.

"Bailey and I are driving down to Morseville in the morning. To the
farm."

Ash looked up. "I didn't know that, did I? Did you tell me and I
forgot?"

"I'm not sure I ever named the day." I was pretty sure, in fact, that I
hadn't, denial being my instinctive response any time the subject happened to cross my mind.

"Well, is that what you want to do?" he asked finally. "Spend the

night by yourself?" He watched my face with a keenness that suggested
I shouldn't even think about lying to him, and I didn't.

"No," I said. "It just seems like I should."

"Why?"

"Because. It isn't right, is it? Climbing out of your bed to go and clear
out my dead husband's things?"

Ash wiped his mouth with the back of his hand, not quite disguising
a smile. "Who are you trying to fool, Lucy?" he said. "God? I don't think
it works that way."

"You don't know how it works."

"Maybe not, but I bet God's got better eyes than you give Him credit
for. More sympathy, too, for us poor humans. Don't forget, He made us
in His image." I just shook my head.

He was quiet for a minute, considering. "You know, Steve Forbert
wrote this really great song. Every verse tells a story, about the way
something used to be—childhood, love, even the planet—and every
verse ends, 'I blinked once and it was gone.' Do you realize that that's
all it would take to lose this, you and me? If either one of us
blinked . . ."

Ash emptied the last of the thermos onto the grass. "Mitchell died,"
he said. "And now you're here. And so am I. With each other. I have a
hard time believing God disapproves of that."

I gazed at him, and couldn't speak. I hadn't come to Ash for a declara-
tion, but it should not have surprised me that I ended up with more than
I counted on. From the day I found those pink roses on the seat of my
truck, he'd been paving the way with offerings, manifest and otherwise.

He took a step forward and circled me with his arms. "Anyway," he
said into my hair, "you've been having nonstop, roof-raising sex with
me for the past week already. You think God didn't sit up and notice
that? All those times you hollered out His name?" I popped his shirtfront with my fist, and he laughed.

"We're leaving at seven," I warned him. "I have to get up really, really early."

"I'll make your coffee."

I tucked my face for a moment into the side of his neck, just a quick hit before I'd be on my way. "Why are you doing this?" I whispered, and Ash raised his head and looked at me.

"Ah, Lucy. You really have to ask me that?"

I came out of the bathroom that night in one of my cotton night-gowns, pretending not to notice Ash's perplexed expression as I slipped under the sheet and then reached behind me and snapped off the light. Beneath the soft tick of the ceiling fan the room seemed to pulse with things unsaid.

"Damn," he said finally. "The end of an era."

"Not the end," I protested. "Just—not tonight."

"You could have just said something, Lucy. I'm not some fiend who can't be reasoned with, who loses his head the minute he sees bare flesh."

I turned onto my side and looked at him in the patch of light that came through the octagonal window over the bed. "To tell you the truth, you're not the one I'm worried about."

We lay quietly awhile, listening to the house settle into its nighttime cadence. "You mind if I ask you something?" he said finally. "About you and Mitchell."

"Okay."

"I'm just wondering, knowing you the way I've come to, how you managed living with him so long without more, um, attention. I mean, didn't it ever occur to you, all those years, what you were missing?"

I propped myself on one elbow and gazed at Ash's profile in the swath of light from the night sky. I remembered being annoyed with Peggy, with Geneva, even with Dove for hinting that sexual attraction was something purely ocular, and yet I couldn't deny that something in me turned, with absolute resolution, every time I looked at Ash, and that it had not with Mitchell, in ways that didn't, in the end, seem to have to do with anything as cut-and-dried as handsomeness. Mitchell had been a good-looking man, broad-backed, windburned, without a lick of vanity. Ash's features were both finer and more animated; you knew at a glance that he was more intrepid, a liver of life. I suppose that, in the end, was the difference, that Mitchell, even before he died, had retreated into stillness and duty and modest expectation, and that Ash was out there, would always be out there, grinning and mixing it up, his arms open wide. The biggest surprise was how motion, not suspension, turned out to be what I was drawn to, the country in which I had found myself an ally.

"I didn't know," I answered, and curled into Ash's side. He lifted his chin an inch and looked at me like he suspected me of pulling his leg. "Okay, here's an illustration," I said. "Imagine you'd never had Willie B.'s pork ribs. How could you miss something you never knew existed?"

"But let's—hm." Ash smiled, warming to the topic. "I'm assuming, at some point, you actually *had* pork ribs. Not Willie B.'s, but some kind. Kinda tough, kinda chewy, kinda flavorless, but pork ribs, just the same." He glanced over at me, and I nodded that I was following him. "Wouldn't you eventually say to yourself, 'There's got to be some pork ribs, somewhere, that taste better than these?' "

"I should've known better than to get into this discussion with you," I said. "The man who's sampled more pork ribs than anyone on the planet."

"Only because all the time I was looking for something as good as Willie's."

I pressed my face against his neck. "That first night we danced together, at the Round-Up? You smelled so, so—familiar to me, and so right, and I got light-headed for a minute and thought it was Willie's sauce I was smelling. I was afraid I wouldn't ever get enough."

"Have you? Had enough?"

"Oh, no," I said. "I feel like I've hardly even started."

He put both his arms around me, and although I stiffened it was a purely reasoned response, not a visceral one; underneath my nightgown everything went loose and liquid, of its own accord. A year ago, six months, even two, would I have imagined having so little command over my own body, that someone might be able to reach into me and switch on my desire as easily as turning a key? It occurred to me with something like panic that Ash had a key but I did not, that he could start me up anytime he chose, while I had no defense against the combined pull of our appetites but a thin wrap of flowered cotton, the masquerade of a fool.

"Turn over," Ash said. "Let me rub your back." I rolled gratefully onto my stomach. "It'd work a lot better without this," he said, tugging at the hem of my gown, and so I sat up and shrugged it over my head and dropped it next to the bed.

I gave Ash a look over my shoulder, stretching out on top of the sheet. "Don't you go getting any ideas."

"Tell you what. I promise not to do anything you don't beg me to."

"Deal," I murmured, burying my face in the pillow as his fingers worked themselves into the hollow of my hips and then inched their way up my spine, remembering, too late, that what I wanted barely mattered, that Ash was the one with the key.

I dozed awhile—the last thing I recall is Ash reasoning, in a perfectly clinical tone, that an orgasm would help me sleep—then woke around three o'clock with a cold start, the feeling of icy fingers around my neck, though in fact Ash's arm and leg were thrown across me, warm and heavy with unconsciousness. His presence, though, was somehow muted, dominated by some other being that seemed to crouch in the corners, breathing its chilly breath, watching me with wide, unblinking eyes. My heart was banging so hard I was sure Ash would wake, and I stole out of bed and into my nightgown.

I turned on every light in the kitchen, and put on water for tea. An old copy of *Guitar Player* magazine was on the table, and I sat and stared at an article on the new wave of flamenco until my tea got cold. The lights helped but did not entirely quench the sense of being scrutinized, and after a while I got up and rinsed out my cup and crept back to bed. Ash mumbled something in his sleep as I slid back under the sheet and burrowed into his side, wishing I could steal his heat, his sureness, his steady-beating heart that seemed never to deviate from its course but tunneled blindly, singularly, forward. He stirred and even hardened slightly under my touch, but when I slung my leg over his he tossed his head like a petulant child and slipped back into the depths of his dreams. Only by fitting myself against his back and deliberately matching my pulse to his was I able to calm myself enough to let my mind float, if not exactly free, then somewhere above what I knew was waiting for me beyond that bed. This way, I made it until five-thirty.

I took a shower and put on jeans and an old loose-fitting shirt, and by that time Ash was up and rattling around in the kitchen. It wasn't yet light out, and under the ceiling fixture's artificially cheerful glare he looked like a sleepwalker, shuffling between the sink and the pantry in his Levi's and bare feet, his hair sticking out in two or three errant directions as he sifted coffee grounds into a paper filter and filled the reservoir from the tap. He gave me a bleary half smile, his jaw bristled with stubble, and I thought what I felt then would literally tear me in two, that nothing, not even the lifelong exile of my family, was worth forfeiting the haven I felt here, in Ash's kitchen, in the orb of his light.

"You should eat something," he said as I sat down at the table, which almost made me smile.

"Since when are you worried about breakfast?"

"You've got a long day ahead of you," was all he said, and my heart started to race again. "I could make you some eggs," he offered, but I shook my head. He pulled out a chair and sat down beside me and held my hand until the coffee was ready, and then he poured two cups and sat down and picked up my hand again. There didn't seem to be anything to say; even Hallmark would have been stumped trying to come up with an appropriate sentiment. We drank our coffee and watched the sky turn pale outside the window, and then we heard Bailey's truck coming up the road.

I got to my feet and set my coffee cup in the sink, and I was so dizzy for a second that I had to hold on to the countertop until it passed. I thought if Ash saw how frightened I was, if he knew without a doubt the blackness I was capable of, he would push me out the front door and lock it behind me.

I went to the door and waved at Bailey to let him know I'd be right out. I found my purse and a sweater, and then stood for a minute with Ash in the dark hall, just inside the screen. Out in the yard the dually's engine chugged like a stallion pawing the dust, impatient to be let out of the chute.

Ash's hand gathered my hair, arranging and rearranging it, as if he was searching for some style he might find more suitable.

"Y'all plan to be back by suppertime?" he asked, and I nodded. "Okay. You have my pager number. You call if anything . . . If there's anything you need. Even if you just feel like checking in."

"I'm not sure the phone down there's still working."

"Your brother has a mobile phone, doesn't he? Use that if you need to. Promise me."

"Okay."

"I'll be thinking of you every minute. Don't you doubt it."

"No."

"Nothing can hurt you there, Lucy. Bailey won't let it, and neither will I."

We stepped through the front door, onto the porch, and I looked at Ash in the pearl-gray dawn, streaks of red like brushfire in the east. I knew, but couldn't tell him, that I was on my own here, that try as we might to convince ourselves otherwise, there are some dances we're meant to do alone. Even knowing how he felt—and I did know, in the way that someone who's been color-blind all her life might suddenly recognize purple or orange, without being told—there were things from which it was not enough to shelter me. He kissed me, and I lay my hand on his cheek and the other at his waist and committed it all to memory, the grainy sandpaper of his face under my fingers, the taut crease where his stomach met his jeans, the way he tasted of coffee and sleep, his face rosy in the early light. "I . . ." he began, then snapped his mouth shut, and smiled. "Never mind," he said. "It'll hold till tonight."

We went down the steps into the yard, and Ash reached out and opened the dually's passenger door. Bailey sat behind the wheel sipping a travel mug of coffee and listening to the stock-market report on the radio as I climbed up. He swung his head our way and he and Ash nodded at each other, but the rancor I might have expected to flare between them in that brief exchange was absent, though maybe it wasn't so much deliberate than a result of the circumstances and the early hour. I squeezed Ash's hand. I had a rare childhood recollection, of having the school bus pull up in front of our house on the first day of the second grade, and how, in spite of the fact that I knew the driver and most of the other kids, that I already knew my school and even my teacher, I had not wanted to let go of my mama's hand, how in that last, uncertain moment I'd clung to the sweetest refuge I had.

"Y'all plan to be back by suppertime?" Ash said to Bailey, and I didn't protest that he'd already asked me the same thing.

"Oh, sure," Bailey said, fitting his mug into the dashboard cup holder. "This shouldn't take more than a few hours, tops. That, plus an hour either way . . ."

"We have to go by the cemetery," I said, and felt both Bailey's and Ash's eyes land, caught short, on me. Then Bailey nodded and looked out the windshield, and Ash let go of my hand. I felt the surrender in the gesture, like he was relinquishing me to Mitchell, to everything my life had been before, and though I knew it was inevitable, it froze me to the bone.

"Be careful," he said, as much, I thought, to Bailey as to me, and shut the door and then stepped back onto the porch, where he stood with his arms folded over his chest in the cool dawn air. Though I raised my hand as Bailey turned the truck in the yard, Ash didn't return the wave.

(seventeen)

I don't know whether Bailey was mindful of the hour or my pricked-up nerves, but we barely spoke on the hour's drive south-west into Leola County. It was a week past the flooding rains, the landscape as lush and green as I'd ever seen it, and I wondered suddenly, with an unease that had once been as familiar to me as my own breathing, whether all that rain had affected the crops, if the corn had taken a beating, if they'd been able to get the sorghum in. Through some arrangement I didn't know the details of, Sam Gill had contracted to lease two hundred of our acres that adjoined his in order to keep them in production until after the sale and the new owners took over. He was working the cattle, too, in addition to his own; Sam had hired an extra hand to manage the load. This had all been told to me over the course of the past several weeks and, I realized now, I had deflected it as neatly as a tennis player returns a backhand, heedless of the fact that, without my guard up, the volley was going to come back and wallop me.

We turned off the main highway onto the county road, and drove for a minute along the fields, the Gill place, that fronted the blacktop. "Corn's early," I said, startled by the way this sounded coming out of my mouth, simultaneously foreign and familiar, and Bailey grunted and said, "Sam knows what he's doing." I stared at him, wondering how he could say this with such authority, and it became clear to me in a way it hadn't quite been before that Bailey and, to a lesser degree, Kit, had handled the affairs of my widowhood so smoothly for the last two months that I hadn't even had cause to notice, that there had been nothing to distract me from what seemed now to have been my single-minded aim, to get myself tangled up, bodily and otherwise, with Ash Farrell.

Bailey slowed and put on his blinker, and we turned up the half-mile drive to the house, bouncing over the cattle guard, the finger of Sims Creek that ran beneath. I gazed at the new green corn, ankle-high, and thought of all the years Mitchell had prostrated himself to the idols of drainage and drought, too little rain or too much. It seemed to me that how you felt about farming depended upon how willingly you accepted incertitude, how you tilled the soil and plowed the seeds under and then sat back and waited to see if the gods would smile on you or curse your name, and that maybe what had seemed like Mitchell's plodding nature had in fact been a reservoir of patience, an endless loop of hope. It amazed me now that I ever thought I'd have the strength to match him, that, for half our marriage, at least, I'd done a pretty good bluff at succeeding.

When I met Mitchell I'd thought farming was romantic, which probably helped to put a bit of sheen on such a somber man. That presumption, though, had vanished almost by the time the ink on the marriage license was dry, but I made do. In fact, the less romantic the life turned out to be, as far as I was concerned, the better. I liked getting up in the middle of the night when the calves were birthing, liked taking the pickup into the fields to check the crops after a storm, liked sitting around listening to the men talk about pesticides and new strains of corn and who was mortgaged up to his eyeballs and who owned his place free and clear. There wasn't much time for bullshit on a farm, and I liked the way it forced me to be levelheaded, to meet every day at dawn with a firm sense of the earth and my place on it. That changed, over the years, got a little frayed around the edges as the seasons passed, different only in the whims of weather, as around me other wives took town jobs, couples split up, children moved away, farms changed hands or sold out to corporations, as I lay in bed night after night listening to Mitchell's measured breathing, the sleep of the hardworking and just.

For a long time I believed that a baby would change things, that it would quiet the voices I felt clamoring in me, that it would tamp down my bursts of what Mitchell called, in his diplomatic way, "impetuosity." A baby would have filled in the blanks, have knotted together the two loose ends, Mitchell steadfast and good, and me, restless, ungrateful, dependent upon something outside my own skin to redeem me. So convinced was I of this, in fact, that I came to believe I could manage it just by wishing it so; it took a few years to come clear that what was missing between Mitchell and me was more than just the spaces in our silence at the supper table, the way he clung to his edge of the mattress and I to mine. There was a spot along our back fence where, no matter how well we fertilized or what we planted, nothing would grow. That, I imagined, was the lay of my interior landscape, stony and barren, sloughing off all prospects. I filed it away as another of my failings, for the day I fully expected Mitchell to announce he'd been keeping score.

He hadn't, of course; it was not his way to stir the pot, only to bear up, to go along, and then he'd died, taking all the things he'd never said with him, including if he loved me, whether or not he ever had. The things he claimed to have been drawn to when he met me—pioneer-sounding things like "mettle" and "spunk"—were in fact the things that fourteen years of life with him had squeezed out of me, so gradually I'd barely noticed, like a slow-leaking faucet, each drop ebbing before the next one forms. What galled me was how complicit I'd been in this process, how, as the house came into sight at the end of the road, flanked by the barns on either side, I could not allow myself, in fairness, to blame it on Mitchell, barely two months dead. He had never struck me, never raised his voice, never strayed; had never expected a thing from me but duty, and so I'd never expected a thing from myself. It might have been true, as Dove said, that Mitchell had put out my light, but the truth of it was that I'd done nothing of my own to prevent that.

The house looked exactly as I remembered, and I realized I'd thought of it, when I'd thought of it at all, as beginning to crumble, to peel and warp and go to seed, a disintegration more fitting to twenty years' neglect than a couple of months. Mitchell had painted both house and barns the spring before, and under the overcast sky, against the backdrop of all that green, the paint looked fresh, even wet. Bailey pulled into the yard and shut off the engine, and I concentrated on breathing in and out, on being, as one of the little carved stones in Dove's garden said, in the moment, although I had to wonder how the concept applied when the moment was one you wanted only to escape.

We sat looking at the house for a while, like we expected the door to open and some welcoming committee to burst forth and sweep us inside, and then Bailey cleared his throat and said, "I guess we'd better get to it."

The scent of the place knocked me back a step, not in that strange, stale way of familiar places that have been closed off, but in the way, even after two months of standing unoccupied, I could separate and identify its individual odors: furniture polish, the starch in the living room curtains, leather from the boots stored in the mudroom, even a hint of the sausage links Mitchell had eaten every morning without fail for his breakfast, scorched black in a skillet. I hung back, and Bailey, who was behind me, reached for my arm, and that was when I remembered that the hand that had gripped mine with such assurance at the steps of the school bus on the first day of second grade had not been my mama's at all, but my brother's, Bailey's, my guardian, my champion.

Bailey stepped around in front of me and got me by the shoulders.

"Listen to me, Lucy," he said. "Whatever happens here today, happens, okay? Don't feel like you have to put a big happy face on it for me. If you get sad, if you get scared, you just go ahead. I'm here to get you through it."

"I'm sad," I said. "I'm scared."

"Well, okay." He led me into the kitchen and pulled out a chair at the table, the same chair, I remembered, to which Mary Gill had led me just after I'd learned the news. Someone had taken up the checkered tablecloth, and the surface of the wood looked bald under the unadorned ceiling light. I longed for a swallow of the bourbon Mary'd fed me that morning, but it was long gone, spilled into the dirt out front when I'd stumbled off the porch and snapped my wrist.

"You tell me, how do you want to do this?" Bailey asked. "Ease into it slow, or get it over with as fast as possible?"

"F-f-fast."

It was early April, but the kitchen had the damp, chilly feel of a place that's been shut up for too many cold nights. Bailey went outside and carried in a stack of torn-down packing crates, and set to work assembling them with strapping tape while I opened and closed the cabinets. The sight of the contents made me feel exhausted, and I sank down again at the table. "Don't touch anything," Bailey said, going out and then coming in again with an armload of old newspapers. "You tell me what to pack."

The twelve place settings of Spode china that had belonged to Mama's mama's mama were in the chest in the dining room, and I managed to convince Bailey that I was steady enough to sit at the table and wrap the cups and saucers and nest them in the packing crates, that

that job was a lot safer, in fact, than my ransacking cupboards and drawers, laying myself open to an ambush that might come from something as innocuous as a trivet or a potato masher.

"Talk to me," I called to Bailey, and obligingly he launched into a story about his and Geneva's anniversary dinner at an oyster bar in Marshall, the comedy of errors that had ensued. I listened attentively, in fact with all my concentration, but the words seemed to rattle around in my head like dice in a cup and when, evidently, he asked me a question that I didn't answer, he came into the doorway and said, "Lucy? Why's it so dark in here?" and yanked back the heavy damask drapes, exposing the view from the front porch down through the pasture to the road, and I burst into tears.

"Oh, shit," he muttered, "I'm sorry."

I got up and went to the window. Bales of hay lined the fence; cows, the Anguses Mitchell had bred since he was a boy in 4-H, dotted the pasture, as bucolic as a folk painting. This, more than anything mortal, was what Mitchell had loved, and even though the fields that had been brown in February were green and the hundred-pound calves now weighed three, it seemed as if the scene was one of suspended animation, awaiting his return. My own presence here seemed fleeting, inconsequential; I had cooked the breakfast, done the laundry, swept the floors. To put it plainly, I had failed: to provide an heir, to be suitably beholden. To leave my mark.

"You know what I really hate?" I said, turning from the window. Bailey shook his head. "I hate this screwed-up notion I've got, because of Mama, about God and Jesus and all that business. That we're punished or rewarded for our, our holiness, whatever that is, and that everything that happens we bring on ourselves, that we've somehow earned it. How did Mitchell deserve to die, to lose all this? I can't get my mind around it. It doesn't make any sense."

"I'm not sure it's supposed to make sense," Bailey said. "I think part of having faith is that you have to trust in things you can't understand."

"He should be here," I said. "Maybe I shouldn't be, maybe I never should have been. But Mitchell should. This was his."

Bailey nodded his head. "Maybe so. But that's not what's really on your mind, is it? You're afraid God's going to smite you for falling in love with Ash."

There was something so matter-of-fact in the way he said it that it took a minute for the weight of Bailey's words to settle in me; and, it was true, as soon as they did, I started waiting for the sky to fall, for the ground to open up and swallow me.

"I . . ..Bailey, sometimes I wake up at night and look at Ash and I wonder, Did Mitchell have to die for this? Did I bring it on, somehow, so that Ash and I could be together? What kind of reward do you think God has for someone who would do something like that, something so greedy and self-serving? Do you think there's a place in heaven for a person like that?"

We turned together to the window at the sound of a car coming up the drive. "Oh, no. Who can that be?" I wiped my eyes on my shirt cuff.

"Don't know," Bailey mused, stepping up alongside me as a white Pontiac came into view. "Maybe the folks from the auction house."

The car rocked to a stop and the driver's door swung open. "Lord, it's Mary Gill."

I opened the front door and met her on the porch, and for once was grateful for Mary's overwrought enthusiasm, the way she hurled herself at you and crushed you in an embrace, like every meeting was poignant and final, even if you just happened to run into her in the frozen-foods aisle at the grocery store. It gave me a minute to hide my face, to come up with some arrangement of my features that would seem suitably grievous, to hope that the wetness in my eyes would be interpreted as mourning and not fear at God's retribution. She smelled exactly as she always had, like early morning in a pastry shop, yeast rising, sweet glaze bubbling on the stove.

"Lucy, Lucy," she crooned into my hair, like we were long-ago lovers and not former neighbors whose circumstances had changed. She pushed me away then and looked at me down the length of her plump white arms. The last time I recalled seeing Mary Gill, Dr. Spikes was explaining to me, as much as propriety would allow, the circumstances of Mitchell's accident, and I was laughing hysterically, being put to bed with a big white pill. Surely there had been some encounter since then, at the funeral or the house afterward, but I didn't remember it.

"Law, you're so skinny!" she exclaimed, shaking her head with its three or four substantial chins. "Not that you had a pound to spare beforehand, but now you're nothin' but bones." She narrowed her watery gaze and focused on me. "How are you, sweetheart? Gettin' along okay?"

And with that, I made a concerted decision; I put Ash away. I couldn't hold him in my head in this place, not and give the occasion the attention it demanded, not when every remark seemed a double entendre, every question hooded with meaning. No matter what Mitchell and I had, or had not, been to one another, I owed him my regard here, today, in what had been his domain. Ash, and God, would catch up with me later.

Bailey came to the door and I turned to introduce him to Mary, though they claimed to recall meeting here the night after the funeral, over Mary's raisin-and-shredded-carrot salad. He held open the screen door as Mary presented a wicker basket covered in a tea towel, saying, "I knew you all was comin' up this mornin' and thought you might care for a bit of refreshment," and we moved into the front hall and all three proceeded together to the kitchen.

"Oh, my," Mary said, setting her basket on the table and raising a hand to her breast. "I just . . . I ain't set foot in this house since you left, Lucy, I just couldn't. It's so . . ." Her blue eyes wobbled with tears.

I wasn't unsympathetic; I knew how this must feel to her. And yet, in a way, Mary's anguish for the loss of us, her neighbors the Brewards, had the effect of removing me from my own feelings about the scene. I had no sense of myself or how I had been in that house, no ghostly image of myself clipping recipes, polishing the glassware, waiting waiting waiting for Mitchell to come back through the door as he'd done with maddening punctuality until the day, finally, he hadn't. Mitchell, I knew, was still here, floating around someplace, waiting to be reckoned with, but Lucy Breward was gone.

"Say, what have we got here?" Bailey exclaimed, peeling back the tea towel to peek into the basket. "Sure smells terrific!"

"Aw, just a loaf of my cinnamon-date bread," Mary said, sniffling a little but composing herself. "Y'all got any coffee?" She went over to the pantry, and Bailey cut his eyes at me. I started to say I didn't think we had, but she'd found a can of Folgers, and the Mr. Coffee was sitting there big as life on the countertop. She made herself right at home.

Mary and Bailey fell into a discussion of the details of the auction, this whim, Mary called it, of Sam's that he might actually bid on and win those two hundred acres to call his own. I sliced the bread with a serrated knife and set out some of the little ivy-trimmed plates we'd bought at an outlet store the first year we were married, and rinsed three china cups under the hot-water tap. None of this stirred anything in me other than the remotest sense of déjà vu, and after a few minutes nibbling bread and sipping coffee I began to be relieved by Mary's presence, for her idle chatter threaded through Bailey's until it wove a kind of web that seemed to catch and hold me, that let my heart keep beating and my hands keep moving.

"Let's see Mama's list," I said to Bailey. He cocked an eyebrow at me. "Come on, I know she gave you one. It's not like her to miss a trick."

He handed over a folded sheet of stationery, the list neatly annotated in Mama's Palmer Method hand. Family photos, Spode china, silver cake plate . . . "Silver cake plate!" I declared. "Why, she claimed she'd given that plate to me!" I rattled around under the counter until I located it and set it ringing on the tabletop, causing Mary to arch an eyebrow and Bailey to smile; I suppose he thought that so long as I was annoyed with Mama I must be all right.

I located the box of photographs Mama wanted in the hall closet, and took it off the shelf and set it on the floor. Lifting the lid, I was momentarily startled to see Mitchell's and my wedding portrait, eight by ten in a silver Carr's frame, and a tiny fissure of discomfort ran through me at the sight of it, of our two faces side by side, looking like any other couple on their wedding day, overdressed and hopeful, slightly dazed. Gazing at my own face, so young and untested, I noted that everything about me seemed restrained: the plain lines of my gown, my simple French twist, the small cluster of, naturally, pink roses I held in my fist. There had been no engagement ring—we'd put a down payment on a pickup instead—but on the fourth finger of my left hand you could see the new gold band, thin as a wire. It took me months to get used to the feel of it on my finger, although in truth it was almost weightless. Mitchell looked as he'd always looked to me, sturdy as a battleship, more handsome than he knew, his hair for once properly cut so that white sidewalls showed at his temples, the rest of him ruddy and abashed-looking, unaccustomed as he was to being the center of attention. I looked and looked but, try as I might, I could not come up with any sense of us as a couple; our faces might as well have been cut out of separate photos and glued into the frame.

What I remembered, better than the wedding, was how the picture came to be in the box in the first place. A few months shy of a decade married, I'd spent all afternoon on a special chicken dish, something with mushrooms and tarragon, different from our usual Tuesday-night fryer, for no special reason other than that it seemed a harmless enough way of spreading my wings. When I put it in front of Mitchell at supper that evening he'd eyed it dubiously for a second or two, then dug in and polished it off without comment, favorable or otherwise. When, finally, clearing the table, I asked him what he'd thought, he'd said only, "Old way's better," and headed out the back door to check the barns before dark.

Well. Anyone who's been married any length of time will know what I'm talking about. Sometimes it's nothing you can name or explain, sometimes the most benign of acts or words. That brief phrase was it for me. I stormed into the living room—pointless, since there was no one to witness it—and took our wedding portrait off the mantel, where it had presided like a holy relic for nine and a half years, and put it in the box in the closet. If Mitchell noticed, he never said so. Probably he didn't, which says something in and of itself. It amazed me now that this had been my idea of rebellion, that it had felt at the time like such a tempestuous act. I hadn't looked at the picture since. Well, maybe Mama would want it, to remind her of the days before her sweet Lucy fell into Satan's hands.

I put the lid back on the box and set it next to the door, and returned to the list. Aunt Min's antimacassars, which were draped over the arms of the living room sofa. Great-granddaddy Munroe's carriage lantern, which had rested for fourteen years on the mantel, nine and a half of them alongside that wedding picture. I gathered the stuff quickly and quietly, like a thief, looking neither to the left or the right, until, finally, there was only one item left on the list: the Munroe family Bible, the whole history of my mama's people lined out in its centerfold like the tenth chapter of Genesis, Ham begat Cush begat Seba, sitting no doubt where it always had, on top of what had once been my bureau, in what had once been my and Mitchell's bedroom, upstairs.

I went and stood in the kitchen doorway. "I don't know," Bailey was saying, "even with all that rain last week it won't be . . ." His voice trailed off, spying me. Together he and Mary, or maybe just Mary, had polished off half the cinnamon-date bread.

"All that's left is Mama's Bible," I said. "I'm going upstairs."

"You don't want to do that by yourself, Lucy," Mary said, starting to push up from the table.

"No, but I do," I said quickly, startling her with her behind halfway off the kitchen chair. "You can come up in a minute and help me, okay? Just let me go up first, alone."

There was dust on the banister, notable in that, when people travel up and down stairs every day, the rail stays more or less clean from the constant tracking of hands. How many times every day had I traveled those stairs in my numb, mindless way, carrying dirty laundry down and clean up, lugging the vacuum, the mop and bucket, my numb, mindless self? Looking back, my life then seems like one long stand against the outdoors, against mud and grass and shit and blood, and that it's no wonder Mitchell and I were fundamentally at odds, his job being to bring it in and mine being to chase it out again. The truly peculiar thing was, I do not remember hating that. I remember only that I didn't object. I remember performing the functions but not being engaged. Looking back, it felt like suspension: always waiting for the next thing.

The big bedroom, the one we'd shared all our married life, was at the end of the hallway. The door was closed, which it had never been a single time that I could remember in all the years I'd lived here, and that rattled me so that I found myself hesitating with my hand on the knob, trying to calm my knocking heart. Finally I turned the knob and threw open the door, leaning back slightly from the jamb like I'd seen TV cops do when they're busting a crack house, in case, I guess, a crazed junkie stood on the other side with a shiv up his sleeve.

There was no junkie, though, no monster, no ghost. Only a bedroom, known yet dreamlike in its details, the rose-patterned wallpaper, the bulky maple furniture, the blue quilt appliqued with tulips that had belonged to some ancestor of Mitchell and whose story had died with him. The curtains, too, were closed, and I went over and jerked them back and let in a flood of morning light. From up here you could see straight between the two barns and over them, toward the back of the property. Mitchell had liked the room because it faced east, so that the sun's first rays crested the sash every morning and roused him, calling him outside, to the land.

I stepped over and opened one of the two closets, although I knew without looking what was inside: three pairs of what Mitchell called "church pants," one blazer, one sports coat with too-wide lapels, a dozen Arrow shirts, and a rotating metal tree of neckties; a single pair of brown brogans, polished every Sunday after church and replaced till the following week. Mitchell's closet had nothing to do with Mitchell's workaday life, which was about denim and leather and dirt and stink, stacks of overalls stored on top of the dryer, high-topped boots that never left the mudroom, thick socks and no-nonsense Jockey shorts in pairs by the dozens. One of the things that had at first amazed me about living alone was that it was possible to go more than twenty-four hours without running a washing machine.

I sat down on the bed; the mattress gave only slightly under my weight, and I seemed to be positioning myself gingerly, as if I didn't want to leave an impression. It was impossible not to think about sex, not to dip a teasing toe into that pool. All the time I'd been married, I'd been in and out of this room probably thirty times a day, and I can say in truth that the action had sexual connotations virtually never. Not even at the end of the day, not even on the rare occasions that Mitchell undressed in front of me, stripping down to his long johns in winter, Jockeys in summer, had I entertained the possibility, so that the times it did happen had the effect of sneaking up and blind-siding me, which usually meant it was over almost before I'd known it was starting.

I'd dated plenty in high school, and Tommy Rupp and I had gotten far enough in the backseat of his Firebird before he finally became convinced, really convinced, that I was saving myself for my future husband, as Jesus had instructed me to do. I knew what arousal was. My mistake was in believing what I'd always been told: that marriage equaled attraction, that you gave your pledge to a man and your heart and your body followed.

And so I'd lost my virginity in this bed, on my wedding night, to my husband, the way Jesus intended, although Jesus had forgotten to warn me beforehand how much it would hurt. Jesus had also failed to provide Mitchell with much in the way of expertise or experience, and so, I think, the awkwardness of that initial encounter, the difficult first penetration and the subsequent searing pain, the seeming buckets of blood that had me swaddled in Kotex for the next five days, had by morning's light daubed a kind of permanent stain upon our union, taking on, over the years, the slightly mottled hue of failure upon failure.

I wondered now if Mitchell had ever hoped for more, if he'd longed for some way we might connect, ring the big bell, see stars. I wondered how he'd have reacted if I'd stood up and voiced demands, if I'd gone in for cut-out panties or X-rated movies in an attempt to light a fire under the two of us. I suspect it would have embarrassed him, but part of me hoped to run across some evidence of a secret life in him, if only a stack of *Playboys* in a dresser drawer. The real shock is that I was able to recognize my own desires when I finally ran headlong into them, fourteen years later. In Ash's words, things had been dark for so long.

There was a stack of neatly folded clothing on top of one of the bureaus, which caught my eye in that I knew it hadn't been placed there by me, it not being my habit, that of the fastidious farmwife, to leave things not put away. I stepped over and lay my hand on top of the stack: T-shirts, a mix of mine and Mitchell's, mostly dark or bright colors.

I stood a minute and struggled with my memory, dug and prodded and worried all the nooks and crevices, until I realized, more than actually remembered, that these things must have been in the washer at the time of the accident, that hours or maybe even days later someone,

Aunt Dove or Mary Gill or some other of the neighbor ladies, must have come along and found them molded in a damp ring to the agitator, and run them through again and finally plucked them out and popped them into the dryer and then folded them and brought them upstairs.

The very fact of them sitting there—a chore, undone, waiting to be performed—made something old and primitive start up in me, something I thought I'd left behind. That the rhythm of this place still lay here, beneath the surface, waiting for some hand to resurrect it, brought my heart to my throat. Soon enough—within days—this room would be empty, the furnishings dragged onto the lawn, if the weather held, and perused, considered, haggled over; as would the house itself, the barns, the fields, the tender shoots of green sorghum, the sleepy, mild-mannered cows. Mitchell had died, sending everything in his realm careening off on its own, like a thousand tiny, itinerant planets, into the world. Everything here had a new life waiting, beating like a secret heart.

Idly, without being conscious of it, I began to separate the folded laundry into two piles, Mitchell's and mine. Mitchell's pile was both more substantial and more subdued; he preferred browns and navies, whereas my own shirts tended to be bright pink or acid green, often with slogans, a quirk I supposed I'd picked up from Dove.

A shirt tumbled from the stack, and I bent and retrieved it and shook it out. It had a cartoon image on a lipstick-red background of a pigtailed woman in coveralls with a pitchfork in one hand and a spotted cow at her side. "Farm Goddess," it read in black script letters. Mitchell had given it to me the previous spring, right after calving season; I remembered the look on his face as I'd unwrapped the package, lifting the shirt out of the folds of tissue paper and holding it up, how I'd laughed in surprise at this rare display of levity, and how, in response to my laughter, his whole face had, for a minute, lost its perpetual careworn look, a look that took its cues from the fields and the skies, and gone radiant with pleasure and pride.

And, just like that, Mitchell was there. I wasn't scared or even surprised; it felt more like something I'd been hunting for, a last, elusive item on Mama's list, without which I couldn't leave. The Mitchell I'd manufactured for myself these two months of my widowhood, the one I'd cursed and blamed, seemed now as flat and one-dimensional as the cartoon Farm Goddess on the shirt, and it occurred to me that I had created that image to suit my own ends, a constant litany of all the ways he'd failed me. Clutching the shirt in my fist, I could see his face in my mind's eye plain as day, the way, through that small act of silliness, he'd purely lit up the room: vivid, imperfect, real. Who knew where we'd have been if Mitchell had laughed more, if sex had worked, if we'd had a child? If he hadn't died? Standing beside what used to be my marriage bed, I liked to think I'd have gone another forty years with grace and humor, sweeping up, scrubbing out the muck, doing and doing as the seasons slid from one to the next and the earth staunchly circled the sun. I hoped I would have. I hoped that hope was enough.

"Lucy?" It was Mary, calling up from the foot of the stairs.

I set the T-shirt back on the bureau, picked up the Munroe family Bible, and walked out of the room, shutting the door behind me.

(eighteen)

Y ou okay up there, hon?" Mary said. "I was just about to come up and see if there was anything I could do."

"There is one thing," I said, descending the stairs, laying the Bible on top of the box full of photographs next to the front door. "Sam has a key to the house, right?" She nodded slowly. "Could you call up Reverend Meeks and ask him and maybe a couple of the church ladies to come out and gather up all the clothes upstairs and donate them to the missionary program, or the next rummage sale? They can't be worth much money, but there's a lot of good wear left in most of it."

"Why, sure, be glad to. Maybe Norma Hornsby will come over tomorrow and help me do it." I nodded my thanks, and Mary stepped over and opened the front door. "Anything else? I hate to run, but Sam'll be wantin' his dinner."

"Is it that late already?" I looked at my watch; it was almost eleven. I walked out onto the porch with Mary. The house was situated on a rise no higher than a respectable anthill, but from the porch everything within the scope of a person's gaze had been ours. It was simultaneously strange and not strange to think of this becoming someone else's dominion, to think of other voices in the rooms, other dishes in the cabinets and towels on the racks, to imagine lives unfolding here with the usual amalgam of gladness and sorrow, sweet and blue. I had loved the place, too, but I had depended upon Mitchell's eyes to see it. Without him to interpret the view, it was nothing but scenery.

"Mary?" I asked. She paused, opening the door to her Pontiac. "There's one more thing."

"What's that, hon?"

"Could you take me there? To where it happened?" Her face clouded over, but to her credit she didn't ask what I was talking about. "Please," I said. "I need to see."

I don't know how I knew Mary would know the place, only that she would. Sam would have walked out there with her, in the days after the accident; she might have asked, even wheedled, him to show her. It seemed to me that if there was anything to be learned from all this, it must be there, in the spot where Mitchell had taken his last step, drawn his last breath, made his last mistake.

She closed the car door and said, " 'Round here."

No one had ever told me the specific location where it happened; I'd always assumed it had been just behind the barns, since that was the spot that had most needed mowing, so I was surprised when we kept walking, beyond the barns and out toward the fence of the back pasture. Mary, in spite of her heft, was a lifelong farm girl, a hardy lady, and if she was puffing a bit by the time we hiked up the last little rise, so was I.

We were standing on that spot where nothing would grow, a patch, maybe a hundred yards square, of little else but rock and weeds. Why in the world was Mitchell mowing back here? What had he hoped to accomplish, turning those weeds under? Unlike me, who'd long since stopped thinking that our rare, fumbling actions in the dark might produce any fruit, it seemed Mitchell was never entirely ready to accept that some things were just the way they were, sterile and unchangeable. Taking in the view from here, the overcast beginning to burn off to patches of blue, his hope seemed both estimable and so dumb that I wanted to weep for it, for the way he trusted, probably even that last morning, probably even the instant before he'd fallen, that things could pleasantly surprise you, might turn out for the best. He was a farmer not just by profession but by constitution; in spite of daily evidence to the contrary, he saw the earth as a bountiful place. Mitchell, better than I, had always had his ear cocked for the possibility of transformation.

"There," Mary said, and gestured toward an irregular spot, a slight, stony outcropping that might or might not have been enough to catch a tire, and for just a moment my breath hitched, and then resumed. I'd had the details of the accident explained to me only once, and those, I knew, had been edited for the sake of decorum and my emotional state, and I'd never asked again. All I knew was that the tractor, or its mowing attachment, had gotten stuck, and that Mitchell was trying to free it, and that he'd fallen while the machine was still in gear. I didn't know if it had chewed him up and spit him out right there or if it had dragged him, whether the tractor had stalled out or kept running until it hit the fence or some other impediment. I didn't even know, truth be told, if there was a body in the casket we'd buried in New Canaan Cemetery two months before, or if it contained only bits and pieces, like those of airline crash victims: a finger, an ear. Remains.

I stepped over and stared down at the rock, looking, I suppose for a clue, something that would tell me why Mitchell, so painstaking and so unyielding in the way he approached the world, would have done this: the one thing in the forty years of his life that was out of character. I guess I was expecting to see something definitive—bloodstains, maybe, or a scrap of the shirt he'd worn that morning—but there were only a couple of dandelions jutting up through a crack in the rock. Of course,

I realized, this might not be the place at all. Mary might be mistaken; Sam might have shown her wrong. I didn't feel Mitchell there, not the way I had in the bedroom, or on the porch looking out across the front pasture to the road. There was just a watery patch of April sun, the wind sighing in the long grass around us. He was gone from here.

Mary stepped up and put her arm through mine, and I received the gesture with gratitude, and we walked that way together, arm in arm, bearing each other up, back through the pasture to the house.

T he boxes, with the china and the Bible and the photos and the linens, were in the bed of the truck, covered with a tarp and strapped down with nylon cord, but I hadn't taken anything else, nothing for myself, not a plate or a blouse. It wasn't that I didn't want to be reminded; it was more as if I wasn't entitled, somehow, to carry a scrap of Mitchell's sturdy rectitude away with me. I didn't turn around one last time at the gate, didn't look in the rearview mirror. In my memory, for the rest of my life, when I thought of the farm I'd think of Mitchell's face floating, not just angelic but Godlike, above it, watching, always watching, with a benevolent and wary eye.

As we passed through the gates of the small country cemetery, I found I had no memory at all of Mitchell's burial. The graveyard itself I knew, from services for neighbors and church members over the years, but I had no picture of myself standing in front of the open plot, no memory of faces or verses or words said in comfort, no knowledge of a box being lowered into a hole. Had there been music? Had anyone cried? The funeral I remembered, in snatches, like stills from a moving picture—a hymn here, a flowered hat there—and receiving people at the house afterward, and falling off the porch and breaking my wrist; I remembered the emergency room of the county hospital in minute detail, down to the mole on the cheek of the young doctor who had set my wrist. Yet I could not remember being present when Mitchell went into the ground.

Neither Bailey nor I knew exactly where the plot was, and so we drove slowly along the looping gravel drive through the cemetery, looking for the stones that looked newest, the spots where the grass had not yet come up over the rectangles of fresh dirt. Right in the middle of the grounds, smack in the midst of a plot of Davises, was a just-dug hole, the earth piled high alongside, a canvas tent and folding chairs awaiting the mourners. A backhoe was parked nearby and a couple of workers were eating sandwiches under a tree, and Bailey slowed and rolled down the window and asked if they could direct us to the stone of Mitchell Breward.

By the time I met Mitchell, he was without living family; other than one elderly aunt who'd escaped to the Pacific Northwest, his relatives were all in the ground themselves, his parents and grandparents down near Lufkin, an older brother, an oilfield worker, dead of a heart attack at thirty-four, in Midland. It occurred to me now as it had not at the time of Mitchell's death that I should have sent the body to Lufkin, to lie with the rest of the Brewards, in perpetuity. I only knew he would not have wanted it, that he'd have wanted to be near home, and that he'd have expected me, in time, to join him.

Death is constant and matter-of-fact on a farm, and yet the times we spoke of it, we spoke as if we understood we would go through eternity as we had in life, side by side. We spoke as couples do, with the assumption that you'll grow old together and die peacefully in your sleep, and be buried next door to each other in the local cemetery. No alternative had been mentioned; we never spoke of accidents, of illness, of the heart that had already outlasted his brother's by half a dozen years. Now here was Mitchell, alone, with a Carter on one side and a pair of Louvins on the other. One Breward, in solitude, now and forever.

The stone was tan granite, modest-sized, with only his name and his

dates, and a small cross twined with flowers inscribed beneath. Someone had left a bouquet of snapdragons and daisies, obviously hand-
picked, wilted and discolored after days of exposure.

"Mary said she comes out here sometimes," Bailey said, prodding the
bouquet with the toe of his boot. "I guess she must've brought these." I
knew he was right; I recognized the snapdragons from the bed under her
kitchen window, which only bloomed for five or six weeks every spring.

"Who chose this?" I said, causing Bailey to look at me in surprise.

"Chose what?"

"This stone."

"Why, you did, Lucy. You picked it out of a book at the funeral
home." We were quiet a minute. "You don't remember that?"

I shook my head. I felt confounded by this, not the fact that I
couldn't remember but by the result, the terrible restraint of it, in spite
of the fact that Mitchell had been, by his own admission, a plain man,
and I thought how unjust it was that he had been gypped, not just of his
life, but in death, too, by this remote and impersonal grave, miles from
any kin, no one but a duty-bound Christian neighbor to bring flowers,
survived by a widow who, instead of missing him, of grieving with dignity, had run right out and jumped into bed with the first man she met.
Where were the carved angels, the floral tributes, the Bible verses or
testaments to the deceased's character or accomplishment? Not
"Adored Husband"—I was more pragmatic than that—but something
to mark his passing through, to set his life apart from the other heaps of
decaying flesh and bone. "Champion Worker," maybe. "Intrepid
Farmer." He'd been plain, but he hadn't been invisible, though I, still
earthbound, seemed to have rendered him that. The bleakness of the
headstone, the raw plot, that primitive little cemetery, ended up saying
volumes more about me than it did about Mitchell.

I saw Bailey glance at me out of the corner of his eye; then he
stepped over deftly and slipped an arm around my shoulders. "What do

you want?" he said. "You want me to leave you alone here awhile? You want to go home?"

"I don't know," I whispered, shivering all over. What I wanted was never to have come. The farm had been the easy part; even the scene of Mitchell's accident had had a seemly finality, a sense of integrity. This place was so crude, so inadequate. I wanted to think of Mitchell in some farmer's heaven, presiding over the crops and the cows from his pearly cloud. I didn't want to consider the possibility that this, a dry yellow field in the middle of nowhere, a hole with a stone, was the only afterlife he might ever know. I couldn't get past the idea that it was my fault, that I hadn't cared enough in life not to dispatch him to such an obscure infinity. "I hate this," I said in a choking voice, and Bailey said hurriedly, "Let's go."

Back in the truck, he started the engine and reached to turn down the air conditioner, which he always kept running full blast, winter and summer both, like he was trying to keep meat from spoiling in the front seat. "There's a poncho back there behind the seat somewhere," he said. "Put that on."

It didn't help, though; the chill seemed more organic than external. Bailey sat behind the wheel with the transmission in neutral, watching me. My hands and head felt only minimally attached, like they were on springs, bobbing with the rhythm of the engine.

"I don't know about you," Bailey said after a minute, in a measured voice, "but I'm starved. You want to go into town and get some lunch before we head home?"

He must have seen I was in no shape for a proper restaurant, and steered into a Sonic drive-in. I let him order me a grilled cheese sandwich and a Coke, although I couldn't imagine actually chewing and swallowing, the whole complicated process. The carhop brought our food and I unwrapped the sandwich and bit off the corner, but it took all my powers of concentration just to manage that and I gave up and sat back and lay my head against the headrest and closed my eyes. Is this what it felt like, I wondered, to be full of the devil? Did he freeze your marrow and turn your blood to ice? Bailey ate hastily and stealthily, like he was doing something embarrassing and was afraid to be caught, though I knew he was really just trying to get us out of there.

"You need something in your stomach," he said, gathering up the paper remnants of his lunch for the trash. "You're gonna make yourself sick, not eating."

"I can't remember how he smelled," I said.

"What?"

"One of the first things I noticed about Ash was the way he smelled. It seemed so . . . Like I'd always known it, somehow. I was married to Mitchell for fourteen years, and I can't remember a thing about how he smelled."

Bailey tossed the wadded-up trash out the window into a metal can. "Why are you doing this, Lucy?"

I lifted my head and looked at him. "Doing what?"

"Why are you tormenting yourself? You didn't kill Mitchell. You didn't wish him dead. Nothing that happened is your fault. You seem, I don't know, determined to beat your head against a wall that isn't there." I didn't have a retort for that. The fundamental difference in our perspectives seemed to be that Bailey couldn't see the wall, and I could; I could feel it every time my head knocked against it, as cold and unforgiving as that granite headstone.

"I need to use the rest room," I said, and wrested open the truck's heavy door.

I stood in the whitewashed cube of a ladies' room and took great gulps of artificially lemon-scented air. In the wavy mirror glass over the sink my face looked pinched, skeletal, my eyes a pair of cigarette burns in a sheet of white paper. I turned on the tap and ran cold water over my wrists, then hot, then cold again, but the change in temperature didn't register, as if my skin had lost its ability to transmit sensation.

Until that morning, I'd experienced Mitchell's loss mostly as absence, a sort of floating blankness, not necessarily unpleasant, in my brain, my chest, the pit of my stomach. What I felt now struck me as the opposite of that, as too much feeling, like the hollowness was suddenly swollen, packed full of emotion like so much cotton wadding, until it seemed my organs were being displaced, jostled, mashed together into half the normal space. I started to sweat. My heart, jammed into its shrunken cavity, raced like a fox with a hound on its heels. How, I thought, was this possible? Where had Lucy Breward gone? Mitchell, I understood, had died, terribly and swiftly, but what had happened to his wife, the fourteen years of shared history?

I blinked once, and it was gone.

There was a soft rap at the door, and I heard Bailey say my name; it reminded me of childhood, his tone impatient, mildly annoyed, like the time I'd kidnapped his G.I. Joe and dressed it up in my Ken doll's clothes. I couldn't answer him, though, could only stare in mild amazement at the eyes in the mirror, like no soul's I'd ever seen before. With every blink I felt Mitchell falling, irretrievably, away, closer to God or whatever lay in that direction, farther from the capacity of me, left behind, to hold on to him, to remember his face, his voice, his smell, his name.

The doorknob began to rattle. Without taking my eyes off the stranger in the mirror, I reached out my hand.

The next thing I knew, I was in Dove's guest bedroom, flat on my back on top of the quilted coverlet, the drapes pulled tight against the afternoon sun. Things were all mixed up in my mind, so that when I closed my eyes and felt her sit down beside me and lay a damp washrag on my forehead, I started to cry, not knowing if I was six years old or sixteen or thirty-three, if my daddy had left and my mama was staggering around tipsy and quoting Scriptures, or if some boy I couldn't live without had failed to return my interest, or if I'd just come from the graveside of my late husband who, it was clear to me now in a way it hadn't been before, had pulled me there somehow in order to hold me accountable, to make sure I'd seen, in all its miserliness, the hereafter to which I'd consigned him.

After a little while Geneva arrived and sat on the edge of the bed, and then she and Bailey and Dove went into the hall to confer in worried voices. Bailey thought I was having a nervous breakdown. "Bosh," Dove said. "It's grieving, pure and simple."

But if you'd asked me what I was grieving for, I wouldn't have said for Mitchell, or for the person I'd been before the accident, but of the person I might, with hindsight, have become. I wanted a chance to do it over, to bring Mitchell back so that I could improve myself before he died, so that I might eventually be a worthier survivor, someone, above all else, capable of keeping his memory. I could not remember Mitchell's smell, had buried him ignobly and alone, had not saved his farm, his life's work, or a single item from it. The only reason could be that there was some fundamental lack in me, and the result was that I would spend the rest of my life running forward with Mitchell's memory wobbling before me, like an egg on a spoon, trying to hold it steady, to keep it from cracking and spilling out upon the ground, lost for all time; that, surely, would be my fate in this life, and possibly the next one as well.

Bailey and Geneva left, and Dove came in and out, offering tea, soup, blankets, TV, tomato-and-onion salad, chocolate-ripple ice cream. My tears, so mysteriously absent for the past two months, seemed endless, like there was some well in me that had finally, belatedly, been tapped. Dove, for her part, didn't seem especially distressed. Occasionally she'd sit beside me and stroke my hair. She seldom spoke, understanding that anything she said to me under those circumstances would have bounced right back, or fallen into the void. She treated me the way you treat a person in a coma, keeping them fed and turned and touched, so that when something finally stirs and they're ready to come back, they can find their way.

It was full dark out when she came into the room and laid her hand on my shoulder. I was on my stomach, my face in the pillow. "Lucy Bird?" she said softly, like she was mindful of waking me. "Ash is here."

I didn't know how to respond to this; it seemed to have so little to do with my present circumstances, this new duty to which I found myself bound, I couldn't think what I was supposed to say or feel. When I'd thought of Ash, letting my mind touch that subject only timidly, the way you probe a sore tooth with your tongue, I believed I must have staggered toward him completely blind with loss, with the pure scream-ing need to connect with something that made me feel anything but what I'd have felt if I'd been mourning properly. My head felt like it weighed four thousand pounds, like I'd need a crane to lift it. I raised my wrist and let it flop back against the pillow, unable to guess how the gesture might be interpreted.

"Maybe it would do you some good to see him," Dove suggested gen-tly. "Pull you out of this a little." But didn't she, didn't anyone, realize I didn't want to be pulled out of this, that I didn't deserve to be? I had been given this assignment, and I meant to apply myself with absolute diligence, like it was my last chance to prove myself worthy, in God's eyes and in Mitchell's, of the clean, white light of sanctification.

"Okay," Dove said, "I'm giving you ten seconds, and if I don't hear you say yes I'm gonna send him on his way. Agreed?" We both, presum-ably, counted to ten in silence, and she stood at my side another minute or so, rubbing the back of my neck with her gnarled old hands, and then let herself quietly out of the room.

I slept and woke, slept and woke. One state was pretty much like the other, the paramount condition of both being a searing loneliness that permeated my waking minutes and my dreams like fever. Ash and Mitchell seemed to drift through my sleep in some sort of prearranged tandem, one taking over where the other left off, so that I was perpetually haunted by all the ways I had failed both the living and the dead. It was hard to know sometimes which of them existed in which dimension; I only felt, in my quick, that I had lost them both, that I had come close and yet never quite crossed that final span, never been known for the glory in me, and that now that glory had been snuffed out, without ever once having had a chance to shine.

I slept through Wednesday and Thursday, two entire days and nights. Now and then I'd wake to the sound of voices outside my door, murmuring their little dirge of worry just out of earshot, but the effort of deciphering what was happening outside that room was beyond my ken. Once I thought I heard Ash, and held my breath and lay still, listening, but there was only the far-off mutter of the TV, and I guessed he must have worked himself loose from one of my dreams. In fact, I dreamed so much and so interchangeably of both Mitchell and of Ash that I thought all three of us were bedmates sometimes; it was a surprise to open my eyes and find myself alone, sweating under the satin coverlet, squeezing my eyes tight shut against the sliver of daylight that had worked itself, despite Dove's efforts, between the drapes. I didn't want warmth or daylight. I wanted dark, cool, blessed absence of stimulation. I wanted the outside world to retreat; I wanted to be left to hone my suffering like a blade, so sharp and deadly I could never take it for granted.

I woke that night to the apparition of my mama, backlit in the open doorway so that she shimmered a little around the edges, her features indistinct, her head haloed in gold. I closed my eyes against the sight and heard Dove's voice, uncharacteristically raised: "I blame you for this, Patsy Hatch, you and nobody else but you. Where do you think she got this from, this notion that she's somehow got to atone for what happened to her husband? What kind of mama puts the fear of God in her child without teaching her about His powers of mercy? It's a wonder she ain't gone plumb crazy by now."

The thought that there was anyone left who didn't see me as plumb crazy was a radical one, even if that person was my fiercely devoted aunt. It forced me to consider the possibility that it might be true. I smiled into the pillow, and felt the reconfiguration of my facial muscles with pure astonishment, that they were set not in plaster, as I'd believed, but in putty. That things were, perhaps, more malleable than they seemed. The idea wedged itself into a crack in my thinking and then stayed there, propping it open, letting in a shard of light, and the light, instead of seeming harsh and unforgiving, appeared to beckon.

I lay marinating under the coverlet and thought of what Bailey had said, that faith meant trusting what you couldn't understand. My mind in the still eye at the center of its vortex kept coming back to two facts, things that stood fixed even while everything around them seemed to tumble and shift: Mitchell was gone, and I loved Ash. All the rest was muddled, but those two things were as staunch and shining as Reverend Craig's cross on the hill out on the Marietta highway. There was both terror and comfort in this. The terror was an old friend; the comfort would take some getting used to.

(nineteen)

The surprise about grief is that it's such hard work, that it chews up everything in its path if you let it. When morning came my head, all four thousand pounds of it, felt as airy as tulle, like it might drift off my shoulders if it wasn't battened down. I hadn't eaten in days, hadn't bathed or brushed my teeth or changed my clothes or spoken to another human being. I felt flattened, like Godzilla had stomped me with his big, clawed foot.

Dove came in, drawn by some psychic ability to the sense of movement, as I was swinging my legs over the edge of the mattress. She rushed to my side but I waved her off, getting unsteadily to my feet. "Better stand clear," I said, "the stench might kill you." She grinned, and I was so relieved by the sight I almost started to cry again. "I thought I'd take a shower," I said casually, like it was something revolutionary I was trying out the sound of.

Dove just nodded. "Fine idea." Her T-shirt read BORN OKAY THE FIRST TIME.

"You wouldn't happen to have something clean I could wear?"

She opened a drawer and took out a stack of clothes: shorts, jeans, T-shirts, underwear. They were my own things, I realized, things I'd carried over the course of the previous week to Ash's house. She separated a top and a pair of jeans from the mix and handed them to me, along with panties and a bra.

"Where did these come from?" I asked.

"Ash brung them."

"When?"

"Last night."

"Ash was here last night?"

"Ash was—lessee. Ash was here Tuesday night, Wednesday morning, Wednesday evening, last night." I looked at Dove in the mirror, but she shrugged and started smoothing the bedspread. "Just settin', visitin' with Bailey and Geneva and me. Eatin' supper. Watchin' TV." I was dumbfounded. Ash, staring at sitcoms and talk shows, breaking bread with my kin? "Mostly he was watchin' and waitin'," she said, plumping the pillows at the head of the bed. "Same as the rest of us."

I had a vision then of Ash as a young man, sitting at Christa Keller's bedside while she died, reading to her from the newspaper, spooning up her custard, holding her hand, his heart broken but his head high, for the time that would come later, for remembering. All around him, every day, Ash kept the past at hand, in the land he lived on made possible by Christa's bequest, in his father's Bible on the nightstand, in the photograph in the plastic frame tucked inside his bureau drawer. It seemed that if you worked at it, it might be possible for love and grief to live side by side, like a pair of old cats, crotchety but familiar, each keeping to its own end of the porch. It occurred to me like a bolt from the blue that Ash could show me. That, even if my mama hadn't taught me mercy, it might not be too late to learn it at someone else's hands.

While I showered and dressed, Dove heated up some soup and a basket of corn bread, and I sat at her table, my hands trembling with gratitude, and ate everything she put in front of me. The world felt new and too bright to me, like I'd been away on some long space voyage and was having to get my earth legs back under me. I began to be afraid, suddenly, that I'd been gone longer, and farther, than I knew, that I'd step outside and find that ten years had passed instead of three days, that nothing was the way I remembered it. I went to the front door and gazed through the screen at the little Buddhas, the sturdy tomato plants struggling to reach the lowest rungs of their cages, the newly planted bean poles with their little plastic markers: Tenderpick, Blue Lake, a whole entire row of Kentucky Wonders. Three days isn't long in the grand scheme of things, but I felt I had to hurry.

I went back into the kitchen, where Dove was washing the dishes, and asked, "Did anyone talk to Peggy?"

"I did, sure."

"Do I still have a job?"

Dove looked at me over her shoulder. "You forget, Lucy, Peggy's mama and I was dear friends. I seen that gal through plenty of tough times, when she lost her mama and again when Duane passed. I knew she'd spare me a favor without too many questions."

I looked at the clock over the stove; it was a quarter till twelve. "I think I'll wander over there for a couple of hours," I said. "Maybe she could use some help this afternoon."

Dove set a plate in the sink and turned to me, wiping her hands on a dish towel. "She ain't expectin' you for another day or two at best. Why'nt you just set awhile and take it easy, get your feet back under you?"

"Is Ash still working at Mrs. Tanner's?"

"Matter of fact, they're finishin' up today. She's havin' some kinda open house thing tomorra, to show off the work." Dove rolled her eyes. "I knowed Harlan Tanner since we was kids together. Boy loved to kill stuff more'n anyone you ever seen. Was bad enough that he made it his hobby, now Ginny done made an everlastin' shrine to it."

"Well, I think I'll wander over and have a look."

Dove laughed. "Why, Lucy, I never knew you to take such an interest in taxidermy."

It was only half a dozen blocks, but I was winded by the time I reached Mrs. Tanner's house, and the absence of Ash's truck in the driveway sucked what little breath was left out of my lungs. The front door stood ajar, the sofa and coffee table and a couple of wing chairs out on the lawn, and I walked across the grass and peered inside.

In the past three days, the room had been transformed. The shelves were all in place now, wall to wall, floor to ceiling, and stained a beautiful dark cherry; the wood had the wet, rich hue of raspberry syrup, gleaming in the sunlight, and there were swirls and cornices I hadn't seen before, etched into the corners. Carved above the top shelf in elegant curved letters that seemed to strike me square in the heart were the words "Harlan Tanner, Sportsman." This, I saw, was a genuine memorial, a true widow's offering. The display—all those stuffed and glaring birds and rodents—might be questionable, but no one would ever, could ever, question Virginia Tanner's devotion to her dead.

I stepped over to look more closely at the inscription. My fingers itched to work themselves into the whorls and crannies, as if that would make the one who'd done the carving appear before my eyes, but the shelves had been painstakingly polished, and in the end I could only stare; the work was so beautiful, so full of tender regard for wood and for memory.

"Oh, hello," Mrs. Tanner said from the doorway, not seeming surprised to find me, a relative stranger, in her living room, admiring her new shelves. "I thought I heard someone. The carpet cleaners set the furniture outside and then left for lunch and I haven't seen them since." She was a small, tidy woman with steel-wool hair trained into a bun and a trace of an accent left over from her girlhood in Derry, England. How in the world she'd ended up in Mooney, Texas, married to Harlan Tanner, who sold farm equipment and loved beyond all else to slaughter and stuff wild creatures, was one of those small-town mysteries we all exclaimed over but never unraveled.

"Is Ash here, Mrs. Tanner?" I said, though it was plain he was not.

"No, dear, I let them go, him and Isaac both. They finished the last of the trim this morning, and helped me put Harlan's trophies on the shelves, but there's nothing left now but for the carpet people to finish up and carry my sofa in off the lawn."

"I don't . . . He didn't happen to say where he was going?"

"Not in so many words. He and Isaac have been talking about fishing for the past two weeks, though, once the rain passed and the weather turned warm."

"Well. I guess I'll be heading along. Thanks anyway." I fixed my eyes one more time on the engraved words above the shelving. "This is really extraordinary," I said. "I had no idea."

"Yes, well, he's an extraordinary man."

I glanced in surprise at Mrs. Tanner, who was smiling at some point in the distance only she could see, and I saw we were thinking of two different men. "Was," she amended, patting her bun. "I mean, he *was* an extraordinary man. It's been six years, but I still sometimes forget he's gone." The road to the past is paved in different colors for different people, I suppose, and for Mrs. Tanner it was paved in gold.

I walked slowly the three blocks to my mama's house. Out front, in her driveway and along the curb, was an assortment of cars sporting bumper stickers claiming various high-flown associations with the own-ers' Lord and Savior. I opened the door and let myself quietly into the front hall. From the living room came the murmur of voices, reciting, in unison, the Twenty-third Psalm: "Surely goodness and mercy shall fol-low me all the days of my life. . . ." I'd never understood the "surely" part. How was it they were so sure? I waited until they said, "Amen," and then I stepped into the room and said, "Excuse me."

Mama got rapidly to her feet, laying her prayer book on the seat of her folding chair. "Everybody," she said in a quavering voice, "you know my Lucy!" The group was staring at me like they expected me to break into an exotic dance, something with finger cymbals and veils.

"Sorry to barge in," I said. "I just need one thing."

The boxes Bailey and I had brought from the farm were stacked in one of the back bedrooms; they'd been riffled through but not yet unpacked, although the Munroe Bible and Great-Granddaddy's lantern were sitting on a nearby chest.

I dug around in the box of photos until I found the one I wanted. It had been taken at the entrance to the county fair, the third or fourth year we were married; Mitchell had been invited to judge the dairy-cattle competition, and wore an old-fashioned ribbon with the word JUDGE on the bib of his overalls, a plaid shirt, a cap from the local feed store. His nose was sunburned, and he was smiling, no doubt at the prospect of all those cows. He was engaged in something useful, which would have pleased him. The other particulars I couldn't remember; maybe it had rained just enough that spring, or corn prices were up. Maybe I'd gotten the meat loaf just the way he liked it at dinner. I would never know, other than that, in an instance of cosmic convergence, the man in the photo, at the moment the shutter had clicked, was a satisfied one. I thought that if I could fix him there, steady in that moment, I might start to learn who he'd been.

Mama stood watching me from the doorway like I might be burgling the place. I turned the photo around and showed it to her, and she nodded, as if she was granting me a concession.

"Mama, will you do something for me?" I asked. "Will you and your group say a prayer for Mitchell? I keep trying, but I'm not sure I'm getting through. Say one for me, too, while you're at it," I added. "I'll be at Ash's, if you want me."

I walked back to Dove's; she'd fallen asleep in front of the TV, watching another of the countless shows that pitted minor criminals against tough but charismatic men and women of the law. In the guest room I pulled my armload of clothes out of the bureau and jammed them into a big flowered tote bag of Dove's, tucking the picture of Mitchell inside a folded pair of jeans for safekeeping. I sat for a while in the living room alongside Dove, who snored gently on the sofa, and looked out the window, waiting for her to wake up, and that's where I was when Bailey drove up.

I went out onto the step and closed the screen door softly behind me. He was halfway out of the truck when he saw me coming down the walk toward him, shouldering the tote bag.

"Hi," I said. "You're just in time to give me a ride." He continued to stare at me, goggle-eyed, as I swung the bag and then myself up into the passenger seat. "You're not busy, are you?" I asked. "Can you run me out to Ash's?"

"Man," he said, fitting himself back behind the wheel. "Talk about Lazarus rising from the dead."

"Bailey, how do you think all this seems to Ash?" I asked when we were out of Mooney and on the highway west of town. "You talked to him, right?"

Bailey considered this for a minute, squinting through the windshield. "I don't know, Lucy," he said finally. "I guess I'd have to say he seemed perturbed. He couldn't understand why you wouldn't see him."

"But I—"

"Hey, you don't have to defend yourself to me," Bailey said. "I just—well, I got the idea Ash thought he could just lay his hands on you and you'd be over it. He didn't agree with the idea to let you alone."

"So, he's mad? Is that what you're saying?" It had not occurred to me that Ash, after all those visits to my Aunt Dove's house to keep vigil for me, would be anything but eager to see me, that I might have a fight on my hands.

" 'Mad' would not be the word I would choose," Bailey said. But he didn't say what that word was.

He turned off the highway onto Ash's dirt road, and I told him to pull over. "I think I'll walk the last little piece," I said, dropping down from the seat, swinging the tote over my shoulder. "Maybe I'll come up with some way to acquit myself in the next ten minutes."

"What if he's not home?"

"So it'll be my turn to wait on him for a change." I shut the door. "Bailey?" I said through the open window. "I think maybe you saved my life the other day."

"I did no such thing."

"Still. You're the best man in the world. The best of all time."

"God, Luce." His ears were bright red. "You haven't had some kind of weird religious conversion or something, have you? You're not gonna go off in the woods and start handling snakes and speaking in tongues and stuff?"

I laughed. "No, I guess I'm still a heathen."

"You hear Ash out, okay? Don't just get your back up and run."

"You're sticking up for Ash? Talk about a religious conversion."

"Go on," he said, revving the engine. "We'll see you at the Round-Up tomorrow night."

Little Hope Road was not quite a mile long, red clay and lined with pines, no different from a hundred other small rural roads in Cade County. Even at a saunter it was barely a fifteen-minute walk. I'd told Bailey I wanted to gather my thoughts, but my thoughts were all over the place, churning like wash in a tub; it was impossible to sort a single item from the pile and examine it for any length of time before the agitation began again, turning everything into a sopping muddle.

The fact was that I wasn't sure I could acquit myself. I didn't know if the things Ash wanted to hear were within my reach. Was it possible for something so new to stand this sort of blow, or would it fold like a tent in a storm? I felt myself being pulled by him, not just the gleam of him, the heat and scent, but by some nameless thing I knew was old and deep; and at the same time I wondered if it might not be too late, that maybe what I'd had to pass through in order to get to this place might be more than he could accept, that with every ruinous tick of the clock he'd been moving the other way.

His truck was there, the keys dangling in the ignition. The front door was open. I took the three porch steps on my tiptoes and stood for a moment outside the screen door. Ash's voice came down the hall from the direction of the kitchen, all the pipes open, full bore, the way he could only have done if he knew no one was listening: "Don't you hear the bells a-ringing, don't you hear the angels singing? It's the glory hallelujah jubilee . . ."

I eased open the screen door and stepped inside, shutting it gently behind me. Underneath Ash's voice was a background chorus of water running from the tap. I crept up the hall and into the kitchen doorway.

His back was to me, and he was bent over the sink, engrossed in some work with his hands I couldn't see. The sun came in the window like the first day of creation, shining on his head. His shoulders worked under a faded blue T-shirt; the smell of apples filled the air. "In the far-off sweet forever," he sang, "just beyond the shining river . . ."

Abruptly, Ash stopped singing. I watched him lift his head, his neck tensing above his collar, and then something clattered into the sink.

"Shit!" he yelled, and spun toward me, gripping his right thumb in the opposite fist. A bright bead of blood glistened.

"I didn't know whether to knock or just let myself in," I said. His face registered not surprise so much as pure stupefaction, like I was a pygmy or a cannibal woman and he'd never seen anything so astounding.

"That depends. Are you visiting, or planning on staying awhile?" He eyed the tote over my shoulder.

"I guess that would be your call," I said as he turned and put his thumb under the running water. "It's your house, after all."

He laughed, a kind of cheerless guffaw. "It's my house, all right," he said, "but I seriously doubt it's my call."

I let the tote bag slump onto the kitchen table. "Dove told me you came by her house every night."

Ash cocked his head, hypnotized by the stream from the faucet. "You knew that, didn't you? She told you I was there, and you said you wouldn't see me."

"Only the first night," I said. "After that, I didn't know." Looking into his eyes was like looking into a crater, black and bottomless. "I didn't want you to see me like that."

"Like what?" He turned off the tap and reached for a length of paper towel, which he wrapped around and around his thumb like an exaggerated cartoon bandage. "You mean, sad? Scared? In pain? Don't you think I know what those things look like, Lucy? Don't you think I've been there myself, a time or two?"

"Not like that," I said.

"Yes, like that. Exactly like that." I saw that he'd been slicing and coring an apple; he arranged the pieces on a saucer and set it in the middle of the table, like an offering.

"How," he said, then fell silent, then began again: "How could you think there was anything you could do that would turn me away from you?"

"You don't know how it was," I said, looking past him to the bright square of the window. "I was . . . I was lost."

"You were never lost. I knew where you were, all the time. Wherever you went, I knew I could find you."

"Ash, my Lord—it wasn't even about you! Don't you get it? This was about Mitchell! My husband, Mitchell, who died!" My husband, Mitchell, whom I'd never known. Unlike Ash, whom I'd known on sight and in my blood, whom I would know after this or twenty life-times passed, whom I would find no matter what shores we washed up on, whatever strange skins we put on as camouflage.

"I never meant to ask you to forget Mitchell," Ash said quietly. "I only wanted to remind you of what you had waiting for you, here and now."

I stared at the tabletop, those slices of apple fanned out like a picture in a magazine. "I'm scared," I blurted. "I let go of myself, all those years with Mitchell. My light went out without my even knowing it." Ash lifted his gaze from the floor. "I can't do it. I can't give myself up that way again."

"So—what, your aim is to back off now, before I bleed you dry?" His voice rose. "Is that what you think you mean to me, Lucy? Or is it that you think it makes you the winner, somehow? Because you backed off first?"

I took the tote bag off the table. "Look, this was a bad idea. I shouldn't have come. Bailey said you were mad."

"Mad?" Ash laughed, a mix of bitter and sweet. "You mean 'mad,' like pissed off? Or 'mad,' like inflamed? Impassioned? 'Mad,' like nuts? For three whole days you were in trouble, Lucy, and no one would let me near you, not even to see you or touch you! Don't you think I'm entitled to be a little mad?"

Without warning the earth went sideways, and I found myself grip-ping one of Ash's ladder-back kitchen chairs, the way I'd had to do in the first weeks after Mitchell died, when it seemed the whole world was off its axis. Maybe after a certain age it's impossible for us to come to each other whole hearted. Maybe too much has been sacrificed, peeled off along the way; maybe there are too many nicks and dings, chunks carved by loss and vanquished expectation. And yet, in seconds, as I stood in Ash's kitchen, my heart resumed its regular rhythm. Even in its compromised state, it was capable of so many extravagant things.

"I went by Mrs. Tanner's earlier," I said, "looking for you. I saw the shelves, the inscription. Ash, it was . . . It knocked the breath out of me. It's so—reverent." He kept his eyes level, his arms folded across his chest. "Do you know what Mitchell's tombstone looks like? His name and his dates, nothing else. Like he was no one to me. A stranger."

"Bailey said you didn't even remember choosing it."

"I didn't. I don't."

"Did it ever occur to you that you did the best you could? Some people, no matter how hard you try, just won't let themselves be known."

"If I . . ." I swallowed hard, gathering the words I wanted, holding them close for a last moment before I let them loose in the world, knowing there was no taking them back. "If something happened to you today, there are a hundred things I could write about you. A thousand."

"Yeah? Name one."

"Just one?" I smiled to myself. "Flag planter."

"What?"

"Nothing. A joke between Geneva and me."

"Try again."

"Countryman," I said. "Beloved countryman." I watched the words take wing and fly right into Ash's grasp and roost there. I sensed an opening, and before the next thing could get said I went around the table and slipped in. *Ah*, he breathed, into my hair. The scent of his throat was the way the earth must have smelled first thing in the morning to Mitchell, damp and dark and full of expectancy under its glorious, mutable surface.

"Let's see this," I said, lifting his hand and slowly unwinding the paper towel. The bandage was bloody but the wound was clean. Still, I held the pad of his thumb against my lips until he smiled, and then I drew it between them and licked the sliced tip. It tasted slightly salty, piquant. I might have sold the recipe to Willie B. for a hundred bucks. But it seemed to me more priceless than that, a mystery worth protecting.

"I have something to show you," I said, and reached for Dove's flowered tote bag. I rummaged among the folded clothes until my hand found the photograph of Mitchell outside the county fair, and passed it to Ash.

He glanced at it, then up at me, then back at the photo again. "I don't remember him much like that," I said. "He worked so hard, all the time. But he looks happy there, don't you think?" My voice caught, and I turned my head away. "He must have been happy sometimes, isn't that true? I mean, statistically, he couldn't—"

"Lucy," Ash said. "It wasn't your fault, nothing about the way he lived or the way he died, either one. You did what you could with what was in front of you. Sometimes you just have to cut your losses and go," he said, and I guessed he was thinking of Marlene. "But sometimes, if you're lucky, you get to go around again."

"Are you talking about reincarnation?"

He laughed, working a hand into my hair. "I'm talking about real life. *Your* life. Right here, right now."

"I decided, at my Aunt Dove's, that you could teach me about holding what you've lost. That you, more than anybody, understand how to—to be reverent." I took the photo out of his hand. "I need someplace to keep this. So that I don't forget."

I followed him down the hall into the bedroom, carrying the tote bag. I'd never gotten around to making a space for myself in Ash's house, but without a second's hesitation he jerked loose one of the bureau drawers and tipped the contents—umpteen pairs of boot socks—onto the bed, then stepped back and offered the empty drawer with a little flourish. I eased my armload of folded clothes out of the tote bag and into the drawer, then picked up the photo of Mitchell, taking a second to fix in my mind the image of him as content, whole, and slid it under the stack. Maybe in that dark nest, in between my shirts and blue jeans, some truth would be revealed that I least expected.

I sat down on the patchwork blanket, and Ash sat down beside me and took my hands. It seemed to me the trick must be in learning to keep the past moving beneath the present, always flowing, so that in a moment of stillness you could summon it up, hear it running down under the passage of your life, informing it, keeping it fed, like a creek feeds a river; that we had to learn to stand for a minute every day in the middle of that stillness and listen for what had been, that that was the only way the dead would be free of our yoke of sorrow and failure. That was my final vow to Mitchell and the first of my life with Ash, one I would carry like a secret scar, a hidden but lasting part of me, a cargo I'd earned and that I deserved. There would be no way to judge if I succeeded, no way, in this life, to know if I'd helped Mitchell gain his peace. It was possible that nothing would come back but the sound of my own heartbeat, the sound of what my brother called faith. I lay down in Ash's arms, to see what I could learn.